T0169983

PRAISE FOR RICHARD ZIMLER

The Incandescent Threads

ONE OF THE *SUNDAY TIMES*' BEST HISTORICAL
FICTION BOOKS OF 2022

'A memorable portrait of the search for meaning in the shadow
of the Shoah.' **The Sunday Times**

'exceptional . . . This is a richly drawn, original portrayal of tenacity
and sacrifice.' **Publishers Weekly** (**starred review**)

'succeeds with its strong emotion, memorable characters, and
mosaiclike structure . . . moving and unsettling. A thoughtful
and affecting novel about generational trauma.' **Kirkus Reviews**

'emotionally charged [and] moving . . . compelling and powerful . . .
a contemporary classic.' **The Jewish Chronicle**

'a fine wide-ranging novel.' **Tikkun**

'a sublime novel . . . An extraordinary premise and exquisitely
written.' **Buzz Magazine**

'Deep [and] moving [with] an enormous emotional charge.'
Time Out

'beautifully written' *Jewish Book Council*

'Readers already familiar with Zimler's exceptional gift for multigenerational storytelling will find this work among his best'
Hadassah Magazine

Hunting Midnight

'From Midnight's first words . . . the reader is charmed. Zimler's ability to lay bare the horror of injustice, to find universal truths and poetry in everyday existence, and his faith in the human spirit, make reading *Hunting Midnight* an uplifting experience.'
Jerusalem Post

'Zimler's book is a triumph of modern fiction: an absolutely gripping narrative of love and loss set against a backdrop of fantastic historic drama. Zimler rises to the incredible quality of his bestselling *The Last Kabbalist of Lisbon*. The characters are rich and fully realized, and their conflicts are vital and real. They grow throughout the book, so that by the end you feel a real intimacy with them. I loved this book. Read it at once.' **Andrew Solomon, winner of the National Book Award (USA)**

'An ambitious historical epic from a superbly talented historical novelist, capable of combining fascinating broad-canvas glimpses of history with the most intimate portraits of the human heart in turmoil.' *Booklist* **(USA)**

Guardian of the Dawn

'The strength of *Guardian of the Dawn* lies in its rich historical setting and in Richard Zimler's creation of an idiomatic language that reflects the religious and cultural diversity of place and period . . . remarkable.' **Times Literary Supplement**

'A terrific storyteller and a wizard at conveying a long since vanished way of life.' **Francis King,** *Literary Review*

'While this novel is a testimonial for the thousands who suffered under the Inquisition in India, it is also a riveting murder mystery [by a] master craftsman.' *India Today*

'This is the third volume in Zimler's luminously written series about the Zarcos, Sephardic Jews from the Iberian Peninsula. While the beginning reads like a nostalgic coming-of-age story—though in an exotic locale—a more suspenseful tone steps in halfway through. Its last sections deliver a warning on the dangerous sweetness of revenge, and how it can lead to a tragedy of Shakespearean proportions. As haunting and mysterious as India itself can be, this novel delves into the darkest currents of the human mind and heart. Few readers will emerge untouched.' **Historical Novel Society**

'Crime and punishment work their usual spell in this deeply absorbing work.' *Kirkus Reviews*

'Parallels with Shakespeare's *Othello* are not accidental but nothing, to the smallest detail, is accidental with a writer who has fairly been called an American Umberto Eco.' *The Advertiser*

'An exciting adventure story . . . Scrupulously researched . . . Fascinating.' *The Independent*

The Search for Sana

'a bold investigation of the Palestinian-Israeli conflict . . . By obliging readers to see the past, [Zimler] illuminates the sources of injustice today . . . He writes in calm, clear prose adorned by the occasional glistening image like a jewel in a fast-flowing stream.' **Michael Eaude, *Tikkun***

'beguiling' *The Guardian*

The Seventh Gate

'A gripping, heartbreaking and beautiful thriller . . . unforgettable, poetic and original.' **Simon Sebag Montefiore**

'*The Seventh Gate* is not only a superb thriller but an intelligent and moving novel about the heartbreaking human condition.' **Alberto Manguel, author of *The Library at Night***

'Mixing profound reflections on Jewish mysticism with scenes of elemental yet always tender sensuality, Zimler captures the Nazi era in the most human of terms, devoid of sentimentality but throbbing with life lived passionately in the midst of horror.' *Booklist* **(starred review)**

'Adding a touch of Jewish mysticism to his historical thriller, Zimler . . . excellently captures the gamut of tumultuous emotions in his intense and detailed portrait of a city destined for war, and his exceptionally drawn characters struggling to survive in a world gone mad make for an unforgettable story.' *Library Journal* **(starred review)**

'Zimler, a seasoned American writer living in Portugal, combines sexy coming-of-age adventures with coming-of-Hitler terrors in this powerfully understated saga.' *Kirkus Reviews*

'*The Seventh Gate* is unforgettable . . . The reader will be haunted by these brave characters and the stirring murder mystery . . . *The Seventh Gate* builds frustration and anxiety into a devastating and haunting conclusion . . . gripping, consuming, and shocking . . . unforgettable.' *New York Journal of Books*

'Zimler . . . surpasses himself with this coming-of-age epic set in Berlin at the start of the Nazi era . . . the whodunit is captivating enough, but the book's power lies in its stark and unflinching portrayal of the impact of Hitler's eugenic policies on the infirm and disabled.' *Publishers Weekly*

'Zimler [is] a present-day scholar and writer of remarkable erudition and compelling imagination, an American Umberto Eco.' **Francis King,** *The Spectator*

'Zimler has this spark of genius, which critics can't explain but readers recognise, and which every novelist desires but few achieve.' **Michael Eaude,** *The Independent*

THE INCANDESCENT THREADS

Richard Zimler was born in New York in 1956 and now resides in Porto, Portugal. His twelve novels have been translated into twenty-three languages and have appeared on bestseller lists in twelve different countries, including the United States, the UK, Australia, Brazil, Italy and Portugal. Five of his works have been nominated for the International Dublin Literary Award and he has won several other accolades for his fiction across Europe and North America. *The Incandescent Threads* is the latest in his *Sephardic Cycle*, an acclaimed group of independent works that explore the lives of different branches and generations of a Portuguese-Jewish family, the Zarcos.

zimler.com / @RichardZimler

THE
INCANDESCENT
THREADS

A Novel in the Form of a Mosaic

RICHARD ZIMLER

Parthian, Cardigan SA43 1ED
www.parthianbooks.com
First published in Great Britain in 2022 by Parthian
This English edition © Richard Zimler 2022
Paperback ISBN: 978-1-914595-33-2
Ebook ISBN: 978-1-913640-73-6
Excerpts from *The Troll Garden* and *Youth and the Bright Medusa* by Willa
Cather courtesy of the Willa Cather Archive
Cartouche of Cleopatra courtesy of Patrick Guenette / Alamy Stock Vector
Edited by Robert Harries
Cover design and typesetting by Syncopated Pandemonium
Printed by 4edge Ltd, Hockley
Published with the financial support of the Books Council of Wales
British Library Cataloguing in Publication Data
A cataloguing record for this book is available from the British Library.

For the men, women and children forced to spend months and even years in hiding during the Nazi occupation of Poland and other European countries. And for the courageous souls who hid them.

THE MOSAIC PIECES

Maybe none of us is ever aware of our true significance.

—EWA ARMBRUSTER

SHE HAD ONLY
ONE CHANCE
(2007)

The Smile

After my mother died, my father would sometimes stop in the middle of the street, tuck his head into his shoulders and swivel around in a slow, suspicious circle, his eyes in search of imminent peril. Dad was seventy-six years old then – tiny, slender and fragile. My wife claimed she still spotted an optimistic bounce in his walk, and my nine-year-old son, George, trying equally hard to cheer me up, said that Grandpa looked like one of those amazing old guys who competed every year in the Boston Marathon.

As for me, every one of my strained and hesitant breaths seemed like a pledge to never accept the injustice of Mom leaving us when she was only sixty-four years old.

The morning after she passed away, Dad brought his clunky cassette player into the kitchen before making his coffee and started listening to an interview she'd done with a Sephardic singer from Istanbul whom she'd befriended. A few minutes later, he found me standing by the back fence of our garden. He'd brought me the bowl of oatmeal I'd left behind in my desperation to get away from my mother's cheerful voice. As he handed it to me, he said, 'I'm sorry, Eti, but I won't be able to go on without hearing your mother every morning. So just be patient with me.'

Three days after Mom's funeral, while my father and I were walking through the parking lot of his Chase branch, he stopped and peered around, his hands balled into fists.

'Is it a ghost you're looking for, or an old enemy?' I asked.

'What do you mean?' he shot back. His eyebrows furrowed into a V, implying that he found my question nonsensical.

My father has eyebrows like hairy caterpillars. When I was a kid, they sometimes seemed ruthlessly critical of me – especially when I dared to ask him about his childhood in Poland.

'You seem convinced that somebody dangerous is going to show up around here,' I told him, trying to sound casual.

'Around here where?' he asked.

Rather than say *I have no idea*, I swirled my hand around to indicate the shopping centre, the bank parking lot, Willis Avenue and the rest of what we normally consider reality.

'Bah!' he said, flapping his hand at me as if my version of reality didn't count for much from where he was standing, but he also shivered, which was when a familiar latch opened inside me and I felt time slowing down, and I made the old mistake of gazing into his big, black, watery eyes for far too long, and when he started gulping for air, tears leaked out through my lashes, and that's when I started thinking that he really was a marathon runner, and not just him but me, too. *I've been running behind you, you wayward lunatic, since I was maybe eight years old*, I thought, *trying to catch up while you look around frantically for a secure hiding place.*

In answer to his worried glance, I told him it was the frigid wind that had made my eyes tear. I also tied his woollen scarf around his neck and kissed him on the forehead.

Children of Holocaust survivors learn to hide their irritation early on, of course.

All the time we were in the bank – while he was writing out his withdrawal slip and bantering with our favourite teller, Lakshmi, and drinking a cup of coffee with the bank manager, and making a quick pit stop in the employee bathroom – I kept imagining my father as a panicked eleven-year-old boy standing at the window of the tailor shop where he spent his afternoons inside the Warsaw ghetto, waiting for his parents to return home.

As a kid, I used to try to imagine what my father's parents looked like. From clues he dropped, I ended up picturing them as rumpled, ravenously hungry versions of Edward G. Robinson and – if you can believe it – Barbra Streisand.

Why Barbra Streisand? Dad said his mom used to sing to herself while she cleaned their apartment. He once hummed a bar of her favourite tune to me. Mom later told me its title: 'Chryzantemy złociste' – *Golden Chrysanthemums.*

My father had a sweet baritone, but he only sang when he got a little tipsy or when a synagogue service called for us to join in on a hymn or psalm. It always seemed to me as if Dad believed that showing too much happiness or love in public might get him selected for the ovens – though that speculation of mine turned out to be slightly off target.

The lyrics of 'Chryzantemy złociste' begin like this: *Golden chrysanthemums in a crystal vase are standing on my piano, soothing sorrow and regret.* Occasionally, I find myself singing that verse to myself. My own voice has come to sound to me like a form of defiance – of the way the world has tried to keep my father and me apart.

Dad always grades the public bathrooms he uses for cleanliness, but this time he had no comment. 'I didn't notice a thing,' he said when I asked for his report.

Though he looked a bit weary on shuffling back to me, he regained his energy the moment Lakshmi fetched him a second cup of coffee. He appreciates coffee more than anyone I've ever met – even the bank's stale brew. He licked his lips after every sip as if it were honey – and to make Lakshmi grin at him.

I admired how he charmed everyone, even now, after Mom's

death, and also how he jabbered away so knowledgeably with the bank manager, Ed, about the upcoming baseball season, his coat open to reveal his University of Utah T-shirt – a gift from an old friend – unconcerned about its fraying collar and holes.

When Ed gave me the familiar signal with his eyes, I told Dad it was time we let our friends at Chase go back to earning profits.

Just before he and I walked back through the Chase parking lot to my car, I did up the top button of his overcoat, and he smiled at me – a tight, boyish one meant to look sweet-natured and to cover what he was really thinking.

The smile, my mother and I called it.

Did Dad learn how to shield himself with that smile when he first entered the ghetto in November of 1940, or only after his parents were loaded on a transport to Treblinka a year and nine months later? I never asked; I learned to avoid leading him back to the cramped, nearly lightless ground-floor apartment where he lived in the ghetto with his parents.

Dad told me only the vaguest outlines of this story; it was my mother who filled in the details.

After his parents disappeared and until his escape on April 7th, 1943 – for eight straight months – Dad stood every afternoon at the window of Willi's Tailoring Workshop on the third floor of his apartment house on Koszykowa Street. It afforded him a wide-ranging view over the entire block, and my father figured he'd spot his parents from up there the instant they appeared on the sidewalk.

Throughout the many months he waited, he guarded in the inner pocket of his coat a topaz ring and some other jewellery that his grandmother Luna had given to him; she'd told him to use them as bribes if he ever found himself arrested or threatened by Nazis.

During the first two months his cousin Abe would join him

in Willi's workshop, and they'd sometimes play chess. Abe was a wizard at the game. When he was thirteen, he'd played the great Paulin Frydman to a draw. 'He'd have become a grandmaster, for sure,' Dad would assure me every time the subject came up.

Then Abe was arrested by the Nazis and taken away.

My father was lucky to escape when he did – the Warsaw Ghetto Uprising started twelve days after he was smuggled out, and his chances of surviving the bloody battles the Jews fought against the Nazis would have been close to zero.

Willi the tailor had already vanished by the time Abe was captured. Once an apprentice on Savile Row in London, he'd insisted on speaking English with my father, claiming that Jews had no future in Poland and that Dad had to learn to speak like a British gentleman if he was going to survive in this world. He'd gone out to buy bread and cigarettes on August 6th, 1942, however, and never returned. Dad was pretty sure that he was one of the fifteen thousand Jews who lined up for a fake bread giveaway organised by the Nazis and forced onto a freight car to Treblinka.

Two weeks earlier, the slender, long-haired, dandyish tailor had handed Dad his scissors and shown him how to cut woollen fabric. Each fabric had its own personality, Willi had told my dad: wool was stubborn but generous, cotton straightforward and honest, linen deceptively complicated but often comic. Then, while Dad watched his neighbour sewing the collar on a shimmering-blue waistcoat that he was making for a friend, my father realised that great skill and beauty resided in his hands, though Dad couldn't have expressed it that way at his age. When the tailor winked at my father and called him over for a hug, Dad discovered that he wanted to study with him – and follow the same path in life.

If Willi had survived, would he have learned to shield off his friends and family with a smile like my father's? I suppose I could have found out how common such a strategy was by spending time with the handful of leaky-eyed, joke-telling veterans of Auschwitz and Treblinka at our synagogue, but I avoided them; one old Jew stifling my questions about his childhood with his eyebrows and showing me *the smile* was more than enough.

A Plan Inside the Pain

My father's great-grandmother, Rosa Kalish, was a famous matchmaker from the Polish city of Garwolin. That was also where Dad was born, but his parents moved to Warsaw when he was just two years old. Rosa's family name was Zarco. Her ancestors on her father's side had come from Portugal, she said, which was why she could speak Ladino. And why she had been named Rosa and not Róża. She had a fox-like face and short silver hair. Her hands were affectionate and slender.

Rosa was murdered at Treblinka in May of 1943, at the age of ninety-three. Before her death, her family and neighbours believed her to be the oldest woman in the Warsaw ghetto. And probably one of the smallest, too. Forty-two kilos – that's what Rosa weighed just before she was picked up by the Nazis. 'Boy, was she skinny!' Dad once told me, bursting out with a short, dry laugh that seemed uncharacteristically mean-spirited to me. 'Her ribs stood out like . . . like the beams of one of those Roman ships. What's the English word for them?'

'Galleons.'

'Galleons – right!'

When I was at college, a friend whose mother had survived Bergen-Belsen told me that the laugh of my father's that I described to her wasn't really a laugh. 'How could you not know that?' she shrieked at me, and I had nothing to say to her except what seemed like the truth – 'I guess I was afraid to know more about what had happened to him and his great-grandmother.'

Dad knew her weight because his paediatrician father insisted on giving Rosa a check-up every week to see if he was succeeding in fattening her up with the cheese and *schmaltz* he requested as payment from his patients.

Putting weight on Rosa didn't work, my father told me. Although he never told me why, I picked up clues from the sprinkling of stories that he told me about her that she must have offered most of her grandson's high-calorie treats to the kids in the family – to Dad and his cousins, Abe, Esther and Shelly. Shelly was the only other person in the family to survive the war.

Four months ago, after Dad's Valium overdose, Shelly told me in a conspiratorial whisper that their favourite meal in the ghetto had been pumpernickel bread smeared with *schmaltz*. Though Shelly didn't say that these treats came from Rosa, he implied it when he held his finger to his lips and warned me not to tell my father what he'd said. 'He'll scream bloody murder at me if you let on that you know!' he whispered.

Dad's father used to summon him up onto the scale just after Rosa, but my father always claimed not to remember his own weight. Still, I know that his ribs must have stuck out like a Roman galleon as well, because I overheard him telling my mother once that when he ate a boiled potato covered in sour cream just after finding refuge in the home of Christian friends on the other side of the ghetto wall, he threw up because his stomach wasn't used to so many calories.

Though Dad was named Benjamin, after Rosa's long-dead husband, everyone in the family called him either Benni or – because he was small and slight – *Katchkele*, which was Yiddish for 'little duck'.

Rosa didn't want to go for a medical check-up every week but she agreed in the end because she realised it helped keep her grandson – Dad's father – hopeful.

As to why her grandson, whose name was Adam, insisted on weighing her, Rosa told Dad, 'He's found a plan inside his pain.'

'What do you mean?' my father had asked the old woman.

'A strategy.'

'And what's his strategy?'

'To keep his grandmother and his *Katchkele* alive long enough to make it out of here. And it wouldn't be very nice for us to spoil his efforts, would it?'

Do You Really Think So?

After he retired, my father started studying kabbalah every day with help from a professor of Jewish mysticism at the University of California. Whenever I was over his house, I would sneak into the bedroom and look at the esoteric texts he stacked in rickety towers on his desk and wonder what the hell he was looking for.

The book he always kept on his night table was *Major Trends in Jewish Mysticism*, by his hero, Gershom Scholem, who had single-handedly revived interest in kabbalah among both scholars and practising Jews in the 1940s and 50s. The text had dozens of dog-eared pages, and so many of Dad's notes in pencil – and even his tiny illustrations of the mythological beasts that Scholem describes – that I once told my father that he ought to try to publish an annotated version, but he scoffed and said that he had never gone to university and nobody would be interested in his opinions, and in any case his notes were really just for himself.

Dad always lacked confidence in his own intellectual abilities, though Mom always said that he had trained himself to evaluate all her articles on Sephardic music with such uncommon depth and insight that she would never have considered publishing one without getting the go-ahead from him.

Once, when Mom and Dad were on vacation in the Bahamas, I slept at their house while on a trip to New York, and I read all his hundreds of notes in the margins of *Major Trends in Jewish Mysticism*. One particular comment he'd written in blue pencil caught my attention: *Do you really think so, Mr Scholem?*

The sentence next to that comment read: 'The long history of Jewish mysticism shows no trace of feminine influence.'

Another of the books I found on Dad's night table on that visit was *Greek Religion* by Walter Burkert. My father was always reading about the ancient Greeks. When I was maybe just five or six, he told me that in a previous life he'd worked at the Library of Alexandria.

'What did you do there?' I'd asked him. He was walking me to school and we were holding hands.

'Nothing important – I just kept things neat and tidy,' he replied, as if it were completely reasonable to think so.

'Did you like working there?'

He showed me a delighted face. 'Boy, did I! I could read all the scrolls I wanted, and I was fluent in Greek and Egyptian, and at lunchtime I'd go swimming in the Mediterranean. Warm seawater, pretty women, sun, beer, good books . . . Eti, I had it all!'

From that brief list of delights, I discovered what Dad's vision of paradise was. And it sounded pretty good to me, too, but a few days later I realised that the list didn't include me, and I was upset about that for years, though it embarrasses me now to admit it.

While Dad was in the hospital recovering from the Valium overdose, I'd go to his room and sit on his bed and wonder when he'd be able to come home. One time, I found a second book under his copy of *Major Trends in Jewish Mysticism*. It was *They Came*

Like Swallows, a novel I'd recently given him. On the first page, he'd written in Yiddish: *Present from Eti. Excellent writing – too good, in fact.* After that, in parenthesis, he'd written to my mom: *Tessa, I think the author would understand how much I miss you.*

They Came Like Swallows was written by William Maxwell. It's about a young boy whose beloved mother dies in the flu epidemic of 1919. Maybe I ought to have given my father a more cheerful novel to read, but he had told me many times that he preferred tragedies.

'When I start to sniff a happy ending, I always look for the doorway out,' was his exact quote.

All I'd Failed to Understand

My mother's father, Maurice, had come to America from Greece in 1937, when he was twenty-four years old. He was the only grandparent I got to know, since Dad's parents were long dead and Mom prevented me from seeing her mother, whom she described as toxic.

Imagine leaving home just after completing your master's degree in music history and never seeing your parents again. All the time I was with Grandpa Morrie – every time he took me to a jazz club or classical concert – I never thought once about the hardships that must have still been throbbing inside his old man's heart. Or about his terror at having to raise two little daughters alone. These days, there are times when my youthful obliviousness seems unforgivable, but maybe it's a blessing that kids don't ever feel the need to gaze out over the length and breadth of their grandparents' lives.

Once, when I was drawing with my father, he told me that we never saw Mom's mother because she was a mean person and didn't want what was best for me.

'Why not?' I'd asked him.

He put down his crayon and looked at me, and I could see him trying – and failing – to find the right words in English. He lifted me up and sat me on his lap. I must have been about four or five years old. We were in the kitchen at our dinner table.

'Listen, Eti, your grandmother . . . I think she got lost and never found her way back home,' he said, but he spoke in an unsure voice.

Confusion made me study my father's eyes, because I'd learned I could sometimes find emotions there that he tried to hide from me. This time, I wasn't sure what I saw, but it might have been distress or fear, because it made me want to stay on his lap for a long time.

'How did she get lost?' I asked.

He took a deep breath, which made me think – in the itchy way that insights come to kids – that he wasn't going to tell me the truth. 'If I said she was jealous of your mother and Grandpa Morrie, would that make any sense to you?'

'I don't know.'

'She's angry, baby,' he tried next. 'Though that's not exactly what I mean. It's more like . . .' Dad looked past me, and I didn't understand that he was looking for a more perfect term, so I turned around to see if Mom was there, but she wasn't. Neither of us found the right words at the time, or maybe Dad really didn't want to tell me the truth, though an odd and angry letter I would receive from my grandmother fifteen years later would make it clear what he ought to have said: *Your grandmother holds a deadly grudge against your mother.*

Grandma's letter was handwritten on four sheets of light-blue paper, front and back, with her name engraved at the top in gold: Dorothy Spinelli. I received it two weeks after I'd spoken to her on the phone. She said she would be overjoyed to make me lunch at her apartment in Great Neck, on Long Island, but also said that she thought it only fair for me to know her feelings about my mother first.

At the time, I was studying painting at the City University of New York, and I'd found my grandmother in the Nassau County phone book. The letter she sent me two weeks after our phone call listed a series of injustices my mother had inflicted on her. The first one was, *When she was five years old, your 'oh-so-sweet' mother refused to eat the moussaka I'd made for your grandfather's birthday, and she ran out of the room shrieking when I took some on my fork and held it up to her mouth.*

'Oh-so-sweet' was written inside quote marks, as though I wouldn't otherwise understand she wasn't really praising my mother.

Grandma Dorothy had pressed so hard with her pen while writing that sentence – and again while warning me to beware of my mother's 'vicious temper and horrid betrayals' – that she had torn both times through the paper.

To hold a grudge against a five-year-old girl who refused to eat moussaka seemed insane, of course. And vicious temper? My mom had raised her voice at me on a number of occasions when I was little, but she'd never spanked me or humiliated me in any way. Though I thought of calling my grandmother to give her another chance, it seemed a lot safer for me to reply with silence. And she never wrote me again.

Every Friday night, Mom and Dad and I would have Sabbath dinner with Grandpa Morrie at his apartment in the East Village. He lived inside three small rooms that he painted in bright colours to highlight the black-and-white photographs of Mom and Aunt Evie that he hung all over the place, even in the bathrooms. The picture he kept above his bed was of himself and his daughters with his hero, Louis Armstrong, and he'd had it blown up to twice the size of a record cover. In it, Morrie, Mom, Aunt Evie and Mr Armstrong are standing in front of Saul's Bagels & Bialys, where my grandfather used to pick up breakfast every Saturday morning. It is October 24th, 1953. Mom is ten years old and Evie is eight. Mr Armstrong is laughing sweetly while gazing down at Evie, whose lips are pursed and cheeks sucked in. She is making her famous *tropical fish face*, and, as anyone in my family can tell you, her elbows jutting out are her fins.

Morrie is gripping Evie's shoulder to keep her from moving, since her tropical fish imitation usually involved swimming around in circles. Louis is holding my mother's hand.

Mom's eyes are wary. Her painfully slender shoulders are hunched. 'I was on the FBI's Most Wanted list at the time,' she tells people whenever they first see the photo and ask her why she looked so terrified.

'Your mother was just crazy shy,' Morrie explained to me when I asked if Mom had been upset that day. Then amusement widened his eyes. 'But that changed when she got interested in boys. Thank god for oestrogen!'

Morrie used to play bootleg albums of all the great jazz musicians for me and Dad when we'd visit, though sometimes we'd also watch Mets games on Channel 9. When Mom would join us, the three of them would talk about Richard Nixon, Henry Kissinger and all the other *warmongers*, as they called them. Their voices were contemptuous. Mom and Dad despised Nixon more than anyone else, it seemed to me. As for Morrie, he never referred to the president by name but nearly always as *that Jew-hating fijo de puta* – 'son of a bitch' in Ladino. He kept a newspaper on his upright piano of two New York City cops arresting him and Dad during a protest against the Vietnam War. 'One of my proudest moments,' he used to tell me.

Grandpa Morrie died of a heart attack when I was twenty-one years old. He was seventy-four. After the funeral, I played in a baseball game organised by old friends at a local park, and the first time I came up to bat, I knew I was right where my grandfather wanted me to be.

During high-school baseball season, Morrie used to come see me play as often as possible. Once, when I'd hit a triple down the line in right, I looked up from third base to see him weeping. He told me later that while I was running the bases, he'd realised with growing excitement that our family genes had skipped two generations. 'Papa was a really fast runner, just like you, Eti. He almost made it to the Olympics in Stockholm in 1912 – in the 400 metres.'

I overheard him once saying to my mom, 'Me, a near-sighted Greek Jew with bad knees, and I've got two gorgeous daughters and Willie Mays for a grandson. Who'd have figured it?'

That remark seems so typical of him – and so generous – that I often think of it when I study the picture of him and me that I keep on my night table. It's a photograph that my father snapped of us just after a baseball game. All these years later, I can still feel the soft perfection of my blue-and-grey uniform and how it made me want to show off for my family. I've put my baseball cap on Grandpa Morrie, and my arm is over his shoulder because it makes him feel proud that I'm taller than him and nearing manhood. His eyes are a bit tentative and embarrassed, since he suspects that a little old Greek Jew might look ridiculous in a baseball cap, though everyone who sees the picture invariably says something like *Your grandfather looks so cute*. My wife Angie never knew Morrie but came closer to the truth when she said, 'He looks like he never stopped being a kid!'

I once asked Morrie what it felt like to know he'd never again see the family of his childhood – his parents or his little brother and sister.

He replied, 'Every morning I light four candles inside my mind, and I'm aware that it'll never be enough, but it's all I know how to do. And I've been doing it since 1947, when I began to accept that no one survived.' He also added in a conspiratorial whisper, 'The secret I'll only tell you, Eti, is that sometimes I'd like to blow out the flames, just for a day or two, and forget what happened.'

I questioned how he could talk about missing his parents so easily with me but my dad could never talk about them. 'Benni lost them too early. He was only eleven years old. Me, I was twenty-four and already a man. I understood what had happened. He didn't.'

On weekends during the summer, Morrie would take me to the pond in Central Park that's near Fifth Avenue so that we could sail the little wooden boat we'd made in his apartment. He would puff gleefully on his pipe as we watched the boat make its way across the water.

The pond seemed a world unto itself back then – a sea of possibilities shimmering in the summer sun.

Morrie warned me never to tell my mother he still smoked when he and I were alone. He'd draw a finger across his throat and say, 'If she finds out, she'll cut off my head!'

How adult and important it made me feel to have my grandfather confide in me!

Morrie sometimes asked me to draw his portrait when we were alone, and when I was finished he'd sketch me. He'd lean forward and study me with his small, experienced eyes – eyes that suggested contemplation and refinement – and after a while I'd become aware that there was a great deal between us that I couldn't explain but that made us seem like the only two people in the world.

A couple of years ago, just after Mom was diagnosed with breast cancer, she and I walked all the way up to Central Park and went to the pond where Grandpa Morrie used to take me. I almost blurted something out about the sweet smell of his pipe tobacco, and how it used to make me feel protected, but I heard him shout inside my head, *Dear God, Eti, don't you dare tell her!* Which made me laugh to myself, of course.

When we finally reached the pond, I discovered – to my astonishment – that it was tiny.

While Mom and I watched two slender little Chinese kids fixing the sail on their tall-masted toy boat, I wondered what else I had failed to comprehend when I was young. And would never now understand.

First Signs

Twelve days after Mom's funeral and seven days after my return home to Boston, I got a call from Dad's mailman, Peter, saying that he hadn't seen my father for a while and that the mail was piling up in the metal box on his stoop. He said he'd knocked on the door that afternoon, but that my dad didn't answer.

When I called my father, he said, 'Oy, zat Peter is such a *nudnik*!' thickening his Yiddish accent for comic effect – and to conceal his true feelings.

I laughed so he wouldn't realise how worried I was. 'So, is everything okay?' I asked.

'Hunky dory.'

Dad always loved to use corny American slang like that because it made him feel like he was no longer a youthful immigrant lost in a gigantic, foreign city.

'Peter knocked on your door today,' I told him. 'Didn't you hear him?'

'No, I must have been taking a dump or something.'

'So why aren't you picking up the mail?'

'It's mostly just bills. Who needs that *tsuris* right now?'

Dad's reply seemed genuine, so I said, 'You don't have to pay anything – I'll visit you in a couple of weeks and write out all the cheques – but please just take the mail in so Peter can stop worrying.'

My father agreed to my request without any fuss, but Peter called again three days later and said the mail was still piling up. Worse, Mrs Narayan, Dad's across-the-street neighbour, phoned that afternoon to say that a young man driving a van had brought two big brown bags into my father's house that morning. 'That driver looked frightfully suspicious,' she told me.

Mrs Narayan uses adverbs like *frightfully* because she went to a British school in Mumbai and got her degree in political science at King's College in London.

'Suspicious in what way?' I asked.

'Well, his trousers were too large. And he looked Mexican.'

'Was he wearing a sombrero and eating a taco?' I joked.

'Ethan, my darling, you may laugh if you want,' she said with regal reserve, 'but I'm telling you, it all looked very odd.'

I had a drawing class to give in ten minutes, so I thanked Mrs Narayan and waited until I was done with my teaching to call Dad.

'Did you get a delivery today?' I asked.

'A delivery?'

'Two bags of something brought by a young man who looks Mexican.'

'Eti, what in God's name are you talking about?'

'Mrs Narayan called and she said the delivery boy looked Mexican.'

'Why is Mrs Narayan calling you? And how the hell does she have your number?'

'I gave it to her after Mom fell down at home – near the end of her radiation treatments. Mrs Narayan is worried about you.'

'I wish everybody would stop worrying so much about me!' he snapped.

'Okay, but who brought you a delivery?'

'He's a kid from Waldbaum's. And he's from Iran. His name is Farid. He's a senior at Hofstra majoring in psychology. And he's about as suspicious as matza ball soup.'

'You're getting deliveries now?'

'Why go out in this cold? I could fall on the ice and wake up dead.'

'But you always liked going to Waldbaum's.'

'I liked going with your mother.'

I made no reply; I felt as if Dad had clobbered me over the head. 'Are you there?' he asked.

'I'm here. So, is Farid reliable? We could hire someone to bring you groceries on a regular basis, you know.'

'Nah, it's not worth it. I just buy scraps. Who can bother cooking for just one person?'

Would you please stop making this more difficult than it needs to be! I screamed at him in my head. 'Listen, I'm coming to visit this weekend,' I said instead. The words just popped out of me. The regret I felt for speaking them was like a corrosive, rusty weight in my chest.

'I told you, I don't need anyone checking on me!' he snarled. But his voice wavered and he seemed close to tears.

'Yeah, well maybe I need to visit you!' I shot back.

'What's that supposed to mean?'

I almost shouted, *My mother just died, or have you forgotten that?* Instead, I told him I needed to come down to New York to meet with the owner of the gallery in Queens where I had an exhibition coming up.

Shelly

Dad's cousin Shelly was eleven years older than him. He'd been forced into the ghetto when he was twenty years old. After escaping through a tunnel, he fled through the forests of Poland to the Soviet Ukraine and ended up in Odessa, where he boarded a freighter to Marseille, and from there he'd taken another boat to Algiers. 'I lived out the war offloading cargo ships, drinking cheap wine and fucking,' he told me while staying with us on the weekend of my bar mitzvah.

Shelly was the first adult who ever spoke to me about sex, and about three years later, when I was a skinny, pimply and unhappy sixteen-year-old, he told me – sitting with me on my bed – that he'd had relationships with both men and women in Warsaw, Algiers and Montreal – 'And everywhere in between!' he said with his infectious, big-hearted laugh. He also assured me that anything I wanted to do in bed was just fine, and that I shouldn't allow anyone – even my parents – to tell me what to do with my cock or ass. He probably thought I was gay, and I wasn't sure myself, but in the end it turned out I was just hopelessly awkward.

A year later, while Dad and I were visiting him in Montreal, Shelly stayed up late with me one night and got drunk on rum and told me about Claude, a French stevedore he'd fallen in love in Algiers. 'But the man who really takes my heart,' he said, thrusting up his hand as if to stop an onrushing bus, 'is George Bizaadii.'

When he was drunk, Shelly would forget how to form the past tense in English, so he tended to talk mostly in the present.

'Uncle George?' I asked.

'Yeah, boy is he handsome when he is young!'

George was the half-Navajo, half-Jewish artist whose paintings were all over our house. He'd helped Shelly locate Dad after the war. Me and my cousins called him Uncle George. His long-time partner was an architect named Martin. We celebrated Passover with them every year at their adobe home on the outskirts of Moab, Utah.

'You and Uncle George were in love?' I asked.

'Absolutely!'

'For how long?'

'A few years. That is when we take a boat to Poland and find your dad.'

'So why'd you split up?'

Shelly fluttered his lips as if he were a balloon losing air. 'George once said that I speak French, English and Yiddish but not Monogamy. He kicks me out. Lucky for me, I spot your Aunt Julie a few months later, and that is that.'

'Love at first sight?' I asked.

'Absolutely! Julie's face, it radiates a kind of light. And it still does. What a knockout! And when I sleep with her, it's as if . . . well, how can I explain . . . ?' He lit a cigarette while trying to come up with the right words. In a no-nonsense voice, he added, 'It's like this, kiddo, we all know that Julie is smart as a whip, and she has a great sense of humour, and she is the most good-natured person I have ever met. But I'm going to be honest with you. After all, you're not a little kid anymore. I was young, and I was always ready to fuck, and what I like most – at least at first – is that she has a pussy made in heaven.'

Shelly used the word *minette* for 'pussy' and *paradis* for 'heaven'.

'And just like that, pow!' he said, snapping his fingers, 'I have two hungry little girls and a mortgage on a three-bedroom house in the suburbs.'

Shelly offered to take me that night to what he called a *swanky cathouse* near Mount Royal where I could get anything I wanted, but I was too scared to go with him and he was way too drunk to drive, in any case.

Throughout my childhood, Shelly would stay with us for two weeks every Christmas, and we would drive up to visit him and Julie and their kids every summer. He seemed like a movie star from the 1940s to me back then, with his slicked-back hair and stunning green eyes.

Shelly would always bring me fancy sneakers as a present, since he owned a sporting goods shop in downtown Montreal.

Shelly's grandmother – his mom's mother – had been from Rouen and had taught at an international school in Kraków for nearly twenty years. After moving to Warsaw just before the Second World War, she became good friends with the French cultural attaché and his wife, and that was how Shelly ended up with the papers he needed to make it to Algiers and later Montreal. It was Shelly who also managed to bring Dad to Canada two years after the end of the war, and from there my father made it down to New York, where he began working as an assistant to a fashionable Midtown tailor in the autumn of 1949.

'I won't ever apologise to anyone about who I fuck or anything else,' I once overheard Shelly telling Rabbi Simon, who had performed my parents' wedding ceremony, in an angry whisper. They'd been conversing in my parents' kitchen. 'Not you, not anyone! All my apologies ended in the ghetto!'

We Missed Every Chance

I insisted on visiting my father over the coming weekend because I suspected that his refusal to shop at Waldbaum's meant that he was hiding some illness that kept him housebound. I drove down from Boston early Saturday and arrived around eleven in the morning. Upstairs, I found a shard of blue porcelain in the hallway. Had a robber broken in? My heart dove toward panic, but Dad was comfortably asleep on his bed. A smashed blue cup was on the floor by Mom's dressing table.

The bedroom smelled like a pet shop and books were scattered across the blankets.

It looked as if he hadn't shaved in a week and his thick silver hair was scattered in wild tufts. The whiskers on his cheeks were white, but they were grey on his upper lip. His head leaned back against two pillows and his mouth was wide open, and he was taking wheezing breaths. Now and again, he'd lick his lips. It seemed as if he might be talking with someone in his dreams.

A book was open on his chest: *On the Mystical Shape of the Godhead*, by Gershom Scholem. I started thinking that maybe what he had been studying in kabbalah had upset him and made him scared to leave the house. I sat on the end of the bed and started rubbing his feet through the blanket.

Isn't it strange how we do things before deciding to do them? One minute I was wondering what the hell was going on with my father, and the next I was sitting beside him and caressing his feet and wishing that my mother was around so she could order him into the bathroom for a shower and a shave.

While I tried to nudge Dad awake, I imagined what I'd want to say to him after he was gone, and I decided it would be this: *You and I missed every chance to talk to each other about what life was like when you were a little boy in Poland and how you suffered. I wish we hadn't.*

I made him a strong cup of tea, brought it up to him and kissed him on his forehead. 'Eti?' he asked once his eyes were opened.

'Yeah, it's me. I made you tea. With lemon and honey, just like you like it. I'll help you sit up.'

'I was dreaming,' he told me, gripping my arm.

'Were you in trouble in the dream?'

'Yeah, I was in the ghetto, and Rosa was there – your great-great-grandmother.' Tears welled in his eyes. 'There was a gigantic wolf or dog in the room with us, and he looked like he was starving, and he was going to eat us.' Dad looked past me and said something in Yiddish in a panicked voice.

'I don't understand,' I said.

'I think there was a dead wolf on the ground with us, too,' he continued. 'Grandma Rosa, she shot arrows at the one that was alive, and the arrows formed this kind of mesh in front of him, so he couldn't get at us. He picked up his dead friend in his jaws and dragged him up the stairs. He wanted to lock us in the house – to trap us. He had a key hanging around his neck, on a chain. And then ... then I woke up.'

He looked at me questioningly, blinking his eyes as if startled by too much sunlight. 'I'm glad Grandma Rosa was there to protect you,' I said.

He stared at me in shock, as if I'd understood too much. Then he showed me his smile that wasn't a smile and apologised for bothering me with what he called *my silly memories*.

'I like hearing your memories,' I said, but I was thinking, *How could two giant wolves or dogs be part of a memory?* Did they represent the Nazis who'd nearly discovered him in his hiding place on the Christian side of Warsaw?

After I brought Dad a second cup of tea and some toast, I asked him to tell me more about Rosa. I think I may have already sensed – without knowing it – that she held the key to his troubling behaviour.

He furrowed his eyebrows at me. 'There's nothing to say,' he replied.

'You just don't want to tell me,' I told him in a hard tone.

After I reached his doorway, I looked back to see if he would at least show me a little regret, but he had already opened *On the Mystical Shape of the Godhead* and put on his glasses.

When I Find It

Dad came downstairs in his blue flannel pyjamas. Around his neck was a bolo tie of the sun god that Uncle George had given him as a Hanukkah present before I was born. The solar disc was made of shimmering mother-of-pearl rimmed with turquoise and made me think of how he'd lived in near total darkness while hiding in Christian Warsaw, much of the time reading by candlelight in a small alcove at the back of a storage room belonging to old friends of his mother, Piotr and Martyna. This was after he'd escaped from the Jewish ghetto in the early spring of 1943. In December of that year, after eight months in hiding, his Polish saviours rolled him inside a rug and took him to a more secure hideout in the countryside, where he lived with an elderly and childless piano teacher named Ewa. She knitted Dad a gorgeous blue pullover that he still hid in his underwear drawer, though I was pretty sure I wasn't supposed to know that.

'Hey, how about some banana pancakes?' my father asked with a big smile.

Whenever Dad was rude or thoughtless to me or Mom, he would make it up to us by cooking us pancakes or French toast, or by buying us little presents, or by being particularly affectionate to us over the next few days. Simply saying *I'm sorry* was never enough for him.

My heart leapt out toward him, but I wasn't ready to let go of my anger and didn't answer. Undeterred, he grabbed a banana from the wooden bowl on the counter and handed it to me. 'Your job, *Katchkele*, is to mash it.'

Dad nearly always turned making pancakes into a comedy routine. Sometimes he'd flip one up to the ceiling and miss catching it with the pan on purpose and it would splat on his foot. Mom would always laugh – even if it meant having to clean the kitchen floor – because with Dad, clowning around was an important part of his love for her and me. It sometimes also seemed as if she understood things about him that no one else did, and because of that, she could forgive him anything.

I stood next to Dad while he made our pancakes and he gave me pointers about how to cook them evenly. After he breathed in their aroma and faked a swoon, he held the pan up to my nose. 'Heaven on earth, no?'

There was only a little maple syrup in the jar in the refrigerator and Dad poured it all on mine. He ate his with brown sugar instead.

Such easy and spontaneous generosity made me feel selfish for wishing he would reveal the secrets of his past to me. *Isn't it enough for him to have always tried so hard to make me feel secure and cherished?* I'd ask myself, though I knew it wasn't.

After we'd eaten too many pancakes and while we were drinking the decaf coffee I'd made, he asked me for a cigarette.

'I haven't smoked for fifteen years,' I said.

'Nobody smokes anymore,' he said with an ugly frown.

'I think Shelly still smokes on the sly.'

'So where the hell is Shelly when I need him?'

'In Montreal.' I looked at my watch. 'It's a safe bet that at this very moment he's trying to convince Aunt Julie to hop under the bedsheets with him.'

Dad laughed merrily – kidding Shelly about his sexual appetite was part of our family comedy routine.

I might have tried to throw my arms around my dad and kiss him while he was giggling, but he got up to fetch one of the beanies he wears on his head when it gets cold.

Had he sensed I was about to embrace him?

Dad had often held my hand when I was a kid, and he'd cuddled with me all the time at home, but I remember him kissing me only once in public. I'd fallen while ice skating at a pond in Queens and opened a gash on my forehead. I started crying, and he picked me up and ran me to our car. Just before we got in, he kneeled down to my height and dried my eyes, and he held my head in both his hands and told me everything would be all right. 'Don't be scared,' he said, 'I won't ever let anything bad happen to you.' He whispered my name and pressed his lips to mine, and he told me that he loved me beyond the edge of the world. And then he kissed my gash as if his love could heal it. His lips and cheek ended up bloody but he didn't care.

Neither of us ever mentioned that amazing moment, but I often polished the memory as if it were made of gold.

Now, while Dad was fetching his beanie, I looked in the fridge and found four cartons of Tropicana orange juice, a half-gallon of skim milk, two eggs and some mouldy strawberries. I threw out the strawberries. The only other food I spotted was a can of tuna, two bananas and a limp-looking tomato that was sitting on the microwave.

'What are you eating these days for dinner?' I asked as soon as he returned to the kitchen.

'Try looking in the freezer, Inspector Poirot,' he replied.

I found nine bags of Libby's Steam and Go frozen peas. 'All you eat for dinner are peas?'

He was licking the brown sugar off his plate but paused long enough to say, 'Don't knock it if you haven't tried it.'

'You need to eat something else.'

'Says who?' he said with a scandalised expression.

'Says me. I'm taking you out for dinner. We'll go to the Sea Cove.'

'Eti, the Sea Cove hasn't been any good since you were peeing in your diapers.'

'We lived in Manhattan when I was peeing in my diapers. We never knew the Sea Cove even existed.'

He looked up to heaven. 'What did I do to deserve a kid who can always argue better than me?'

'We'll go to Cactus Taqueria,' I said. 'You love their burritos.'

He thought about that. 'Call them up for takeout. Get me a vegetarian burrito with no cheese and extra hot sauce. I'll give you money.'

'You need to get some air. We'll pick them up together. And you can save your money.'

'So, did your medical degree from Harvard finally come in the mail?' he asked with his eyebrows making a stern V.

'And you need a shower,' I told him. I held my nose for comic effect.

'Bah!'

'And take off those pyjamas. I need to put them in the laundry.'

'Are you finished with the lectures?' he asked, showing me a nasty frown.

'I'll finish them when you tell me what's going on.'

'Nothing's going on.'

'Well, what's with the bolo tie?' I asked.

'I felt like dressing up,' he said defiantly. 'Can't I dress up in my own house?' He looked past me as though enchanted by a memory. 'When you were small, I used to always wear a suit and tie whenever I'd go out. Those were the days!'

'You know what, you should put on a really nice shirt – one of the linen ones you made for yourself – and show everyone at the taqueria how handsome you look in your bolo tie.'

'Nah, I'm tired of being in the world. I've been out there,' he said, flapping his hand in the general direction of the street, 'for seventy years. When do I get to stay home?'

It seemed a reasonable query for a recently widowed man to ask, so I backed off. And I picked up vegetarian burritos for the two of us. But after I'd fluffed up his pillows and neatened his sheets that night, I questioned him if he was looking for anything special of late in all his kabbalah books. He was seated on the armchair in his living room, watching a black-and-white movie on TV.

'No, nothing,' he answered.

'I'm not sure I like you reading all the time about angels and demons and spirits, and all that other weird stuff.'

'Why not?'

'You're exhausted. We both are. You need a break.'

'I don't see what one thing has to do with the other,' he said.

'Look, Dad, if you tell me what you're looking for, I won't tell anyone, not even Angie.'

He turned down the volume on the TV and said, 'There's this piano player, and he plays only one note, and everybody in his family thinks he's crazy. And then one day . . .'

'No jokes,' I said, rolling my eyes.

'Ssshhh! And one day the piano player's son asks him why he only plays one note, and the piano player, he says, "Everybody else is looking for it, but I found it!"'

Dad looked at me defiantly.

'What exactly are you trying to say?' I asked.

'Isn't it obvious?'

'In the Yiddish original, maybe. In your English translation, no.'

'I'll know what I'm looking for in my books when I find it.'

Standing High Up on a Cliff

My father refused to leave the house with me even once that weekend, and I don't think he ever ventured further than his own front yard over the ensuing weeks. I insisted that he tell me why on my next visit, which was about a month after my first one, but he just kept repeating to me that he was too tired to participate in the world any longer.

Had he developed agoraphobia? My sister-in-law Mariana was a clinical psychologist in Denver, and she raised that possibility with me when I called her, but she also said that Dad's grief might simply have sapped all his energy. 'If that's the case,' she added, 'he ought to recover his vitality bit by bit. But either way, you ought to get him into therapy.'

He isn't ever going to sit in a room and tell a stranger or anyone else about his life, is what I didn't tell her. Instead, I thanked her for her help and told her I'd do my best.

In late May, three months and a week after Mom's death, I had trouble reaching my father on the Friday before I was supposed to come for another visit, this time with my wife, Angie, and our son, George. He didn't answer the phone all morning, so at about eleven-thirty I called Mrs Narayan and told her where I'd hidden a spare key to his front door.

'There's a problem,' she told me when she phoned about ten minutes later. She was crying.

I felt as if I were standing high up on a cliff and that I'd fall a thousand feet straight down if I made a false move. 'He's dead, isn't he?' I whispered.

'No, I thought he was, but he's not.' She took a deep breath. 'I've called an ambulance. They're on their way.'

I sat down because the world had started revolving slowly around me. 'What happened?'

'I don't know. I found him lying on the kitchen floor.'

'Where is he now?'

'Still where he was. I didn't want to risk moving him – in case something is broken.'

'Is he breathing?'

'Yeah – but slowly.'

'And where are you?'

'Sitting in the dining room.'

'Would you hold the phone to his ear so I can talk to him?'

'I'm afraid he . . . he isn't going to hear you.'

'A part of him might hear some of what I tell him.'

'Okay. Wait a minute.'

I waited for Mrs Narayan to tell me she was ready, then started telling Dad that help was on the way. Without intending to, I also told him that I loved him in Yiddish, over and over, as if I were keeping him in the world with those four little words: *ikh hob dikh lib*.

All They Meant to Each Other

Shelly joined us at the hospital two days later. Dad was out of Intensive Care by then and in his own room, and eager to complain to me about the wretched hospital food. He assured me that he'd had no intention of committing suicide; he'd simply had trouble sleeping and lost count of the number of Valiums he had taken and had maybe drunk one or two schnapps as well. 'To settle my stomach,' he told me.

The combination of alcohol and tranquilisers must have dangerously lowered his blood pressure and caused him to pass out when he went downstairs in the middle of the night for a glass of orange juice. His forehead had hit hard against the kitchen floor and a big bandage covered the wound. He and Shelly joked in a mixture of Yiddish and English about how hard his skull must be not to have been cracked by the impact.

When Dad got up to pee, his hospital gown opened, and I saw how skinny he'd become; it occurred to me that he was slowly but surely turning himself back into the lonely orphan he'd been in the Warsaw Ghetto.

Do we prepare for death by going back to our worst times? I began to wonder.

A couple of days earlier, when I'd first seen him in the Intensive Care Unit, attached to tubes and with an oxygen mask over his gaunt face, I began looking for ways to make sure he would never suffer alone again. My mind began spinning out toward the ways I would get him to rejoin the world, and a few of them seemed reasonable at two or three in the morning, but when I woke up at dawn they seemed absolutely impossible, especially because I knew he would never accept having a live-in nurse or healthcare worker.

Insomnia assailed me the entire time he was in the hospital, and on his fourth day there, I nodded off in his room while Shelly was reminiscing with him about his mother's gefilte fish, and how she would keep a live carp and pike in the bathtub until she was ready to make it. When I woke up, Shelly had moved real close to Dad, who was propped up by two pillows. My father frowned and said something abrupt in Yiddish, but Shelly replied to him in English. 'Are you kidding?' he said. 'You did great, Benni. I'm really proud of you. *Vraiment fier!*' Then he pressed his lips to my father's, and he kept them there for far longer than most men would consider appropriate, and he held my Dad's shoulders as well, and when they finally separated, Dad was crying, and my arms and legs were tingling, and my head seemed to be encased in glass. I pretended that I was still asleep so that they would keep talking, but for a long time they didn't say anything, and I found myself drifting back to another time and place, to the first time I met Shelly, and I remembered him tossing me high into the air and catching me – and kissing me all over – maybe because that's when I first realised that he had a boldness that was missing in my dad, and all of a sudden the easy, affectionate way the two cousins had always complemented each other made perfect sense, and I realised that they had meant even more to each other that I'd thought, and that their lives were far more nuanced and complex than I'd ever suspected.

Schmuel the Candlemaker

I drove Dad home the next day. The crab apple trees in his yard were fluffy pink clouds, the breezes were warm and welcoming for the first time in months, and blue jays and squirrels were darting everywhere. Once my father was settled in his bedroom, Shelly asked me to come with him for coffee at the Starbucks on Willis Avenue. The moment we were outside, he requested that I tell him everything that had happened with my father over the past few months.

I got the story out of me without choking up, but while Shelly was buying a chocolate *mandelbrot* for Dad at the Seven Dwarfs Bakery I had to go outside to keep from crying in front of the salesgirls.

Dad's favourite food in the world was chocolate *mandelbrot*. Mom told me that for years he used to hide a piece under his pillow at night – folded in a napkin – in case he woke up hungry.

'Hey, kiddo, we'll figure this out!' Shelly told me when he got outside. He handed me the bag to carry. 'Don't you worry, Eti.'

We walked home arm in arm.

Would my life have been easier if Shelly had been my dad? I tried not to ask myself that question, but I did.

On his last night at my father's house, Shelly and I got drunk after Dad was already sound asleep, and we sat around the kitchen table talking about what life was like in Algiers in the 1940s. In the middle of his story about how he and a friend once stole a bunch of car tyres from a French cargo ship, Shelly shook his head and said, 'Jesus Christ, why do I talk about such bullshit?'

I shrugged. 'Because we're both upset.'

'*Non, c'est pas ça*. I just try to keep from breaking my word to your dad,' he replied. 'But I'm going to. Listen, kiddo, your father, what is happening to him now . . . It has to do with Grandma Rosa and the ghetto. I think your dad is on strike.'

'On strike for what?'

'Fuck if I know, but that's what people do who don't have power – they organise a strike.' He swirled his finger around the rim of his whisky glass while trying to locate the right words. 'I need to tell you some secrets . . . secrets about Rosa. I mean if you're going to understand your father and me and everything else – even yourself.'

Shelly's slurred speech made me realise he was smashed and that he probably needed to be in order to divulge secrets to me that had been hiding in his heart for sixty years.

I wasn't sure if an eighty-seven-year-old man ought to drink so much, and I almost confiscated the whisky bottle, but I figured that if Shelly survived the Nazis hunting him down in the forests of Poland, he could survive a couple of glasses of Jack Daniel's.

He leaned forward in his chair and, in his slurred, idiosyncratic, French-accented English, told me that my great-great-grandmother Rosa wasn't the simple matchmaker I'd thought. 'Once, you know, she revives a man who has died,' he told me in a menacing voice.

He explained that the resurrected man was a candlemaker named Schmuel. A rooftile had fallen on his head during a snowstorm in January of 1941 and killed him.

'Rosa brings Schmuel back to life with one of her prayers,' Shelly said. 'And just a few days later, he returns to work.' Shelly shrugged. 'As if nothing at all has happened. After that, people start whispering about Rosa and her special talents. She is . . .'

'But wait a minute,' I cut in, 'was Schmuel really dead or just knocked out?'

'No pulse, no breathing – you tell me!'

He stuck a cigarette between his lips but didn't light it because his doctor had told him that his lungs were shot and he couldn't risk it. He rubbed his eyes as if he needed a break, so I stood up and gazed down at the crab apples by the back fence, and it was while I was admiring how the moonlight turned their branches to silver that I remembered what Dad had written in blue pencil: *Do you really think so, Mr Scholem?*

I went back to Shelly. His eyes were closed and his breathing was shallow.

'We could go up to your room. I'll get you into bed, and you could tell me what you need to, then go straight to sleep.'

He patted my leg and smiled. 'I'm okay, kiddo,' he told me. 'Don't worry about me.'

Shelly sat up straight and rubbed a hand through his thinning grey hair to rouse himself. I noticed then how beautiful his long-lashed, green eyes still were. They seemed to indicate that he was chosen in some way – perhaps to tell me all the stories my dad wouldn't. 'Pretty soon, Shmuel begins coming to our Sabbath suppers,' he continued. 'And he brings us little gifts.'

'What kind of gifts?'

He waved his hand at me with disgust, just like Dad. 'Molasses candy, bad books, bags of sawdust . . . And that horrible ghetto soap that melts when it sees water! And candles, *mon Dieu*, we have enough candles to set Poland on fire. And you know what, maybe we should have!' He laughed in a burst.

'Why sawdust?' I asked.

'The makeshift ovens we have – they burn sawdust.'

Shelly said that the gifts stopped a few months later when Schmuel was picked up by the Jewish police and put on a crew working outside the ghetto.

'So you never saw him again?'

'Nope.'

'Was he killed?'

Shelly shrugged. 'Probably. Just after the war, I hunt for everyone. I have to find my sister Esther and your father. And then I go back a second time with George, of course. After that visit, I realise that the Nazis murder nearly everybody. So I do what I can to forget.'

Rosa the *Mekhasheyfe*

The first time Dad ever took me to Montreal was when I was six years old, and that was when I discovered that Shelly kept a framed newspaper clipping of Grandma Rosa's ninety-second birthday party on the piano in his living room. The article was written in Yiddish – which uses Hebrew characters – so I was unable to read it. The postage-stamp-sized photograph of my great-great grandmother impressed me as a kid, however. Rosa's face was as wrinkled as a walnut but her deep-set eyes were so keenly intelligent and mysterious that they made me shiver. My father told me that they'd been light brown, but when I drew Rosa with my crayons I made them emerald green; they seemed that bright to me.

In the photo, she sits behind a small round cake topped with two slender candles. She wears a pursed and amused smile, as if she is indulging the photographer, who is clearly someone she adores.

The photographer was her youngest son, Karl – or Carlo, as most everybody called him.

On that same visit, Mom told me that Shelly had inherited

Rosa's stunning, Arabian-Nights eyes. I hadn't noticed their frame of dark lashes until I studied them from afar a little later. And when he noticed me staring, he swooped me up, and I touched my fingertip to them, which made him growl and bite my neck. After I'd finished laughing, he put me down and whispered, 'My eyes are powerful magic, Eti.'

'Can you even kill Germans with them?' I asked.

'You bet!' he replied with a confident nod.

But I only found out what Shelly really meant years later when I overheard Dad telling a customer – while pinning the bottom hem on a dress he'd made her – that his cousin had bedroom eyes like nobody since Rudolph Valentino.

Now, seated opposite each other in Dad's kitchen, Shelly told me that the article he'd kept on his piano said that Rosa had revived Schmuel the candlemaker with a kiss and not a prayer.

When I suggested that it must have been a great temptation for a half-starving ghetto reporter to make life seem like a happy fairy tale, Shelly disagreed. 'No, Rosa must tell him about the kiss. She never likes to talk about her special ways.'

'Are you saying she knew spells and incantations?' I asked, though that suggestion seemed absurd the moment I spoke it.

He drizzled more whisky into his glass and considered how to reply. 'She is a kind of holy woman,' he finally said. 'People whisper that she is a *mekhasheyfe* – a Jewish sorceress. Eti, I know you don't believe in all that stuff – and that you don't even believe in God. And I'm with you on that. Back in Poland, I realise that there isn't anybody up in heaven who cares about any of this shit down here. But the world is so different then. It is normal for everybody to think that Rosa is maybe a *mekhasheyfe*. For Christ's sake, people pay her to make marriages! And there are anti-Semites hiding under every bush, and some streets in big cities are still just dirt, and the synagogues are huge wooden castles. People like Rosa . . . She cures you with her hands and prayers. You might think I'm lying, but I see her help people. It works sometimes. Maybe because most everyone is convinced that she has that kind of power.'

I felt as if a gate had just opened, and I became anxious to rush through it to where Shelly wanted to take me, which was back to his childhood. And my father's, too. 'Rosa the *Mekhasheyfe*,' I whispered to myself, as if it were the title of a novel that my dad might have spent many years writing in secret.

'Did you ever learn any of Rosa's incantations,' I asked.

'Me? No. She tells me they would be dangerous to me.' He winked and made a fist the way he does to indicate an erection. 'She knows I'll use whatever she teaches me to have my way with pretty girls!'

The Direction of the Soul

After I made Shelly and me a pot of coffee, he recited the prayer that Rosa had used to bring Shmuel the candlemaker back to life:

בָּרוּךְ אַתָּה ה', אֱ-לֹהֵינוּ מֶלֶךְ הָעוֹלָם, אֲשֶׁר קִדְּשָׁנוּ בְּמִצְוֹתָיו, וְצִוָּנוּ לְהַדְלִיק נֵר שֶׁל שַׁבָּת.

Blessed are you, Lord, our God, sovereign of the universe, who has sanctified us with His commandments and commanded us to light the lights of Shabbat.

Jewish women speak this prayer when they light the candles at the supper table just before the traditional Friday-night dinner. Shelly told me that Rosa whispered the blessing over Schmuel seven times.

A minute or so earlier, she'd seen him crumple to the ground. She'd been sitting in the clock repair shop where Luna, her eldest daughter – my father's grandmother – was employed. 'Rosa spends her afternoons there,' Shelly told me, 'because the owner bribes the Nazis to get coal for his stoves, and it is well heated.'

It suddenly seemed as if the past were too complicated for me – that I might get tangled in all of Shelly's details and never find my way out. 'It's really good to find all this out,' I told him, 'but I don't see what this has to do with my dad's refusal to leave the house over the last few months.'

'Wait, kiddo, I'm coming to that!' he replied, and he took a big, satisfied sip of his coffee.

He told me that when Rosa made a match between a young man and woman, she would look deep into each of them to see the direction that their souls were facing. An individual soul, she'd explained to Shelly, Benni and their other cousins, normally faced either north, south, east or west. In rare instances, however, a person's soul might face up or down. 'Grandma Rosa tells me that souls that face up should not marry,' he said.

'Why?'

'They focus on God's hidden life and other loony subjects – all those things that your dad likes to read about. They tend to make bad husbands and wives – too distant. And they never earn a decent living.'

'So does my dad's soul face up?'

'At the moment, I think it's facing west. It makes a turn when your mom . . . when she leaves us. His soul is kind of unique – it can twist around. That's part of what I need to tell you. Anyone with a soul facing west . . . They get depressed. The world to them seems really dark at times. Rosa told me once that that was why they make the best poets. Like your Aunt Julie. She works on poems in her diary. And some of them are pretty good. Though she only reads them to me. She has a western soul. Me, I face east, as you've probably figured out.'

'And my soul?' I asked.

He shrugged. 'I don't know. I can't see into you like Rosa. But what I mean to say is that your father has developed a type of . . . inclination toward sadness. Because of the current direction his soul.'

'Shelly, do you really believe all this?' I asked.

'*Oui, absolument.* Because east and west and north and south aren't just physical directions. It's more subtle than that. Though I'm not sure I really understand it. But what's important is that your dad believes what Rosa tells us. And maybe *he* understands.' Shelly took another long sip of his coffee. 'And now we come to the last part of what I need to say to you.' He raised a hand over me as if to partake in a ritual, closed his eyes and whispered what sounded like a Yiddish blessing.

When I asked him what he'd said, he replied, 'A protective incantation that Rosa taught us.'

'So she did teach you some of what she knew!'

'Yeah, she figured we needed a little extra help if we were going to survive the Nazis. So back then, when I'm by myself, when I'm frightened, I whisper that incantation over and over. Your dad does the same. Rosa tells us that the human voice . . . It is very powerful and protective.

'Okay, so we come to July 22nd, 1942,' Shelly continued. 'Your father goes out hunting for discarded clothes and anything useful in the rubbish heaps near Sienna Street. That is where the wealthiest people in the ghetto live. But on the way back home, a Jewish policeman in a wagon, he stops your dad and orders him to climb up. About a dozen men and women are there. A second policeman is with them. Your dad doesn't know where they will go. But an old man in the wagon . . .' Shelly's voice faltered and he cleared his throat. 'He tells your dad they go to Umschlagplatz.'

Foreboding gripped my heart; the freight trains that took Warsaw's Jews to Treblinka left from Umschlagplatz.

'Why did the Jewish policeman choose my father?' I asked.

Shelly replied that Dad had been holding a torn lampshade that he'd found on the street and very likely the policeman had taken a liking to it. He confiscated it from my father right away.

Shelly shook his head at the sad impossibility of it all.

'I'm sorry I've made you speak about these things,' I told him.

He patted my hand and said, 'No, I want to remember.' He took a steadying couple of breaths. 'Anyway, the wagon goes by the clockmaker's shop where Rosa visits her daughter. The owner – Mr Kessel – sees your dad. He grabs our Grandma Luna and they run outside. Rosa hobbles out after them, and they all shout at the policemen to stop. "Give me back my grandson!" Luna yells. But the head policeman says it is too late. "Go away!" he tells her. So you know what, Eti? Luna lays down right in front of the horse. My God, what a woman!'

By then, a crowd began to gather, Shelly explained. And Rosa limped up to the wagon. '"Give me back my boy!" she orders the policemen.

'"The Nazis give me a quota," one of them tells her. "If I don't make it, more people die." He points to his colleague. "Ten Jews for him, and ten for me. If the boy leaves, who will substitute him?"

'"I will," Rosa tells him, so the policeman says, "Why should I accept you instead of him?"

'She shouts back, "Because if you don't, I will curse you and your family, and all of you will die in the ghetto! And no one – not even a rabbi – will say any prayers for you, and you will walk the earth as a spirit – a *dybbuk* – for all eternity!"'

Shelly looked at me with blazing eyes – he was still fighting the Nazis after all these years.

'So what happened then?' I asked.

'The policemen, they give up. Rosa scares them too much.'

'And my dad goes free?'

'Yes, Benni jumps down off the wagon. But then,' he added, his voice darkening, 'Mr Kessel and some other people help Rosa into the wagon. And that is that.'

'That is what?'

'They go off to Umschlagplatz.'

'Grandma Luna just let her mother go?'

Shelly tilted his head and waved his hand at me, as if to indicate I'd said something silly. 'Sorry, Eti, that you even ask such a question means you were never there.' He leaned forward and took my shoulder. 'Don't get me wrong, I'm not criticising you. I'm happy... more happy than you can ever imagine that you were not with us in the ghetto. But what you ask – it's just not a question that means anything... not to Luna or me or anyone else who was there.'

In case I had any doubts about the significance of what he'd just told me, Shelly whispered, 'Your father cannot forgive himself for substituting Rosa. He thinks he sends a holy woman to a death camp. When he is young and strong – when he has your mom – he can fight against all that guilt. He knows he must give you a good home, he knows he must help your mom, he knows he must make suits and dresses and earn decent money. But now that your mom isn't with us...' Shelly reached for his coffee and downed the last of it. 'Our little Benni can't go on the way he always has. Maybe he doesn't think he deserves a good life anymore. He looks in all those kabbalah books of his, but still he does not find the doorway out of guilt. And maybe there isn't one.' Shelly leaned back in his chair abruptly, which made his spine crack.

'Hey, be careful!' I told him.

He shrugged as if it were of no import. 'It's just old bones.' His expression grew serious. 'Let me tell you something, kiddo. Guilt – after a while, it's like swallowing stones. And your father swallows thousands over the years. All that weight inside him . . . He can't get up anymore. I mean, he walks around, but he's not really walking.'

A little later, I helped Shelly get into bed, and his eyes closed as if he might not open them again for a long time, and I kissed them because he'd seen too many terrible things in his life, which made him caress my cheek. 'Go to bed, kiddo, you're tired too,' he said.

I went to my father's room and made a nest for myself in the armchair where he tossed his clothing and watched him sleep, picturing the moment he stepped down from the horse-drawn wagon in Warsaw as both the best and worst I could ever imagine.

After a while, I moved to Dad's bed, but I didn't touch him because I wanted to feel my need to comfort him as deeply as possible, and only when I couldn't bear it any longer did I lay my hand on his chest, and I thought, *No wonder you always had to say you were sorry with more than words*.

I sensed that I'd arrived somewhere new and unexpected – a place where I forgave him for everything he had ever done wrong. And where he forgave me too.

But it was Rosa whose pardon he needed, wasn't it? She had been fighting with her prayers and incantations – with a thousand years of Jewish mystical knowledge – to protect her family and friends, and maybe everyone in the ghetto. It must have occurred to my father – probably not long after his rescue – that he could never hope to replace her.

No One Is Ever Ready

I tried to act normal around Dad and Shelly the next morning at breakfast, but my expression must have given away how jittery I felt.

'You look like you're coming down with a cold,' my father said. 'Lean down.'

He was seated at the kitchen table opposite Shelly. He held his hand to my forehead. 'You don't feel hot.' He glanced over at his cousin. 'I don't think he has a fever. You check.'

I stood back up. 'I'm not coming down with anything,' I told him with a put-upon sigh.

Shelly held up his fist. 'The poor kid just needs to get laid,' he said to make us laugh.

He packed his bag after breakfast, and I got ready to take him to the airport.

He and my father kissed cheeks at the front door and spoke in rapid-fire Yiddish. I heard Dad say *Julie* very clearly, so he must have asked Shelly to give her his love. When my father finally let go of his cousin's hand, he said, 'See you later, Shel.'

'*À plus tard*, Benni,' Shelly replied, fighting to smile.

They always spoke the same formula when they had to say goodbye. The idea of a definitive parting was simply too terrifying.

Once Shelly was buckled up in the passenger seat of my Volvo, he patted my leg and said, 'You look like shit.'

'I'm okay. Just a bit disoriented. I feel like I've finally stopped running – after forty-five years of trying to catch up to my father.'

'That's probably a good thing.'

After we were on the freeway, Shelly looked over at me as if he were afraid to ask something.

'Go ahead,' I told him.

'What do you plan to do with your father's secrets?'

'I don't know yet.'

'He's going to scream at me because I told you, you know.'

'I'll make sure he screams at me instead of you.'

He shrugged. 'I guess it no longer matters. Living with the Angel of Death changes things. Can you believe I'm eighty-seven years old?'

'No. And I'm not ready to say goodbye to either of you,' I told him.

'Here's another secret, baby – no one's ever ready.'

Who Has These Conversations With Their Children?

For dinner that evening, I picked up burritos again from Cactus Taqueria. Dad ate his with his hands and ended up licking the hot sauce from each of his fingers and also the aluminum foil.

'You have a tongue like an anteater,' I said, laughing.

'So, who wouldn't want a tongue like an anteater? Anyway, this hot sauce is my cocaine.'

When it came time for me to carry his dish to the sink, I squatted next to him, and I saw him as a man and not just my father, and we seemed to have been connected forever, since even before I was born, and I pressed my lips to his.

I felt a jolt inside him, but he didn't lean back or fight me.

When I pulled away, he looked like he'd swallowed another one of his guilt stones, so I told him that everything was okay – that he didn't have to say or do anything. 'I just love you,' I said in a confessional voice.

He blinked twice, unsure of what to say, and then he motioned me forward and whispered in my ear, 'I love you beyond the edge of the world.'

The unfallen tears in his eyes took away my voice and started me crying as well. We looked at each other as if we'd reached home after a long journey – and were completely safe. Soon, however, our intimacy became too much for him and, with a pat on my shoulder, he said that there was an NBA basketball game on TV that he wanted to watch, since the San Antonio Spurs – his favourite team – were playing. I have no recollection of how the game went or if the Spurs won. Dad kept his hand on my leg like he used to do when I was small, and whenever our eyes met he showed me the smile of his that meant that he was just where he wanted to be. It seemed that we both knew that something amazing had happened but that talking about it might spoil it. I ended up thinking of Mom and wishing that she was with us, and my mind travelled back to all the times the three of us had been together in this house and watching *Poirot* or *Inspector Morse* on Channel 13.

The next morning, I woke up thinking, *It's now or never*; I'd told Angie that I'd drive home that evening, so I had to come up with a way of convincing my father to rejoin the world right away.

I think that the kiss I'd given him the night before must have given him insomnia, because he yawned through breakfast. Just after he'd taken his blood pressure pill, he said, 'I think you must have seen me and Shelly.'

'Seen you in what way?' I asked.

'In the hospital room. When we ... hugged.'

I was eating a second bowl of oatmeal and paused just long enough to say, 'Yeah, I saw that.'

'You were only pretending to be asleep,' he said.

'Guilty as charged, your honour.'

'He shouldn't have hugged me like that.'

'Why not?'

'Didn't it bother you?'

'Why would it bother me to see two men who love each other kissing?'

'I don't know.' He twisted his lips back and forth while considering what to say. 'It's not so very normal.'

'It seems perfectly normal to me.'

He took a deep breath. 'If you want to ask me, you can.'

My gut tensed up because he looked so upset. 'Ask you what?' I said.

'Ask about me and Shelly.'

'I don't need to ask anything. That's between you and him.'

Dad gazed down. I could tell his heart was battering against his ribs.

'No more stones,' I said. 'Not with me.'

'What?'

'You don't need to feel guilty about this – not with me. It's a very good thing that Shelly loves you so much. You two . . . I think it was maybe the most beautiful kiss I've ever seen.'

Dad gazed down again. 'Shel was my first. I mean, I was lost. He helped me. He had returned to Poland to try to locate Esther and me. When he found me . . . I was just sixteen.'

'I'm glad your first time was with a real expert.'

Dad laughed as if he might soon start crying. 'This conversation is *meshugge,*' he said, rubbing his hand over his face as if to wake himself up. 'Who has these conversations with their children?'

'Well, maybe we should have them a lot more often.'

She Had Only One Chance

While I was cutting tomatoes for lunch, Dad came up beside me and studied my technique as if it were the most interesting thing in the world, which meant he had something urgent to say but wasn't going to say it. Or so I thought. When I put my knife down, he held my hand in both of his and moved his fingertip over the lines in my palm. 'Your hands were so tiny when you were a baby. And so beautiful.'

When I looked up at his face, he was fighting tears so hard that he'd folded his lips inside his mouth.

My heart seemed to leap inside my chest. 'Are you okay, Dad?' I rushed to ask.

'Yes, I'm fine.' He wiped away his tears. 'I used to study your lifeline and think, I want this boy to outlive me by fifty years, no matter what. I want him to be happy. I don't want him to be burdened with any of my sadness.'

'I've had a good life,' I said.

'No thanks from me,' he said with a frown.

I suddenly understood the conversation he'd had with Shelly in the hospital. 'You did the best you could,' I told him. 'That's all any kid can ask his father, isn't it?'

'It wasn't nearly enough,' he said, misery creasing his face.

'You did great. I always knew you loved me. You were a wonderful dad! And you used to make me and Mom laugh all the time. And I'm doing fine. I've got a good life.'

He didn't seem comforted by my words, so I sat him down at the kitchen table and took his hand. I studied the lines in his palm just like he'd studied mine, but they didn't tell me anything that I didn't already know. 'I think Grandma Rosa realised she had no other choice,' I told him.

He pulled his hand back. 'What are you talking about?'

'Shelly told me about you and Rosa.'

His face turned accusatory. 'What did he tell you?'

'About the Jewish policemen who chose you for a transport to Treblinka and how Luna stopped the wagon.'

'That bastard!' He looked toward the front door as if he still might be able to catch Shelly and scream at him.

'It was my fault,' I rushed to say. 'I made him tell me.'

'That's crap. No one can make Shelly do anything he doesn't want to do! No one!'

'I guess he did what he felt was right.'

'With my life – he's playing with my life!'

'It's my life too.'

Dad fumed at me with his eyes bulging – his dragon face, I used to call it – then got up and started looking in kitchen drawers.

'What are you looking for?' I asked.

'My goddamn cigarettes!'

He couldn't find where he'd hidden them. I tried to calm him down, but he pushed me away.

'Listen, I know I'll never know what it's like to have been where you've been,' I said. 'And I know that there are things you don't want me to know. But I also know that if you hadn't lived, I wouldn't have been born. I wouldn't be here.'

'Don't you think I know that?!' he shouted.

'And my kids wouldn't be here.'

'Listen, there's nothing you could say to me that I haven't already thought of. I'm not a dummy. And I've had seventy years to think about what happened.'

'Maybe Rosa saved you for a reason. Maybe she saw something that you could do but she couldn't – something really important.'

'Listen, smart guy, why do you think I've been reading Gershom Scholem all these years? But you know what I learned? That God can't be known. Which means we can't know our destiny either. Because there's no such thing! Grandma Rosa didn't have to die in a camp.'

'All I know is that if she thought she had another option, she'd have taken it. She had insights into the way things work.'

'You don't really believe that!'

'I don't know what I believe anymore. But Shelly told me that he believes. And that you do too. Rosa must have known that she had only one chance to save you. People can know things like that. They sense them. I'm sure of it. She must have wanted to go on living, but she . . .'

'Of course she wanted to go on living!' he shrieked.

'So the only possibility is that she couldn't have lived with herself if you had been taken to Treblinka.'

'That's idiotic! She could have lived with herself. You weren't there. You don't know anything. People gave up their grandchildren and children all the time.' To himself, he whispered, 'If she'd never figured out about . . .' And then he said something in what might have been Yiddish, that sounded like *mesrat nesh*, though I discovered later that the correct term was *mesirat nefesh*.

'I don't understand,' I said.

'Rosa could have gone on without me just fine, Eti. That's what I mean. Christ, the whole world went on after my parents were turned to ash. And who the hell remembers them now? Who the hell remembers them or Rosa or any of them?!'

'I remember them. And you and Shelly remember them.'

Dad opened the big drawer that held all the kitchen implements. I thought he was still looking for his cigarettes, but instead he grabbed his corkscrew and took it in his fist and hurled it at the kitchen window as hard as he could. Astonishingly, it made only a single small crack.

Dad held his head in his hands. 'Look at me, I can't even break a fucking window!'

He looked as if he might retrieve the corkscrew and try again, so I rushed to it and snatched it up.

'You're a big help,' he sneered.

'Dad, imagine having to give me up to the Nazis.'

He faced me as if I had gone too far, vibrating with rage. 'If I had to give you up, I would have!' he said in a trembling voice.

'I don't believe that.'

'Believe what you want. I was there, you weren't!' Tears gushed in his eyes. 'Oh, God, you don't understand anything.' His shoulders hunched and he began to sob. Then his legs gave way and he dropped to the floor and curled his arm over his eyes.

I sat with him and embraced him while he shook.

'Dad, I'll never know Rosa, but Shelly told me that she believed she could see the destiny of every person's soul. So if that's true, then she saw yours when you were up in the wagon. And she saw what you would do in the future – or at least she sensed it. And whatever she sensed must have convinced her that she had to save you. And not just you. She had to save me and your grandchildren. And she knew that she wouldn't get a second chance to do it, and it was so incredibly important to her that she got up into that wagon and did what she had to do.'

When he grabbed my hand, I thought he was going to tell me again that I understood nothing, but he said in a sad voice, 'I've thought of that too, Eti, and I hope you're right, but I just don't know.'

Dena and the Potato Chips

Dad went to a kennel in Glen Cove when I was seven and brought me and Mom home a Shetland sheepdog named Dena. It was love at first sight for me and my mother.

Dena learned to go up the stairs in our house over that first week, but she was too terrified to go down them. She would shiver and whine until one of us picked her up.

Mom overcame Dena's fear by placing a Lay's potato chip on each step of the staircase; Dena loved potato chips more than anything in the world, and by the time she got to the ground floor, she was licking the salt off her lips and her fear was cured.

Things didn't work out quite that well with my dad, but I used the same technique.

By then, Angie had come down from Boston, since I'd told her I couldn't go home yet. She and I coaxed Dad to come with us to the Seven Dwarfs Bakery by telling him they had a sale on chocolate *mandelbrot*.

My father had a panic attack while we walked there, but we sat with him on the curb, her arm over his shoulder. While he panted and sweated, I squatted down in front of him and told him that we wouldn't let anything bad happen to him, but that only made him snort at me and tell me to make myself useful and get him some water.

Shortly before he finished the bottle I bought, he stopped panting, and I handed him a napkin to dry his face and neck.

'Should we go home, Benni?' Angie asked.

'What, and miss the sale at the bakery?' he said in disbelief. 'Are you nuts?'

Once he'd picked out the *mandelbrot* he wanted, we convinced him to come with us to Starbucks for coffee. From there, we walked all the way to Waldbaum's – a half-mile away – to get him chocolate sorbet and pick up a pack of Marlboro Lights, though I talked him out of the cigarettes once we got there.

Two Costa Rican workers from Mineola Glass came and replaced the cracked window in the kitchen while we were eating our sorbet. Dad offered each of them a bowl with a couple of scoops to thank them for working so quickly.

After they'd gone, he started eating the sorbet out of the container and announced that he wasn't going back out for a few more days at least. 'That was the panic attack from hell,' he told us. 'And I'm getting too old to risk anything worse.'

'You've got to go out again,' Angie told him. 'It's really important.' She gathered her long brown hair behind her head and got out a hair-tie and made herself a ponytail, which was a sign that she was steeling for a battle.

'No, in point of fact, I don't,' he replied. 'And it's not important – not even for me.'

'So, what does a panic attack from hell feel like?' she asked.

'I'll put it like this – it's like my heart is going to explode,' he said.
'And if it does, what'll happen?'

'I'll drop dead, of course.'

'Benni, my love, we're all going to drop dead one day.'

He pointed his spoon at her, and some sorbet dripped on the floor. 'But not with a heart explosion!' he snarled.

Angie tore off a paper towel. 'I'm pretty sure that from where you've been, you can imagine deaths a whole lot worse than a heart explosion.'

While she cleaned up the spill, he squinted at her, as if she'd outsmarted him. Still, he wasn't about to give up. 'You know something, Miss Anthropology Professor,' he said dismissively. 'You're even worse than my son.'

B-plus

Peter the mailman called me five days after Angie and I returned to Boston to say that the mail was piling up again.

Was that Dad's way of asking for additional help?

By then, I'd spotted what I thought was a workable plan inside all my crazy, wayward solutions, so I drove down the following Thursday, since I didn't have any classes on Friday. After supper, I gave him a big glass of port wine and he fell asleep in the living room in front of the TV. I tiptoed upstairs and packed a bag of his favourite T-shirts and trousers, and another with all his books on kabbalah and a selection of my mother's cassette tapes.

The very next morning, before doubts could undermine my resolve, I told him I needed to buy spring clothes and coaxed him out for a ride to Macy's. 'You won't even have to get out of the car,' I told him. 'I'll go shop and you can listen to WQXR.' That was Dad's favourite classical station; Grandpa Morrie had turned him into an avid listener long before I was born.

'I guess that'll be okay,' he told me.

When I kept on going past the exit for Great Neck, he said, 'You missed the turn-off, Eti.'

'Did I?'

'Absolutely.'

When I didn't get off at the next exit, Dad showed me a suspicious look. 'What's going on? Are you kidnapping me?'

'It's your grandson George's birthday tomorrow, and I told him you'd be there.' I showed him a challenging look. 'He adores you. And you're not going to turn me into a liar, are you?'

'Are you nuts?'

'Yes.'

He pounded the dashboard. 'Turn around!'

'Too late.'

'I can't go to Boston. I don't even have a change of clothing.'

'You do – I packed a bag for you.'

'You did what?'

'I packed a bag of clothing for you. And put everything Gershom Scholem ever wrote in a box. And I have all your medications, too. It's all in the trunk of the car.'

'Who gave you permission for that?'

'No one.'

'This is *meshugge*!'

'Yeah, welcome to my life.'

'But I can't go without tapes of your mother!' he said, groaning.

I congratulated myself on being able to predict his deepest worry. 'I packed them, too, Dad. Including the one of Mom and Belle where they sing together.'

Belle was an elderly Appalachian woman who became a good friend of my parents back in the 1960s.

My father gazed out the window while considering what move

to make next. 'I haven't heard your mom and Belle in years,' he said in a dreamy voice.

'Then you've got a treat in store,' I said.

'I seemed to have raised a dictator!' he snapped, which made me flinch, but when I turned to him I spotted amused admiration in his eyes, and when I rested my hand on his leg, he let it stay there. A little later, while we were crossing the Throgs Neck Bridge, I asked how he was doing. He was looking out the window back at the houses along the north shore of Long Island. 'It's a really nice view from up here,' he said. He flapped his arms. 'It's like we're flying.'

We stopped for Mexican food in Mystic, and he wolfed down his guacamole tacos with a big cup of coffee. While I was enjoying how he licked his lips, I realised that I had no idea where the two of us were headed – and didn't care.

Is half the trick in life learning to improvise? And if Angie and I timed our request just right, could we get him to stay with us indefinitely?

Dad needed to pee, so I waited for him out by my car, and I found myself humming 'Chryzantemy złociste' to myself. As he came to me, he smiled and said, 'The toilet didn't flush so well, but the sinks were spic and span and the mirrors were shiny. B-plus.'

'Not bad,' I said.

After I helped him into the passenger seat, I started thinking that B-plus is about as good a grade as any of us can expect to have at the end of our days.

After I'd buckled Dad in, I started the car, and as we left the parking lot, he asked in a hopeful voice if I'd mind stopping at some swanky clothes store in Boston before going home so that he could buy something wonderful for his grandson. 'And I want to go to your studio right away, too. I haven't seen any of your new paintings.'

I felt a click in my chest as he said that – a sign of renewed trust, it seemed to me – and I rose to meet his enthusiasm, telling him that I wanted him to pose for me at my studio, and he nodded his agreement and turned on the radio to find a jazz station, because he'd had enough of Bach and Mozart and was in the mood for some Louis Armstrong or Chet Baker, and we drove down the main street in Mystic toward everything that we didn't yet know would happen.

THE DEAD
THINK SO TOO
(1952-1977)

When Dr Lai told me that Shelly had collapsed in the stockroom of his shop because he'd had a stroke, I felt the blood shooting up through the top of my head like a missile. Soon after that, sweat began pouring from my neck and the hospital corridor started gyrating around me. My daughters led me to a chair, and I lowered my head between my legs. Sometime afterward, without knowing exactly how I'd gotten there, I was seated next to my husband and I had a paper cup filled with water in my hand. Shelly was asleep. He had an IV in his arm and had kicked off his blanket, so I stood up to cover him. He was wearing a loose-fitting blue smock that made him look like a schoolboy in art class. A television monitor to the side of his bed tracked the jagged line of his heartbeat, which oscillated between fifty-five and sixty beats per minute. That seemed slow, but Dr Lai assured me that the medications that Shelly had been given were keeping him calm and that his heart didn't need to pump any faster.

I rubbed Shelly's hand for a time, moving my fingertip over the calluses on his palm, because they meant he was a lot tougher than he looked and could withstand more than his fair share of troubles. His thick brown hair was tufted at wild angles, so I stood up and smoothed all of it down, then made two greying wings extending back over his ears – just as he likes it.

None of our marriage difficulties mattered while I was sitting with him – not even his affairs. My grievances and doubts were still there, but they seemed to belong to a woman standing behind me, observing me from the doorway while I whispered to the wonderful, big-hearted man with whom I'd been travelling for the last twenty-five years.

Do other women ever consider that it would be best not to love their husbands or boyfriends quite as much as they did?

When Shelly woke up, he spoke to me in drowsy Yiddish. He kept licking his lips, so I lifted up his water cup and put the straw in his mouth and he sucked away contentedly. I had the feeling that he thought he was a little kid. Maybe he imagined that I was his mother.

Shelly's face is more expressive – more pliable – when he speaks Yiddish. And he makes more exuberant hand gestures, as if he's the lead in a silent movie. I kept nodding as if I understood him, figuring – wrongly, as it turned out – that he'd switch to French or English at some point.

Among other words, I learned one for sleepy – *farshlofn* – that seemed soft and fuzzy in my mouth, like a word invented by the broken-hearted Jewish angels that had roamed the Warsaw Ghetto in his youth and that his cousin Benni had once told me about.

When he nodded off again, his mouth remained open. I stood up to cover him with his blanket and noticed I could see nearly all his fillings – even the two gold ones in his molars that Uncle Abraham had given him back in Poland.

I didn't want to leave, but when Dr Lai came back in, he told me that Shelly was stable and that it was a good sign that he'd been rambling away in Yiddish. With a reassuring nod, he added that it was only natural that he'd be confused after his stroke, but that he was certain that it was just a minor one. 'He'll be mostly himself again soon,' he said.

'Mostly himself?' I asked.

'Well, it'll take him a while to get all his powers back.'

Dr Lai's use of the word *powers* made it sound as if Shelly were a comic-book superhero, which seemed perfectly in keeping with my sense of having awakened in a universe that wasn't the usual one I lived in. An hour or so later, still holding Shelly's hand, I let my daughters talk me into having them escort me home, since he didn't look as if he might wake up anytime soon.

I wrote him a note on a napkin I took from my bag: *See you in the morning. Kisses big and kisses small, Jules.* I left it next to his plastic water cup.

Diane drove my ancient Ford Fairlane because I didn't trust myself. Margot crumpled into sobs beside her. I leaned forward from the back seat and rubbed her slender shoulders and assured her that her father would be fine. And yet the whole time I was comforting her, I was asking myself, *When in God's name will I ever be able to stop pretending that I'm a cheerful person?*

At home, Diane heated up the lentil soup I'd made the day before and Margot chopped up tomatoes for a salad. The banging of cupboards and clanging of plates confirmed that they'd inherited my strategy of survival-through-frenzy.

I started up to my bedroom to change into my pyjamas, but each step seemed to be taking me further and further from anywhere I wanted to be, so I stopped on the landing and contemplated the painting by Shelly's old friend George that we'd hung there a decade earlier. And for the first time, I saw what it was really about.

How do you live ten years with a painting and never notice anything below its brushstrokes? At the centre of the composition is a youthful bride and groom clinging together, panicked, cornered by a thick forest of trees that are growing upside down. Their tangled roots climb and spread through mud-coloured clouds, and their sparse, pale-green, diseased canopies are pressed to the barren ground. The young man wears a giant, hand-me-down coat, and his trousers are too short, revealing pale, needle-thin ankles. His white yarmulke covers unruly black hair – the hair of a young rebel. The young woman wears a billowy rose-coloured dress with golden bells at its hem. She has a beaky nose and is balanced on one slender leg, so that she seems part flamingo or egret. The couple stands in the angular shadow of their *chuppah*, the ceremonial canopy used in Jewish marriage ceremonies. At the left of the painting, obscured by the woods, are the turrets and garlic-bulb towers of Warsaw.

Here is the revelation that I had while peering at the disquieted couple: they and their city are about to be overcome – strangled, in fact – by the upside-down trees. They will be killed by something that makes no logical sense – that seems impossible – just as Shelly's parents and little sister, Esther, were murdered by a machinery of death that had once seemed beyond belief.

But I wasn't about to let that happen – not in Montreal in 1977. At least, not in my own mind. In the daring escape I scripted for the bride and groom, they raced through the murderous woodlands, hid aboard a night-time train for Gdansk and stowed-away on a ship to New York.

I decided that George's painting was about the need to flee at the right moment. And about believing that the unthinkable can happen at any time.

I also realised that he had painted for those of us who would see it in the future, to tell us: *You must work to make sure that all those who are being persecuted find safety*.

After I pressed my hand to the bride and groom – to thank them for making me understand – I tiptoed back down the stairs, wishing to see how silent I could become. In the kitchen, I grabbed a bottle of Portuguese red wine from our pantry. Shelly had bought a case the previous week.

'If only Rosa were here to drink a *bissel* of wine with us,' he'd told me after he showed me the label, which indicated that it had been made in the Douro region, upriver from Porto. He said that because he could trace his ancestry through his great-grandmother to Lisbon. Shelly's last name was Zarco, and back in the fifteenth and sixteenth centuries, the Zarcos had been manuscript illuminators and mystics.

Diane called me to the dining table and handed me a bowl of lentil soup. I ate it without looking up because I couldn't face my daughters' expectations. Margot then served the salad. The girls must've found the silence oppressive; Diane jumped up and showed us how her father had imitated a rabbit while playing charades – when she was a teenager, she said. It was while she was hopping around the dining table that I decided that my best option would be to go to my bedroom and bury my head in Shelly's pillow so that I'd always remember the earthy scent of him.

Yet I didn't leave; the girls might regard my absence as a betrayal of their needs and I was not up to having a quarrel.

Diane nibbling a make-believe carrot and rubbing her nose with her paw . . . Her gestures seemed all wrong, like the upside-down trees in George's painting. But such determination lit her long-lashed brown eyes that I didn't ask her to stop. It was as if she were fighting on the front line of a war.

How is it that our children inherit our worst traumas, even when we do everything we can to raise them as confident and happy?

'Dad looked just like that!' Diane exclaimed to me and Margot, and she laughed too loudly. My own attempt to giggle sounded so false that it made me cringe.

I poured myself a second glass of wine, hoping for its deep-red amnesia to overwhelm me. A little while later, I started shivering, and it was then that I realised why Diane's imitation of Shelly imitating a rabbit seemed so inappropriate to me; it was an elegy she ought to have given her father only after his death.

Margot noticed my trembling.

'Mom, are you cold?' she asked, as if it weren't obvious.

'I've fallen into a snowbank in my mind,' I replied. It was a line of Shelly's, though he used it to mean that he was at a loss for words.

Shelly loved the word *snowbank* in English. He said it sounded noble to him.

Grapefruit, loaf, roundabout, broomstick, knapsack . . . Shelly kept a list of his favourite English words in the notebook where he wrote down memories of his life in Warsaw and Algiers.

Sophie, Carole, Robert, Denis, Rosalie, Sharif 1, Sharif 2 . . . The back page of the notebook lists his lovers in Algiers. It used to always fill me with envy. My goodness, what would it have been like to have the freedom of a man when I was twenty years old!

Margot fetched the shawl my mom had knitted for me when I graduated from high school and draped it across my shoulders, and because of that, everything we said to each other that evening now seems filtered by the warmth and weight of old black wool.

I picked around the lettuce and spinach with my fork but managed to eat the cherry tomatoes. Shelly's absence seemed like a rope around my neck, tugging me toward hopelessness. At some point, my eyes settled on the portrait of him hanging over the fireplace. George had done it in oil pastel, and the romantic glow in his emerald eyes – and the generous spread of his arms – reminded me of all the magical evenings that George, me and Shelly had spent together in the Utah desert, when my husband and I were young and didn't yet know about how quickly a stroke could change everything . . .

Margot stirred me from my trance by asking if I wanted more tomatoes – and just like that a scream was again embedded in my chest. *We should never have moved to the fucking suburbs!* That was what I would have shouted if I could have.

Isn't it odd how a panicked mind will seek out a circumstance of life that is of little importance and ascribe cataclysmic meaning to it?

Would I have managed my frustrations and fears more successfully if we'd stayed in the city?

'*Arsène Lupin, Gentleman Cambrioleur,*' Diane said as if it were an announcement.

'I don't understand,' I told her.

'That was the name of the movie that Dad tried to communicate to us – when we were playing charades, I mean.'

She told me that he'd imitated a *lapin* – a rabbit – in the hopes of giving her *Lupin*.

'So we were playing in French?' I asked.

Margot reached for my hand. In a worried tone, she said, 'Dad preferred French to English when we played. It gave him an advantage. Don't you remember?'

'Of course, I remember,' I replied in a resentful tone. But I didn't; I was convinced, in fact, that Shelly had insisted that we play more often in English so that our daughters could show off.

Was it possible that we devoted so many evenings to charades because it was Shelly's way of telling us that we would have to guess things about him that he could never openly reveal?

To take my daughters' inquisitive looks from me, I asked Diane how long ago we'd played the game of charades in which her father had imitated a rabbit. She leaned her head back just like Shelly does when he's working out a puzzle in his head and told me she'd probably been eleven years old.

'So I was fourteen,' said Margot, and she shook her head as if it were an impossibly long time ago.

'So I was thirty-seven,' I added. For no reason I could think of, I also said, 'I must have just started working again as a nurse.'

Only when Diane told us that she had lifted up her cousin Tom onto her lap did I remember that he had been with us as well. He was just four at the time and he was on Shelly's team.

'I need Tommy on my team,' he'd announced, grabbing the little boy's hand, and when I asked why, he said he had to have another man with him, which was just like Shelly, since he always grumbled that he was outnumbered by the women in his life.

The truth was very different, of course. In the company of an attractive woman, Shelly's eyes would light up and his hands would begin to shake. He was like some wild beast out of the Old Testament – sniffing at the air, making ready to pounce. Though to be fair, his interest wasn't uniquely sexual; he also adored gossiping with my fussy, French-speaking, lavender-scented aunts, for instance. He'd ask them about their best recipes for tarts and cobblers, and his sweet-natured, insistent eagerness – peering over their shoulders while they were baking – was enough to convince them that he was the most charming man in the world. He never seemed to trust men, however, especially the salesmen he dealt with at work. Though his cousin Benni and Benni's son, Ethan, were exceptions; those two could do no wrong. And George, too. To Shelly, George would always be the man who had saved him from a spare, lonely, pointless life.

Benni and Shelly . . . When they were talking together in Yiddish, imitating their nutty relatives back in Poland, giggling mischievously, they became the stars of their own black-and-white comedy – one that they'd started filming in Warsaw before the war.

When anyone asked my husband about his parents and the rest of his family, he would say, 'Everyone died in the camps except my cousin Benni, and he's of the thirty-six righteous men who keep God from destroying this *meshugge* world of ours.'

Deference always deepened his voice when he spoke of Benni to people who'd never met him.

In Jewish lore, the *Lamed Vav Tzadikim* – the Thirty-Six Righteous Ones – are chosen by the Almighty to sustain both the physical universe and the world of spirit. By fighting for what is virtuous and beautiful in their daily lives, without any thought of earthly or heavenly reward – and without calling attention to their works – they guarantee the continuation of Creation. They never speak of their crucial role, and it's not even clear that they know how important they are.

Benni's son, Ethan, once told me that his father was a mystical clown, and I think that's true. Maybe that's characteristic of some of the *Lamed Vav Tzadikim*.

Even if other people didn't grasp the depth of Shelly's esteem for Benni, I did. And I am convinced that Shelly would have taken his own life if his cousin hadn't survived the war. If for no other reason than to complete the family tragedy. Yes, my husband regards his own life – and probably mine too – with that sort of theatrical breadth and scope. In fact, it's one of the things that I find so exceptional and courageous about him.

He never told me that he ever considered suicide, but I saw it in his self-incrimination and manic despair when, early in our marriage, Benni had to be rushed to New York University Hospital with a burst appendix. Even after his cousin recovered, Shelly suffered terrible insomnia for weeks afterward. He told me, 'The thought of never being able to hug Benni again or hear his voice ... Jules, I just couldn't go on.'

Once, shortly after our first vacation in New York with Benni, I dreamed of a wicked old Pulcinella with long, crusted fingernails and cruel yellow eyes pushing my husband from the roof of a wooden synagogue covered in snow, and when he slipped off the eave, he became a little boy, and he began falling through darkness. I don't know how, but I found myself falling next to him, and I thought we'd never reach the bottom, but Benni caught us as if we weighed nothing – one in each arm – and he giggled at our astonishment.

In the dream, snow was falling over us – cold but invigorating. Those tens of thousands of white flakes – that resplendent and ordered whiteness – seemed to have a grand purpose, to be summoning us toward a realisation, and it seemed to be: *No matter what happened in our past, we have a chance to start over.* On waking, that wondrous feeling made me start to cry.

When I told the dream to Benni, he shrugged and said that it was all backwards, since Shelly had saved him. Then, a couple of months later, he called me early one Saturday and said, 'Listen, Jules, I've been thinking about that dream of yours, of Shelly falling, and I think that it was his grief that was nearly bottomless. But after he and George found me, I became a kind of bottom. I was the ground that kept him from falling further.'

'And the Pulcinella with the crusty fingernails?' I asked.

'Well, I'm afraid the world played an evil trick on us, didn't it?' he replied.

After that phone call in which he interpreted my dream, Benni became my confidant, though it took me a few more years to realise that. He helped me survive Shelly's betrayals by letting me rant on about my humiliation and anger in our phone conversations. And by making me laugh.

Once, after Shelly had disappeared for a weekend, Benni said, 'It's got nothing to do with you. It's him – he has always had way too many hormones.' And he told me an old Yiddish joke to explain:

A ten-year-old boy is bathing and his mom comes in, and he lifts his pee-pee out of the soapy water and says, 'Mom, is this my brain?'

'No, sweetie,' she says with a put-upon sigh, 'not yet.'

Benni sometimes made me laugh until I cried. Maybe it was because I always see his wish to please me in his sharp, black, little-boy eyes . . . Even today, all these years after first meeting him, when I catch his glance, the effect of his seeing me and not turning away goes straight to the deepest part of me.

That power to reach down into my unseen life and hold me motionless is something the two cousins have in common. Perhaps their Zarco heritage has given them that gift.

Margot and Diane drew me out of my daydreams of Shelly and Benni when they started pestering me to take more salad or have some fruit. I told them I'd already eaten more than I'd wanted to and – to divert their attention – asked them tell me more about our long-ago game of charades.

Diane said she'd guessed *lapin* right away. Shelly had swooped her up into his arms and given her what we call his boa-constrictor hug, though she remembered that he was unable to convey to her and Tom the film's full title and they had been forced to give up in the end. She said, 'How could anyone expect us to guess the word *gentleman* in English when the rest of the title was in French?'

She pretended to be outraged by the injustice until I said – as was expected of me – 'Well, you know as well as I do, your father loved to play games with you two girls. You two were the only people on earth he didn't mind losing to.'

One thing I've noticed over the years: Margot's complaints to her father are nearly always a form of jousting – a way for the girl to safely test her limits – while Diane's are born of true anger.

Now, Diane wrinkled her nose in that fussy way that she has had since she was a baby and said, 'Dad smelled of rum when he gave me his boa-constrictor hug.'

She sounded resentful, but I realised a few minutes later that maybe she only meant to imply to me that we were playing on a Friday evening; Shelly drank a big, icy piña colada during our Sabbath dinner and never touched anything but wine during the rest of the week. It also occurred to me that Diane may have inherited her father's oversensitivity to smells, though Shelly always claimed that he never paid any attention to the deeper meaning of scents until he began to make his way through Polish woodlands and farms to Kraków, walking always at night, often just one step ahead of his German pursuers.

On our first date, Shelly gripped my hand tightly and said, 'Those bastards could track me as silently as they wanted, but I still smelled their tobacco and their food. And I learned to trust the crows and pigeons and sparrows. They'd fly off at the first sign of Germans. I'm telling you, Julie, Polish birds hate Nazis as much as I do!'

2

I saw Shelly for the first time when I walked into his shop, Cagney's Sporting Goods, to pick up the sneakers my little brother had ordered a week earlier. It was the spring of 1952. I was nineteen years old, and I'd been walking around heartbroken that my beloved Montreal Canadiens had lost the Stanley Cup Finals for the second straight year.

Imagine being so youthful and innocent that your biggest problem is a hockey puck that ends up in the wrong goal too often!

Shelly was standing at the counter, writing a receipt, and when he looked up at me, he squinted from the smoke curling up from his cigarette, and his handsome, menacing eyes told me exactly what he wanted.

His short black hair was slicked back, and he'd let the whiskers on his cheeks and chin grow for a couple of days. He wore a snazzy grey suit and his vest was white silk. He looked like he'd stepped out of *Guys and Dolls*, which my parents and I had seen on Broadway about a year earlier.

I named him Guido in my mind. I still call him it on occasion. It never fails to make him grin like a devil.

On the wall behind him – inside a gold frame – was a signed picture of James Cagney dancing down a long staircase. On our first date, Shelly told me that he'd named his store after him. He said, 'An Irish-American movie star who can dance like an angel and speak Yiddish like a pickle peddler – now that's a *mensch*!'

I pretended I was studying the women's sneakers in the window so I could glance back at him without being noticed. He was telling an old woman with a knot of white hair atop her head what she should buy her grandson for a present. They were speaking French, which I understood quite well because my mother was French Canadian, though I spoke it only when I was forced to, because my accent was appalling. Listening to his patient voice, I felt as if a clock inside me had finally stopped ticking. And I was such an inexperienced and optimistic young woman that it seemed inevitable to me that sooner or later I'd find my Guido.

I must have not only seen too many hockey games but also read too many private eye novels, because I longed for a tough-guy lover who would take my virginity and use me any way he wanted – a handsome, no-nonsense sexual professor, of sorts. Now, more than two decades later, I can finally admit that that was what I wanted without any embarrassment – proof, I suppose, that becoming middle-aged can be liberating for timid souls like me.

Shelly was only thirty-two years old, but he looked like he had done everything with a woman that a private detective posing as the owner of a sporting goods store could ever hope to do.

I handed him the receipt for my brother's sneakers and spoke to him in the best French I could muster, but he answered in English. His accent wasn't Quebecois. He told me he'd lived in Algiers during the war but had been born in Warsaw.

After he came back from the storeroom with a shoebox containing the sneakers, he walked me to the door and said that he hoped he would see me again because he'd have a really nice surprise for me next time I visited him.

'I think I know what your *belle surprise* is,' I told him, trying to imitate Lauren Bacall's husky, knowing voice.

'Do you really?' he asked with a sly laugh.

He came outside with me. He grinned because he understood he'd enchanted me. I turned and headed down the street toward home, feeling his dark stare on me, hoping my trembling legs wouldn't buckle.

3

Our first date was at Enrico's, a Sicilian restaurant and bar owned by an elderly couple who were always snapping at each other. It was the only place in town where he could eat his beloved *arancini*, fried rice balls stuffed with peas and tomato sauce.

My heart started pounding the moment he waved to me from his booth. I've always suffered from low blood pressure and thought I might pass out as I walked to him. He stood up to greet me. He held his hat in his hand – a black trilby with a silver band. He asked me to sit next to him. 'We'll be cosier that way,' he said while standing up to let me slip past him.

I have no idea what we talked about over our first few minutes together. All I can recall is Shelly pouring me too big a glass of red wine, and when I protested, taking my hand and kissing it. With a confident smile, he told me then it was time for my *belle surprise* and moved my hand below the table and pressed it into something hard and warm, and it took me a moment to realise he'd taken his cock out of his pants.

I pulled my hand back as if I'd been burned, which made him grin.

'I know I'm vulgar,' he said in an apologetic tone. 'But I want you to see how hard you make me. Are you angry?'

I shook my head; my thoughts were turning somersaults.

He summoned the waiter and asked me what I wanted for an appetiser. 'Just . . . a bit of water,' I croaked.

'For an appetiser?' Shelly asked, laughing generously.

I nodded. After he ordered us a big bottle of mineral water, he chose two appetisers – Sicilian sausages and grilled octopus.

The big black flashlight Mom kept in our broom closet . . . I thought of the perfect way it always fit in my hand as I wrapped my curious fingers around Shelly's cock again.

Where had I found the courage to do that? It seemed as if I'd become someone else.

Shelly closed his eyes and bit his lip as I squeezed him. When I eased off, he sighed as though he'd been through a battle and said, '*Mon Dieu*, I can see that my life is in danger.'

He had us toast my brother's sneakers, since they had brought us together. Then he flinched and said, 'Oh, shit, I hope you're not kosher! Or vegetarian! I ordered all that *tref*.'

'No, it's okay, I'm not Jewish and I eat meat,' I replied.

'Maybe you feel that I am,' he said in a whisper. 'Jewish, I mean.'

'I don't understand.'

He leaned close to me. 'I'm circumcised,' he whispered.

'Right,' I said, as if I knew what he was talking about; his was the first erect cock I'd ever touched.

Shelly told me that night that he'd wanted me to know he was Jewish right away because he'd discovered that many French Canadians believed all the worst stereotypes about Jews. When he asked about my background, I explained that my dad was an English Quaker and professor of genetics, and my mom a French-speaking Catholic and history teacher. 'But she thinks all religions are pretty much rubbish,' I added.

'And you?' he asked.

'Me, I think I'm an atheist – and I'm studying to be a nurse.'

His eyes brightened. 'I lucked out – a nursing student who doesn't believe in God!'

'So that's a good thing?' I asked with a laugh.

'Well, it's always very good when a woman knows her own anatomy,' he said. 'Makes finding things for her boyfriend much easier.' He leaned toward me and whispered confidentially, 'And it's good that you won't be worrying about what God might think of you when you climb on top of *ma belle surprise*.'

At that, I risked squeezing his cock again, which made him close his eyes and take a hesitant, tormented breath. I felt as if I'd chanced upon some very powerful magic.

As our appetisers arrived, he lifted my hand off of him gently and gave each of my fingers a little kiss. 'Let's eat, kiddo,' he said, and he wiggled around a bit while inserting his cock back in his pants.

He forked octopus and pieces of sausage into my mouth. I thought about telling him to stop, since I didn't want to appear helpless, but I'd already drunk half my red wine and couldn't come up with a single good reason why I wouldn't want a handsome and charming man with a large penis to feed me tasty Sicilian appetisers for the rest of my life.

After our pasta was served, we got onto the subject of Poland, and he told me how he used to hang out with the actors at the

Yiddish theatres. 'I wanted to go on stage,' he said. 'I wanted to make people laugh and cry. I wanted to take long bows in front of cheering audiences. I was such a *dummkopf*!'

During that first meal together, he told me that all of nature was on the side of the Jews in the war – every bird and tree and stream – and yet his whole family except for his cousin Benni had been wiped out. He spoke of his past with a kind of lopsided, ironic smile that made me uncomfortable. Later, when I met Benni, I realised that he and Shelly hid behind nearly the same counterfeit grin when they talked about all they'd lost.

I was too jittery to eat more than a few mouthfuls of my linguini with clam sauce, so Shelly insisted I take it home to my parents in a doggy bag.

As he encouraged me out the door of Enrico's, he patted my behind. A minute later, when we kissed under the awning of a nearby stationery shop, he held me tightly and told me I was extraordinarily beautiful. I eased my head against his chest so I could catch my breath, and when he placed a delicate kiss on my brow, I felt a knot coming undone inside me, and I was pretty sure that now that it was open, I'd never get it tied again.

4

How much of our destiny – both good and bad – is determined by our physical appearance? It's a question that most women married to handsome men must ask themselves on occasion – though, if they're anything like me, they already know the answer before they ask it.

To catch my husband's eye, women in restaurants would cross their legs suggestively or fiddle with the fabric of their blouse or take their lipstick and hand mirror out of their bag. Back in the

1950s, when nearly every adult in Montreal seemed to smoke, youthful *femme fatales* would ask him for a light right in front of me. And although almost nobody was out of the closet back then, I'd notice guys giving Shelly suggestive glances whenever we'd eat souvlaki at Apollo's, which was on St Catherine Street and close to a few of the gay clubs.

Just before I moved into his apartment, Shelly told me – when he was a little bit drunk and in one of his playful moods – that he'd slept with a number of Arab men in Algiers, in part because their women were unavailable and he didn't like going to prostitutes.

'How many is a number?' I'd asked.

'I don't know, maybe thirty,' he told me, adding as an afterthought – to set the record straight, it seemed – 'Though, of course, that number does not include *mes petits amis français*.' When he noticed my stunned expression, he shrugged as if his adventures in North Africa were just a boyish lark and said, 'It would have been a crime to turn down all those lonely young men!'

Was he just kidding? It seemed likely, because I thought that homosexual men were rare and invariably effeminate. And it had never occurred to me that anyone could be bisexual. When he assured me he was serious, however, I decided that he was exaggerating, that he might have slept with a couple of men over the years – to avoid having to pay prostitutes, like he'd said – but that he was trying to shock me. Or test me. Maybe he'd wanted to see if I'd be horrified.

Later, I came to believe that back in the ghetto he'd vowed that if he ever survived the war, he would find love anywhere and anyhow it came to him. Also, I figured out that sex had taken on a life-affirming – and mystical – significance for him. Once, while we were driving to Toronto for a weekend, to visit his old friend George, he told me that for many years, he thought that *l'infinie beauté de risquer la fusion avec un inconnu* – the infinite beauty of risking union with a stranger – was just about the only blessing of God he could find in our world. Such poetic directness was unusual for Shelly, however – mostly he claimed that he simply had no willpower when it came to a good-looking woman or man.

After I'd managed to incorporate Shelly's unabashed bisexuality into my internal image of him, it made him seem even more worldly and adventurous to me – and more powerfully masculine, too. I was too embarrassed to reveal my fantasies to him at the time, but I was sure that he would have been tickled to learn they included a host of equally bisexual, tough-talking French stevedores and Arab sheiks who couldn't get enough of me.

The only person I told about Shelly's fondness for both men and women was my father, who was close friends with the only out-of-the-closet gay man I'd ever met, a theatrical director from Toronto named Martin Jay. After I'd revealed exactly what Shelly had told me, the only question that my father asked was, 'But does he love you, and do you love him?'

The answer was yes in both cases.

And yet, over the next few months, when Shelly began disappearing for a day or two at a time, I began to doubt that what we had together was love. At first, I believed what Shelly told me – that he was going fishing or hiking with his buddies – but I learned the truth when I cornered Benni on one of his frequent visits to Montreal and demanded that he tell me what was going on with his cousin.

To his credit, Benni didn't try to lie to me. And when I confronted Shelly, he didn't either. At the time, we were spending most of our evenings together, though I still slept every night in my old bedroom in my parents' apartment.

I began to weep when he confessed that he occasionally slept with someone else.

'Men or women?' I asked.

'Both,' he said. 'I know I should have more willpower – I wish I did – but I don't.'

I pushed him away when he tried to embrace me. He said, 'Listen, Jules, I know it's hard for you, but there are times when I've just got to be with someone. I start thinking I'm going to die if I don't have sex right away, and if you're not there, then what am I supposed to do?'

'If you really loved me, you'd never want anyone else!' I told him harshly.

'I love you something crazy. Even just holding your hand is exciting! And whenever we kiss, it feels like I've come home after being away for far too long. But it's not in my nature to be with one person. This big need just grabs me and . . . and I can't stop.'

'Nature? You have no fucking nature!' I shrieked, and I ran out of his apartment and didn't come back for two days. When I did, he rushed to me as I opened the door and threw his arms around me. He began to sob so hard that he shook. In a quavering voice, he said, 'I was sure I'd lost you forever.'

When I told him I still loved him, Shelly kissed my hands and face as if we'd been a winter apart. A little later, while I was in the bathroom washing my tearful face, he kneeled down and asked me to marry him.

After we were wed, Shelly still craved his sexual adventures, but he also didn't want to lie to me, so he started pleading with me to join him in threesomes on occasion. I suspected that amorous triangles weren't going to work for me, but I regarded his effort to include me as honourable, and I was too young and inexperienced to simply say no. Our first escapade was with a sweet-natured young waitress who worked at the Sheraton Hotel downtown, but when Shelly buried his head between her legs and she started moaning, I turned to ice. A few weeks later, we decided to see if I wouldn't be more comfortable with a second man, and Shelly invited a buddy of his named Gilles to spend an evening with us. He was a muscular little carpenter and amateur hockey referee with salt-and-pepper hair. My heart started banging against my ribs when Shelly took his cock down his throat, but after my husband had swallowed all that Gilles could give him, our guest came to me and started kissing my nipples, and Shelly was watching me with rapt eyes, and I felt like a monkey in a zoo, and I had to make a quick exit from our bedroom to keep from getting sick.

My husband rushed out after me and said he hoped I wasn't upset or angry at him. I gave him a quick kiss and said, 'I'm sorry, I guess I'm just no good in groups.'

'Hey, nobody's perfect!' he shot back, which irritated me at the time, but in years since it has often made me laugh with greater and greater admiration for Shelly's unstoppable delight in sex.

Shortly after Shelly and I were married, I missed my period, though I didn't become certain I was pregnant until few weeks later. When I told him, he danced me around our kitchen as if he were his beloved Jimmy Cagney. And he made love to me insatiably – at all hours of the day and night – right up until I went into labour, nearly seven months later.

My being pregnant turned him on like nothing had before; he'd push me on my side and curl up behind me and caress my gigantic belly and in a few seconds – *bang!* like birds mating – it was over.

We used to laugh about how quick a trigger he'd developed.

'I can't help it – I love you so much,' he used to tell me, and his eyes – endlessly tender – convinced me I'd never heard anyone say anything so true.

The relief in me was like flying, I told Benni, since I could see a clear and tranquil landscape spreading before me and seeming to go on forever.

While I was pregnant, Shelly came home after work every evening, and he didn't even glance at anyone else when we were out at one of our neighbourhood restaurants. He couldn't pass by me without giving me a kiss, and every time he helped me out of bed in the morning, he'd caress his hand over my belly, needing to know the exact shape of me and the baby. Once, he told me, 'I'm only completely at ease with two people in the entire world – you and Benni. Christ, even the smell of you . . . it goes straight to my heart.'

When Shelly discovered that I craved Italian food, he learned how to make pasta with all sorts of homemade sauces, and my favourite dish soon became what we called *Shelly's Leeky Pasta* – Portobello mushrooms, peas and leeks over fettuccini.

Shelly also brought me breakfast in bed when I was too lazy to get up. Benni pitched in too, and made me two stunning maternity dresses out of vibrantly coloured cotton prints from India, with extra fabric at the seams so that Shelly – who had learned how to sew when he was a kid – could let them out every couple of weeks. I started to think that there was nothing those two couldn't do together. *The Warsaw Wizards*, I began to call them.

I also realised that Shelly and I had started a new journey together the moment I got pregnant. And I couldn't imagine anything I wanted to do more than have children with him.

Shortly after I gave birth to Margot, he confided in me that he had promised himself while dashing frantically through a Polish forest at night – just a mile or so ahead of the Germans who were hunting him – that he would have at least two children.

'If I survived, I'd do my part to keep the Jews from perishing from the face of the earth,' he told me in a tense, hushed voice, as if his Nazi pursuers might still hear us.

After Margot was born, Shelly proved himself a playful and attentive father, as well. Then, three years later, Diane came along, and neither of the girls could get enough of him. What he loved most was reading to them. He'd sit with his legs crossed on our bed and impersonate all the different characters in *Charlotte's Web* and the *Dr Dolittle* books.

Shelly as Charlotte, spinning her web up the wall and down the dresser and across the Persian rug in our bedroom … Margot's jaw would drop open as her father spider-walked around the room, and Diane would talk to him in her tiny voice as if he really were Charlotte.

'How do I know you won't bite me?' she asked him once.

'You don't!' he growled, and he attacked her arms and neck while she shrieked with delight.

Benni always told me that if the Nazis hadn't occupied Poland, his cousin would have become an acclaimed actor, but I only began to believe him after the girls were born. Though perhaps all his monumental, wild-hearted gestures – his eccentric passion – might only have worked on stage and not on film.

And yet, I can see now that the girls required far more than their father's playfulness. They needed him to tell where he'd grown up in Warsaw, and what his school had been like, and who his friends had been, and what their beloved Uncle Benni had been like when he was a kid. But most of all, I think, they needed to know how their brave and handsome dad had outwitted the Nazis and come to live in Montreal. But Shelly never invited them into his past. And so – perhaps without intending to – he turned all that happened before his coming to Canada into an unmentionable secret. And a dangerous one, too. That become clear when Margot was in eighth grade. Over dinner one evening, she gathered up her courage and told her father that her history class was studying the Holocaust, and her teacher – Mr Muller – wanted him to come and talk to the students about his experiences.

I'd just served the girls their spaghetti and meatballs, and Shelly was holding out his plate for his portion. His face turned pale, and his lips drew together into an angry slit, and I was certain he was going to explode at Margot, but instead he put down his plate and stood up and walked to our bedroom. And he didn't come out until the morning.

Margot blamed herself, of course, and she sobbed in my arms.

In such ways, our daughters learned never to question their father about his life in Poland, and though I told them what I knew, their impatience with me made me realise that it wasn't just the names of their grandparents and other details that they needed, but their father's confidence in them. *He doesn't trust us with his deepest self.* That's what they grew up thinking, even if they couldn't have put it into words until they were much older.

Around the time Diane started kindergarten, Shelly's need for sexual experiences outside our bedroom returned, and my bouts of rage and resentment – and our quarrels – would send me on long, sulking walks. Once, I grew so angry at him that I threw my Montreal Canadiens mug at his head, and I would've been glad to have knocked him out, but I missed.

Of course, I occasionally had the chance to sleep with another man, and early on in our marriage, before I got pregnant a second time, a number of good-looking physicians made their interest in me explicit. But the guilt churning in my gut when I permitted one of them to give me a kiss in his office made it clear that infidelity was never going to be an option.

Thankfully, my daughters became a deep source of comfort to me, and Benni – bless him – always listened to my complaints about Shelly without passing judgment on me or my marriage.

And then, a last affront made me realise how ashamed of him I was – and that I had reached a limit. When the girls were seven and ten, he came home one night pretty smashed, and I could smell another woman's perfume on him. After he undressed, he collapsed on our bed and fell fast asleep. Him lying there, oblivious to the world and indifferent to my feelings seemed so insulting that I began to tremble with rage and frustration. And I felt dirty, too – as if soiled by our life together. I grabbed my pillow and moved to the couch, and the next morning, before he woke up, I dressed Margot and Diane and drove off to my parents' house in Toronto. I phoned Shelly late that night and told him we weren't coming back, and I could tell from his choking voice – while he pleaded for me to come home – that he was in dire despair.

After I refused to return to Montreal, he asked me to permit him see me in Toronto, and he flew in early the next morning. When he arrived at my parents' house, he looked as if he hadn't slept. My mom took the girls outside, and Shelly and I sat opposite each other in the living room, amid Dad's piles of books and records, and he started to tell me why he'd come home drunk, but I told him I didn't need or want any more explanations for his behaviour, because I could no longer share him with anyone else. 'Not ever,' I told him. 'And under no circumstances.'

'So you haven't . . . haven't fallen out of love with me?' he asked timidly.

'No, but I see clearly now that if this goes on, I will. And I can't permit that to happen.'

I think he understood at that moment what our marriage required of him, and he gave me his word that he'd never again have sex with anyone else.

Did he live up to his vow? I could never be entirely sure. But I grew convinced that he fought as hard as he could against his mad urges and never came home again with anyone else's scent on him.

I'll say this for Shelly – even at our worst times, he never blamed me for our difficulties or tried to undermine my confidence. Quite the contrary – when I wasn't sure if I should resume my nursing career after so many years away from work, he called in some favours and got me a job in the Obstetrics ward at the McGill Health Centre.

When Margot was in her last year of high school and we felt comfortable leaving her in the care of her sister for a few days, Shelly and I would fly to New York once every few weeks to visit Benni and his wife, Tessa, over a weekend. On one of those stays, we found ourselves alone in an elevator at Macy's, and he brought my hands to his lips and kissed them and started to cry. 'I hate it that I used to make you unhappy,' he said. 'And that I lied to you sometimes. I'm sorry – more sorry than you can ever imagine.'

'It's all right,' I told him, trying to sound casual, but his confession – and the scent of distress on him – moved me deeply. While we were hugging, he said that he was looking forward to another twenty-five years of trying to figure out why a woman as intelligent as me had fallen for a *nudnik* like him, and we laughed with the easy complicity of old friends, and a moment later, I discovered that I could no longer find any residual anger at him inside me.

As he dried his eyes with his thumbs, Shelly said, 'You know, the most exciting thing that ever happened to me was you walking into my shop.'

That stunned me because I was sure that the pivotal moment around which his entire life had turned was finding Benni after the war, and when I said so, he replied, 'Maybe that's true, but things with Benni are different.'

'Why are they different?'

The doors opened on the housewares floor, and we stepped together out into all that glaring light. After a reflective pause, he said, 'I already knew Benni and loved him. And at some level . . . It's like Benni and I are the same person. So finding him sometimes seems like it was another way of finding myself.'

'And with me?'

Shelly wrinkled his nose like he does when he's thinking hard. 'With you, it was like I'd been swimming in the sea for twenty years, really far from shore, and it was exhausting,' he said. 'And now I could come back to land and finally rest – and be with you.'

Shelly also told me on another of our trips to New York – with such good humour that it didn't seem vulgar – that my pussy was the absolute greatest thing since the invention of writing. And a few months later, while we were making love inside our freezing tent in Algonquin Provincial Park, he told me that he could imagine fighting to the death over me. 'Christ, Jules, your ass alone could start World War Three!'

Shelly made me laugh till I cried when he said such things in that overly serious way of his – as if fucking was a form of philosophy. Once, when Benni and I were discussing my husband's successes with young men and women in North Africa, I told him what Shelly had said about me and the invention of writing. By then, we'd both had a couple glasses of wine, and I expected to set him shaking with merry laughter, but instead his eyes grew glassy and he began to sniffle.

'What's wrong?' I asked.

'It's just that Shelly has so much good in him . . . such a big desire to express his love through his body that he can't contain it. That's why he says those things to you – things no other really good man would say in a million years. You know, Jules, sometimes I think he's the one who's a member of the *Lamed Vav Tzadikim*.'

'Oh, Benni, you can't be serious!' I said as if it were impossible.

'Why not? After all, if sex and love don't sustain the universe, then what the hell does?'

While considering that possibility, I examined my highs and lows with Shelly from a different angle. Maybe having an oversexed husband – one who got hard every time he saw me in the shower or even just pictured my breasts – was wonderfully good fortune.

Our daughters understood without my ever mentioning it that they'd been born to a Jewish Don Juan – which was one of the reasons they'd laughed so hard when he hopped across our living room while imitating a rabbit. That's another thing I'll give Shelly – despite his good looks, he wasn't fussy about his appearance and never worried about looking silly on occasion.

5

I mention all this about our sexual escapades and difficulties because of the nagging problem that Shelly's stroke would soon cause him, though at first we were both simply overjoyed that he was still alive, of course.

'I never thought I'd make it here again,' he whispered to me when my daughters and I finally got him home from the hospital.

Once he'd sobbed with relief on the sofa in our living room, he grew ravenous. 'That hospital food wasn't fit for a dog!' he growled.

I'd made stuffed zucchini for lunch because it was his favourite meal, but he wanted to go out to Schwartz's Deli. In a pleading, little-boy tone, he said, 'I need to be somewhere that's full of life. Please, Jules, we'll have your zucchini for dinner.'

He was as frail as a kitten, and his left side had been weakened by the stroke, so he leaned on me as we walked to my car. It turned out that he'd been craving cheesecake, so he ate two gigantic pieces with a cup of coffee.

Marianne, his store manager, came by just before supper and assured us that there was no reason for him to rush back to work – sales were brisk, in fact. To celebrate the good news, we invited her to stay, and we polished off a bottle of Portuguese red wine along with my zucchini.

The next day, the doorbell rang in the late afternoon and I opened the door to find Benni and Teresa standing on the stoop. Benni held a big pink box tied around with twine. He'd come up to see Shelly in the hospital and stayed in our guestroom for two days, so I didn't expect him to return so soon.

'How's Shel?' he asked even before we kissed.

'He's good,' I said. 'You'll see.'

After Teresa and I hugged, I led them both into the kitchen, where Shelly was sitting in the spring sun cutting in through the open windows. When my husband saw his cousin, he started to quake and fought to stand up.

'Just stay where you are!' Benni called out, and he kneeled next to Shelly.

After they'd kissed and cried, Shelly opened the big pink box and discovered a shimmering chocolate *mandelbrot*. '*Mein Gott*, it's absolutely gorgeous!' he said in a reverent voice, and he cut off such a big piece with the knife I handed him that I thought he'd share it with Benni or Teresa, but I was wrong.

Shelly snorted when I told him he was being rude and said,

'Just give them plates, and take one for yourself, and try not to interrupt me when I'm eating!'

Everything was easy over the three days that the four of us had together, and we made one another laugh all the time, and often too wildly, like people who'd been through hell. I was sure that everything was about to return to normal and that I could go back to work, but then – just after Benni and Teresa returned to New York – Shelly stopped getting dressed and shaving. He watched old movies on the small television in our bedroom and started re-reading the Willa Cather novels George had sent him years before. He lost his appetite, too; he wouldn't even eat the poppy seed *hamantaschen* I made him.

'It's weird, kiddo – I'm tired all the time,' he told me.

'It's not weird,' I told him. 'You had a stroke.'

But it wasn't his fatigue that was truly preoccupying him. I found that out the next Saturday afternoon when I overhead him talking to Benni on the phone, and though he spoke mostly in Yiddish, at one point he yelled in English, 'Yeah, my *putz* is dead! Kaput! We'll pay a rabbi to say *kaddish* for it when you visit.'

To whatever Benni replied, Shelly snapped something that had to do with his cousin being a *dummkopf* and crashed the receiver down.

After he was asleep that night, I crawled under the covers and took him in my mouth.

'Hey, what d'ya think you're doing down there?' he snarled, and he tapped me on my head.

'Getting you hard,' I replied.

'Christ, not now, baby. I'm exhausted.'

I sat up and turned on the light. In a gentle tone, I said, 'Listen, Shelly, maybe you need to talk to someone.'

He blocked out the glare of the lamp with his hand. 'About what?' he asked in a falsely innocent voice.

'About your cock,' I said.

'What about it?'

'I overheard you talking to Benni.'

'You . . . you little traitor!' he sputtered. He looked up toward the ceiling and, as though speaking to God, snarled something in Yiddish.

In the confident voice I decided to use, I said, 'I'm sure this sort of thing is normal. Your erections are bound to come back in a few weeks.'

He sat up and reached for the cigarettes on his night table. He placed one between his lips, sneered and said, 'So you're a penis expert now?'

'I've had yours in me a few thousand times,' I replied, trying not to raise my voice. 'So, yeah, I know a little something about the way they work.'

He lit his cigarette, stood up and hobbled out of the room.

'For Christ's sake, Shel, take it easy on yourself,' I called after him.

He came back into the doorway. 'Tell me, Jules, what the hell could be normal about a dead *putz*? I'm only fifty-seven.'

'Did you ask Dr Lai about it?'

He glared at me as if hanging might be too good for me and said, 'You think he cares about my penis? And what's this got to do with you, anyway?'

'Remember me? I'm your wife,' I said.

'Yeah, but not everything is about you, you know.'

'Jesus, Shelly, you must be watching too many American sitcoms to come up with a line like that.'

He chewed the inside of his cheek, like he does when he is about to start yelling. 'You know something, Jules, you've always been too clever for your own good.'

'So you'd rather have married a *dummkopf*?'

An ugly frown creased his face, and he told me to shut up, which set rage pulsing through me. I said, 'Listen up, you asshole! One thing I could always count on was your cock. It's been good to me even when you've been a total schmuck.'

'Well, the party's over, baby,' he said. 'I'm like your beloved Montreal Canadiens – I wilt in the second period.'

That night, Shelly began whimpering in bed. I curled up behind him.

'What's going to happen to me?' he whispered.

'Nothing's going to happen to you, you silly boy. Nothing's changed. We'll figure this out together.' I pinched his behind. 'Listen, Guido, I'll put you back in working order if it's the last thing I do!'

When he turned to me, he said in a grave voice, 'You might as well just pack me off on a cattle car to Auschwitz.'

I made no reply to that; his words formed a fist around my throat. I had to sit up to breathe.

'Try to sleep,' I told him. And after a while he did. But I was up all night.

The next morning, while Shelly was eating breakfast, I made a call to Dr Lai's office from our bedroom. He assured me that impotence among stroke patients of my husband's age rarely lasted more than a few weeks. Then, he told me something important: 'Julie, listen, you and Shelly will spare yourself a month or so of sleepless nights if you'll just have a little faith in the miraculous design of the human body and the healing that Shelly is now experiencing.'

The wisdom in his voice made me start to cry, but Shelly scoffed when I repeated the advice. 'It's easy for a thirty-year-old hot-shot doctor to talk about the miraculous design of my body – he doesn't have a dead dick!'

Shelly moped around in his bare feet for the next couple of days and watched black-and-white movies in our bedroom. On the third morning – as a way of forcing him to spend some time outside the house – I convinced him to drop me at work and pick me up that evening.

As I would later learn, he walked a couple of miles through downtown Montreal that afternoon. When exhaustion overwhelmed him, he called a cab and went to the Museum of Fine Arts and ended up sitting on a bench in front of a bird-headed god from ancient Nimrud for a half hour. He told me that he understood for the first time that the Assyrians wanted their gods to be as sensitive and good-natured as birds so that they could alert them to the approach of enemies.

I didn't understand a lot of the other conclusions he came to about the gods of Nimrud and Persepolis that he told me that evening, but I didn't mind because he was so cheerful.

While I chopped up shallots for potato soup, Shelly snuck up behind me and threw his arms around me. 'Montreal in the spring is beautiful,' he whispered, and in the warm weight of his head on my shoulder, I felt his gratitude for Canada having given him refuge after the war.

At such times, it has always seemed to me that Shelly was overjoyed that he'd fallen for a girl from his adopted country.

'I have to take you to smell the lilac bushes in La Fontaine Park!' he told me as I served him dinner. His eyes seemed to glow and he faked a swoon. *Mon Dieu, quel parfum!*

The next evening, Shelly rushed to me as I got home from work, holding a landscape painted in bright, crazy colours that he'd found in a dumpster on the Avenue des Pins. It showed a cockeyed row of Montreal's plex houses. Their outdoor staircases were twisted and curved, and one of them – painted silver – led straight into a pink sky. On the top rung stood a tall, painfully slender man with his arms open, as if to say, *All this is mine!*

When I agreed that it seemed to be about the world's peculiar and difficult-to-fathom beauty, he kissed me and said, 'I'll have it framed and we'll put it in our bedroom – behind our heads. I want to sleep under a painting I found in a Montreal dumpster. And this guy will be our guardian angel,' he added, pointing to the wire-thin man on the silver staircase.

'I'm all for guardian angels,' I replied. 'But what were you doing hunting in a dumpster on the Avenue des Pins?'

'Jules, don't you occasionally pick over trash for what might be useful?' he asked in a dumbfounded voice.

'No, never.'

He shrugged as if I were hopeless and said, 'Then I'm afraid you'll never find what you're not already looking for.'

At the time, my shift in Obstetrics ended at seven in the evening, and over the next two weeks, Shelly would pick me up in his clunky old Saab at the entrance to McGill Health Centre and take me out to dinner. He was generous and playful, and the only difference in our lives was that we never had sex, but I had decided to take Dr Lai's advice and allow myself a bit of faith for a change.

Shelly went back to work a month after his stroke. By then, he was able to walk without a limp and his left hand had regained his usual firm grip.

Two days later, however, I caught him sobbing at the kitchen table in the early morning. I had just come downstairs and there he was, curled over himself. Tears were rolling down his cheeks.

'What happened?' I asked.

'I had a dream. Except it wasn't a dream.'

When I came to him, he grabbed my hand and pressed it into his cheek. 'What did you see?' I asked.

'She came back to me.'

'Who?'

He looked up at me with despairing eyes. 'I can't tell you,' he whispered.

'An . . . old girlfriend?'

'Are you nuts? You're my only girlfriend.'

He let go of my hand and stood up. After he looked around the room, he went to the refrigerator and opened the door.

'Shel,' I said, 'I'm sorry, but I've had enough of this secrecy of yours.'

He took out the carton of milk and took a long sip.

'Tell me,' I repeated.

'You'll think I've lost my marbles,' he said, wiping off his milk moustache.

'I was never convinced you had any to begin with,' I shot back, grinning and hoping he'd do the same.

Instead, he trudged upstairs to our bedroom and closed the door behind him and called Benni. I pressed my ear to the door, but he spoke only Yiddish. That night he didn't come to bed. He sat slumped on the sofa and guzzled down half a bottle of Bacardi rum and passed out in his clothes.

He complained of a hangover the next morning, so I made him oatmeal and a pot of strong coffee before we both headed off to work. He still refused to tell me about the dream that wasn't a dream.

Apparently, Shelly didn't go to his store that day, and Benni arrived from New York just before lunch, and the two of them went out to Schwartz's Deli. Benni had a smoked meat sandwich and a glass of red wine; Shelly had a piece of strawberry cheesecake and a decaf coffee. Just before leaving, they spotted a local celebrity at the counter – the singer Leonard Cohen – and Benni found the courage to thank him for 'Chelsea Hotel #2', one of his favourite songs. When Cohen complimented Benni on the sleek cut of his blue linen shirt, Benni told him proudly that he'd made it himself, and they ended up conversing about tailoring for a little while.

I found all that out that evening after I discovered Benni in our living room, sitting in the armchair by the window, reading a recent issue of *Paris Match* that I'd pilfered from my dentist's office. On the cover was an ancient-looking, downhearted, misty-eyed Jean Gabin. He seemed a perfect match for my mood.

After we hugged and talked about how he'd spoken to Leonard Cohen at Schwartz's, Benni told me that Shelly had sobbed on and off all afternoon. He'd ended up exhausting himself, and Benni had just put him to bed.

'Do you know what's going on with him?' I asked. 'I mean, I understand he's upset that his *putz* isn't working right, but all this frustration and anger . . .'

Benni put his finger to his lips and motioned me into the den, then closed the door behind us.

'The problem is Esther,' he said.

'Who's Esther?' I asked, but a second later I knew exactly what had happened. *The great big careless schmuck has gotten some poor young girl pregnant!* I told myself.

But Benni had a different surprise in store. He grimaced to make it clear I ought to expect something bad and said, 'Esther – his little sister.'

'What about her?'

'You have to understand, Jules, All That never really ended for Shelly.'

All That was Benni's code for the Holocaust.

'I understand, but why is Shelly—'

'Esther's come back to him,' he cut in. I must have made a sceptical face, because he said, 'And she's still just sixteen years old. It seems that the dead don't age.'

'Come back to him how?' I asked.

'It's hard to explain.'

'Benni, just tell me what the hell is going on or I'm going to scream!'

He patted at the air to have me stay calm, then lit a cigarette and stared out the window at our back garden. Without turning back to me, he said, 'It sounds too crazy in English.'

'Sometimes I think crazy is all I've got,' I told him.

He nodded as if he understood me perfectly, but didn't reply. He smoked thoughtfully. I decided not to interrupt, but the silence soon began to throb all around me, so I said, 'Look, Benni, why don't you say what you need to say in Yiddish and then translate for me?'

He grunted. 'That's the point – it's untranslatable.'

Tears of frustration welled in my eyes. 'Benni, honey,' I said, 'I'm losing my mind. The two of you . . . it's like two against one sometimes. I can't win.'

'I'm sorry it seems like that. Listen, Jules, it's like this . . . Shelly says that he always worried that Esther was wandering the earth as a *dybbuk*. You know what a *dybbuk* is?'

'A Jewish ghost, right?'

He drew in hard on his cigarette. I had the feeling he was about to reveal perilous secrets to me. 'More or less,' he said. 'It's a spirit without a body. Shelly thinks that while he was unconscious in his shop, after his stroke, Esther found him and kind of went . . . went into him.'

I felt as if I were no longer where I was meant to be – that I'd gotten lost somewhere between Shelly's stay in the hospital and this moment. In a hesitant voice, I asked, 'Esther went into him how?'

Benni stared out the window again and mouthed something to himself in Yiddish. In profile, he looked like a little boy anticipating disaster. I could easily see him as the kid who'd gazed for months out of a window on Koszykowa Street in Warsaw, waiting for his parents to return home.

When I called his name, he turned to me with a startled face.

'How did Esther get into Shelly?' I repeated.

'In old Jewish stories, *dybbuks* do pretty much what they want,' he told me, adding in a menacing whisper, 'They can even get into bed with you.' He shook his head disapprovingly and said, 'All kinds of spirits used to hang around Warsaw. Mom said that we had one who lived on the roof of our building in summer. She used to warn me against doubting God's existence, too, because an evil *dybbuk* would take me over as punishment as soon as I fell asleep.'

My thoughts seemed to slide slowly away from me. Benni sat me down on the sofa. 'You want a cigarette?' he asked.

When I nodded, he lit one for me, and though it tasted filthy, I didn't put it out. He remained standing, observing me worriedly.

'What does Esther want from him?' I asked.

'To share his life. You've got to understand, she lost her whole family except for Shel. And she was just a teenager.'

I swirled my foot around a bald spot in the old kilim that Shelly had told me he'd bought at a flea market a few years after we were married, but it occurred to me just then that he might really have found it rolled up by the curb in front of some scuzzy tenement, waiting for a garbage truck. I looked around the room at the Rembrandt and Cézanne posters he'd framed and hung proudly on the walls, suspecting now that he might have rescued them from the dumpsters behind some art gallery. The image of him hunting through piles of trash set me crying, and to keep from giving in further to despair, I tried to be amusing. 'Your cousin is part raccoon,' I said.

'I don't understand,' Benni replied.

I dried my eyes. 'He scrounges around in garbage heaps. He brought home a painting the other day that he found in a dumpster on the Avenue des Pins.'

Benni laughed affectionately. 'Was it any good?'

'Yeah, but everything in it is cockeyed.'

'Cockeyed?'

'Crooked. At a weird angle.' My throat was suddenly dry. 'Listen, Benni, there's a bottle of Gewürztraminer in the fridge. Could you get it?'

He rushed away and returned with the wine and two glasses. 'Esther, she talks to Shelly,' he told me as he poured.

I stubbed out my cigarette. 'So what's Esther say?'

'For one thing, she tells him about all the places she's been.'

'Hasn't she been in heaven?'

He lifted his wine glass, so I did too. '*L'chaim*,' we said as we chinked them together.

'Esther said that after she was killed in Treblinka, she wandered around Poland, looking for her family,' Benni told me. 'That lasted years, she thinks. She's not sure – she's not so good at time. I guess she's . . . oh, what's the word?'

'Disoriented.'

'Yeah, but more permanent than that,' he said. He made a frustrated, clucking sound with his tongue.

I patted the sofa and said, 'How about sitting next to me? You standing there, looking so nervous – it scares the hell out of me.'

He did as I asked, and when I smiled my approval, he smiled back in the same fond way. Had our love for the same man turned us into mirrors?

I leaned back, crossed my arms over my chest and said, 'So does only Shelly hear Esther or do you do too?'

'No, I can't hear her. He tells me what she says.'

'And you don't see her, right? After all, she's inside Shelly.'

'That's right, she's inside him.'

'Did she say how she got to Montreal?'

'She told him she woke up one morning in a strange city, and snow was on the ground, and people were speaking English and French, but she understood them, though she didn't know how. Sometime later, she spotted Shelly. He was going into a store downtown, and—'

'Hold it!' I said, cutting him off. 'How the hell could Esther recognise her brother after not seeing him for thirty-five years? My voice surged with triumph because I'd found a logical flaw in his story – which meant that Esther was really only a product of Shelly's disturbed mind.

Benni searched for a reply. 'I guess . . . guess she recognised his soul,' he said.

'Are you telling me that *dybbuks* can see souls?'

He pursed his lips and raised his eyebrows – his signal for an esoteric subject that was beyond his understanding – then said, 'Look, Jules, I've read quite a lot about *dybbuks* but this is the first one I've . . . actually met.'

I moaned and said, 'Benni, you *do* realise that we sound like we've lost our minds.'

'Only in English. In Yiddish translation, all we've said makes perfect sense. Anyway, Shelly said that Esther came to him a little less than four years ago. He told me that she's been with him all the time since then, but she only snuck inside him when he passed out. I guess that he left his door unlocked, so to speak.'

'So he actually thinks she's been hanging around him for four years?' I asked with an increasing sense of dread.

'On and off. He didn't think much about it because he didn't think she was real. He thought she was a kind of hallucination produced by his feelings – by the slow accumulation of sadness.'

The Slow Accumulation of Sadness seemed like the right title for the book someone – not me – might write about the hidden lives of Holocaust survivors.

'Benni, do you really believe that Esther has come back as a spirit and that she's inside him?' I looked him straight in the eye because I needed him to see that his answer would determine the path our lives would now have to take.

He took a last quick drag on his cigarette while considering how to reply. While crushing it out, he said, 'I don't know. Really strange things happen sometimes. And me and Shelly ... I sometimes think that I attract things that are odd and improbable. Who could ever imagine I'd be living in New York and that Shelly would be in Montreal? When I was a kid, I'd never have believed it possible!'

His look told me that it was now my turn to reply with something meaningful, so I said, 'You two did great to get out of Poland. And I feel blessed to know you both – to have become part of your lives. But this is something different – something that has to do with ... with the soundness of Shelly's mind.'

He made his counterfeit smile and took another cigarette from his pack. 'Your husband was going to be a great actor,' he said. 'And Esther was going to be a concert pianist. And me, I was going to be an archaeologist.' He gave a sad little laugh. 'It's like I told you once, when you dreamt of that Pulcinella – life had some dirty tricks in store for us.'

'So did you want to go to Egypt?' I asked, because he'd told me once that he had lived in Alexandria in a previous life.

'That's right. My dad had told me about the Library of Alexandria. And I think I'd already seen a mummy at some museum. But you know what, our cousin Abe was the one who had a real chance of making his dreams come true.' Benni let his cigarette dangle from his lips. 'Everybody knew he'd be a chess champion.'

After he lit his cigarette, he stood up and opened the window all the way. 'Sorry about all this smoke,' he said. 'I've tried to stop but I can't.'

'It's okay, I don't mind.'

'I think of Abe a lot,' he said, and his eyes grew remote. At length, he added, 'I keep a list in my head of all the things he and Esther didn't get to do. And I always find new things to add.'

'That was a long time ago,' I said, since I seemed to be in danger of losing him to his never-ending list.

'It sure doesn't seem so'. He sat down next to me again. 'Though I know you're right in terms of years,' he said in a conciliatory tone, 'because here I am, a tailor living in New York, and I've got a kid of my own. And Shelly . . . He sells sneakers and tennis rackets to little *pishers*, and he's got you and the girls and this beautiful house.'

I knew from the way his hands were shaking that he was fighting back tears. To distract him, I pointed out a male cardinal – scarlet red with a black mask – that had just alighted on the lowest branch of our cherry tree.

'Beautiful!' he said with renewed cheer. 'We've got lots of them in New York. And blue jays. America and Canada have really good birds. Poland's birds kind of suck.'

I poured us both more wine and said, 'Shelly thinks God might have the head of a bird. Like those sculptures from Nimrud in the Museum of Fine Arts.'

'Good for Shelly – and God, too,' he said, and he flapped his arms. 'I'm pretty sure that wings and a beak could prove useful if the Nazis come back.'

'Benni, honey, does Shelly's little sister have something to do with his impotence? I don't seem to get what's going on.'

'Shelly thinks that Esther doesn't want him to ... be with you. Apparently, it upsets her.'

As my stomach clenched, I asked in a resentful tone, 'She wants him all to herself?'

'I think that's the general idea.'

I felt as if I'd just enlisted in an undeclared war, though it seemed to me that I'd have little chance against an hallucination of a frightened little sister who'd perished thirty-five years ago in a death camp. 'Can this really be happening?' I asked.

Benni sipped his wine and said, 'I told Shel that he probably needed to see a psychiatrist.'

'We both know that that's not going to happen. He's only going to talk to you. And maybe me, if I can convince him that I'm on his side.'

'And George,' he said. 'He called him yesterday to tell him about Esther.'

'Did it do any good?'

'I'm not sure. But he needed to speak to another man and he couldn't reach me. He's too embarrassed to talk to you. I thought if he spoke to a psychiatrist in French he might remember that he lives in Quebec, and that the war has been over a long time. You see, he speaks to Esther in Yiddish. And it's bad for him. Thinking in Yiddish ... It's reassuring for a few minutes, but then he starts remembering everybody he used to talk to back in Poland, and pretty soon he can't get enough air in his lungs.'

Benni and I looked at each other, and this time we seemed to reflect each other's apprehension. For a moment, I imagined us alone on the deck of too large and too fast-moving a ship, and we had no idea where it was headed.

'Does Shelly know anything about *dybbuks*?' I asked. 'How to get rid of them, I mean.'

'Maybe, but the thing is, he doesn't want Esther to go. Now that she's come back, he's hoping to keep her around.'

6

Shelly camped out on the couch again that night. Benni talked with him for nearly three hours the following morning behind the locked door of our den. I'd taken another sick day, so I was home, doing laundry and ironing to keep myself busy.

When Benni finally emerged for lunch, he joined me in the kitchen. 'How's it going?' I asked.

'It turns out that Esther remembers me well.' He took himself a glass of water and gulped it down. 'And she doesn't mind my being with Shelly, so things are calm at the moment.'

That seemed a bit of good news, but despair shook me when I considered that she was being reasonable just to gain Shelly's confidence. Maybe she was going to order him to leave me.

Half a croissant was sitting on my breakfast plate. Benni pointed to it. 'You going to finish that?' he asked.

He was famous at our family dinners for eating leftovers. 'Be my guest,' I told him.

He began to eat it with those mouse-like bites he took when he wanted to savour a pleasure. My expression must have given away the question I wanted to ask, because he said, 'Esther asked me about what I've been doing these last thirty-five years, so I told her. She especially wanted to know how I made it out of Warsaw.

I suspect she's considering how she might have survived instead of me. It's like she's trying to redo her past and give it a happy ending. I mean, there's no rational reason why I should be here and she should be dead.'

'You believe that's what she thinks?' I asked.

'That's pretty much what all survivors think. And I'm beginning to believe that the dead think so too.'

Benni had to return to New York late that evening because his son, Eti, had a baseball game the next day, and he'd promised to be there. He said he'd come back as soon as possible. I didn't drive him to the airport because neither of us thought it was a good idea to leave Shelly alone. Instead, I called our regular taxi driver.

Just before he left for the airport, Benni said, 'This afternoon I phoned a couple of religious friends who live in Brooklyn. They say they know an old Jew – a healer – who was born in Danzig and who might be able to help. His name is Levi – Mordechai Levi.'

'Shelly won't talk to any rabbi,' I said in a warning tone.

'Levi isn't a rabbi. He's an expert in this sort of thing.'

'But what if this expert turns out to be a nutcase?'

'I guess we'll just have to improvise.'

'Oh, great,' I said glumly.

Benni took my hand. 'Don't you worry, Jules, All That made me damn good at improvising.'

Over the next few days, Shelly barricaded himself in the den while I was at home. What he did while I was at work, I have no idea.

Every evening, at supper time, I'd knock on the den door and ask if he wanted me to bring him some food, but he would tell me that he wasn't hungry and needed to be alone. His rancorous, resentful voice was like a knife at my throat.

Once, I summoned my courage and came downstairs while he was making ready to go to sleep on the couch. I asked him what he did all day long while I was working. He gazed right through me and said that there were lots of forgotten details about his life in Poland that he had started to remember. When I reached out to his arm, he flinched and took a step back, and from the way he looked away, I understood that Esther had told him not to touch me.

My next few days were full of fear and self-recrimination, and dizziness occasionally overwhelmed me at work. Once, when I was close to fainting, I had another nurse take my blood pressure, and we discovered that it was dangerously low. I'd had that problem before and had solved it by drinking an extra coffee every morning and afternoon, and I tried that strategy again, but it didn't help this time. I thought it was a bad idea for me to start taking medication while under such an emotional strain, so whenever possible, I'd lie down for a half hour in the supply room near the Cardiac Centre where the staff maintained a couple of cots.

At night, during my frequent bouts with insomnia, my mind would travel downstairs to Shelly sleeping in our living room. I would tell him we'd get through this together, but in my imagination he often refused to even look at me.

Sometimes, while Shelly slept, I'd sneak into the den to open all the windows to clear out the stink of sweat and cigarettes. I'd sit at the desk where I pay our house bills, switch on the lamp and read my French thesaurus for hours, improving my vocabulary. I kept thinking that if I could memorise enough key words, I'd be able to tell Shelly exactly what was in my heart in the language he most loved, and he'd learn to trust me.

But maybe the truth behind my obsessive behaviour lay somewhere else – perhaps I'd needed to give myself a task that was nearly as impossible as fighting a ghost.

The realisation that I was most afraid to tell Benni or anyone else was that what had happened to Shelly had revealed that he has always had a hollow inside him in the exact shape of Esther.

It seemed sometimes that it was inevitable that he and I would get lost in the tangle of all he had refused to tell me or anyone else about his family.

Every morning when I left for work, I worried that he'd take his own life. I'd picture him in the bathtub, covered in blood, his eyes closed, his right hand still holding his Swiss Army knife.

The ambulance medics were French-speaking in my fantasies. I'd tell them, '*C'était sa soeur qui l'a tué.*'

'*Sa soeur*? *Où est elle*?' they'd ask.

'*Morte en Polonie il y a trente-cinq ans.*'

They'd look at each other and start making a list in their heads of all the synonyms for crazy that I'd recently learned: *dingue, folingue, maboul, foldingue, désaxé, cinglé, azimuté . . .*

I imagined Shelly killing himself because Esther would tell him that his death would ensure that they'd remain together forever.

I knew he'd use his old Swiss Army knife, because it was the only thing that he managed to save from his life in Poland. And I became convinced that he'd want to decide on the exact time and place of his death. That seemed obvious now – a consequence of everything that Shelly had ever told me about himself.

Benni and I spoke on the phone every evening, and five days after he returned to New York, he said that he'd finally managed to get Mordechai Levi on the phone. The old Jewish healer had a calm, confidant voice and seemed to be deeply knowledgeable about what Benni called *practical kabbalah*, meaning magic. He and Benni would be coming up to Montreal in a few days.

I hadn't told our daughters anything about their father's troubles with Esther, since they'd have insisted on Shelly consulting a psychiatrist, and he'd have ended up shouting rebukes at them. Instead, I told them that going back to work had exhausted him, and in the evenings he wanted to be alone. I said that he sent them all his love.

Had Shelly ever spoken to our girls about his sister? I thought not. In more than two decades of marriage, he'd spent no more than ten minutes telling me about her. Here is all I knew: she had been an unrepentant tomboy as a girl, but during her fourteenth year – in 1940 – she had grown five inches and become a willowy young lady. Still, she detested sewing and knitting and all the other activities considered proper for middle-class Jewish girls. She would play Beethoven sonatas for hours on end in the family living room, often in a kind of trance, humming to herself, as though unable to contain the ceaseless flow of music in her head. In the evenings, she'd sometimes go dancing with Shelly and his friends, and in winter she'd go ice skating with her parents. Her idol was the Norwegian figure skating champion and actress, Sonja Henie, and her favourite author was Julian Tuwim, a Jewish-Polish poet from Łódź; when she was eleven, she'd met Tuwim at a reading that Shelly had taken her to, and the famous author had taken a liking to the excitable little girl and exchanged letters with her. For a couple of years, she'd slept with his correspondence under her pillow.

My work at the McGill Health Centre became my refuge. I remember a frightened young mother from Eritrea giving birth one afternoon after seven painful hours of labour. Her gaunt, harried, sweat-soaked face shone with otherworldly light when I placed her wrinkled little son in her arms. She kissed his shiny black hair and sobbed, and I stood before the two of them as before a landscape as wide and deep and noble as the Grand Canyon, and I decided to speak as little as I could over the rest of the day and to keep repeating in my head a prayer for their safety: *Please let nothing bad ever happen to her and her son.*

Although I didn't believe in any traditional conception of God, I sent those words out to whoever or whatever was able to hear them, which was how I knew I'd started to believe in Benni's practical kabbalah. And that I'd come to accept that Esther was every bit as real as the slow accumulation of Shelly's sadness.

Two days before Benni was scheduled to fly up to Montreal with Mordechai Levi, Diane called and pleaded to see her father. She told me she no longer believed my excuses. 'I'm really worried about him – and you,' she said.

I told her that her father wasn't home, that he'd begun putting in a lot of overtime to make up for the month he'd missed. Some hesitance in my voice must have given away my lie, and she demanded to know what was really going on, so I told her that I was just worried about him taking too many risks with his health. 'I really wish he'd spend more time at home,' I said, which proved a mistake.

'I take that to mean he's already cheating on you again!' Diane snarled.

'No, that's not what this is about,' I said.

'Mom, how can I believe you?' she asked.

'Look, all I can do is tell you how things stand. And what's in my heart. If that's not good enough for you, then there's nothing I can do.'

My desperate tone convinced her that her suspicions were unfounded, but she went to Cagney's Sporting Goods the next day to see how her father was doing, and when his store manager, Marianne, told her that he hadn't been going to work, she sped over to the house and accused me of hiding what she called *Dad's monstrous behaviour!*

Her face was so distorted by rage that it chilled me. And all I could think of to defend myself was the truth, so I told her that Shelly's stroke had started him thinking too much about his dead family and that he'd hidden himself in the den. 'His past has finally caught up with him,' I said.

She apologised for yelling at me and reached for my hand. It was such a relief to see her fondness for me in her eyes that I shivered.

'Mom, shouldn't he see a psychiatrist or some sort of therapist?' Diane asked in a gentle tone.

'Maybe, but he wouldn't go. It seems to me that your father is having a mid-life crisis. He needs some time by himself – to go over all that's happened to him. It'll probably take a few months, so please just be patient.'

She accepted my explanation, probably because it sounded eminently normal for Canada in 1977 – and curable. Despite my warning, however, she walked to the den a few minutes later, knocked on the locked door and asked her father to let her in.

Shelly told her in a gruff voice to leave him alone.

'Dad, it's just me,' she said in her little-girl voice, which seemed like a tactic that might at least get him to open the door a crack, but then she added in a motherly tone, 'You're being silly.'

'Go away!' he yelled, and so loudly that my heart jumped inside my chest.

Diane ended up pounding on the door and telling him he was being selfish. I stood up and was about to go to her – to plead with her to stop making herself miserable – when she marched into the kitchen. She was holding the brass door handle. 'It came off in my hand!' she snarled.

She held it up and shook it at me as if I were responsible.

Her self-righteous pose seemed symbolic of the wayward direction of my life, and I was about to give way to tears, but

I gathered my forces and made light of what had happened. I even managed a brief laugh at the absurdity of the situation. Unfortunately, that deepened her irritation at me and her father, and she crashed the door handle down onto the kitchen table.

'You married a very selfish man!' she shouted, and she targeted me with such contemptuous eyes that I realised that I must have represented to her just about everything a woman ought not to be – forgiving of a cheating husband, most of all.

'I know you don't understand, but trust me when I say that I'm doing the best I can,' I replied, which made her scoff.

'Just tell me this – why do you always defend him?' she asked.

'Do I always defend him?'

'Yes.'

'I don't think that's true. In fact, I recall a number of times when I admitted to you and your sister that he'd hurt me badly. But before his stroke, our life together was really good. He doesn't have affairs anymore. Your father isn't the same man he was.'

'If he's changed so much, then why doesn't he come out of the den and talk to me?'

'Oh, I see what you mean. No, that hasn't changed – he's still holding on to his secrets. But you need to see things from his point of view. He has always wanted to protect you and Margot.'

'Protect us from what?'

'From all that happened to him in Europe. He didn't want you burdened with so much sadness and loss and—'

'So he burdened us with other things!' Diane cut in. 'We lived with way too much silence, you know!'

'Yes, I'm very much aware of that. I guess it seemed the lesser of two evils to him. Maybe it still does. I don't know. Maybe after this crisis, he'll talk to you more openly. I hope so.'

'Mom, I can't stay here right now, this is too much for me,' she said, and she picked up her bag from the kitchen table and dashed out of the room.

I was fairly certain that she'd slam the front door closed, but I heard only a delicate click. My mind grasped on to that small concession, and I began to hope that Diane might one day understand and forgive her father.

Benni came back the next day. It was a Sunday, exactly nine days after he'd last seen Shelly. I answered his knocks carrying salad tongs because I'd been polishing all our silverware. He held up his hands as if to surrender and said, 'I've been mistaken for lettuce in the past, but I'm actually Jewish.'

When I didn't laugh, he nodded and said, 'You're right, Jules, my timing was off.' After I explained what I was doing with the tongs, I asked where Mr Levi was.

'He didn't come! The son of a bitch screwed me! Give me some orange juice, I'm dying of thirst, and I'll tell you the whole story.'

As I led Benni to the kitchen, he whispered, 'Is Shel still barricaded in the den?'

'Yeah, unfortunately.'

While I went to the refrigerator, Benni dropped down at the kitchen table. 'Get this, Jules, Levi told me that his friends called him Rikhter, which should have set alarm bells ringing in my head, but sometimes I'm pretty dumb.'

I poured him his juice. 'Why? I don't understand.'

'Thanks,' he said, taking the glass from me. '*Rikhter* means judge. Judge Levi, that's what he liked being called! Pretty ominous, don't you think?' He took a greedy and breathless sip of juice. 'But he seduced me with his crazy stories about flying rabbis and chickens that lay golden eggs and brides coming back from the dead. And he told me about a demon that he pulled out of a German soprano while she was on tour in Kraków in 1933. That was what convinced me that he could help Shelly. He wrote out a list of what we'd need to get for the exorcism, and I—'

'The exorcism!' I cried out. I nearly choked on the word.

'Well, that's kind of what we've got to do.'

'You make my life sound like a horror movie.'

'Sorry about that. But listen, everything was set – I bought a first-class plane ticket for Levi and booked him a room at a fancy hotel, and then, this morning, he spoiled everything. Or nearly did. In the end, we came up with a plan that I could carry out alone.'

'How did he nearly spoil everything?'

Benni downed the last of his drink, so I poured him more. 'He'd already told me that Shel would have to start eating kosher food and going to *schul*, and that it would be best if he started showing a little fear of God and saying the right prayers over meals, and all the rest. So, you know me, I lied and said none of that would be any problem, and maybe I went a little overboard and told him that Shelly never intended to become a secular Jew, that it just happened, kind of somebody waking up one day and finding out he's become a little bald. But this morning, when he asked about you and found out you weren't Jewish, he went berserk. He screamed at me for what he called *withholding pertinent information*, like he was from the FBI – and anyway, it wasn't true, because he hadn't asked before about your religion or what you looked like or anything else.'

'Does it matter I'm not Jewish? I'm not the *dybbuk*, Esther is.'

'Wait, this is the best part!' Benni exclaimed triumphantly. 'He called you a *shiksa* from the North Pole! And he told me that Shel would have to divorce you. "Divorce Julie?!" I said. "Are you nuts?" But he said Shelly had to do what he said or he couldn't work his magic, so before I was tempted to kill him, I told him I was very sorry, but that he and the other FBI agents he worked with would have to look elsewhere for someone's life to ruin and that he was fired!'

'So what did you do?' I asked, and I sat down opposite Benni at the table and played with the silver candle holder that Shelly had bought me shortly after we were married.

Benni patted his belly and said, 'Listen, Jules, I didn't eat lunch today. Can you make me an omelette or something? I'll tell you what happened while you're cooking.'

'Sure.'

I took the carton of eggs and some cheddar out of the refrigerator.

'Levi had memorised all of Deuteronomy,' Benni continued. 'When I found that out, I should've known that he was going to give me some trouble.'

'Benni, honey, I don't know what you mean. I haven't read the Old Testament in thirty years.'

'Deuteronomy is like God's book of baseball rules. Every last regulation is written out.' He sighed. 'But I probably shouldn't make fun of it. I guess I should try harder to be a good Jew.'

'I think you're a good Jew,' I said, cracking open an egg.

'That's because you're too sweet for your own good. But I'm only kosher because I'm mostly vegetarian, and I haven't been to *schul* since Ethan was born, and I'm not sure I even believe in God, which is rule number one.'

'But you love Jewish history.'

'And mythology,' he said gratefully. 'And kabbalah, too. I guess I love nearly everything except the rules.'

I cracked open a second egg. 'All right, Benni, so what did you do?' I asked.

'As I was leaving Levi's place, he called out to me and told me to wait a minute, then got a piece of paper and ended up writing out a list of things we'll need to convince Esther to leave Shelly. I was suspicious at first, but he apologised for being so rude to me. He took my hand and said that it was his obligation to help Shelly because he was a Holocaust survivor, even if he didn't go to synagogue and was married to a *shiksa*. I wasn't sure what to do – I got a little confused. But he told me that our only hope was performing the ceremony he had in mind. He seemed to know what he was talking about. And he said he was sorry again. Anyway, I accepted the list. I've got it in my wallet. So after I eat a quick lunch, we'll go to a good antique store.'

'Why an antique store?'

'They've always got a lot of old mirrors. And we'll need ten.'

7

As Benni ate his omelette, he explained why we'd need mirrors. He said that Esther – looking out of Shelly's eyes – would expect to see a reflection of herself in them, but that instead she'd see a middle-aged man. That would disorient and upset her. 'So, with any luck, we'll be able to convince her to leave Shelly without a fight,' he told me.

In an excited voice, he added that Levi had discovered the mirror trick in the writings of Isaac Luria.

'Who's Isaac Luria?' I asked.

Benni stared at me with shocked eyes and said, 'He's one of the most powerful kabbalists of all time! Haven't you looked at those books I've sent you and Shelly?'

'Benni, I'm sorry, but when I read about Judaism I just get sleepy.'

He sighed as if I were hopeless. 'Luria lived in the sixteenth century, and he was good friends with Berekiah Zarco. You remember who Berekiah is, I hope.'

'How could I forget? Whenever Shelly wants to establish his pedigree, he talks about your illustrious ancestor and what an important mystic he was.'

'I'll tell you a secret, Jules – I think about Berekiah a lot. Sometimes, when I'm lying in bed, I wish I could get in touch with him.'

'Why? What would you tell him?'

Benni forked up his last bit of omelette. 'I'd say, "Send me back to my family's apartment in the ghetto, in the fall of 1940, but only for a minute, because I'm not planning on staying, and help me bring everybody back with me to New York."'

'Benni, there really is a Mordechai Levi, isn't there? You're not making all this up to make me think that you know how to help Shelly?'

'Of course I'm not making it up!' He stood up and took a folded-up piece of paper from his wallet and handed it to me. 'Look for yourself. That's Levi's list of things we'll need.'

I unfolded it and found a page of jagged Hebrew script. All those words I'd never be able to read seemed a message from a place and time I didn't want to know anything about. I handed the note back to him and sat at the table opposite him.

Benni put the note between us and pointed to a word. 'That's how you write "mirror" in Yiddish,' he said in a voice of rescue. 'And see there?' he said, moving his finger. 'That's the number ten. In short, we need ten mirrors. One for each of the *sefirot*.'

'Do I want to know what the *sefirot* are?' I asked.

'All you need to know,' he said authoritatively, 'is that Levi told me that no *dybbuk* is able to turn away from a circle of mirrors. And when Esther looks into them, she's going to realise that Shelly has been made in the Lord's image, and that she has been . . . oh, I forget what it's called in English.'

'Creating bad problems for us.'

'That'll do.'

Benni had finished his meal, so he wiped his mouth and blew his nose.

'You seem like a little kid sometimes,' I told him.

'I feel like I'm back at Ewa's house whenever I eat eggs. She got them fresh sometimes from nearby farms.'

Ewa was the Christian woman who'd hidden him toward the end of the war.

Benni took his plate to the sink and started washing it, and I asked him if he'd said anything special to Levi to win his sympathy.

'I told him that Shelly's parents and sister were murdered by the Nazis, and my parents, too, and every last one of our cousins and aunts and uncles. And you know what, as a peace offering, he gave me a cinnamon donut he had in his pocket, but it was old and hard, and once I was on the street, I threw it in the trash.'

I laughed in a burst because of his comic grimace, then covered my eyes with my hands because a surge of tears was spilling out of me. In a lost voice, I said, 'I'm losing my mind, and so is Shelly, and here I am laughing.'

Benni hugged me. 'Sorry, Jules. I shouldn't have tried to be funny. It's a personality flaw. But it's true that Levi gave me a donut. He goes every morning to a Dunkin' Donuts in downtown Brooklyn.'

'This is all just too much for me,' I confessed. 'Sometimes I think I've wandered into an old Yiddish play and need to get off the stage because I'm the wrong woman for the part.'

'Of course you do. You're a smart-as-can-be Quaker girl from Canada who fell in love with a Holocaust survivor who never learned to keep his *putz* in his pants. None of us needed a crystal ball to know that it wasn't always going to be such a smooth ride.'

My brother's son, Johnny, was an architect, so I called him to ask where I could pick up some large, sturdy mirrors, and he told me about a wholesale dealer named Kauffman on the Rue Notre-Dame who cut his own but who also kept some fancy ones around for special customers.

While I was getting ready to drive there, Benni came to me and said that it was time that he went in to see Shelly. 'He must have heard me arrive and is wondering what happened to me.'

'So I have to buy the mirrors alone?' I asked.

'Yeah, that would be for the best. But you'll do fine. Just make sure you get ten.'

I chose eight new mirrors and two gorgeous antiques in gilded, acanthus-leaf frames. Mr Kauffman's Vietnamese assistants stood them up in his truck, and they drove behind me all the way home, then carried them into the house.

'Wow, beautiful!' Benni said when he saw the fancy ones. 'I've convinced Shelly and Esther to go with me for a bite to eat, and while we're gone, you put them around the den. They're not too heavy, are they?'

'No, I'll manage. But what are you going to say when you come back and he sees them?'

'I'll explain that he needs to look at himself in them.'

'And Esther?'

'I'll tell her that only when she leaves him will she be able to join her family on the Other Side. I think that the really hard part will be convincing Shelly that it would be selfish to hold on to his sister – that she needs to be with Rosa and the rest of our relatives.'

8

Benni and Shelly returned while I was reading about *dybbuks* in one of the Gershom Scholem books that Benni had sent us. I was sitting in the kitchen and had closed the door, so I didn't see them enter, but I heard their steps in the hallway and a brief conversation in Yiddish, and then the squeal and click of the den door being pulled open and locked behind them. About ten minutes later, Benni came to see me.

As if he were showing his mom an unexpected treasure, he held a clear plastic bag filled with water, and a small orange-and-white goldfish with bulging eyes was swimming around in it. The contours of the fish – elongated and squashed by the water – made me think of the strangely endearing painting that Shelly had found in a dumpster and hung over our bed.

Benni smiled and said, 'Be an angel and get me a glass bowl.'

After I fetched one, he spilled the goldfish and water inside.

'How's my husband?' I asked.

'Not so hot. While we were starting on our egg rolls, Esther told him she doesn't want to ever leave him. He hardly ate a thing.'

'Swell. So what's the goldfish for?'

'*Dybbuks* and other spirits have no power over fish.'

'Benni, what exactly is that supposed to mean?' I demanded, picturing myself cornered by all the things I'd never understand about his way of thinking.

'I'm not sure, but it's what Mordechai Levi told me.'

'So what are you going to do with him?'

'You'll see,' he said confidently.

'I will? Can I watch what you do?'

'Sure. I want Esther to meet you. I want her to see that Shelly's in good hands. I wouldn't want her to leave us without knowing that.'

Just before he turned the handle I'd re-screwed to the den door, Benni told me in a warning tone, 'Even if Shelly snaps at you, try not to speak to him.'

We found Shelly sitting forward on the sofa with his head angled down. He was naked. The blinds had been drawn. Benni had lit ten candles and placed them around the room. They gave the mirrors surrounding us a yellowish glow.

Benni eased the goldfish bowl down on the coffee table.

Shelly's eyes were hooded and fearful when he gazed up at me. *We're all back in the Warsaw of his youth*, I said to myself. And when I spotted myself in the mirror across the room from me, I added with resentment, *because that's where Esther has taken us*.

While studying my husband's sunken cheeks and the grim pouches under his eyes, I realised he was in a place where I could not reach him.

Benni told me to sit at the old desk in the corner. I envisaged myself crossing a bridge as I stepped there. My breaths came shallow and hesitant.

Benni spoke a sentence in Yiddish that included my husband's name, then raised his hand over his head and muttered what must have been a prayer, because I heard the familiar words *Baruch Adonai*, which meant 'Blessed is the Lord'. Shelly stood up and closed his eyes tight, as if he might not ever open them again.

Successive reflections of Benni and Shelly extended – ever smaller – into the endless depths of the mirrors. The candlelit figures seemed a metaphor, but for what, I didn't know – maybe for survival against all odds. Gazing at them, it occurred to me that the three of us had been brought here by all that my husband had failed to tell me and his daughters and maybe even Benni.

When Benni spoke again, it was in a trembling chant. And yet when our eyes met in one of the antique mirrors, I saw what looked to me like confidence. Had he witnessed such a ceremony as a boy?

After Shelly raised both his arms above his head, Benni scooped the goldfish out of his bowl, clasping it securely in his fist, so that only the wriggling tip of its tail was visible. He touched his dripping hand first to Shelly's forehead, then to his hands, his chest, his belly, his sex, his legs and his feet. He spoke at the same time, in an abrupt and determined mixture of Yiddish and Hebrew.

I distinguished only one word clearly – *keter* – which I later discovered to mean 'crown' in Hebrew. Benni pronounced it as he touched Shelly's forehead.

After he dropped the fish back in the bowl, he spoke what I presumed to be a command, because my husband shuffled toward the larger of the antique mirrors and grasped it firmly, one hand on each side of the golden frame. A moment later, Benni stepped behind him and closed his eyes and spoke a few words in a whisper.

After letting silence surround us once more, he spoke Esther's name softly, followed by what sounded like a fervent payer. When his eyes opened, he repeated her name six more times, each time louder and more defiantly. I had the feeling he was groping his way ahead – ever closer to her – with his own voice.

And then he called out Rosa's name, and I sensed he was pleading with Esther to go to her.

Did she? It seemed not, because Benni began to speak to her beseechingly. He pointed with his index finger toward Shelly's reflection as though to compel her to gaze at him.

But my husband gazed down instead. Benni – angry now – stepped behind him and gripped his shoulders. He shouted Esther's name and some words in Yiddish, and so loudly that I jumped to my feet. While continuing to shout, he pounded on Shelly's back. It seemed like a scene out of the Old Testament.

Slowly, hesitantly, fearfully, Shelly lifted his gaze and studied his own reflection. Tears slid down his cheeks. As he wiped them away, a morbid chill crept through me, making me shiver, and I thrust my hands over my mouth, because I thought I might call out for help.

I next remember Benni staring at me, his eyes filled with worry, and it took me a moment to remember where I was. I'd later wonder if Esther might not have left my husband and entered me for a moment. Had the chill I'd felt signalled her passing through me? In my more rational moments, I decided that I'd simply experienced a shudder of panic.

Shelly's eyes were now closed and he'd covered his ears with his hands. Had Esther told him not to look again into the mirror?

The need to protect Shelly drew me forward, but Benni told me to stay where I was. He took down my husband's hands from his ears and spoke to him in Yiddish, ending with the name Rosa, which he pronounced with reverence, and I came to believe that he was telling Esther that their great-grandmother expected her to leave her brother and go to her.

My husband began to weep, and he shook his head as if in physical torment. Benni came to me and reached out for my hand. 'I need you to grab a hold of Shelly,' he said, adding with an encouraging smile, 'Don't worry, Jules. You'll do fine.'

Benni moved my hands to where he wanted them on Shelly's shoulders.

I was convinced at that moment that Shelly was right: Benni was one of the *Lamed Vav Tzadikim*. How else could he know how to help his cousin?

Benni scooped up his goldfish and touched his dripping hand to my lips and said, 'Speak to Esther. Tell her Shelly will be safe with you.'

The tenderness in Benni's eyes suddenly made me realise that this ceremony was about love more than anything else – about the need to do whatever it asks of us.

He returned the fish to his bowl while whispering a quick blessing.

Shelly had begun to shiver by then. While watching him, I grew certain that nothing that happened to me mattered any longer. As long as I could save him from any more terror in his life, I'd be all right.

Do I need to add that it made no difference to me whether or not my husband's terror had taken on an illusory form?

'Tell Esther about you and Shelly,' Benni told me. 'You can be honest – even about your difficulties. Levi told me that *dybbuks* can hear all our lies.'

What I remember most of the next few minutes was my self-doubt. I felt as if it were all I was. Yet as I spoke, I realised that I was making a second marriage vow – a far deeper pledge than the one I'd made at my wedding, when I'd understood so little of what that love would ask of me.

Did I tell Esther that nothing could ever be as important to me as her brother? Mostly I remember talking about the journey he and I had been on for twenty-five years, and that it was the measure of the person I had become. I said that I didn't want it to ever end – not even with death. I remember that at some point, I noticed the mirrors around us, and the endless repetition of our candlelit reflections. Looking between myself and Shelly, I had the feeling that we had become one person. When I turned to Benni, he was watching me with admiration in his eyes, and an overwhelming sense of well-being and belonging came over me, and I said to myself, *Everything makes sense now, even all those terrible moments of anger and loneliness.*

And then the feeling of belonging was gone, and I hugged my hands around Shelly and lay my head against his back. I began to cry, but not because I was sad, but because I'd finally told him what I'd needed to say for a very long time.

Benni came to me and took my hand and led me to back to my desk.

Shelly was studying himself in the mirror when I looked at him, and he began to speak in Yiddish. From the sad, hesitant rhythm in his voice, I came to believe that he was saying goodbye to Esther. After he drew silent, he nodded in reply to something she must have told him. A moment later, his eyes opened wide with excitement and he laughed sweetly. He spoke then to Benni, who tucked his lips inside his mouth like he does when he wants to keep from crying.

Shelly gazed at his reflection again, though I imagined that it was Esther he was seeing. Was Rosa there as well? He spoke both their names, using gentle, reassuring gestures with his hands to emphasise whatever he was telling them.

As I would later learn, he taught Esther the protective prayer that Rosa had entrusted to him before he made his escape from the Warsaw ghetto.

When Shelly closed his eyes, Benni led me outside and closed the door behind us. He whispered, 'He needs to be alone to say goodbye to his sister.'

'So she's agreed to go?' I asked.

Benni kissed my cheek. 'Yes, you convinced her.'

I shivered.

'I knew you'd be able to do it,' he said.

'How?'

'Who else has as much power as you do over Shelly? Jules, you're the one. You've always been the one. Don't you know that?'

Benni's affirmation left me sobbing. Because I hadn't known.

He led me to the kitchen, and I asked him what had moved him close to tears near the end of the ceremony.

'Esther told Shelly that she hoped that wherever she was going with Rosa . . . that there'd be a piano. She couldn't remember the last time she had played, and her fingers ached something terrible from not being able to give voice to all that she had lived – to all that was inside her.'

9

Shelly came to bed that night after I was already asleep. He must have crawled under the covers without making a sound because only after three in the morning did I notice that he had curled up behind me. His arm over my hip grew too heavy, but I didn't dare take it off me or turn around for fear of waking him.

I awoke again at dawn and felt Shelly's penis stiffening in the crack of my behind, and when he bit my neck and growled, I felt myself falling toward a place where I had no power, and had to trust him, and I let myself fall – gratefully, blissfully – because I was sure now that there was no bottom to what I felt for him.

Afterward, while we were cuddling, I said, 'You're back, aren't you?'

'Yes, I'm here now. I'm sorry I was so mean to you, but I wasn't in control of myself. Can you forgive me?'

'Of course I forgive you.' I combed his beautiful wings of hair over his ears and said, 'When you're ready, I want you to tell me all about Esther.'

'You want to hear about my sister?' he asked apprehensively.

'Yes, she wanted desperately to be remembered. She deserves me knowing who she was, and what you felt for her. And I think you need to tell the girls, too.'

'You really think they should know?'

'Yes, I'm sure of it. Will you tell them?'

'If you want me to, yes.'

We kissed again – softly, like the old married couple that we were – and Shelly looked as if he wanted to say more about what had happened to him, but then he curled into me like a tired little boy and closed his eyes. A minute or so later, he was asleep again.

I watched him for a long time. He never once even stirred. It was as if he'd been drugged.

When I tiptoed downstairs, I found Benni seated at the kitchen table. He was wearing a pyjama bottom but no top. I noticed that his chest hairs were turning grey and found it moving that he didn't try to hide how he was ageing from me – that he felt so at ease with me. He was huddled over his steaming coffee cup as if it were a treasure. He'd opened the back door to let in some air, which was sweetened by the lilac bushes I'd planted years before, and I breathed in appreciatively on their heartening scent.

Benni and I kissed good morning. His eyes were red and tender – probably like mine. Something clenched in my gut as I poured myself cereal, and I realised then how badly I needed his reassurance that his cousin would be all right. And yet I wasn't ready to speak of what had happened. I put the radio on at a low volume. Stevie Wonder was singing 'Sir Duke'.

I sat down opposite Benni. My apprehension must have been obvious, because he said, 'He'll be all right now, you'll see,' but I could tell he was trying to convince himself as much as me.

'Did you know Esther well?' I asked.

'Not really. I was just a kid when everybody vanished.' He tapped the kitchen table with his fingertip as if he'd just made a discovery. 'You know what, I'm going to tell you something I never told anyone but Teresa.'

'You never told Shelly?'

'Nope, not even him.' He gazed away. At length, he said, 'When I get depressed, everything I've ever done seems covered with a kind of dye. It wipes out all the colour in my memories. Nothing escapes. Even the most wonderful times, like Tessa giving birth to Eti, or being found by George and Shelly. They go all grey in my mind. And nothing seems to mean anything anymore. Even the best moments don't seem important.'

'Does that happen a lot, Benni?'

'Not as much since falling in love with Tessa. But I get worried sometimes that my depressions will come back one day. And be worse than ever. And if that happens, I think I might not be strong enough to withstand them for very long, and it scares me.'

When Benni turned to me, he showed me his counterfeit smile, and a kind of wild courage surged inside me. I squeezed his hand, and I forced him to promise me that if the grey dye ever returned – and robbed him of colour again – he'd let me know. 'Because I'll grab Shelly,' I told him, 'and we'll come to you wherever you are, and we won't leave you until you tell us that you're okay.'

Benni looked away from me and rubbed a hand back through his hair to keep from ceding to too much emotion, and I didn't want to intrude on his feelings, so I went and took myself an orange from the counter. I peeled it back at the table, giving him a section and taking one for myself, and we ate the whole orange together. The sharing became a kind of ritual – even the stickiness on our fingers was a part of it – and when he smiled at me for real, the trust between us became a third presence in the room, and I knew that he and I would be linked forever.

It was just after noon when I heard my husband pounding around on the upstairs landing. I met him at the bottom of the stairs with a welcoming hug. He was wearing a pair of pale-blue boxer shorts and was still heavy with sleep. With a moan, he told me that he was dying of hunger.

Benni had been out weeding in the garden, and he shuffled in while Shelly was devouring a lox-and-tomato sandwich he'd thrown together.

'You okay now, Shel?' Benni asked.

'Yeah, just starving,' my husband replied, and he yawned like a cat.

Benni pulled off one of his gloves. 'Hey, how about some pancakes?' he asked excitedly.

'If you pour on lots of maple syrup,' Shelly told him.

'You, Jules?'

I wasn't very fond of pancakes, but I didn't want to disappoint him. 'Sure, why not?' I said.

I noticed then that I was still in my bathrobe, and that it looked terribly shabby, so I headed to my bedroom to get dressed. By the time I returned to the kitchen, Benni had already made the batter and was heating up the oil in a pan, and he asked me to wash some blueberries for him. While I was at the sink, the crazy Jew I'd married snuck up behind me and bit me again on the neck, and I knew from the way his warm hands circled my waist exactly what he was planning for us later that afternoon.

Toward evening, my husband finally got dressed and we all drove to La Fontaine Park and dropped Benni's goldfish – Shelly had nicknamed him Poseidon – in one of the ponds. It was a relief to see him swim happily away into the depths of the murky water, and I thanked him for his help. And then I whispered aloud to Esther. '*A dank*,' I said in Yiddish – thank you, followed by, 'Tell everyone that Shelly and I will be all right now.'

After my husband hooked his arm in mine, the reflection of

broad maples on the surface of the pond rippled in a breeze. All those trees growing downward seemed to reveal another secret to me. 'The world is always as upside down as in George's painting,' I told Benni and Shelly. 'At least, if you know where to look.'

10

Maybe Esther truly was a *dybbuk*. Or the summation of everything that Shelly refused to say about All That. Or simply a childhood that had caught up to him. But whatever she was, she was now where she was meant to be, which is what counted most.

Several days after she left us, I was at work, taking blood from a young mother, and I gazed out the window at the gold-and-russet sunset, and I remembered the pond in La Fontaine Park as if I had dreamed of it throughout my whole life. Right away, its murky water seemed to conceal my future, and its surface was a mirror, and Poseidon and I were one and the same, swimming toward a distant horizon. Then, everything in and around me seemed to clear and become transparently beautiful. And for a timeless moment, the world shed its usual meaning, and I saw that it was much more open and wider than I'd ever imagined, an unfolding narrative in which all the characters were linked, and I was eager to know more about my place in the story. But the young mother asked me when her blood tests would come back, and just like that, everything returned to the way it had always been.

VARIATIONS ON AN ANCIENT MELODY (1944–1954)

I had just finished giving my second lesson of the day and was pouring myself a cup of linden tea in my backyard when I heard a motor car grinding over the bumpy lane in front of my home. The wild rush of delight in my chest caught me off guard and made me laugh – I'd not suspected that I'd missed my younger brother so much.

I searched the threatening sky – all those heavy, slate-grey clouds that had come in from the east that morning – and grabbed my cane, wondering if it would be safe to drive in a downpour. While making my way through the music room to the front of the house, I began practising how I'd tell Karol that we ought not to go very far until the weather cleared – to which he'd say, *Ewa, you're always such a frightened little mouse!* Then he'd head to the back door to evaluate the weather for himself, and his gaze would be drawn by the ponderous gravity of our childhood over the farmlands and hedges he knew so well, and when he turned back to me, he'd curse our parents for what he regarded as a miserable upbringing.

I stopped at the window at the front of my house and saw the swirl of dust kicked up by the wheels of Karol's car, which was dark and large.

Ewa, I've purchased a Mercedes! he'd written in his last letter to me, three months before. *It's essential for getting around such a huge city, and since I wish to advance in my career, I must show my senior colleagues that I am to be taken seriously. In the summer, I shall drive to Łódź to see my old friends from school, and while I'm there, I'll stop by and take you on a ride.*

I'd wanted to write back, *Would the owners of a German insurance company really promote a Pole to vice-president?* But my reference to his foreign origins would have irritated him, so I simply congratulated him on his wise decision and asked for a photograph of him with his car.

He'd signed his letter *Karl*, the German version of his name – and what our father, a native of Gdansk, had always called him.

When I stepped outside, I saw that my anxiety was pointless; my brother had not come for a visit after all. The driver of the car that had just parked under my sycamore was Piotr, who had studied with me for several years when he was a boy, until his family moved to the capital. I'd last seen him two years before, when he and his wife had stopped by for a chat while on a visit to his aunt, who lived on the outskirts of Brzeziny, a twenty-minute walk from my farmhouse.

The relief at seeing Piotr instead of my brother made me thank my good fortune. I was astonished that I could have experienced a flash of joy at the possibility of seeing Karol – of embracing the sad and taciturn young boy that he'd been – just a few moments earlier. What little-girl fantasies my heart still invented for me!

I recognised Piotr's sad, deep-set eyes right away. The scruffy beard he'd grown made him look like the lonely and otherworldly Jesus that Orthodox artists painted on their icons.

He got out of the car and hailed me with a wave. 'Yes, Ewa, it's me!' he called. 'Give me a moment.'

He seemed to have become more slender and frail since I'd last seen him. Had he gone through very hard times of late?

After opening his back door, Piotr dragged out a rolled-up Persian rug – brick red and brown with a golden fringe – and unrolled it on the bare ground to reveal a surprise: a dark-haired young boy. He was dressed in loose-fitting black trousers and a white shirt. He wore no shoes. His hair was mussed and his face was caked with dust.

He didn't stir. He lay across the arabesque pattern of the rug with his eyes closed, his arms crossed over his chest, which reminded me of a photograph I'd seen only recently, though I couldn't recall where. In his right hand was a tiny scroll tied with a black ribbon.

The boy is dead, I told myself, *and Piotr has come to bury him where no one will ever find him.*

I reached back for the door frame because my legs had gone all weak.

After Piotr kneeled down on the rug, he brushed the dust from the boy's face with a handkerchief that he took from his pocket. 'Benjamin, we're here,' he said in the soft, summoning voice that an adult uses to awaken a child.

The boy's eyes opened. Piotr smiled reassuringly. 'We made it!'

Piotr introduced me to his young friend, who gazed off beyond me toward the horizon. It was at that moment that I noticed a bruise on his forehead, but it seemed nothing compared to being rolled up in a rug.

'He's tired after the long journey,' Piotr explained.

He pointed down the hallway to the rear door and told the boy to wait in my backyard. 'You'll be safe there. I'll talk with Ewa for a little while and then I'll come get you.'

The young man did as he was told without any hesitation or sign of distress. As we stepped into my sitting room – just large enough for my sofa, an armchair and a card table – I asked Piotr if his car was a recent purchase, and he replied that unfortunately his teacher's salary didn't permit such luxuries and that he had borrowed it from a cousin. In reply to my subsequent questions, he said that Benjamin was the son of a Jewish friend named Graça who'd been with him at university, and that she and her husband, Adam, were caught in a Nazi round-up more than a year ago. 'Benjamin was at school when they vanished,' Piotr continued, 'so he started waiting every day for them to come home, but they never did. Then his other relatives were taken away. And when one of his great-uncles was the only person left he could entirely trust, the old man gave the boy all the money he had and instructed him to escape the ghetto any way he could. Benjamin already had my name and address, so he showed up one day at my door. He was filthy – he'd crawled through one of the cramped tunnels leading out of the ghetto. And he was infested with lice, too.'

Piotr's resigned shrug reminded me of how we had all grown used to the most terrible news over the last few years. And yet I winced on picturing the boy trapped in a lightless tunnel. 'How did he come to have your name and address?' I asked.

Piotr picked up the deck of cards with which I played solitaire. 'His mother had spoken to him about me. We'd been very close at university. She told the boy that if anything bad ever happened to her and Adam and his other relatives, he was to come to me – that I'd help him get to safety.'

I leaned on the oaken chest where I stored my sheet music and gazed through the open window at Benjamin, who was standing at the edge of the pond that I shared with Bartosz, my nearest neighbour. He'd joined his hands together and was now tilting his head far back.

'What's he doing?' I asked.

Piotr looked out the window. 'Imagining something, I suppose.' He tapped the top of my music chest. 'Do you still store your eggs and cheese with your scores?'

'Yes, and they still don't understand Schoenberg's compositions!'

He grinned, but when he looked out at Benjamin again his

eyes narrowed. I sometimes allowed myself complete freedom to interpret other people's expressions and give them specific meanings. On this occasion, as my former student turned to me, I imagined that he was telling me, *There are things you don't know about the difficulties my mother and I had when I was Benjamin's age. I only alluded to them once with you, and very vaguely, because my father had threatened me. Even today, I find that those old troubles weigh on me, because I could do nothing to help my mother when she needed me most, and it is a terrible thing to fail someone you love.*

Piotr put down my deck of cards and rubbed his eyes like he does when he's anxious. I took his wrist and gave his palm a kiss, exactly as I used to.

'It's good to see you, Ewa,' he said.

'Piotr, you know you're always welcome here,' I told him.

'I wasn't sure where to go,' he said. 'I had to leave in a hurry. The woman who lives in the flat just below us found out somehow about Benjamin.'

'Did she try to blackmail you?'

'No, but we couldn't risk being caught with the boy.' He shook his head. 'The ghetto in Warsaw . . . Have you heard about what's happened there?'

'No, I occasionally get some local news – mainly what my students tell me. But almost nothing reaches me from Warsaw.'

'The Germans started transporting everybody out of the ghetto – thousands per day, I was told. Then the Jews who were left started fighting with whatever weapons they could find. The Nazis used all their firepower against them – tanks and machine guns and God knows what else.' Piotr reached a tense hand up to his forehead. 'Ewa, I don't think anyone got out alive.'

Tears welled in my eyes, but I fought them back. How would my weeping help any of the dead, after all? Piotr helped me to my bathroom so I could wash my face. I then sat for a time in my bedroom, in silence, marvelling at how it took just a few years for evil and vicious people to destroy what had taken centuries to build. When I returned to Piotr, he told me he was sorry to have upset me.

'No, you did the right thing,' I assured him. 'But there's something I don't understand. Where did the Germans transport the Jews?'

'A friend in the resistance told me that they were taken to camps in the countryside.'

'What kind of camps?'

'Ewa, look, maybe it's best if we talk about something else.'

'Piotr, do the Germans murder them in these camps?'

'Yes, that's what I've heard.'

Why kill all those defenceless people? I almost asked, but as we'd discovered since the start of the war, that was a question that made no sense to the Nazis. I returned to the window. Benjamin was now sitting on my weedy lawn with his legs crossed. He held a stick in his fist and he was hitting it into the ground over and over, as though punishing someone in his mind.

Piotr came to me. 'I've got to find a way to keep him alive until the end of the war,' he said. 'Then I'll try to find out if anyone in his family survived. So that's why I'm here, Ewa.'

'But . . . but surely there is someone in a better position to hide him,' I stammered. 'A distant relative, an old friend of his parents. Maybe Martyna knows someone.'

Martyna and Piotr had been married a few years earlier.

'We couldn't think of anyone else we could trust,' he said. He gazed down, pondering alternatives. At length, he added, 'But you're right, it's too dangerous for you. I see that now. I have an old friend in Łódź who might be able to keep him for a while. To have come here to you . . .' He apologised for his lapse of good sense.

Guilt began to prowl around inside me. 'Couldn't your parents take the boy?' I asked.

'No, my mother is a fan of Mr Hitler. She even blames the Jews when we have bad weather.'

'Will he be safe with your friend?'

'For a while. Listen, can I see the music room before we get on our way to Łódź? Your piano and I . . . My goodness, it was love at first sight!'

I laughed, but my chest was aching with shame, and I hid my hands behind my back because I could no longer control their trembling when I was upset. 'Of course, Piotr,' I said, 'though it needs to be tuned. Remember Grzegorz, the piano tuner who lived just opposite the All Saints Church in Łódź?'

'No. I don't think I ever met him.'

'He was murdered by the Germans last year. He'd been hiding a Jewish couple.'

In truth Grzegorz was in good health and had attended to the needs of my piano just a few months earlier, but I lied in order to remind my old student why I could not accept the boy.

After shaking his head at the injustice in the world, he squatted down to take a look at the pedals. 'Remember how much trouble I had reaching them at first?' he asked.

He's so much more alive and worldly than I am, I concluded when our eyes met, and yet all my love for him tethered us together. *It is a blessing to have known the length and breadth of such a good man*, I said to myself as if it were a prayer.

'What is it?' he inquired.

'Just the strangeness of time,' I replied.

'Yes, it passes quickly. I'm thirty-two years old now. Can you believe it?'

'Wait till you're sixty and then you'll know how fast everything passes!'

'Are you sixty? My God, you don't look it.'

'Sit, you little liar!' I told him. 'Play something for me.'

'I haven't played in at least a year.'

'That doesn't matter.'

He sat on my bench and moved his right hand over the opening phrase of *Pictures at an Exhibition*, by his beloved Mussorgsky. He held the final F as if keeping a door open. He looked up at me, waiting for my approval, so I smiled the smile I have been making to my students for forty years. *You are safe to go through*, it means. *I will watch over you wherever you go.*

As he played, however, glum thoughts assaulted me. I sat on the fraying velvet loveseat against the back wall and put one of the big white cushions over my lap. *It's my own fault that he's here*, I thought. *I convinced him that he could always trust me.*

Pictures at an Exhibition . . . When he was just a small and excitable little demon, he heard me play the first movement at one of the recitals I organised for my students. Afterward, he told me that he had to learn it – that it was the most exciting piece of music he'd ever heard. He was too young for it – its complex rhythms and harmonies would burden him like an older brother's overcoat – but he was unstoppable as a boy. And in any case, children must be permitted to grow into the music they play.

Whenever he would come for his lesson, he'd race to my piano, breathlessly determined to show me how perfectly he had mastered the sections of *Pictures from an Exhibition* that I'd asked him to work on. Then, after giving him an opportunity to show off, we would always work on Bach for the first half hour of our lesson.

It is said that if you place a newborn baby in a warm pool, he will swim with ease and grace, as though he had been meant to live out his life underwater. Most children will take to Bach in the same way, I have learned.

Over our last half hour, for nearly two years, we worked on *Pictures at an Exhibition*. He concentrated on it as if it were a mountain he had to climb in order to reach his homeland.

After our lessons, I'd always make him tea and serve him a piece of cake on my mother's royal-blue china, sitting him in my armchair as if he were local nobility, since I'd discovered that such rituals helped him overcome his nervous nature, and we would listen together to recordings of master pianists on my Victrola.

Now, as my old student swept through the chord progressions, I felt as though I always knew that he would end up pressuring me to give up my quiet existence and leave for someplace I didn't want to go. After remarking my discontent and dismissing it as a betrayal of the love I felt for Piotr, I surprised myself by searching for an explanation for the boy that the people in the nearest village would accept.

He's Piotr's son. You remember, my student with the sad eyes. His wife is ill with consumption. He doesn't want the boy in Warsaw right now. He's afraid he'll catch the disease.

He's my cousin Maria's grandson. Yes, Anton, the one who was suspended from school for hitting a teacher. He's going to be staying with me for the summer because Maria feels that . . .

When Piotr finished playing, I said, 'That was quite good,' but I hadn't been listening.

'It was a shipwreck, but thank you for being kind,' he said, giggling.

When I looked out the window at the Jewish foundling by my pond, a cavern of terror seemed to open under my feet and I reached out to the wall to keep from falling. 'If someone discovers that the boy is living here,' I said to Piotr, 'then how will I explain him?'

'I thought you might say he was Hania Nowak's son. I'm still in touch with her. She's in Kraków now. She's a nurse. The old people will remember that she was your most talented student – and that you took her in for a time, when her mother was unable to cope with her and all her brothers and sisters.'

Hearing about Hania and her family reminded me of my own brother, and it now seemed that it was no mere accident that I'd presumed that my brother had arrived for a visit; the world itself was showing me that no matter how clever a story we invented, neither I nor Benjamin would ever be completely free of danger.

'Someone still might guess the truth,' I said.

'I'm afraid that's true.'

I took a deep breath. 'Piotr, I mean my brother. He'll see through any ruse we invent. And he'll be relentless – he always is. He'll contact Hania. And he'll have the boy taken away.'

'You could say that Benjamin is my son. That way, if he calls, I'll confirm the story.'

'Yes, that's what I'd have to do,' I agreed. 'I mean, if I were to take in the boy.'

'I thought your brother was in Berlin. Has he moved back home?'

'No, he's still in Germany, but he bought a car and is planning to visit. In fact, when I heard your car, I thought that you were going to be him.'

Piotr played a chord sequence: C major, A minor, G seventh, C major.

'Putting the world back in order?' I asked.

'You taught me to do that,' he replied with a grin. 'Does Karol hate the Jews?'

I rested my hand on his shoulder. 'Oh, Piotr, I'm not entirely sure that he knows what he likes and dislikes – except our parents. He hates them.'

'Why's that?'

'They were simple people. And too fearful of God to raise confident and happy children. Worst of all, our mother could neither read nor write.'

'Is that a reason to hate someone?'

'Embarrassment turned to hate in him. Does that happen often? I don't know. I only know what happened to my brother.'

Piotr wrinkled his nose, and I remembered that he used to do that whenever he hit a wrong note. 'For some reason, I thought that he was a Communist,' he said.

'He was, but he joined the Nazi Party so he could get a promotion. If he suspects Benjamin is Jewish, he won't hesitate to denounce him.' I paused to reflect, then added, 'And me, too.'

'But that would mean imprisonment for you at the very least.'

I nodded by way of reply. I didn't want to explain that my brother also blamed his older sister for adding to the landscape of affliction that had trapped him as a child.

Piotr stood up, went to the door and called the boy, who pretended not to hear. He turned to me. 'Benjamin hasn't been outside in eight months. And he's been confined in one little room. We couldn't risk his being seen or heard.'

Eight months without sunlight, I thought, trying to understand how always having a ceiling over my head would affect me, and deciding that it wouldn't be so bad if I could play piano – which was a shamefully silly thought, of course, because if I were a Jew doing my best to vanish, I couldn't very well bring a musical instrument into my hiding place or make any noise at all.

Piotr summoned Benjamin again, and this time the boy started shuffling dejectedly back to us.

'Are you hungry?' I asked him as he reached us, smiling in what I hoped was a motherly way.

Benjamin gazed down by way of reply.

I turned toward Piotr. 'How about you? I could boil up some potatoes and carrots from my garden,' I suggested in an enticing voice.

'No, we better get going,' Piotr said. 'I'll take Benjamin to my friend in Łódź.'

As he gazed around the room a last time, his eyes grew moist and he rubbed a nervous hand back through his hair, and I could see that his affection for me would turn to disappointment – or even contempt – the moment he led Benjamin back to his car.

'Ewa, your hands, they're trembling,' he said anxiously.

'It's not a problem – when I play, they're steady enough. It's really something of a miracle. Listen, Piotr, how long would the boy stay with me?' I asked.

'Until the Germans leave. Or until you sense danger.'

'It could be a while before they go. Hitler claims that his Reich will last a thousand years.'

Piotr scoffed. 'Bach and Beethoven will last a thousand years. Handel, too. Hitler – no one with any decency will want to know anything about him in a few years.'

'And Mussorgsky?' I questioned.

'I'll tell you this – if I have anything to say about it, he'll last a million times longer than any of the Nazis or their Polish collaborators.'

Benjamin never spoke to me over our first days together and hardly even looked at me, and I began to sense that there was something ugly or corrupting about me that he alone could see. A disquieting thought assailed me one night in bed and made me so sick that I had to run to my bathroom: *he can see the cowardice I've shown at all my most decisive moments.*

After I'd cleaned myself up, I went outside so that I could revel in the cool air. It was a night full of stars, though I didn't see any guidance in their light. *I'll be hanged in the main square in Brzeziny*, I thought. *I'll die without ever having done anything I was supposed to do.*

And I whispered aloud: 'One life – there are no second chances.'

I spoke those words because it seemed an unforgivable waste for me to have remained on my parents' farm. I ought to have defied my father and left for Kraków when I won a place at the Academy of Music. If I'd done that, I wouldn't have the stillbirth of all my unlived desires in my belly.

Why was it always so hard to admit that I was responsible for the smallness of my existence?

I wanted a few days alone with Benjamin before having to explain him to any of my students. I didn't have a telephone, so I couldn't call them to inform them that their lessons were cancelled for the week. Instead, I hobbled down the road to Bartosz's house and asked his daughter to inform Mr Mirecki, the headmaster at her school, that my back was acting up and that my lessons would only begin again the following week. He knew all my pupils and would tell them.

Benjamin ate the lunches and suppers I served him with meticulous care – as though he were a watchmaker sorting cogwheels and sprockets. Often, he would save his piece of cake for hours later – or even for the next day.

As I say, he never spoke to me. To my questions, he would nod for yes and shake his head from side to side for no. I was tempted to plead with him to say something – even to condemn me for hesitating to take him in – but I was certain that my insistence would only frighten him.

He slept in my brother's old room until a thunderstorm intruded on our quiet existence several nights after his arrival. At just past two in the morning, he appeared at my door in the ancient flannel pyjama bottoms I'd found for him in my brother's clothes chest. As he stood there shivering, I suddenly realised how skinny and frail he was.

What good fortune it was that I'd awakened as well, or I might not have seen the gate between us swinging open. 'Come,' I said, and I lifted the covers for him.

He hugged his arms around his chest, unsure of the way forward. His eyes were brooding.

'Everything will be all right,' I told him. 'Get into bed before you catch cold.'

He slipped under the covers but curled away from me. When I touched his shoulder, he started as if my fingertips were made of fire. But a few minutes later, I reached for his frozen hand, and he took it.

We held hands all night. I know, because I did not fall asleep again.

I felt as if destiny had brought us together. And now that it had, we had to create our own future. And I sensed that our only way ahead – toward safety – was together.

Over the next couple of days, it gratified me to see him racing around in my yard and throwing stones as far as he could. And I was extremely impressed with his concentration as he sketched with the pastels I'd given him. At the time, he always drew sleek, multicoloured animals living in a sunlit desert.

In the night, I'd study this little survivor who'd come to stay with me – the rise and fall of his slender chest, the shine of his dark hair, and the soft curve of his chin. And it began to seem as if I'd never really looked at a young boy before – or at anyone else, for that matter. It seemed as if I'd been given new eyes – that I could finally see another person for who he was. And such clear and accurate vision seemed a very special gift.

He's real, I kept thinking to myself, as if he were one of the exotic and colourful butterflies he often sketched. *He's real, and he has found his way to me, and I must help him.*

During his first few nights in my house, Benjamin often seemed to be reaching out for someone in his dreams.

'Did you have a nightmare?' I asked him one morning when he'd awakened with a shout. He shook his head, but he was drenched in sweat.

As I was drying his hair, I heard him speak to me in grammatically incorrect Polish, though he didn't move his lips: *I no tell you who I see.*

Had I mistaken my own thoughts for Benjamin's voice? 'Did you just speak to me?' I asked.

He shook his head again, so I said, 'But I heard your voice.'

He shrugged and showed me a confused look.

Later that morning, I heard pounding coming from the back of the house and I ran outside to discover him banging his head against the wall near his bedroom window, over and over, and it was then that I understood the bruise I'd first seen on his forehead. I rushed to him and pulled him away from the wall, but he wriggled out of my grasp and looked at me in terror, which stopped me from insisting that he tell me why he'd been hurting himself.

Another strange and disquieting occurrence took place just a couple of days later: while I was brushing my hair at my mirror, I

grew certain that he was observing me through the closed door.
When I opened it, he was sitting on the floor, playing with a
bronze sculpture of a horned Pan – the Greek god – that I kept
on my mantel. He said nothing when he looked up at me, but
his black eyes were questioning, and when he handed me Pan, I
became aware of what he was asking me: *What will you do when
the Germans come for me?*

A week after his arrival, while I was practising some Beethoven
excerpts in preparation for resuming my classes, Benjamin addressed
me for the first time. 'You make the start of the *Moonlight Sonata*?'
he asked in hesitant Polish, with a slight Yiddish accent.

I tried not to look stunned, but I imagine that my mouth had
dropped open. 'Yes, it's by Ludwig van Beethoven,' I told him,
hoping he could not hear the excited thumping in my chest. 'How
do you know it?'

'My cousin Esther makes it for me,' he replied. 'I mean, she
plays it for me.'

'She must be a good pianist.'

'The best!' he said.

'Benjamin, your Polish is good, but it's not perfect. Did you
go to a Jewish school?' I asked.

'Yes. Piotr and Martyna make me study Polish to make my
grammar perfect when I hide with them. They say it is important
that I speak without an accent, too. But I can't get everything right
all the time. I know I still make mistakes.'

Now that he had decided to speak, a great many questions
circled around me. And I realised that a second gate had opened
between us.

'Benjamin, I don't even know your family name,' I said. 'Would
you mind telling me?'

'My father's family name is Zarco. My mother's is Rosenfeld.'

'Zarco – where is that from?' I asked. 'It doesn't sound Polish.'

'It's a Portugal name.'

'Portuguese,' I corrected with a smile.

'Yeah, that's right. Sorry.'

'Don't be sorry. Portugal – my goodness! How lucky you are to have ancestors from so far away!'

'Portugal isn't far. It is just past Spain.'

'True enough.'

'They've come to Poland many years ago,' he said. 'I mean, they *came* to Poland. Rosa . . . She told me that.'

'How many years ago?' I asked, greatly moved by his effort to speak Polish properly.

'Four centuries ago.'

'In the sixteenth century?' I asked, and he nodded. 'And who is Rosa?'

'My great-grandmother,' he said.

'So your Zarco ancestors came in the sixteenth century! That's a long time ago. Even before I was born!' I joked.

He didn't find my jest amusing, and at that precise moment, giving him back his laughter became one of my most important priorities.

'If I remember my studies correctly,' I said, 'then a man named Giovanni Palestrina was the most famous composer in Europe in the sixteenth century. That's a beautiful name, isn't it? Giovanni Palestrina . . . He lived in Rome.'

Benjamin nodded, but I'd clearly confused him.

'We should go to Rome someday. There'd be so much to see! Would you like to go to Rome?'

'How would we go?' he asked.

'I guess we'd take the train,' I said. 'There must be one that crosses the Alps.' A thrilling idea then crept up on me and prompted me to tap my hand against his chest, just above his heart. 'Benjamin,' I said in an enticing voice, 'would you like to learn the first phrase of the *Moonlight Sonata*?'

'I don't play piano.'

'I can teach you.'

He shook his head.

'Why not?' I asked.

He sized me up with a squint and shouted something nasty-sounding in Yiddish, then dashed out of the house. A little later, I spotted him squatting by the pond, studying a leaf that he'd picked up as if its network of veins were a map back to his home in Warsaw.

That afternoon, as I was waking from a nap, I heard his voice again inside my mind. *I should stay with my family and die in the ghetto*,' he said.

Do you really think that? I replied, as if it were perfectly logical to talk to him inside my mind.

Yes, he said. *I think that.*

Your parents wouldn't want you to die, I told him.

They would, he declared.

No, that's impossible. Trust me. I know they could never wish that.

He replied with silence. I sensed that he was considering what I'd told him.

Still drugged by sleep, I took up my cane and limped to his room, but he wasn't there. At the window, I discovered him gazing at a fox sitting at the far edge of the pond.

Who are you really? I thought while watching Benjamin and his new friend, since they seemed to have come to this time and place out of an ancient myth.

After Benjamin came inside, I dared to speak my strange

thoughts to him: 'I occasionally imagine what people are thinking,' I told him. 'The house I grew up in was almost always silent.' I held my finger to my lips. 'So silent that my imagination grew and grew.' I opened my arms wide. 'Do you understand?'

'Yes.'

'But with you, it's different. Benjamin, did you speak to me in my mind a few minutes ago?'

'I don't think so,' he replied. 'What did I say?'

I didn't wish to speak of what his parents had told him. 'You said that you were hungry,' I lied. 'Let's go find ourselves a snack.'

That same evening, after Benjamin had washed up and put on his pyjamas, he fetched the small scroll that had been in his little fist when he'd come to my home and handed it to me. 'You look, but you be careful,' he said in a grave voice.

'I'll be very careful.' I unfurled it only a little – the paper was fragile. The writing was in tiny square Hebrew letters.

'Berekiah Zarco writes it.' He held up four fingers and gestured behind him. 'Four hundred years ago,' he said, and he showed me a big nod.

'Who is Berekiah Zarco?' I asked.

'He knows everything,' Benjamin replied. 'He see things. He maybe sees me and you.'

'What's the scroll say?' I asked, holding it up.

'I don't know. My parents tell me to keep it. Rosa gave it to me – it's a gift.'

'Well, it must be very important.'

'Very,' he agreed.

I handed it back to him. 'Thank you for showing me. You have quite a well-known family.'

He ran off to hide the scroll again and came back in panting. I sat him down on my sofa and put on my recording of Paderewski playing the *Moonlight Sonata*.

At the mysterious first entrance of the dominant chord, he turned to face my Victrola, and he held back his tears heroically. I did not wish to embarrass him, so I began fussing with the sleeves of my blouse, which suddenly seemed too long. A little later, when he began to sob, I kneeled next to him and kissed his hands. I told him that I knew that it was hard to be living with a stranger, and I confessed that it was difficult for me as well.

'We'll just have to do the best we can,' I said. 'And forgive each other for the silly mistakes we make.'

After I apologised for not being able to speak Yiddish with him, he dried his eyes, and I led him to my piano and sat him down. I positioned his fingers on the dominant chord that had struck him so powerfully, and he played it once himself, grinning afterward and pulling in his shoulders, embarrassed but pleased, and I explained slowly and carefully that Beethoven could be a great friend to him at his most difficult moments, just as he had always been to me.

Here's what I always planned to tell the man I'd marry (though I never found him, of course): *My father and mother were always convinced that I would lose my mind one day. They told me never to tell anyone that I could hear people speaking to me inside my head. I felt completely alone as a girl – and tainted. I knew that no one really saw me or cared for me. But then I met you and we fell in love, and everything changed.*

In reality, the person who changed my life was Mr Mazur, my piano teacher. He was a stooped old man in his sixties when I began lessons with him. He had sparse grey hair and dark eyebrows that met over his nose, and little sharp eyes. He wasn't particularly patient or kind, and I realised years later that he didn't even like children. Very possibly, that was even why my parents had chosen him for me. They must have hoped that I'd soon discover that the piano wasn't for me.

But once Mr Mazur discovered I had talent, he revealed a keen insight for how to help me progress. He also taught me all he knew of music theory, and through his guidance, an expanding universe of melodies and harmonies replaced the dungeon of forced silence in which I had found myself prisoner. And when I learned that Bach and Mozart understood me perfectly, I was saved from a life of loneliness. And very likely lunacy, as well.

Every time I begin a new score, here is what I say with my fingers: *Thank you, Mr Mazur, for saving me.*

One evening – a few days after he'd started speaking to me – I called out to Benjamin that supper was ready, but he didn't come.

What would I do if he were dead? I wondered, and an irrational panic – like a frigid gust of wind – made me shiver.

I found him sitting at the table in my backyard, holding a small black salamander with yellow spots in the palm of his hand.

'He's beautiful!' I said.

'I haven't seen one before,' he replied.

'We have lots around here. I used to play with them when I was a girl.'

'He's lost,' Benjamin said. 'He's far away from everything . . . everything that he knows. He needs a home.'

'Where is his home?' I asked.

'Warsaw.'

'Oh, yes, I see what you mean,' I said. 'Unfortunately, a great many salamanders have become lost of late. But I think he will be happy in our pond. It's a comfortable place to be.'

Benjamin stared at me with tense, fearful eyes, and once again I knew what he was wondering, so I took his shoulders and said, 'I'll never tell anyone who you are. Never!'

I felt that I needed to vow that to him or I would never be able to be sure of myself, so I placed my hand over my heart and added, 'You have my word on that.'

The boy nodded, but I could see he didn't entirely believe me.

A thousand worries kept me up that night, and all of them ended with Benjamin's death. A puny and cowardly part of me even wanted him to perish – after all, I could then return to my uneventful life. And yet, in the early morning, when I went to his room to observe him as he slept, I took his hand in mine and realised that the world had blessed me in the most unlikely of ways – or maybe in the only way it still could. And that I was not as trapped in my little life as I'd thought.

The nights began to get warm in July, so on one particularly lovely evening, I decided to serve supper outside, which I hadn't done in years. I'd made a raisin-and-cinnamon cake that day and after he'd eaten his turnips and potatoes, I cut him a big piece, but he put it aside for later. 'You can have as much cake as you like,' I told him, 'so you don't need to save it.'

'I save it and eat it later,' he said in a very serious voice, as if he were a banker talking about a major investment.

I laughed softly, but he didn't take offence, and when I tickled his chin, he curled into me like a kitten. With him in my arms, I felt lighter and more joyful than I ever had. It was as if I had untied every rope that had been holding me down, and I felt blessed.

Or have I finally lost my mind? I asked myself, but then, with a burst of glee, a revelation came to me: *What no one ever told me was that it would feel so good to disregard the dictates of caution and fear and convention.*

At sunset, a chilly wind swept in from the east, and seemed to spread worry over Benjamin's face. I recalled how I'd calmed Piotr with formal rituals and wondered if history might repeat itself. 'Why don't we go to the sitting room and I'll serve us tea on my mother's china,' I said.

'Can we wait a half hour?' he asked.

'Yes, of course, whenever you're ready,' I said.

I brought our dishes into the kitchen.

When Benjamin returned, the knees of his trousers were scuffed and his hands were filthy. He told me he'd been hunting frogs.

He's finding his own way forward! I rejoiced inside my mind, and my relief made me laugh.

After he was washed, I served us cake. As always, Benjamin added two heaping teaspoons of sugar to his tea and held his cup by the handle, with his little finger out, which always struck me as very impressive. I imagined that he was imitating his mother or father, and by then I'd begun to think of them as wonderful parents. I wished that I could have met them, in fact, even for just a moment, to thank them for bringing such a beautiful boy into the world.

Over the next couple of weeks, I remained awake on many nights watching Benjamin as he slept. I suppose I needed to verify that our life together wasn't a fantasy or dream.

On several occasions, his voice entered my mind with astonishing clarity, telling me what he dared not openly say during our days together. For instance, he implied to me once that he had banged his head on the wall because he could not forgive himself for staying alive.

My guilt is also a wall, he told me.

Then I shall help you tear it down, I replied, thinking of Samson.

No one must help me. And only I can see the wall. And it's big – as big as my life. Maybe it is my life.

You know, Benjamin, I can't see Handel's arias either, but they are completely real to me, I said. *I can hear them even when no one is singing. So perhaps we can overcome this problem together.*

No, the wall is mine, no one else's, he declared, as if it were his birthright.

On those occasions when he would speak to me in my mind, I allowed myself to imagine that Benjamin was something far greater than a small, thirteen-year-old boy from Warsaw. *He is like no one I've ever met before*, I told myself. *And he'll never realise how important he is to me – and to all the others who have known him.*

Maybe none of us is ever aware of our true significance. And everyone's life has hidden value. Was that the most important lesson he was teaching me?

I reasoned that I could not successfully hide every trace of Benjamin from visitors, and that he might be glimpsed by passers-by at any time, so I decided that it would be safest to introduce him to all my students and visitors. His name was rare in Poland – and always considered Jewish – so I decided to call him Krystian. That name would also remind him to wear the mask of a Catholic young man whenever we were with anyone else.

I explained to my students that the new boy's father was named Piotr Bajek, and that he had studied with me twenty years earlier. Piotr's wife had recently been struck down by polio after giving birth to a daughter, I said, and she was convalescing in a clinic near Kraków. Piotr had had difficulty coping with both the baby and Krystian, and he had sent the boy to spend the summer with me.

Krystian Bajek. It was a name that seemed to suit Benjamin's skullcap of thick dark hair and big, affectionate eyes.

I never gave him any chance to converse at any length with the boys and girls who had lessons with me because he sometimes said something in an awkward way. Furthermore, his Yiddish accent was noticeable on words that he wasn't used to pronouncing, so that anyone hearing more than a few sentences from him would presume that he was either a foreigner who'd spent a long time in Poland or a Jew – or both.

Miło Panią poznać.

Miło Pana poznać.

I reminded him that those were the proper ways to say *nice to meet you* when greeting either a woman (the first case) or a man (the second). And I asked him to limit himself to that greeting. Then he was to excuse himself and return to his room or play outside.

I made him promise never to speak Yiddish with anyone, of course, and every evening I gave him grammar and pronunciation lessons in Polish. He became adept at declaiming the poetry I brought to the kitchen table for him to study. I sensed that Julian Tuwim's quick and precise rhythms would appeal to him, and when we started on his works, the boy told me that his cousin Esther had once received three letters from him, though he couldn't say why.

How impossible it is to predict the turns we take in life, I often thought while listening to the youthful cadences of Benjamin's voice.

Curiously, he knew some English, and he taught me a song that a tailor friend of his in the ghetto had sung with him. It was entitled 'Blue Skies'.

Blue birds, singing a song,
Nothing but blue birds from now on . . .

'Blue Skies' showed me that Benjamin could carry a tune, so instead of starting him on piano lessons, I began to teach him popular songs. *Later*, I thought, *when he's more comfortable with me, we'll start piano lessons*. And yet, after a time, accompanying him became enough for me – in fact, it became my way of helping him up over the wall that only he could see.

Our first crisis came six weeks after Benjamin's arrival. My toilet backed up and created a stinking mess, so I went to the home of my neighbour, Bartosz, and called our local plumber, Mr Jankowski. The next day, he came riding up on his rusty bicycle with an exuberant yellow wildflower behind his ear.

A man unafraid of beauty, I reasoned, and I understood at that moment why he had occasionally appeared in my daydreams of a less solitary life.

After digging a slender trench across my yard, he discovered that roots from my cherry tree had invaded the piping and created a mass of tiny fibrous filaments that he referred to as a *wolf's tail*. He cut away the obscene tangle – half a metre in length – and showed it to me like a trophy.

'Disgusting!' I said.

He laughed the way men do at delicate ways of women, which I enjoyed.

Benjamin was fascinated with the wolf's tail and also Mr Jankowski, who had a face like a woodpecker and great big callused hands. The boy stood watching the lean, muscular plumber work with such rapt eyes that Mr Jankowski ended up letting him help stir the cement in his pail and apply it to the crack in the piping that the greedy cherry tree roots had created.

I warned Benjamin not to speak more than a few words of Polish – to pretend that he was too timid to speak. I didn't watch over him because it gave me pleasure to think of him learning things from a man that a woman couldn't teach him.

'Too bad about the boy's mother catching polio,' the plumber told me when he came inside to be paid. A minute or so later, after he'd climbed back on his bicycle, he smiled and said, 'Tell Benjamin I hope to see him again soon.'

Those kind words hit me like a punch in my gut. I picked up my cane and rushed to my young houseguest, who was still in the backyard, squatting over the wolf's tail, studying the dense tangle. I grabbed his arm and stood him up. 'Krystian – that's your name, not Benjamin!' I shouted. 'Krystian!'

He burst into tears.

'If Mr Jankowski goes to the authorities, they'll come for you and send you away. As for me, they'll throw a rope around my neck and hang me!'

I was aware that I was out of control, but I was unable to contain my fury.

Benjamin pulled free of my grip and ran away, toward the copse of poplars where my brother and I had hidden from our father when he was drunk. I went outside again a half hour later, but I couldn't find him anywhere. I pleaded with him to come home, but he didn't.

I sat at my piano, but nothing I played sounded right. After a time, I decided to go to Mr Jankowski's house to test him in some subtle way – to see if he'd guessed that Benjamin was Jewish. I put on my floral print dress and brushed a bit of lustre into my hair, but as I stepped outside, I realised the obvious – that I would only succeed in arousing his suspicions.

Benjamin returned home after sundown, his shirt stained with mud and eyes red with tears. I apologised to him and took off his soiled clothes, and I led him to his bed.

'Sleep,' I told him, thinking that he and I might have only a few more hours together.

He reached out for my hand, and I gripped it tight. Soon he had curled into a ball of slumber.

I stayed at his side for another hour or so, recalling Mr Jankowski's goodbye smile, which now seemed to conceal malevolence. Were his parting words to me a coded way of saying he'd be back soon with German officials?

When the Nazis come, I thought, *I'll tell them that Krystian is Piotr's son, just as I've told everyone, and I will speak so confidently that they will have to believe me. And yet if they strip the boy, they'll see that he's circumcised, and how will I explain that?*

When I finally left Benjamin's room, it was to count my meagre savings. I cursed myself for allowing my sister-in-law – long separated from my brother – to keep my mother's jewellery, because if I still had her gold bracelet or wedding band, I could offer a decent bribe.

In the end, however, good fortune was with us; no German or Polish officials visited that evening or on any of the subsequent days, and the bribery note I expected to find every afternoon in my postbox never arrived. So either Mr Jankowski failed to make the connection between Benjamin's name and his religion, or, if my intuition was correct, he hadn't cared.

A man who would put a yellow wildflower behind his ear would never betray a Jewish boy, I reasoned, and though I knew that my logic was naïve at best, I refused to give in to scepticism; I needed to believe that at least a few people I knew were so noble of heart that nothing of what the Nazis said or did could corrupt them.

I suppose I needed to believe, too, that I was one of them.

Still, this anxious little episode taught me an important lesson: I had to be far more careful whom I permitted to converse with

Benjamin, since he plainly did not fully comprehend that a single word of Yiddish might end any chance we had of outlasting the Nazis.

We lived that summer mostly on rice and potatoes mixed with carrots, leeks and turnips from my garden, since meat had become quite expensive. Whenever I saw that Benjamin's energy was flagging, however, I would purchase a perch or trout from Feliks Sitko, the delivery man who came clattering down my road in his horse-drawn cart three times a week, ringing his shrill bell, and who was an old friend of my brother's. I also made my young guest start the day with half a glass of milk or a wedge of cheese. Ducks occasionally lazed around my pond during July and August, and if either of us had ever learned to shoot, we could have fattened ourselves up with a true feast, but it seemed to me that those graceful creatures deserved a trouble-free life as much we did.

In our first conversation about our ducks, I learned that the word for them in Polish was the same as in Yiddish – *katchke* – and that his mother and nearly everyone else in his family called him by the nickname *Katchkele*, meaning 'little duck'. 'Though my dad,' he said in a respect-filled voice, 'always called me Benni.'

I could not intrude on his mother's place in his heart, of course, and I almost always avoided referring to him by his father's preferred name – even when we were alone – lest he fail to grasp the importance of answering only to Krystian. Still, every once in a while, when I would tuck him in, I would whisper, 'Goodnight, Benni' before kissing his brow, and it seemed to put him at greater ease with me. Calling a young boy by one of his true names is an intimate and important act, of course.

That summer, I occasionally detected deep and troubling thoughts assaulting Benni even during our most carefree moments. For instance, I would sometimes catch him staring off at the horizon – his lips closed tight – when he was weeding our flower beds.

I imagined that he still expected his parents to come walking over the nearest hill one afternoon, but maybe he was simply struggling with a particularly troublesome riddle, trying – like me – to understand why his homeland had betrayed him.

'What are you looking for out there in the distance?' I asked him once.

'Just thinking,' he said.

'About what?'

'About how things might be if they weren't the way they were.'

'Oh, dear, ifs can be dangerous,' I said, since this was a topic about which I knew a great deal. 'You might do best to stay away from ifs, at least for the time being.'

I had a curious dream on July 17th. I know the exact date because I wrote it down in my diary. Here is what I jotted down:

A man I have never seen before joins me in my backyard. He has a long grey beard and is dressed in a dark caftan. He thanks me for helping Benni. He has a benevolent smile. I trust him. After he takes my hand, he leads me around the pond several times. I do not question why. It is nice to walk with him. It feels as if I know him – that I met him when I was a girl. He begins to sing to me. He has a handsome baritone. He sings a sinuous and moving melody I've never heard before.

'Lovely, isn't it?' he says when he has finished.

'Yes, where is it from?' I ask.

'It's an ancient hymn,' he tells me, and he asks me to sing it back to him. When I do, he smiles, and then the two of us are no longer in my backyard. We are standing together in a

city of small whitewashed houses. He leads me inside a low
doorway into a cool, damp room. Are we below ground? That's
the impression I have. A tall candelabrum giving off waves
of yellow light stands before me, and behind it is my piano.
Seeing it delights me. 'Can I play something?' I ask.

'That's why you're here,' he replies.

I sit down, and I think of what I might play, and I decide
that I ought to play something very old and intricate – a fugue,
perhaps – but then I wake up.

I noted down the melody the old man taught me in my diary.
And then I went to my piano – still in my nightdress – to make
sure I'd written it out correctly.

I discovered that it was in the key of G major. It rose forthrightly
– as though in declaration – from the D above middle C to G,
then tiptoed down – across delicate steps – to A, and finally –
courageously, despite grand obstacles – climbed back up to D.

I played it to myself several times, wondering where it had
come from. Perhaps I'd heard it in a concert I'd attended as a girl
and forgotten.

My playing woke Benni. He came to me in his pyjamas, half
asleep. I kissed his eyes and took his hand. He smelled like warm
cereal. And something else a bit peppery. 'You need to go back
to bed,' I said.

'What was that melody?' he asked.

By this time, his Polish grammar had noticeably improved and I
detected a trace of a Yiddish accent only on the trickiest of words.

'I heard it in a dream,' I explained.

Seeing Benni's eyes open in astonishment, I realised then who
the old man might have been – or whom I wanted him to be. 'I
think an ancestor of yours visited me,' I told him.

'Who?'

'Berekiah Zarco. He taught the melody to me.'

That didn't seem to surprise the boy.

'Here, listen,' I said, and I played the melody for him. 'Have you ever heard that before?'

'I don't think so.'

'Has Berekiah Zarco ever appeared to you?'

'Once,' he whispered, as if it were a dangerous secret.

'When?' I asked.

He continued to whisper. 'After we moved into the ghetto. He came to me while I was going to sleep and told me to ask Rosa for a protective prayer. And I did. She had me memorise it.'

'Do you remember it?'

'Of course, but it's in Hebrew. You won't understand it.'

'Still, I'd like to hear it.'

'No, I can't tell it to you. Rosa said it was only for me and my family.'

'Oh, I see,' I said, trying to keep my disappointment out of my voice.

He closed his eyes and leaned on me as if he intended to go back to sleep standing up. I kissed his brow and steered him back to bed.

Berekiah intended the melody for Benni, I decided. In fact, I convinced myself that he'd taught it to me because he couldn't reach the boy.

The little melody that Berekiah taught me became the theme for my first composition, which I would work on between my lessons. I'd never even thought of writing music before – which seemed astonishing now that I'd started. What had I been waiting for?

I used the melody as the theme of a fugue in the Baroque style, but the counterpoint sounded clumsy and artificial when I played it for Benni – as though I'd forced the melody to dance in gilded fineries when all it wanted to do was walk up and down a gentle hillside.

While struggling with insomnia over the next nights, I remembered what Berekiah Zarco had told me and used the melody to create a harmonised hymn. Then, over the next weeks, I transposed the theme from the key of G to E minor, and in a third variation, I managed to re-work it without any fixed tonality. *Variations on an Ancient Melody*, I began to call the piece. I didn't believe it was particularly original or advanced, but composing for myself, and without expectations of hearing my music ever played by anyone else, satisfied my desire to have a secret project in my life – a purpose that only Benni and I would know about.

Benni and I settled into an easy routine that August. Mostly he was out and about, playing in the yard by himself or with Pawel, a boisterous but sweet-natured pupil of mine who lived just a mile away. They would kick around the football I bought through Feliks, imagining themselves winning decisive matches in the final minute, shrieking and whooping.

They'd call me outside to watch their penalty kicks, and I'd always root for the goalkeeper, since the odds always seemed so unfairly stacked against him.

When it was raining, Benni would take out the pastels I'd given him and draw on the floor beside me in my music room while I worked on my *Variations*. The boy had read a great deal about ancient Egypt and executed nearly endless sketches of their gods. I found them so curious and charming that I had him do one of the ibis-headed deity, Thoth, on a thick piece of wood and then contracted my carpenter neighbour, Lukasz, to make it into a weathervane. When Benni saw it affixed to the pinnacle of our roof, he whooped with joy and took both my hands and danced me around in a circle till we both got so dizzy that we had to sit down.

Sometimes, too, Benni would help me make repairs on our clothing. Thanks to his tailor friend in Warsaw, the boy was quite good with a needle and thread, and he and I were able to take in a number of my brother's ancient shirts and trousers so that they'd fit him.

On one particularly lovely moonlit evening, after we had polished off the last of the cinnamon cake that he'd helped me make the day before, Benni put on his pyjamas and went off to bed. As I tucked him in, he pulled me down to him. I thought he was going to give me a kiss, but instead he whispered something in my ear. It was in a language I'd never heard before – Hebrew, I realised. And his careful, reverent voice made it clear that it was a prayer.

When I asked him about it, he said that he'd asked God to keep the two of us safe, along with his cousins Shelly and Esther and all his other relatives. 'I included everyone,' he assured me with a big nod.

And so it was that I learned that Benni had decided to take me into his family.

A second crisis . . .

About two months after the start of our journey together, Benni came to me while I was napping, hot tears sliding down his cheeks. 'I've forgotten what my mom looked like!' he said with a moan.

I took his hand and gripped it tight. 'Can you see your father?' I asked, and when he nodded, I told him to picture him with his mother.

'I've tried. It's no good – it doesn't work!' he told me mournfully.

I sat him down beside me on my sofa. He was in such misery

that I started to cry myself. 'Did your mother and father ever dance together?' I inquired.

'I don't know!'

'You must have gone walking with them through Warsaw. Where did you like most to go?'

'To the river.'

'Go with her to the river now, in your mind.'

'I have! But she's not there. She's gone. And she's not coming back!'

I found it an incomparably heartbreaking and momentous experience to hold a child who has ceded to despair. We realise that we could be given nothing more important to do in life than to soothe the little being wrapped in our arms.

After his eyes were dry, I took him for a walk in the countryside, since the beauty of the Polish summer nearly always helped animate me, but he remained as glum as can be until we came to the ruins of an old chapel on the road south. Curiously, it was where I always went when I was most depressed, since the heroic tenacity of those rough grey stones seemed to bring back hope to me.

It was still morning, and swallows were gliding and diving around us, curious to see who this old woman and young boy might be. Benni was enchanted with the ruins and suggested that we might move there and build a special home for the swallows, too. When I told him that they left Poland every winter, he said, 'I know, they go to Africa.'

'So maybe what we should do is go to Africa when winter comes,' I said, but then I grew irritated with myself. *First Rome, now Africa*, I considered. *What does all this talk of travel have to do with anything?*

'Would we come back to Poland in the summer?' Benni asked.

'No, we'd stay far away,' I replied, thinking of Hitler and his thousand-year Reich.

'But we'd have to come back,' he said. 'Everyone I know is here.'

'Unless... unless you still have family in Portugal.' That seemed to be the conclusion I'd needed to reach for many weeks. Maybe it was even why Berekiah had sung me his hymn.

'I don't know if I do,' he said.

'Did you ever hear Rosa or your parents speak of cousins there?' He shook his head.

'Did Berekiah mention them when he appeared to you?'

'No.'

'Portugal isn't involved in the war, you know,' I said. 'It must be quiet there. And you and I ... We'd be perfectly safe if we went there, I think.'

That afternoon, I wrote to Piotr and asked him to try to find out if Benni had any family left in Portugal, though I used the name Krystian in my letter, of course. I also asked him to send me any photographs of the boy's family that he might have.

A bit later, while I was making fingering indications on a Bach prelude I wanted Pawel to practice, Benni came running to me.

'Ewa, we went skating!' he exclaimed joyfully.

'Who?'

'Mom and me!'

'Can you see her?'

'Yes!'

He was jumping up and down – so electric that he couldn't bear to be touched.

'Pick some detail of her clothing,' I told him, hoping that his memory would work like mine.

'What kind of detail?'

'Anything. Her hair . . . the dress she's wearing.'

'She's wearing a flower pinned to her dress.'

'What colour is the flower?'

'Red.'

'Touch the flower in your mind. Can you do that?'

'Yes.'

'Now close your eyes and smell it.'

Benni inhaled deeply.

'What's it smell like?' I asked.

'It smells red,' he said.

I laughed. 'Good, then, whenever you want to see your mother, all you'll have to do is picture that red-smelling flower.'

A letter from Piotr came a couple of weeks later. He wrote that he knew of no one who might have photographs of Krystian's family or who could tell us whether he had any living relatives in Portugal. *We'll have to wait until after the war is over to pursue such a possibility*, he told me.

Brzeziny had become a glum and empty town, and I did not want Benni to accompany me when I occasionally rode there with Feliks, since German officials might stop us, but he would fuss and whine when I left him alone, so I ended up bringing him along for the first time in late August.

Benni and I practised some sentences that he could use in conversation with Feliks, and he repeated them over and over until he was able to say them without even the slightest trace of a Yiddish accent. Feliks' mother had been from Turin, and to my great relief, he volunteered his contempt for the Nazis as we neared Brzeziny, telling me – seething resentment in his voice – that the

Germans all thought that Italians were lazy and stupid. 'Even ones like my mother, from the North!' he snarled.

Feliks asked after my brother, as he always did, laughing heartily when I told him that Karol had bought a Mercedes. 'I guess we always knew that he'd be a rich man someday!' he told me.

Since I detected hidden envy in his voice, I replied, 'Well, I wouldn't be surprised if he's gone into debt to purchase such an expensive car.'

Once we reached Brzeziny, I took Benni past the empty lot where the synagogue had been before it was dynamited to rubble by the Nazis. We then entered the main Jewish section of the city, which was just off the central square. We found it deserted except for hostile-looking feral cats and crows cackling at us from rooftops. It was upsetting to see, though I wasn't surprised; by then, my students had informed me that the seven thousand Jewish residents of the city had been moved to the Łódź ghetto, where they'd joined hundreds of thousands of other prisoners. The kids also told me that all of those Jews had been transferred elsewhere more recently. To another ghetto? My students didn't know. And I didn't ask their parents or any other adults, since it would have been risky to appear interested in the fate of Poland's Jews.

Even though we didn't come across any German officials, Benni kept his head down while we walked. And made not a peep. I imagined that he sensed, like me, that a great evil had taken possession of Brzeziny – and that it would be best to pass through the city unnoticed.

My destination was the house where Ryszard Fuchs, one of my most talented students, had lived with his parents. He was only half-Jewish and I thought that there was an outside chance that he or his Catholic father had been freed from the Łódź ghetto. But I soon discovered that the ground floor windows in the family home had been smashed and an insulting word for Jews – *Żydzisko* – had been painted on the front door in big black letters.

I might have snuck a look through one of the windows to make sure that no one in Ryszard's family had returned, but Benni trembled on seeing that horrible word. I gripped his hand tighter and said that it was time for us to go. He looked up at me with thick tears glistening in his dark eyes – as though pleading for a way to forget what he'd seen – so I said, 'We're never coming back to this place. You and I are going to stay safe at home – for years, if we have to.'

In early September, the chill of autumn came in from the east, and I bought Benni a winter coat and new shoes. I also knitted him a thick blue sweater that he would wear everywhere – even into bed. I'd had to make very large stitches because of my trembling hands, and the sleeves came out too long, but I decided not to redo them, since he still had a lot of growing to do.

I'd certified by then on several occasions that if Benni limited himself to words and expressions that he knew quite well, his Polish wouldn't reveal his origins, so I permitted him to join me and my students before and after their lessons. In addition to Pawel, he befriended my most graceful and charming pupil, Anna Trocki, who was fourteen and just becoming a woman.

From the devoted way that Benni would pour Anna's tea and bring her cake, I suspected that he was experiencing his first crush.

It was Anna who told us that her father had heard on the BBC that the Nazis were losing the war now on several fronts, and I began to hope – too afraid to say so openly, however – that Poland would soon be free. In my fantasies, I rode by train to Warsaw with Benni and searched for his aunts, uncles and cousins, though I admit that

I was in two minds about finding them, since if I had to give up the boy to them, I wouldn't want to go on living.

One Saturday afternoon, while Benni and Pawel were making a spice cake in my kitchen, I decided to read in my room, and a photograph in an old newspaper made me finally understand the pose I'd seen Benni take when I'd first seen him. The picture was of King Tutankhamun's golden sarcophagus. The carved figure of the pharaoh had his forearms crossed over his chest, with his hands pointed toward his shoulders and securing the royal crook and flail.

I asked Benni to join me for a moment in my music room and closed my door. 'I figured out what you were doing!' I whispered, and I showed him the photo.

'I don't understand,' he said.

'*Whisper*,' I told him, and continued, 'When Piotr unrolled the rug in which he brought you here, you didn't move. You had your arms crossed in the exact same way.'

'Oh, yeah – I remember. I was trying to see what it would feel like to be dead.'

'And what did it feel like?'

'It felt pretty much like I was alive except that I couldn't move.'

After the cake was in the oven, the boys sat with me in my bedroom, and Pawel fell soundly asleep. Benni and I went to the kitchen to clean up. He whispered, 'Rosa used to say I lived in ancient Egypt in a previous life.'

'Rosa believed in reincarnation?' I asked.

'Yeah. Mom said she could see people's souls and the traces of where they'd been.'

On Thursday, September 21st, an elderly man in a tweed suit knocked on my door, so I instructed Benni to hide in my music room. The visitor turned out to be the deputy headmaster of our local school. After offering me his card, he told me that he'd heard about my young houseguest from one of my pupils. 'We'll need to enrol the boy,' Mr Popiel told me while standing with me outside my door, and noticing my less-than-enthusiastic reaction, he added in a bullying voice, 'He can't stay here with you all day, you know.'

'His father is supposed to pick him up soon and bring him back to Warsaw,' I told him. 'So there's no point in enrolling him here.'

'But in the meantime, Miss Armbruster, he's missing his lessons. That can't be right.'

I invited him into my sitting room and offered him the armchair, hoping that my hospitality would soften his rigid tone.

'We all know that every child needs schooling,' he said as he sat down.

'Yes, you're right,' I replied, sitting in my usual place near the end of my sofa. 'But I'll have to get his father's permission, of course.'

'If you give me his telephone number, I'll call him from the school.'

'I'm afraid I can't do that. He gave me strict orders not to give his number to anyone.'

Mr Popiel showed me a condescending frown. 'That's perfectly absurd, Miss Armbruster.'

'Absurd it might be, but it's the truth. I will write to Piotr today, and as soon as I have his reply, I will let you know what he wishes me to do. If he says yes to enrolling his son, I will bring Krystian to you right away.'

'I'm afraid that isn't adequate. No, not adequate at all. If you'll just think a moment about—'

I cut him off by standing up and raising my hand. 'You must forgive me, Mr Popiel, but I take my responsibilities too seriously to be cowed into doing anything but what his father authorises.'

I hid my hands behind my back as I led him to my door, since they'd begun to shake. I was dizzy with fear, as well, and pouring with perspiration, but I'd spoken firmly, and just as I'd wanted to, and that seemed a small triumph at the very least.

Benni came to me when I stepped back into the house. He reached for my hand and asked who the man had been. After I told him, he said, 'Will I have to go to school?'

'No, I chased him off.' I laughed then, but out of apprehension, because I'd already reached the conclusion that Mr Popiel wouldn't give up. And since I could never expect Benni to speak in perfect Polish every day – and not let anything slip about his past or his real name – it meant that he would have to leave me much sooner than I'd hoped.

I dashed off a letter the next day to Piotr to tell him that he had to come as soon as possible to pick up Krystian. I might have called from town or a neighbour's home, but I was terrified that my conversation might be overheard or that I might give away the reason for my anguish with an ill-considered comment. Also, I very selfishly wanted another couple of days with Benni before I'd be forced to hand him over to Piotr.

And yet the very next day, I realised that if the school doctor were to examine Benni, he would discover that the boy was Jewish. I rushed panic-stricken to Bartosz' house to call Piotr – to ask him to come for Benni in the cousin's car – but he wasn't at home, so I explained the situation to his wife, Martyna. She told me that Piotr's cousin was away on business in Kraków, that he'd only be back in about a week. She added that they could trust no one else to help them in this way without arousing suspicions.

My apprehension made me cross with my pupils over the next few days. And then, as if to seal us inside a nightmare, a letter from my brother arrived on Monday, September 25th. Karol apologised for not visiting over the summer and informed me that he would soon be returning to Poland. In between the lines, I read that life in Berlin had become impossible for him. Had he lost his job?

If he asks for his old bedroom back, will I be able to refuse him? I wondered, though I knew that I wouldn't be able to do it.

Benni had been reinforcing the buttons on the bright red waistcoat I'd made him when I carried inside my brother's letter. I gave him it to read, but he said the Polish was too complicated, so I told him that my brother was coming to stay for a while – and might arrive at any time.

'Even today?' he asked.

'Yes, the letter took a week getting here, so he might show up at any time.'

I did not explain what Karol's return home meant for us, but Benni must have understood from the worried tone of my voice, because he took the waistcoat in his callused little hands and, with an angry grunt, ripped one of the side seams.

I rushed to him and told him not to worry, but he threw the ripped waistcoat to the ground and dashed out of the house. By the time I made it outside, he'd vanished.

I headed right away to Bartosz' house to call Piotr and Martyna again, and though I tried them every fifteen minutes over the next two hours, no one ever answered.

Benni undoubtedly sensed the movement of battle troops in my head that evening, and that night he came to me in bed, long after he should have been sleeping, and begged me tearfully not to make him go into hiding again.

'No, neither of us is going to hide ever again,' I replied, but I wasn't sure I could keep that promise, so I did not give him my word. Instead, I held him while he cried.

I finally managed to catch Piotr at home the next morning, and he told me that he would be able to come for Benni in his cousin's car at around 4 p.m. the next day. 'Ewa, I can hear how upset you are, but I promise you that we'll figure out how to keep the boy safe,' he assured me. 'We won't let anything bad happen to him.'

Piotr and I might indeed have come up with a solution together, but my brother arrived that afternoon, while I was playing my latest addition to my *Variations*. I didn't hear the car approaching, but Benni ran to me and warned me. As usual, I told him to hide in my music room and not to say a word.

A petite young woman with shoulder-length blonde hair and long red fingernails stepped out of the passenger door of my brother's Mercedes. Her slender shoulders were wrapped in a white fox stole. As for Karol, he wore a dark suit and trilby. How disappointing and oppressive his stiffly handsome face looked to me, but I waved to him. 'Welcome home!' I called out, thinking it safest to appear delighted.

As he took his girlfriend's arm, I noticed the enamelled swastika pin on his lapel.

'I'm Birgit,' the young woman said when we shook hands. 'It's lovely to finally meet you!' She smiled at me as if posing for a movie magazine. She smelled strongly of sweet perfume and cigarettes.

I soon discovered that Birgit spoke Polish quite well, but with a German accent, and when we reached my sitting room, she explained that she'd been born in Danzig to a German father and Polish mother.

'Thank God, Hitler has taken Danzig back for Germany!' Karol announced, plainly needing to make his continued allegiance to the *Führer* clear to me right away.

'Yes, it's wonderful,' I replied, making a mental note to use the German names for all our main cities.

To my surprise, Karol told me that he and Birgit had arrived in Łódź five days earlier.

'Then you got here before your letter,' I said.

He turned to Birgit. 'The mail service in Germany – it seems to have become unreliable,' he said in what seemed an exaggeratedly fearful tone.

'So things aren't going well in Berlin?' I questioned.

'Things?' my brother asked, as if my question were silly.

'Daily life,' I conceded.

'Daily life, as you put it, Ewa, is much as it always has been.'

'That's good to hear.'

Birgit must have sensed the undeclared war between us, because she said in a peace-making voice, 'Karl and I decided to come to Poland before the weather turns cold.'

'I'm sure it will be lovely for you and my brother to have a vacation here,' I said.

I was hoping that she or Karol would either agree that they were here only for a short time or let me know that they planned to stay more permanently, but instead Karol leaned toward me and asked, 'So where's Krystian?'

My heart seemed to stop. 'How . . . how do you know about him?' I stammered.

'I had a drink with Feliks Sitko the other day,' my brother said cheerfully. 'He told me about your little guest'.

'I think he's in my music room.'

Karol brought his hand down indignantly on the arm of his chair. 'Well, bring him out to meet me!'

I went to Benni, who was squatting behind my fire screen. He seemed ready to flee. I wished we could have.

After I helped him stand up, I whispered, 'My brother is here with his girlfriend. Don't trust either of them, no matter what they tell you. With any luck, they'll leave in a little while.' I kissed his brow. 'Remember, we're in this together, and I'll never give you up!'

He nodded, and we walked to Karol and Birgit hand in hand. I introduced him as Piotr's son.

'Was Piotr the one who was blind in one eye?' he asked, squinting in what he hoped was a comical, silent-movie way. To please him, Birgit giggled girlishly.

'No, that was Bohdan,' I said.

Birgit lit a cigarette, kneeled next to Benni and wiped the hair out of his eyes. 'What a cutie!' she gushed.

She kissed his cheeks and left behind lipstick stains. Something about her abrupt movements ... Had she been drinking? I took Benni back from Birgit and told him to go play at Pawel's house.

'What ... what about supper?' he asked hesitantly.

'I'll have the food ready in an hour,' I told him. 'Come back then.'

'Yes, we'll talk over supper,' Karol told the boy with a big smile, though it seemed more like a threat.

When my brother turned to me, the swastika on his lapel shimmered, and I heard him tell me in my mind: *I'm going to hurt you in a way that can never be healed.*

After Benni had run out the door, I asked my brother where he and Birgit were staying.

'With my old friend Werner,' Karol said. 'He has a comfortable flat in Łódź.'

In a falsely eager voice, he said that it had been too long since he had returned home and that he wanted a look around. After he went out to the backyard, Birgit said with a sad smile, 'I'm sorry he was rude to you. He has mixed feelings about being here.'

'Yes, I understand,' I replied.

She stood up and went to the window, and I followed her there. Tender affection appeared in her clear blue eyes as she watched my brother, and just like that all my unfavourable thoughts toward her vanished.

While she adjusted the drape of her fox stole, she told me about the trip from Berlin. She laughed nervously after each of her observations of the towns they passed through, and especially after she said that Karol had got lost on the backroads leading to my home but refused to ask directions. 'Men are such strange creatures!' she said, shaking her head.

I realised that she was nearly as nervous as I was and did my best to make her feel at home with a series of questions about her childhood in Gdansk, which I called Danzig, but all the time I was thinking about Karol, because I was certain he would return to us in a foul mood.

Indeed, he was mostly silent at dinner, and he ate almost nothing, saying that turnips, carrots and potatoes were hardly his idea of a proper meal. I could see that being here made him feel a prisoner of the past, so I stifled my resentment and apologised for not having any meat or wine to give him. I found myself wishing that there was something I could say or do to help him, but I'd learned long ago that he would always see me as one of the people he'd had to overcome in order to break free of our family and become the man he wanted to be. Very likely, he considered me one of his boyhood jailers, in fact.

Birgit did her best to steer our conversation toward safe territories and entertained Benni with stories about the pet dogs that she'd had as a girl, along with a rabbit named Futrzany who'd slept in her bed until he was six months old, at which point he'd disappeared without a trace.

'Did you ever find him again?' Benni asked in a cautious voice, since he probably already suspected how her story would end.

'Yes and no,' Birgit replied with appropriate menace, and she went on to describe her horror when she discovered that the magnificent stew that her mother prepared on the evening after Futrzany vanished included what was left of him.

Birgit's grotesque story must have piqued Benni's interest; afterward, he focused rapt eyes on her whenever she skidded off on one of her odd tales of childhood, which made me jealous. Only much later did it occur to me that something about her might have reminded him of his mother.

My little houseguest decided to save his dessert for later, of course, which struck Karol as curious, and he asked Benni if he'd suffered deprivations in Warsaw, at which point I jumped in and told the boy that he'd had enough conversation for one evening and he was to get ready for bed. He protested by moaning and stamping his feet, but Birgit said she would tuck him in and tell him a bedtime story, which set him running for his pyjamas.

'You'll die in this wretched house, won't you?' Karol said to me after Birgit and Benni had left us.

I felt as if he'd slapped me. 'You always knew how to stop a conversation,' I observed.

'Why did you always support our parents?' he asked.

'What do you mean?'

'You did everything Dad told you.'

'Karol, I don't think that's true. But in any case, I was afraid of him. He'd hit me on more than one occasion. And he'd humiliated me in other ways.'

My brother took a long, pensive sip of his coffee. He looked at me as if he were an entomologist studying a foul-smelling insect. 'Papa hit me too – and often for no reason,' he said.

'I know, and I'm sorry that happened,' I replied, and I thought, *You and I, each in our different ways, will never get over what happened to us, will we?*

When Birgit returned to us, my brother took her by the arm and told her it was time to go.

Karol couldn't bring himself to kiss me goodbye, but Birgit did. While they drove down my lane to the main road, I realised that I might never see my brother again, and the mixture of panic and relief I felt made me wish I could cry over all that he and I had lost, but I couldn't.

When I woke in the morning, Benni wasn't in his bed. I discovered him kicking his soccer ball in the backyard. Over breakfast, I asked him about Birgit's bedtime story.

'She told me about going to the beach in France with her parents. She said the water was warm. She said she learned some French, too. But I didn't understand everything she said.'

'Why not?'

'While she was telling me about their favourite restaurant, she switched to German.'

'That's odd.'

'She said she could tell about her life much better in German.'

'I see. But why did she think you'd understand her?'

'I don't know. After a while, I told her I couldn't follow her, and she switched back to Polish.'

Had Birgit heard some inflection in Benni's voice that gave her to understand that he was a Yiddish speaker and would understand her German if she spoke slowly enough?

He shrugged when I asked him about that possibility.

'She didn't see you naked, did she?' I questioned hurriedly.

'No, of course not! She just tucked me in and told me her story about France.'

I'd waited too long all my life to make decisions, but not this time. I put all my money in a beaded handbag that I'd inherited from my mother and told Benni to dress for a trip. Then I packed a suitcase with extra clothing for the two of us and, at the last moment, grabbed my *Variations*. He retrieved the scroll he'd inherited from Berekiah Zarco. He also showed me a stunning pair of sapphire earrings that his great-grandmother had given him to use as a bribe. The little devil had hidden them from me the whole time we'd been together!

After we'd walked a few hundred paces, Benni gasped and told me he'd forgotten something important. More secret jewellery? He dashed off before I could ask.

He held up his beloved blue sweater as he ran back along the road to me.

We walked hand in hand to Mr Jankowski's house. The plumber spotted my anxiety right away and asked me what was wrong. 'I'm sorry to bother you,' I told him, 'but I have to count on your goodwill.' I put my hand atop Benni's head. 'I need to get our little friend here back to Warsaw.'

'What's happened?'

'His grandfather is very ill – may even die.'

'I see. All right, if you wait a few minutes for me to finish what I'm working on, I'll take you to Łódź in my wagon.'

'I don't know how I'll ever repay you,' I said.

He gave a little laugh. 'There's nothing to repay.'

Before we all went out to his wagon, I asked to use his telephone and called Piotr. Martyna answered and told me her husband was giving classes but would be leaving to pick up Benni in about two hours.

'No, tell him to stay there,' I told her. 'We're on our way. I'll explain when we get there.'

Mr Jankowski helped me and Benni into the back of his wagon and gave us a thick grey blanket to keep warm.

'Where will we go from Łódź?' Benni asked.

'To Warsaw.'

'How?'

'By train. And if anyone asks, we'll say you're my grandson.'

Later on the trip, Benni started repeating his protective prayer to himself, so I asked him to teach it to me and committed it to memory: *The Lord and I are one, and it is He who turns my soul to light, and it is that light that always guides me to safety. And may the Lord gift each soul under threat with this same holy radiance.*

We reached Warsaw late that afternoon and went straight to Piotr's apartment, which was in the suburb of Praga. Benni knew the way. He led us past the Orthodox cathedral down a bleak side street. I'd twisted my ankle a bit on climbing into Mr Jankowski's wagon and had to go very slowly.

I told Benni to run and not look back if Nazis were waiting for us at Piotr's apartment.

'But what about you?' he asked.

'Me? I'll keep them from going after you any way I can.'

'But they'll hurt you.'

'No, they won't do anything to me. I'm not Jewish.'

I could tell from his eyes that he knew I was lying and refused to leave me.

The moment Piotr opened his door to us and smiled, a shiver of relief swept through me. After he greeted us, he took me by the hand and led me to the upright piano in his sitting room. An old photograph of me was standing on its lid, inside a silver frame. My face had been full and round, and my hair was dark, but there was a mistrustful look in my eyes.

'See!' I said to Benni, pointing to my picture. 'Proof that I wasn't always a dinosaur!'

He disregarded the opportunity for humour and tugged on my arm. 'I'm starving,' he said.

Piotr chuckled. 'I'll get you something to eat.' Before he left us for the kitchen, he patted my shoulder. 'Ewa,' he said, 'it's not such a good piano, but you could play us something.'

I tested the theme of my *Variations*, but I discovered that it sounded rather frail at that moment. Benni came back to me devouring a chicken wing.

Piotr brought in the rest of the bird on a big white ceramic plate. He sat on the arm of his couch and asked what I'd played.

'A little composition of mine,' I said, wondering why I'd told the truth. Did I really expect to earn anyone's praise at this late date?

'Wow – you're composing!' he exclaimed happily. 'That's wonderful!'

Why do I always expect the worst from people? I asked myself, though I was pretty certain I knew the answer.

'Listen, Piotr,' I said, anxious to take the focus of our conversation off of me, 'I told everyone that Benni was your son. So if he's been reported, the authorities will come here. We've got to get going right away.'

'But how will they know where to find me?'

'My brother will track down my former pupils and ask them for your surname.'

Piotr phoned Martyna, who was at her travel agency, and they talked over where to take the boy while Benni and I ate. He and I talked of his favourite places in Warsaw. He told me that his cousin Shelly once took him to a big flower market, and from that moment on he knew that he wanted to live in a really big garden.

When Piotr and Martyna returned to us, they said that we'd be taking Benni to her widowed father. 'He isn't fond of Jews,' Martyna confessed, 'but he hates the Germans even more.'

She told us that he lived alone in a village twenty kilometres from Warsaw.

Benni and I sat in the backseat of the car that Piotr had borrowed that morning. I watched the scenery without speaking, drifting toward slumber despite my apprehension. Benni played a word game with Martyna that made them both laugh and squeal with delight. We reached the village at sunset.

Piotr's father-in-law, Augustyn, was a brawny, heavyset man with knobby hands who wheezed as if he were nearing a heart attack. His fingernails were crusted with dirt and he reeked of brandy. Martyna talked with him in the house while Piotr and Benni and I remained outside.

'I can't leave Benni here,' I kept telling myself, sensing it would be a fatal mistake.

I was tempted to grab the boy's hand and start hurrying away, but Piotr told me to have faith in Martyna. 'She's her father's favourite,' he murmured.

A little later, she came back to us, smiling, and told us that her father had agreed to their plan.

I took Benni with me into the musty storage room that was to serve as his bedroom and handed him an envelope containing all my savings.

'Use it for bribes if the authorities come for you. And if Martyna's father isn't good to you, then make your way back to Piotr. Do you think you can do that?'

'Yes. I'll walk all day and night if I have to,' he said proudly.

'Good boy.' I handed him the *Variations*, which I'd begun to think of as belonging to him, since his ancestor, Berekiah, had given me its melody.

'But how will you work on it without what you've already composed?' he asked.

'I won't. When you bring it back to me, I'll start on it again.'

There was so much I needed to tell Benni – about how deceitful people can be, about the grammatical mistakes he still sometimes made in Polish, about how grateful I was to have had our few months together – but now there was no time. I felt as if all my previous life had just been preparation for this moment. 'Only now – when I'm already old, am I the person I was meant to be,' I told him. 'You changed everything. Helping you has made all I've done seem important and worthwhile.'

He shrugged, since he was too young to understand me.

'The war will be over soon,' I said more sensibly, trying to sound cheerful, 'and then we'll be able to live together again.'

'When will it be over?' he asked.

'I don't know. Maybe in a year.'

'A year? I want to go back home with you!' he cried.

'Ssshhh! Please, Benni, you need to stay here.'

He pressed himself into me. His quickened breaths against my chest terrified me. 'I'm coming with you,' he said in a moaning voice.

I hugged my arms around him. 'Listen, Benni, people back home are starting to ask questions. I need you to stay here. And your parents do too. They need you to stay alive.'

He leaned back away from me. 'How do you know that?' he asked in a resentful voice.

'I understand a few things that you don't understand yet – about the way the world works. Now, listen closely, I'm going to go back home, and if I'm wrong . . . If the authorities don't come and question me, I'll know that no one has denounced you. And then I'll come back for you.'

'You promise?'

I tapped the top of his head playfully. 'Of course, silly!'

When we embraced again, I breathed in deep on his warm, cereal scent, knowing it might have to sustain me for a long time – perhaps forever. Piotr came into the room while I was wondering if I could continue to fight off my tears much longer. 'We better get going,' he said. 'At night, the roads are difficult.'

I whispered Rosa's prayer over Benni, and, when I kneeled down, he whispered it over me.

As an amen, I said to myself, *May these Hebrew words build a wall around us both – bigger even than Benni's guilt.*

Just before leaving, I stepped up to Augustyn and asked him to keep the boy safe for me. 'It's the most important job you could ever be given,' I told him, and though he nodded, I could see in his dull, drunken eyes that he thought I was just a silly old lady.

I didn't dare gaze back at Benni as we drove away, but I heard him speak to me in my mind: *I don't like it here*, he said.

I know, I told him. *But I need you to stay alive. I can't live without knowing you're safe. So be patient and strong.*

I've been patient and strong all my life, he replied. *When do I get to be what I want?*

I made it home the next day. To my relief, no one had searched the house.

In Benni's dresser I discovered several pieces of cake, and one of them was covered in mould, so I tossed it into my pond.

That night, when I was nearly asleep, Benni said to me, *I didn't just save my treats in case we ran out of food. It was also because I wanted to show you that I wasn't a child – that I knew how to plan and wait.*

I gave my lessons as usual over the next three days. At night, I fell asleep on the sofa in my sitting room. My dreams were often darkened by anxiety. And I had no appetite; I lived on vegetable soup and tea.

A Mercedes came grinding down my lane on the fourth day. I expected to see Karol again, but a slender man in a German uniform stepped out. He was young – in his late twenties, perhaps – with dark hair, and a crescent-shaped scar on his forehead. To my astonishment, his eyes were warm and he gave my hand an enthusiastic shake when I met him on my stoop. His driver remained in the car.

He started by telling me his name – Wilhelm Brandt. He also told me that he was from the regional Office of Racial Hygiene. He spoke Polish with a heavy accent.

'Welcome to my home,' I told him.

'You *are* Ewa Armbruster, aren't you?' he asked. 'I hope I haven't come to the wrong house.' He laughed in a boyish way.

'Yes, I'm Ewa,' I told him.

'I understand that you're a piano teacher,' he said with a hopeful smile, and when I said I was, he asked to see my instrument.

I led him into the music room, wondering if perhaps his visit had nothing to do with Benni after all.

'A Broadwood!' he said in an astonished voice.

'You seem surprised,' I said with a little laugh.

'To find such a wonderful piano out here in the countryside ...'

'It belonged to my old teacher. He left it to me in his will.'

'Do you mind if I play a little something? It's been too long.'

'No, I don't mind at all. Give it a try.'

He sat very upright and played the opening of the overture of *The Barber of Seville*. I could tell from his sure touch that he had once been a fine and accomplished pianist.

He turned to face me. 'I used to accompany my father and sister,' he explained. 'They're opera singers.'

'How wonderful!'

'I know mostly the Italian repertoire. My sister was a lyric soprano. She lives in Cologne. Do you have many students?'

'I have seven at the moment.'

'Good for you! It's important to give youngsters a musical childhood.' He caught my gaze and shook his head as if facing a sad duty. He stood up stiffly. 'Miss Armbruster,' he said, 'I'm afraid I must become unpleasant now. You see, I've been told that you had a boy staying here with you for some months.'

'Who told you that?'

'It doesn't matter. What was the boy's name?'

'Krystian.'

'A student?'

'No, the son of a former pupil of mine – a professor of mathematics in a high school in Warsaw. Unfortunately, his wife has contracted polio. His father sent him to me for the summer.'

'A Jew?'

My legs went weak, but I feigned calm. I sat down on my loveseat and placed my shaking hands under my bottom. 'Why do you ask me such a silly question, *Herr* Brandt?' I asked.

His face elongated with shock. 'Is it silly?' he inquired.

'To me it is.'

He joined his hands together and declared, 'And yet I was told that he was a Jew.'

'Did my brother tell you that?'

'Are you saying that your brother is also responsible for hiding a Jew boy?'

'No, of course not. What I *am* saying is that Krystian isn't a Jew.'

'Even if he spoke like a Jew?'

It's Birgit – she must have guessed! I thought, and the room and everything around me grew a great deal darker. To the Nazi, I said in what I hoped was a cheerful tone, 'You ought not to pay attention to rumours spread by visitors. I'm afraid that it's so very boring around here that people from big cities like Berlin and Warsaw invent stories just so they can have something to talk about.'

He glared at me menacingly. 'Where's the boy now?'

'I don't know.'

'You've hidden him somewhere, you mean.'

'Hidden him? No, I brought him to his father. But I have no idea what Piotr will do with him while his wife is ill. I imagine he'll send him to a relative.'

'Are you related to this Piotr?'

'No, I told you, he's a former student.'

'And what's his family name?'

'Bajek. And I don't know if you realise it, *Herr* Brandt, but that's a good Christian name in Polish.'

His face showed such contempt for me that I gazed away. Terror was now lodged now in my throat.

The Nazi sat at the piano again and played a few bars of the first of Felix Mendelssohn's *Songs Without Words* with great sensitivity. I was certain that he chose that piece because Mendelssohn's family had been Jewish. Perhaps he meant to tell me that he knew I was lying. Very likely, he thought he was being clever.

When Brandt was done, he turned to me and said with cold and formal ease, 'I could have you hanged, Miss Armbruster. You do know that, don't you?'

I cleared my throat and took a deep breath. I felt strangely powerful. Probably because I knew that nothing he could do could ever compel me to betray Benni. 'What I know is that you Germans control our country,' I told him.

'Yes, we do. And hanging is a quick death.' He stood up, and his eyes were now remorseless and cold. 'Enemies of the German Reich – enemies who hide Jews – ought to be made to suffer far longer, don't you think?'

At that moment, I was certain that all the beautiful music he'd learned had taught him nothing about what was important in life, and that seemed a great failing. 'You play very well, but if Mr Mendelssohn were here, he'd find you a great disappointment,' I said.

'If Mr Mendelssohn were here, I'd have him executed along with you!' he shot back, and made to leave.

At my front door, he turned to me with an icy glare and said, 'Your piano needs tuning, but it's the best I can find in this wretched backwater, so I'll send a truck for it tomorrow.'

Shortly after his departure, I fetched my axe, and I knew what I had to do – for Mendelssohn and Rossini and all the others – but my Broadwood seemed like the closest friend I had ever had, and I couldn't do it. Instead, I used a knife to engrave my name under the lid, thinking that I would claim it back if I lived to see Poland free of Brandt and his friends.

Late that afternoon, I walked out my front door and never looked back. I brought only a little food and some keepsakes from my mother with me. I felt astonishingly light, freed from a destiny I'd never really wanted in the first place – the destiny of leading a small, isolated and docile life. I realised I was no longer afraid of what the Nazis might do to me. I wanted only to be with Benni for as long as I remained alive.

I remembered a dream as I walked down the main road to Brzeziny. In it, the boy and I were standing on the roof of an old wooden synagogue. A great wind was blowing around us. We were cold. A man's voice called to us. When we walked to the rim of the roof, we discovered Berekiah Zarco looking up at us with curious eyes. He wore long robes and a silver crown. 'Come down,' he said. 'It's time we set off.'

We climbed down a ladder to him. He hugged us. When I looked around, I discovered that the synagogue had become a train station. 'Where are we going?' I asked.

'Home,' he replied.

A wagon on the road behind me stirred me out of my memories of the dream. When I turned around, Bartosz waved and called out to me. As he reached me, he asked, 'You off again, Ewa?'

'Yes. An old friend is ill and has sent for me.'

'What should I have the headmaster tell your students?'

I thought about that for a while. 'To keep practising. And as soon as the Germans go home, we'll celebrate with a recital.'

Bartosz laughed and told me that that would be the first musical recital he'd ever voluntarily go to. A little later, he dropped me in

Brzeziny. I remembered just in time that I had no money for my journey to Warsaw, so he also gave me a loan.

'I don't know when I'll be able to repay you,' I told him.

'You let me come to that recital of yours free of charge and we'll call it even!'

I arrived in Warsaw that evening and spent that night with Piotr and Martyna. They took me early the next afternoon to Benni.

He ran out to greet me, and while crying in my arms, he said, 'I was sure they were going to kill you, like they killed my parents and Rosa.'

'No, I didn't give them time to get me,' I replied, and as I kissed the top of his head, I recalled the afternoon I'd turned down my chance to have a career in music, when I'd choked on the belief that I'd never escape my parents' farm. 'You know what, Benni,' I added, 'I guess I'm finally learning when it's time to go.'

Benni and I spent the last months of the war with Augustyn. For reasons I didn't entirely understand but which had to do with his deep disappointment in the world and himself, the powerful man got drunk most afternoons and would awaken only near dinnertime, famished and sniffing at the supper I was making like a hunting hound. He was generally silent, but occasionally, in the morning, we would talk together about the old days, and he spoke with a gentlemanly authority about his work as a carpenter that I grew to greatly respect. He was a devoted fly fisherman, and he soon taught Benni how to cast and where the best fish would congregate, so we often had trout or perch for dinner.

Benni and I decided that he would learn a trade while we were waiting for the war to end, and Augustyn managed to secure him an apprenticeship with a kindly tailor who lived in the nearest town.

As for me, I discovered that I didn't need a piano to compose – I could hear all eighty-eight keys in my mind with no effort at all, and they never needed tuning. I wrote three more variations that fall and winter, and a fourth by the early spring.

After the war ended in May 1945, Benni and I began to learn what the Nazis had done to the Jews in Auschwitz and the other death camps. We reasoned that if anyone in his family had been among the few to survive, he or she would naturally come hunting for relatives. Unfortunately, the home he'd always lived in near Łazienki Park – and much of the neighbourhood – had mostly been turned to rubble. The only shop left standing that he remembered had been where his mother and aunt had bought pastries and cakes. The elderly owner had a red, painfully thin face, and he walked with a bad limp. His name was Wieczorek, and he was selling mostly canned goods now.

At first, old Wieczorek seemed quite nervous to talk to me. With a grim frown, he said he didn't remember the Zarco family. I knew from the vehemence of his repeated denials that he was lying. I suspected at the time that it was because he'd collaborated with the Nazis, but a few weeks later I learned that the Soviet secret police had already begun arresting Poles who'd worked in the resistance and others whom they considered a threat, so it's possible that he was instead terrified of being interrogated by our new rulers.

'But I know that my mother once bought my birthday cake here!' Benni insisted to me when I told him that the shop owner didn't remember him or his family.

He refused to leave, so I stepped to Mr Wieczorek and took the pearl ring that had been my mother's off my finger. 'Take it,' I said.

'What for?'

'The boy needs to find his family. Are you sure you don't remember them?'

He examined my bribe, then motioned me to the back of his shop. There, surrounded by the damp darkness and the sweet scent of perfume he must have been stocking, he said, 'I remember the boy's mother and aunt, but they haven't come back.'

From my bag, I took out one of the papers on which I'd written my name and Benni's, as well as Piotr's address and my home address. 'If anyone from his family should stop by your shop, or if you hear that they've come back, please give them this note and tell them we're waiting for them. It's very important. We'll stay in Warsaw another couple of weeks, then go back home.'

Although he promised he would do as I'd asked, his cold and abrupt manner inspired little confidence in me, so when we returned to the front of the shop, I said, 'Mr Wieczorek, this is our chance to make up a little for what was done to our Jews.'

'Our Jews? I assure you they weren't *my* Jews!' he snarled. 'There were way too many of them, in any case. I sold them their birthday cakes, but I never liked them!'

We stayed for three more weeks in Piotr's apartment, until the end of the first week in June, and a number of Jews returned to Benni's neighbourhood from where they'd fled – mostly the Soviet Union – but no one in his family appeared.

Back at my home, we discovered that everything of value had been stolen, even my mother's china and my sculpture of Pan, and though that made daily life a bit cumbersome, red poppies were carpeting the fields, the swallows had returned, and the ruins of the old chapel on the road south could still be counted on to revive our spirits with their tenacious spirit. I put the boy to work planting a vegetable garden and helping me clean the house while I made enquiries about tailors in Brzeziny who might need an apprentice. In his free time, Benni embarked on wild-hearted adventures with Pawel and Anna.

We thought it best to continue to keep his true background a secret from everyone, since we'd heard rumours of Jewish survivors who'd returned home only to be murdered by Polish neighbours. A few weeks after our arrival, old friends in Brzeziny helped me locate my piano at what had been Nazi headquarters in Łódź. It took several weeks for me to take ownership, and I was only able to do so after hiring an attorney. The first thing I did after movers rolled it into my music room was to clean all the keys with a mixture of vinegar and water, since I did not want to touch any residue left by a pianist who'd learned nothing from teachers like Verdi and Puccini.

My brother never contacted me. Four months after our return, in October, at the celebratory recital I organised for my students, a school friend of his informed me that he'd moved to Gdansk with Birgit just after the end of the war. And that he'd become a Communist again and started working for the regime put in power by the Soviets.

By that time, Benni had secured an apprenticeship with a meticulous young tailor in Brzeziny named Kowalczyk.

Who had betrayed the boy and me to the Nazi authorities? We didn't have to wait long to find out ...

On the day after our return, Mr Jankowski came round to tell me that it was my delivery man, Feliks. Apparently, Feliks had spread rumours about the boy being Jewish to all of his customers in the days before Mr Popiel, the deputy headmaster, paid me a visit. As to how Feliks had discovered that I'd lied to him about Benni's identity, I have no idea, though it was possible that he had caught the boy in a grammatical error that no native Pole would be likely to make. Or, at some point, Benni might even have slipped up and revealed the names of his parents – Graça and Adam – or other relatives. Their Jewish names would have exposed his religious background right away.

A speculation . . . Perhaps Feliks' envy of my brother had been far more violent than I'd at first imagined and he had decided to hurt Karol by wounding me. Can people be so perverse and evil? The answer, of course, is yes, they can. And frequently are. The Nazis taught us that lesson if nothing else. What Feliks never knew, however, was that my brother would likely not have wept a single tear if I'd been hanged.

Six months after our return, I crossed paths with Feliks for the first time, at the main market in Brzeziny. Curiously, I wasn't tempted to question him about what he'd done because I'd learned by then that the Poles who'd collaborated with the Nazis all found good and noble reasons to betray the Jews and those of us who had hidden them. Just as those Poles who stood by while their Jewish neighbours were arrested, put in ghettos and turned to ash had found any number of justifications for their silence.

If Piotr had not brought me Benni, and if I had refused to take him in, then I, too, would have likely been guilty of the same unforgiveable crime. The boy saved my life, in that sense, and permitted me to go on composing my *Variations* and teaching little children how to play Mozart and Beethoven, though I realised soon enough – seeing clearly where duplicity and silence had brought my country – that I ought to have done much more to fight the Nazis from the very start.

Benni stayed with me for more than two years after the liberation of Poland. Once in the spring and once in the autumn, we would go to Warsaw to see if any members of his family had returned or left word for him, but we never came upon even a trace of them.

We also located Portugal's consular office in May of 1947 and left our address with a nice young lady named Mónica, who promised to give it to any of Benni's relatives who came looking for him.

Then, one day in early September of 1947, a taxi dropped two young men at the end of my dusty drive. One was Benni's cousin Shelly. The other was a close friend of Shelly's – a Navajo Indian named George. We would later learn that they had indeed found us through the consular office.

Benni and Shelly . . . Their reunion was the most wonderful testament to love I have ever witnessed, and I shall carry the vision of them embracing and laughing till the end of my days.

Too soon, however, Shelly and George took Benni off to Canada, since the government had made it possible for Jews to leave the country without even a passport. Although the boy and I began to write each other nearly every week, he was unable to accumulate enough savings to visit me for many years – and, in any case, I instructed him to use all his earnings to make a good life for himself on the other side of the ocean.

Then, this past July – nearly seven years after I'd last seen him – a handsome young man with tender dark eyes and a skullcap of black hair appeared at my door in a beautifully tailored charcoal-grey suit. At first, I did not let myself believe that he was my Benni, but then he raised a hand of blessing over my head and whispered Rosa's Hebrew prayer, and my legs gave way, so that he had to hold me up and walk me to my sofa and hand me a glass of water. He told me that he'd have come sooner, but it had taken him more than two years to obtain a visa. Then, in his tearful embrace, I ceded to all the emotions that I had denied myself for far too long.

Over the next three weeks, until he left again for America, I often watched Benni sleeping at night, in his old bed, and I would hold his hand, as when he was little, but by then he was already a man, of course, and a successful tailor in New York. He is there now, in his little apartment in Greenwich Village – safe from all of Europe's evils – so the rest of his story I must leave for someone else to tell.

THE TAILOR
WHO LEAKED
WHAT HE COULDN'T
PUT INTO WORDS
(1965-1968)

While taking a class in non-Western music during my junior year at college, I began daydreaming about heading out to the Amazon rainforest with a tape recorder, mosquito netting and all the notebooks I could fit in my backpack, and transcribing the traditional songs of the indigenous peoples of Brazil before they were lost or forgotten. I came to regard it as a calling, in fact, and one that nearly perfectly matched my talents, since I'd become fluent in Portuguese and – after sixteen years of flute lessons – could memorise even dissonant and unusual melodies quickly. To be honest, I also imagined myself imbibing a cup of hallucinogenic ayahuasca and dancing around a grove of palms while wearing only a feathered headdress, and making love to a bronze-skinned shaman while wading in the warm river-water embracing his village, but it was the 1960s and such wild-hearted fantasies seemed perfectly reasonable. Or had I read too much William Burroughs? Very likely. Need I add that none of it came to pass? Although I was accepted during my senior year to music graduate school and was scheduled to begin my PhD in ethnomusicology at the University of California in early September of 1965, my father had a major heart attack about a month before that, which sent my life spiralling off in another direction.

Dad collapsed while walking his wire-haired dachshund, Radley, on Third Avenue, a block from his apartment on East 11th Street. He was then just fifty-two years old.

After getting an early-morning phone call from my father's upstairs neighbour, Daniela, I flew in to New York from Berkeley late that evening. The next morning, when I reached his room in the Intensive Care Unit of New York University Hospital, Dad was asleep. An oxygen mask was clamped over his face, which was gaunt and pale – the colour of cigar ash under the fluorescent lighting.

I leaned against the door frame because I felt as though I were falling inside myself. And I sensed that I wouldn't hit bottom for a long time.

I took off my coat, folded it neatly over the chair by my father's cot and sat down. Does a mind seeking solace sometimes stumble instead upon a trauma long forgotten? Of all the things in the world I might have thought of while watching my father snooze, my mind seized on Zencefil, a hook-nosed, yellow-skinned marionette – a witch – whom my father had imbued with a seductively menacing voice in his version of *Hansel and Gretel*. Even though she got baked in her own oven at the dramatic end of Dad's performance, Zencefil remained very much alive in my young mind and climbed into my dreams that night. She stood on my chest, hands on her hips, like a victorious general. And then, with meticulous calm, she strangled me in her cords.

All those years before, when I tearfully related my nightmare to my father, he grabbed the marionette and knocked on her ugly nose with the bulb of his pipe and tossed her to the floor to show me she couldn't hurt me or anyone else. 'She's nothing, Teresa,' he said. 'She's just wood and porcelain. She's only as powerful as you make her.'

But pressing my fingertip to her cool ceramic face – touching her rouged cheek – seemed an encounter with death itself. Since I was unable to put that into words – I was too young for that – I told my father that I hated her.

Dad gave her away that day. To whom? He never said and I never asked. All that was important was that she was gone. 'You've taught me something I should have realised sooner,' my father told me when he served me supper that evening, and when I asked him what it was, he said, 'That you and I are a lot alike. I've always been afraid of witches too!'

So did I think of Zencefil while sitting by my father's hospital cot so that I could be certain that he and I had a special bond? And had Dad also come to the same conclusion that I had – that Zencefil got her power over me from my equally menacing mother?

So many questions circled around my head that day, but none of them had a definite answer.

Half an hour or so after my arrival, Dad opened his eyes. Slowly, their gooey opacity cleared and he smiled. He signalled for me to help him take off his oxygen mask. 'Gosh it's good to see you,' he said in a croaking whisper. He snatched up my hand. With a grimace, he added, 'Please tell me that Rad is okay.'

'He's just fine,' I said. 'He's with Daniela and Mr Cupcake.' Mr Cupcake was Daniela's overweight basset hound.

'Thank God. That silly mutt is all I've been able to think about since waking up in this place.'

I sat back down and questioned him about what had happened to him, and he explained about the shooting pains in his chest and left arm. 'And then nothing,' he said with a shrug. 'Did they tell you I had a heart attack?'

'Yeah,' I replied.

He frowned. 'I wish I had my pipe.'

'I'm sure you can't smoke.'

When our eyes met, Dad sensed my worry and told me not to work myself into a tizzy, one of his favourite English expressions, and one that he'd learned while doing odd jobs for a wealthy British family in Salonika throughout high school. 'There's enough money in the bank for you to get your PhD. Everything's going to be okay.'

On his request, I helped him sit up. I fixed his pillow behind him because his back was sore.

He strained to smile. 'Listen, Teresa, if the worst happens, I don't want you being upset for me. Really. I've done everything I had to do.'

I glared at him. 'I won't be okay if something happens to you! Don't you dare say that!'

He jiggled his hand like he does to plead for calm. 'I'm sorry, I didn't mean it like that,' he said. 'I just meant you wouldn't have to give up school.'

When I sat back down, he told me – slowly, choosing his words carefully, because he could see how upset I was – that he was proud of me for being kind and beautiful and courageous, and he used the Ladino word for beautiful – *formosa* – so that I'd know he was talking about a great deal more than my appearance. He only began to cry when he asked me to look after my little sister, Evie, though not to 'crowd her' – which made both of us laugh through our tears, since she'd snapped at both of us the week before when we'd dared to question her about her new boyfriend.

When he asked about my flight in from San Francisco, I told him about the retired accountant who'd sat next to me. His name was James and he was on his way to Paris. 'He'd been stationed in Normandy during World War One,' I said. 'His best buddy – Claude – had been killed there. He told me that he was nervous to be going back. He sounded real embarrassed about that. He even raised his hand to cover his mouth and said so in whispers. And he also confessed that he was frightened to be flying. While we were descending toward JFK, he groaned and reached out for me, and he held on to me real tight till we landed.'

All through my story, I wondered why I was talking about James, but then I said something that surprised me: 'His hand was gigantic, and it was really warm. It moved me – how this handsome old war veteran with big warm hands trusted me.'

And just like that I was sobbing, and I realised I'd needed to talk about a stranger and the way he had confided in me, and feel all my gratitude, so that I would be free to weep about something other than my father being so frail and helpless, though we both knew that that was what my tears were really about, of course.

Dad motioned me to come to him, and I lay my head across his belly, and he rubbed my head. I was seven years old again, and he a young father wondering how he would be able to raise two little girls all by himself – though he'd kept that from me at the time. When I was finally old enough to understand how terrified he'd been, he told me that whenever he'd thought of telling me that he was scared, he played Beethoven on his piano instead.

'Did it work?' I asked.

'Yeah, most of the time – if there's anyone who understands terror, it's Beethoven.'

After I nodded my understanding, he asked, 'So why was James going back to France?'

'He said he was seventy-nine years old and he figured it was his last chance to let Claude and his other friends who'd died know that he'd never forgotten them. He kept calling them his buddies. I liked that. It was like he was still eighteen years old. Anyway, the thing is, whenever he talked about the war and his old pals, his eyes . . . they opened real wide and got all glassy, as if they were reflecting a magical landscape.'

'Maybe World War One was his Golden Age,' Dad said, and I said, 'You think so?' and he replied, 'For the men who fought . . . if you read what they wrote, it was always the war that made them feel most alive.'

'How about you? When was your Golden Age?' I asked.

'Me?' He scratched the whiskers on his chin, and I knew he'd have filled the bowl of his pipe if he'd had it with him. 'I think it was when you and Evie were little. Just after your mom . . . after she left. There was always one more emergency around the corner, and there was never enough money, but I never felt more alive. It was wonderful!'

'I guess it was another kind of war,' I said.

'Yeah, I think you're right,' he said with a quick laugh.

Dad grew short of breath after that, and I helped him put his oxygen mask back on. He sensed my apprehension and took my hand. I knew what he'd have said if he weren't wearing the mask, and it was, *Everything is going to be okay, I promise*, which he'd told me a thousand times after my mom left us. After a while, I felt the world withdraw, and his moist brown eyes told me all I needed to know about the kind of man he was. For a few minutes, it seemed to me that he and I were alone on an island, and that we had always been there even when we thought we were somewhere else.

The sound of people walking in the hallway broke our intimacy, and he took off his oxygen mask again. He said he needed to tell me about his finances.

'Now?' I asked, and he shot back, 'Yeah, do you know a better time?'

While he was listing what he kept in his safety deposit box, I started combing his thick brown hair out of his eyes.

'Tessa, are you listening?' he snarled.

'Of course,' I lied.

After a while, all his talk of things that didn't interest me made me want to plead for a coffee break, but I didn't, because his precise tone told me how important this was to him.

Once he'd finished his list, he asked me to put some of the balm I always kept in my bag on his crusted lips. Then, while I was fixing his blanket, his eyes fluttered closed. I planned to tiptoe out, but he awakened the moment I stood up. 'You still here?' he asked.

'Yeah, you okay?'

He nodded. After I helped him drink some water he asked me to go to Daniela's apartment and bring Radley back home. 'He must have been terrified when I fell over, so please tell him I'm doing well and that I miss him and that you'll give him his regular dog food.'

'I'm not sure his vocabulary is that large.'

'No, but he'll sense your relief. And listen, a warning – he might jump in your bed tonight and whine a lot and want to snuggle with you.'

'As long as he sleeps with his muzzle facing away from me, that's fine,' I said.

'Why, what's wrong with his muzzle?' he asked in an offended voice, which was what I'd hoped, since I was eager for a bit more humour.

'Sorry, Dad, those wholewheat dog biscuits you bake him give him really bad breath!'

My father shook his fist at me, and in his squinting brown eyes I saw a decade of back-and-forth banter, which made me understand that my effort at humour was also about trying to go back to the way things had been before his heart attack. But when I took a last look at him from the doorway, his eyes were closed and he was again making a whistle on every exhale, and I realised that I'd failed to get there.

Radley and I did indeed share my bed that night, but he hunted for Dad in the morning – sniffing in every corner of the apartment, and when I got his leash, he dashed into my father's bathroom and refused to go for a walk, so that I had to pick him up and carry

him outside. I'd been up most of the night juggling my options –
trying in vain to keep a dozen alternatives in the air – but while
strolling with him on St Mark's Place, past a shop with garish,
tie-dyed T-shirts in the window, I realised that only one of them
was realistic.

Had Dad reached the same conclusion? The moment I walked
into his room, he waved me over and said in a hoarse whisper,
'Teresa, I'll be furious with you if you put off graduate school!'

When I hesitated to reply, he told me that I'd be a fool to give
up my plans. I didn't dare risk a quarrel, so I told him we'd talk
about it later.

'No, now!' he ordered.

'Later!' I shot back. 'So how did you sleep?'

'A lot you care!' he snapped.

I sat with him and kissed his brow and said – with what I hoped
was an encouraging smile – that his unshaved cheeks made him
look like his father in one of the photographs he'd brought with
him to America, which I thought would please him, but misery
crossed his face and made his throat catch when he tried to speak.

'What's wrong?' I asked, and he whispered, 'If only Papa could
have once held you as a baby. He'd have loved you like crazy.'

Dad cried while I rubbed his frozen hands. Afterward, we
sat together without talking for a long time. He slept on and off.
When we did speak, it was mostly about Evie and the misfits that
she'd had as high-school boyfriends; it was a safe topic, and one
that had become part of our family comedy routine.

That afternoon, I spoke to Dr Johnson, the chairman of
Berkeley's Music Department, and he agreed to postpone my
enrolment – and my scholarship – to the spring of 1966. Over
the next few days, Dad did his best to make me reconsider – even
lectured me about being true to myself in a dramatic voice – but

I'd inherited what he called *Sephardic stubbornness*, and he began to grudgingly accept my decision.

A week or so later, I was able to sublet my apartment near campus to a graduate student in French literature from Seattle.

My father started walking by himself about three weeks after his heart attack, and he was so grateful for his renewed independence that he would erupt into peals of laughter at Radley's antics, especially the way he'd gnaw on a carrot while holding it between his paws, and how he'd bark and pounce when the carrot slipped out of his grip. Sometimes Dad laughed so hard that he had to hold himself up on the nearest wall to keep from sliding straight to the floor.

My father's doctors were pleased by his progress, he and Radley kept each other in high spirits, and I was pretty sure he wouldn't start smoking again after I left, so in early November I gave notice to the graduate student subletting my apartment that she'd have to move out by January 15th. Meanwhile, my father went back to work part-time at New York University Press, where he managed printing and graphic design. In early December, however, his diabetes created circulation problems in his right leg, and he had to go back into the hospital, and a surgeon called in on his case told me that if the problem continued much longer he'd have to operate.

'Operate in what way?' I asked.

'I'm afraid I'll have to amputate the leg,' he said.

The choking panic I felt while trying to fit the words *amputate the leg* in my head reminded me that Dad telling me in the hospital that I was courageous was wishful thinking – perhaps the greatest wish he'd ever had for me, in fact.

Once again, my dad seemed at peace, however. Sitting up in his hospital cot, he told me that he'd be fine in a wheelchair as long as he could still get to work and play electric piano with his

Dixieland band once every few weeks and watch NBA games on Sunday with Radley. His smile was genuine, but when I came back unexpectedly quickly from getting coffee, I caught him sobbing into his pillow, his knees up by his chest, and his eyes were so red when he looked up at me that I thought they'd been bleeding.

Evie had visited us over two weekends by then. She had recently cut her blonde hair into bangs – in imitation of Cher, I guessed – and stopped putting on all the goopy make-up she'd used as a teenager to try to make herself look older. She was tall and willowy and fair – like a girl from the prairies. Just before she'd started college, Dad had remarked that even her shadow now seemed a lesser form of light, and it was true.

Sometimes it seemed to me that Evie and I were different species; like my father, I was olive-skinned and dark-haired. He'd referred to me as his Sephardic princess when I was little.

The day after I caught Dad sobbing, Evie visited us again – it was a Friday – and I took her out to lunch at the Second Avenue Deli so that I could tell her about the possibility of him losing a leg. Dad was convinced that she would come to terms with it more easily without having to speak to him about it in the hospital.

'Evie likes circling around her troubles,' he'd told me. 'She's like Rad when he's picking a place to sit.'

'Next you'll tell me that she barks at garbage trucks and sheds on the sofa.'

'No, but she once drank out of a toilet bowl,' he observed.

I laughed so hard that I began to sneeze – an idiosyncrasy I'd had since I was little. 'Is that true?' I asked.

'Absolutely. It was when we visited Washington DC and stayed at the Mayflower. The hotel sink was too high for her, poor thing.'

Dad spoke as if Evie's behaviour were admirable, and maybe

it was, but his serious face only made me laugh again, which gave him a chance to pretend to be angry at me.

At such moments, I knew I'd never find someone as unintentionally funny as my dad.

Just after Evie and I ordered our lunch, and while I was planning my strategy, she engaged me a conversation about the furniture she'd bought for her new apartment, and from there she moved on to her favourite class at Bard College, which was topology. While she was telling me about what she called the *uniqueness of manifold spaces*, I picked around my stuffed cabbage and realised – astonished – that she'd turned into a mathematician.

After we left the restaurant, we started ambling down Second Avenue, and she began looking over at me – her shoulders hunched, her hands joined behind her neck – as if she were terrified. 'It's bad news about Dad, isn't it?' she asked timidly.

'It might be. But let's not talk on the street.'

We walked to Washington Square Park, where I sat her down on a bench and told her about the complications that diabetes might cause.

She cried in my arms while I rubbed her back, and we held hands on the way home, swinging them between us as if we'd gone back in time a decade and were walking together to school, which is how I re-learned the shape and feel of her.

That afternoon, as we made dinner, she kissed me a couple of times for no reason, like when we were kids.

I checked on her before going to bed. While I stood in the doorway, she made the compressed face she makes when she's too upset to talk, but she fought to find her voice – a sign of maturity I hadn't seen before – and promised me, as though speaking a vow, that she'd help me and Dad any way she could, even if it meant quitting college. I sat with her and told her that leaving school was out of the question. She nodded, and I nodded back, and silence spread between us, and she yawned real big, and then I did, and we ended up laughing. I was about to stand up and go when she threw her arms around me and buried her head at my neck, and the fresh, warm scent of her was like the answer to a question I hadn't even known I'd asked – a question about how much Dad and I might still mean to her. And I remembered again what I'd already forgotten a dozen times over the course of my life – that she was as devoted to us as we were to her.

Happily, Dad, me and Evie never had to learn how we'd react to his being confined to a wheelchair; blood thinners helped partially restore his circulation a few days later, and after a week he was doing well. Still, to be safe, I decided to postpone my graduate studies to the fall.

'What's a few more months?' I told him.

'Bunny Rabbit, you don't understand,' he said, shaking his head – and using the name he's had for me since I was a little girl.

'What don't I understand?' I asked.

In a menacing tone, he replied, 'A few months can last a lifetime.' Dad often used Ladino as an exclamation point, and he added, '*Un minuto puede cambiar todo.*'

A minute can change everything.

I was too young to consider that what he was telling me wasn't nearly as glib as it sounded, that it was, in fact, the slender tip of a great mystery – of how we become the person we will one day be, when we could have become so many other people.

I knew that if Mom had been willing to help, I'd have been able to start graduate school, but she had made it clear four years before that she didn't want any contact with me and Evie and Dad. I'd last spoken to her at the beginning of my freshman year at the state university in Binghamton. At that time, I decided to try to restrain my anger at her for abandoning me and Evie when we were little and try to track her down. I soon discovered that she was living in West Hollywood, and although she didn't hang up on me when I called, she spoke to me in a deeply suspicious tone, as if I were about to start shrieking at her or reveal some terrible ulterior motive for getting back in touch. She told me that she wouldn't be able to visit me during parents' week, which I'd used as my pretext for re-establishing contact. In a voice permitting no dissent, she'd said that she was about to fly to Rome with her new boyfriend. He was an Italian-American cameraman named Franco Spinelli, and he was set to start work on a movie being shot by Roberto Rossellini.

Hearing her voice again – after eleven years without speaking – made me feel so fragile and needy that tears rose into my eyes, and I wanted to tell her how much I'd missed her, but I sensed it would only distance her further from me.

'Going to Rome is my chance to meet some really big European stars!' she said excitedly.

Once she realised that I wasn't going to berate her or ask her questions she didn't want to have to answer, she became a lot more friendly, and despite my disappointment that she wouldn't be able to visit me at college, we ended up giggling like star-struck teenagers about Anna Magnani, Marcello Mastroianni and all the other Italian actors she might meet. I had hopes that we could be back in touch with each other on a regular basis, and that I might be able to finally tell her how badly she'd hurt Evie and me, but after she returned from Rome, she never called. When I tried to reach her, I discovered that her phone had been disconnected. Evie eventually got a hold of Franco Spinelli's phone number, and he told her that he and Mom had moved to Santa Monica. 'We had dinner the other night with Warren Beatty!' he boasted, doing his best to imply they'd become Hollywood A-listers. After I conversed with him for a little while, Mom got on the phone and said that she'd had lunch with Mastroianni at a fashionable trattoria in Rome and that he was 'incredibly handsome and incomparably charming,' which seemed so clichéd a remark that I began to wonder if she might not have met him after all.

In any case, Mom told me that she'd secured work as an assistant scriptwriter on *Bonanza*. When I summoned the courage to ask her why she'd moved without giving me her new phone number, she said, 'I'm sorry, Teresa, but I've had enough of mothering for one lifetime. *Basta*!'

Over my first few months with Dad, my qualms about putting off my studies abated, in large part, I think, because of my need to care for him and do our household errands. Whenever I'd sense myself trapped by circumstance, I'd learn a new piece on my flute or take Radley on a walk or go to a museum with one of my old friends. I'd make dinner for me and my father nearly every night, as well, and I enjoyed shopping at the cramped Asian markets in Chinatown and inventing unusual recipes. My ungenerous and occasionally murderous daydreams about my mother – about how she had always failed me and Evie when we needed her most – ought to have convinced me that something dangerous had taken root in my spirit, but I never stopped to consider what my unspoken desires were trying to tell me.

I thought I knew myself well, but I was just twenty-two years old, after all.

Right after our Hanukkah celebrations, a mist of despair seemed to seep into Dad's apartment, however. I remember that I was watching a light snowfall out my bedroom window one afternoon when I had my first ever panic attack. I felt as if my heart might burst, but I didn't call out to Dad or dial 911. I suppose I sensed that the true origin of my pain was in my mind. I lay down on my bed and closed my eyes, and I listened to 'Jesu, Joy of Man's Desiring' in my head, and after a few minutes I was able to get enough air into my lungs. It was while I was staring at my sweaty face in the bathroom mirror that I grew certain that my plans for Brazil had been foolish. And I saw – in my lost eyes, most clearly – that I had no idea what to do with my life. What had made me think that any musicians in Amazonia would trust me? Very possibly, none of them would know enough Portuguese to understand what I was asking them.

After a second panic attack a few days later, the idea of dining out with friends or going to the movies with Dad would start my heart racing. And by the beginning of the new year, playing my flute became nearly impossible; the music itself – all those thousands of notes – started to make me feel as if I were being slowly suffocated.

I was reminded that I wasn't so different from the shy and moody twelve-year-old girl who refused to attend her elementary-school graduation because her mother wouldn't be there. And I began to dislike everything I'd loved. I wondered if the ambitious and enthusiastic young woman I'd been had been merely a role I'd adopted to fool myself and everyone else. Even my father's delight in Radley began to enrage me.

A word of advice: if you become jealous of a dachshund, it's time to get back to the life you really want.

The only thing I forced myself to do was read the news section in the *New York Times*, because I was determined to keep myself informed about the Vietnam War. Looking back, I think that the rush of moral outrage that the articles brought out in me made me feel as if I was still the same young woman I'd been before I'd postponed my plans for graduate school.

My father continued working half-days in January, and I'd do my best to appear alert and cheerful at breakfast, but as soon as he left the apartment, I'd go to my room and watch TV. I'd only leave the apartment to walk Radley and do our food shopping at a neighbourhood market. Whenever *Bonanza* would come on, I'd imagine my mom writing all the worst lines of dialogue and – to the cringing embarrassment of her boyfriend and his Hollywood buddies – being really proud of them.

In my mind, the mother I pictured was nearly always laughing at me – at the defeated young woman I'd become. If I had been a fan of gothic novels or low-budget horror movies, I'd have said she was haunting me and had used her spells to drain away all my self-assurance.

Once in a while, I'd stop what I was doing and wonder how a mother I hadn't seen in fifteen years – and whom I'd never trusted – could have so much power over me. And how I'd changed so quickly. But perhaps I hadn't. Maybe the abandoned little girl inside me had been waiting for a convenient reason to give up on all her plans.

Whenever an old high-school friend wouldn't take no for an answer and insist on coming over, I'd say that my father had taken a turn for the worse and that we weren't permitted guests. I was sure that no one would understand my panic attacks or sympathise with my rage at my mother. Maybe, too, I secretly understood already that I didn't want anyone looking below my surface, because what they'd find there wasn't particularly *formosa*.

After a time, my father sensed how despondent I was, and he started telling me I had to go back to Berkeley, but I swore to him that I was fine and asked him to 'stop hounding me,' as I put it. He ended up giving me an ultimatum in mid-February – if I didn't go back to California within two months, he'd change the lock on his front door without telling me, and not even my begging or sobbing would convince him to let me back in.

His anger seemed misdirected and cruel. I was furious with him.

'But my plans for Brazil were silly,' I finally admitted to him at supper one evening.

He crashed his fork to the tab. 'Teresa, I won't permit you to put yourself down! Your mother used to do that all the time, and I hated it! Now listen up . . . I've known since you were seven years old that you were unusually talented. And if you think I'm going to let you waste your life, you've got another thing coming!'

'How could you be so sure I was so talented?' I asked, and he replied, 'Don't you remember?' and I said, 'No,' so he said, 'You learned to play songs from my collection of seventy-eights when you were this tall.' He held his hand about two feet from the floor. 'I remember that one day I came home and slipped Fred Astaire singing 'Puttin' on the Ritz' on the record player, and afterward you tooted it back for me *note for note*! Don't you recall?'

'No.'

'You played in perfect syncopated rhythm! Seven years old and you already knew how to swing!' Dad sang the first verse of the song in a snappy voice he uses to imitate Fred Astaire, and then added in a conspiratorial tone, 'Your mom and I used to say that she'd given birth to an extraterrestrial!'

Dad burst into delighted laughter. And I burst into tears. In his arms, my fantasies about Brazil drifted back to me, hesitant and shy. In bed that night, gazing out my window at the crescent moon, I discovered that the tropical waters were still soft and warm, and my handsome, bronze-skinned shaman whispered, *I've been waiting for you for months, hoping you'd come back.*

I learned that night that the whispers of a dream lover – even one as unlikely as an English-speaking Brazilian shaman – are a disguised form of hope.

The next morning, I took out my flute and tested my ear by playing back jingles I heard on the radio, and when I played 'Puttin' on the Ritz' from memory, I realised that there was a kind of hidden magic working through me, though I had no idea where it had come from.

A few days later, I sat in on a couple of songs with Dad's Dixieland band – the Black Cats – at a bar mitzvah in Brooklyn, and my high-flying solo on 'Young at Heart' – all those bird-like notes at the top of my range – made realise I had nearly become myself again. How had I become such a stranger over so many agonised weeks? It seemed improbable – almost too peculiar to believe.

Toward the end of February, when I told Dad I'd go back to Berkeley in April, he raised his hands and started singing Handel's 'Hallelujah' chorus.

That evening, he took me to our favourite restaurant – Arezzo – to celebrate. Radley came too, and he sat under our table, moaning with delight while gobbling down our pizza crusts. The tingling of the pepperoni on my tongue made me feel as if I'd re-entered my body after a long absence.

Only a few days later, however, my best friend from high school insisted that I meet her and one of her housemates for dinner because she wanted me and other friends to model at a fashion show they were organising, and everything started off in a different direction yet again.

Fia Simonetta and I had been inseparable in high school, and after college at NYU, she moved into a dilapidated old apartment in the

Lower East Side that smelled like cat pee and discarded clothing because one of her flatmates owned six cats, and the other – Margerie 'Moonlight' Levitsky – was a hippy fashion designer who kept rolls and rolls of garish, bargain-basement fabrics in the living room.

Moonlight later helped some of the members of the Symbionese Liberation Army flee arrest after they kidnapped Patty Hearst, but that crime was eight years away from happening, and at the time she seemed perfectly harmless to me and Fia.

The three of us agreed to meet at my favourite restaurant, a small Turkish place called the Bosphorus. It was on Bleecker Street, just a block from the Bitter End. I wore a stunning wine-coloured woollen coat – with 1920s-style wide lapels – that Moonlight had made for me, since I knew it would please her. I arrived a few minutes early and stood in front of the panoramic photograph of Istanbul in the window. Droning music was coming from the record player inside.

By six-fifteen, I figured that Fia and Moonlight had been held up, and I was about to go back home and wait for them to call when a short man with shaggy black hair stepped up to me. His big, dark, sad-looking eyes and fancy grey suit made him look like a well-dressed raccoon.

I'd noticed him standing for some time on the other side of the doorway, smoking nervously. I figured he was waiting for his date.

'This is my favourite restaurant in the whole world,' he said.

Mine, too, I almost replied, but I didn't want to give him any hope of picking me up, and simply nodded.

'Are you okay?' he asked with an accent I couldn't identify.

'Sure,' I replied, 'why wouldn't I be?'

My gruff tone must have unnerved him, because his English grew shaky and he said, 'You have looked a bit worried. Maybe you wait for someone?'

'Old friends,' I replied, and just to be safe, I added, 'And my boyfriend is joining us later.' He flashed a smile that seemed more of a call for help. 'I'm waiting for a friend too,' he said. I gazed down, hoping he'd go away.

'I'm a tailor, and my name is Benjamin,' he said. 'I tell you that because your jacket is lovely, but the lapels aren't sewn correctly. If you want, I could maybe sew them again for you.'

'Listen, I'm sure you mean well,' I told him, 'but I want to wait for my friends by myself.'

I spoke more harshly than I meant to, and his eyes teared up. After he moved back to the other side of the door, he lit another cigarette and gazed away from me as if he'd been punished.

Thankfully, Fia and Moonlight came along a minute or so later and rescued me from my guilt.

On March 26th, Dad and I marched in a rally against the Vietnam War with twenty thousand other protestors. The atmosphere was festive and zany, and for a while we walked behind a heavily made-up British cross-dresser impersonating Queen Elizabeth, who held up a sign reading THIS WAR IS A ROYAL DISASTER! At one point, Dad and the rest of the Black Cats got him and everybody else around us singing 'When Our Troops Come Marching Home' to the tune of 'When the Saints Go Marching In'.

As we were passing the Metropolitan Museum, I spotted a short, dark-haired man in a powder-blue suit holding up a sign on the corner of Fifth Avenue and 81st Street, and what it said would give me insomnia over the next several days. In handwritten black letters, it read HOLOCAUST SURVIVORS AGAINST THE WAR. Underneath that slogan was a big yellow Jewish star.

I looked from the sign back to the Metropolitan Museum, then up to two pigeons perched on its rooftop, and when I looked behind me, I saw a woman with red hair at her window, observing the protestors and eating what looked like a baked potato, and everything around me – even my father's questioning smile – seemed to have been staged. Later, I realised it was because I became so aware of the separation between my own self and the rest of the world. And I think that was because I needed to remember exactly where I was when I figured out why reading about the Vietnam War often made me feel physically ill. When my father asked if something was wrong, I pointed out the man in the powder-blue suit.

'Look what his sign says,' I said.

From the dispirited way Dad gazed at me afterward, I knew he was thinking of his parents and brother and sister, and his seven aunts and uncles, all of whom had been dragged from their homes in Salonika and sent on transport trains to Auschwitz, and of how there was a hollow in his life where there ought to have been an entire world, and how no one he knew could speak Ladino with him except me and Evie. I took his hand, and we continued walking without saying a word, because there was nothing we could say that was as eloquent or important as *Holocaust Survivors Against the War*.

That afternoon, I remembered that when I was a girl, I used to fantasise about our relatives in Salonika, and how, if Hitler hadn't been born, they'd have put me up in their little whitewashed houses by the beach and insisted on fattening me up with moussaka and dried figs, and . . .

It seemed astonishing and shameful to me that no one until that spring day had had the courage to say, or even think, that America's bombs and bullets and flamethrowers were creating a Holocaust for the Vietnamese people.

The man holding the sign stood arm and arm with a heavyset elderly woman in a floral dress. They were conversing with an easy complicity that made me think she was his grandmother. Only when I got closer to 81st Street did he look familiar, and a little later, after we were already a couple of blocks away, I realised that he looked like the tailor I'd met outside the Bosphorus.

I left the march and walked back to 81st Street, and, from a safe distance away, listened to him talking to the old woman next to him in what sounded like Polish or Russian, and I was soon certain that he was the man I'd met. My shame at having treated him badly made me shiver.

I thought of stepping up to him and apologising, but a slender blonde woman in an unflattering low-cut dress strode up to him and shouted that he was a disgrace to the Jewish people and to all the victims of the Nazis. Benjamin asked her to please leave him be, his voice admirably calm, but she pointed a damning figure at him and snarled that he would go to hell for embarrassing the Jews in front of the *goyim*, and her enraged face made her look like a demon in a medieval illumination. He must have thought something like that too, because after she rushed away, he fumbled the cigarette he was trying to light and started cursing to himself, and he seemed about to melt into tears. When his grandmother reached for his arm and started whispering to him, I realised my chance to approach him had vanished.

A few weeks later – four days before my flight to California – I was moving around the antennas on Dad's television set to try to get better reception on the Channel 2 news, and when I finally got a decent image, I saw Benjamin the tailor sitting on an outdoor staircase. A reporter I didn't recognise explained that he'd chained himself to the railing of the military induction centre at 39 Whitehall Street in lower Manhattan. He was holding in his lap a small version of his sign I'd seen him carrying on Fifth Avenue – HOLOCAUST SURVIVORS AGAINST THE WAR.

I shouted for my dad to stop playing Scott Joplin on his piano and come see what was on the news. He rushed in, Radley in his arms, as a reporter asked, 'Are you really a Holocaust survivor?'

The journalist's tone was sceptical, but Benjamin replied in that slow and even voice of his – which I now realised wasn't so much calm as controlled – 'I spent more than a year in Warsaw ghetto when I was a boy, and then I went into hiding, and at one point I lived for more than eight months in a room not much bigger than a closet, and I could never go outside. The Nazis murdered my parents and all my aunts and uncles. So, do I pass your test, Mr Reporter?'

'I love that man!' Dad said, beaming.

The journalist asked, 'But what do you hope to accomplish, other than getting yourself arrested?'

Benjamin's eyes narrowed. 'Have you seen the photographs of Vietnamese men and women and children being burned to death by napalm? I have, and it's a crime against humanity, and I intend to do what I can to stop it.'

My chest heaved, and I began to sob, which set Dad off, too. 'I've got to find that man and shake his hand,' he said through his tears, and I wanted to say, *I've already met him*, but I was too ashamed of how I'd behaved to admit it.

I flew back to Berkeley at the end of April, and, to my great relief, the professor I'd asked to supervise my thesis – Dickson Applewhite – agreed to work with me. In June, after I'd read and annotated every book and paper that he could find for me about Irish and Scottish traditional music, we flew to Asheville, North Carolina so that he could direct my first experiences in the field. Over the previous seventeen years, he'd collected traditional Scots-Irish songs sung by the people of Appalachia.

Dickson had a memory for melodies that far surpassed my own – he called it his *music catalogue* – and in his pleasantly warbling voice he could sing more than three hundred songs that he'd recorded in Appalachia, Ireland and Scotland. He looked like a television version of a Southern lawyer, sporting an impeccably ironed white shirt, often with the sleeves rolled up, and a colourful bowtie. He had a Piedmont accent that he tended to thicken into a syrupy drawl around young women, and over our first week together he took great pleasure in telling me endless stories about all the mishaps with insects, floods and hunters in his fieldwork, exaggerating his own bumbling nature in an effort to make me laugh. Pity the innocent nitwit I then was; only when he tried to kiss me one evening over the pasta I'd made for our supper did it occur to me that he'd been trying to seduce me from the moment I'd first stepped into his office. I might have even ended up his summer girlfriend, but he was fifty-seven years old, and too paunchy and pale for my liking. Although he kept up a barrage of seductively humorous stories over the next few days, he eventually shifted his attentions to a young waitress working her way through college at the Little Pigs restaurant in Asheville, and she ended up sharing his bedroom at the cramped little house near the Blue Ridge Highway that we'd rented.

What I remember most from my first few weeks in the field was the shocking poverty. That summer, I encountered families living in one-room shacks with dirt floors and foul-smelling outhouses. Most of the adults had never set foot in a schoolhouse or visited a doctor's office. Mothers cooked on wood-burning stoves, made their kid's clothing on handmade looms and kept chickens and pigs in makeshift pens. Boys and girls ran around everywhere barefoot, even in town.

Yes, there were tens of thousands of illiterate men and women in the mountains of North Carolina in 1966.

The insistent mosquitoes and oppressive, sluggish heat made me think that the chills and fevers some of the people suffered from might even be symptoms of malaria, though the doctors I later consulted in New York were dubious. Malaria in America? Of course, they had no idea of the America that was hidden inside the Blue Ridge Mountains. I often wished I could've handed out antibiotics and hundred-dollar bills to everyone I came across.

Dickson interviewed all the men who agreed to talk to us, because he said they'd either distrust me or try to get me into bed, so I collected songs exclusively from women.

The woman who most influenced me that summer was Belle, a quick-tongued, wiry, sixty-four-year-old widow, though her dark, sun-toughened hide and deep wrinkles made her look a good deal older. She had long, beautiful hands, and a keen-eyed, intelligent expression that made me certain that she could teach me a great deal of what I hadn't learned from my mother. I took a roll of photos of her before flying home, and the good-natured humour in her expression – and tolerance for the over-excited graduate student taking the pictures – always reminds me of the generosity of most of the women I interviewed.

On her front door, Belle kept a plastic laurel wreath, and under it was a sign that read ALL ARE WELCOME HERE, FOR ALL OF US WERE ONCE STRANGERS IN EGYPT.

Belle often spoke in such Biblical language. She explained that her father had been a fire-and-brimstone preacher who'd roamed throughout the Carolinas and Tennessee, and that he'd sing verses of Genesis to her in improvised lullabies when she was small.

Belle had had eleven children, but two had died at birth and another three hadn't lived long enough to start first grade at the little wooden schoolhouse – topped by a weathervane of a coyote – four miles to the east. She made stunningly patterned baskets out of oak splints cut by her oldest son, Jeremiah, slept under a thick cotton quilt stitched by her grandmother in every kind of weather and made the most delicious apple sauce I ever tasted in a kind of leveraged press that her ancestors had carried with them from Scotland two hundred years earlier.

Belle confessed to me one day when we were walking to her youngest daughter's house for lunch that if she'd have had her own money hidden somewhere, she'd have left her late-husband after having her first child. 'Levon wasn't much of a likeable man when he was on the juice,' she confided to me. 'It made him lazy and downright mean.'

When I inquired where she'd have gone if she'd left him, she said, 'To the ocean.' And when I asked why, she said it was because the ocean embraced every beach and shore in the world, and she was certain that those mighty waters would tell her what to do.

Belle was also a clairvoyant and a healer, though it took me months to feel comfortable using those terms. On several occasions, she put a hand of blessing on my head in an effort to 'join what has been broken inside your soul,' as she put it, and once, when we were alone, she told me details about my life that were impossible for her to know – for instance that I was nearly always worried about my little sister, because our mother had abandoned her and me when we were too young to understand why. After I told Belle my sister's name, she looked me straight in the eye and told me what I was most afraid of hearing, that Evie – like me – sometimes blamed herself for our mom's departure. She also said that my sister had kept a keepsake from our mother. When I called Evie that evening to ask, she said she couldn't recall holding on to anything of Mom's, but then she called me back in the morning and exclaimed, 'Yeah, it's true – I grabbed her lipstick – that dark shade she used to wear. I'd completely forgotten!'

Whenever I'd visit Belle, the first thing she'd do was put my hands in hers and bless me, and I grew certain after a time that I was touching holiness.

'Everyone should have the chance to know someone as magical as Belle,' I told my father when I first spoke to him about her.

In my dreams about that summer, Belle and I are often floating around her yard, above the rusted old Ford that had belonged to Levon, and we stay up in the air without any effort, and when I wake up, I'm convinced that it is her love for me – her selfless love – that keeps us aloft. The most important *reading* of me that she made came after I told her about my dad's heart attack, and how I'd isolated myself afterward. She was silent for a long time after that, darning a grandson's socks, and then she told me something *you won't want to know*, as she put it.

'Tell me anyway,' I said.

'I'm pretty sure your mom had never liked you from the start.'

It was just before I was set to leave Appalachia for good, and by then, I didn't need to ask her how she knew what she knew, so I asked her instead why Mom had never taken to me.

'I don't know that, child, but you'll have to figure that out if she ever returns to haunt you.'

Among other songs that Belle taught me that summer was 'Creeping Dan', which Dickson discovered to be a variant of 'Creeping Jane', a song that he'd collected near Knoxville a decade earlier. In the song, Dan is the Angel of Death, and each verse is about how he creeps up on his victims and tosses the bitter candy of death in their mouth. Belle could no longer hold a tune so well, but she taught me the melody by plucking the top string of a guitar brought to her by her eldest grandson, Luther, who lived just a few hundred yards away.

She also surprised me one day by calling Luther's girlfriend his *doney*, which seemed related to the Ladino word *dona*. I was the first person to tell Belle it wasn't a word in standard English, though she refused to believe me. Later, I learned that the word probably made its way to Scotland with Spaniards taken prisoner during the Armada.

From Belle, I learned that sharing our childhood songs can deepen trust and respect. After teaching me the words to 'Creeping Dan', for instance, she whispered something to me that she'd never confessed to her husband or any of her children – how her Uncle Sonny – her father's brother – had stood her in front of her mother's mirror when she was eleven years old and put his hand under her dress and told her that she mustn't ever tell anyone what he was going to do to her or Creeping Dan would come and toss a bitter candy in her mouth.

'But I'd already seen what men have between their legs,' Belle told me, 'and I said that he'd better get away from me or the Lord'd strike him down. That didn't stop him, of course, and he started puttin' his big ugly fingers in me, so I told him I wasn't scared of Creepin' Dan because the Lord was my shepherd, and I started hollerin' for Momma, and he clasped his hand over my mouth so tight that I tasted the dirt on his palm. But Momma came running up onto the porch a few seconds later, and Uncle Sonny took his hand back quicker than summer lightning.'

'Did you tell your momma what he'd done?'

'No, 'cause she'd have grabbed Daddy's shotgun and shot him down dead.'

In mid-July I flew to New York before returning to Berkeley. By then, my face had tanned to the colour of cinnamon, and I was covered everywhere with little scabs where I'd scratched my mosquito bites. I'd also clipped my hair real short in an effort to stay cool. On first seeing me, my father said I looked like a porcupine and smelled like one, too, which gave him the bright, mischievous laugh that always made me think he must have been a terror when he was young.

Over that first blessed week in New York, Dad's air conditioning seemed like the most important invention of all time, and I stayed up late with him every night, rejoicing in all that chilly air, hugging my sweater around me, telling him about Belle and the other good people I'd met. I realised while answering his questions that the songs their ancestors had brought with them from Scotland, Ireland and northern England seemed a noble heritage. And that transcribing their lyrics and melodies had become a great responsibility.

My plans were to go back to Berkeley in early September, when I'd start teaching music theory to undergraduates. I was also going to study with a fluent speaker of Ticuna – one of the indigenous languages of Brazil – whom Dickson had found for me. Her name was Líria Conti, and she was a graduate student in genetics at Stanford. Líria had spent the first eight years of her life in Amazonia, in her mother's village, but her father was of Italian heritage, and he'd brought her and her mother to Manaus when Líria was nine. In January, she was returning to her mother's village for a few months. I'd already spoken to her twice, and she'd agreed to find me a place to live among her kin.

A few days after my arrival, Dad said he'd invited a special guest over for dinner – 'A Sephardic Jew like me,' he said.

'You're not trying to set me up with someone, are you?' I asked. 'Because I spent a month fending off a horny old professor who wears bowties and talks like he's in a Southern novel.'

'What a suspicious mind you've got!' Dad said, feigning

irritation. 'It's just somebody I thought you'd like. Besides, he's over thirty – way too mature and gentlemanly for a little Bunny Rabbit like you,' he said dismissively.

For supper, my father was making his mother's couscous with eggplant, carrot and cilantro. As a starter, we were having her zucchini-and-parmesan fritters.

Dad had immigrated to America in 1937, when he was twenty-four years old, carrying only two books with him, and one of them was a handwritten collection of his mother's recipes. The other was Stendhal's *Le Rouge et le Noir*, a gift from his French-speaking father. For years, Dad slept with those two books under his pillow, though he kept them now in his safety deposit box.

His parents' strategy was to get their children to America before the Nazis invaded Greece – which seemed a certainty to them – but they'd only managed to save up enough money to send Dad – their eldest – to safety. His younger sister, Tamara, ended up in Auschwitz and his baby brother, Ari, was shot by the Nazis or Greek police while trying to escape across the border to Turkey near the town of Orestiada.

I recognised our guest the moment I opened the door to his knocks. 'Oh, my God,' I said. 'It's you.'

Benjamin the tailor took in a quick intake of breath and grimaced. He was dressed like Jay Gatsby, in a pale-pink linen suit, a cream-coloured shirt and a mother-of-pearl bolo tie that I'd later discover to be a representation of the Navajo sun god. In his right hand he carried a showy bouquet of violet-coloured tulips and in his left he secured a shopping bag printed with the name *Cagney's Sporting Goods* in big black letters.

'Didn't I . . . didn't I meet you a few months ago . . . at the Bosphorus?' he stammered.

'Yes, that was me,' I told him.

'You look different.'

'Because I cut my hair, and I'm all tan.'

'I don't understand. Do you live here, in this apartment?'

I nodded. 'I grew up here. My dad still lives here. I'm visiting him. Did he invite you over?'

Benjamin heaved a sigh. 'Is your father ... is he Maurice Sasportes?'

His reticent, uneasy tone made it clear that he was hoping I'd say that he'd come to the wrong apartment, leaving him free to turn and run back down the stairs. But it was too late to lie. 'Yes, that's my dad,' I said.

'He and I met the other day,' Benjamin said. 'He invited me to dinner. But maybe it would be better if I ... you know ... if I left.'

Radley was standing next to me, and he was panting as if he'd just run a marathon, since guests – particularly men – put him in a frenzy. I leaned down, grabbed the rhinestone-studded collar I'd brought him from Asheville and told him to shush.

'That you, Benjamin?' Dad shouted from the kitchen.

Our guest didn't reply. He stared at me and raised his eyebrows questioningly.

'Yes, it's him!' I called back, since my father might come in at any moment and see us.

'Bring him in here, Tessa!' Dad called out.

Radley started barking since he wasn't getting what he wanted. Benjamin squatted down and petted his ears and muzzle, telling him that he was very handsome, which set the mutt moaning and licking at the air in an effort to get a taste of the man's face.

'You'd think he was starved for affection, but my father spoils him rotten,' I said.

'What's his name?' Benjamin asked, standing back up, so I said, 'Radley,' which made him squint and ask in surprised tone, 'Like Boo Radley?'

My mind did a happy little hop; it seemed that we'd at least be able to talk about books. 'Yes, my dad loved *To Kill a Mockingbird*,' I told him.

I picked up Radley and carried him to his mat in my father's bedroom. After I'd closed the door behind me, I steered Benjamin into the kitchen. My father had his pipe clamped in his mouth, though he never smoked anymore – at least not in front of me. He beamed at our guest as if he were Mozart, then held up his hands, which were covered in shredded zucchini, took out his pipe and said, 'I can't hug you; I'd soil that gorgeous suit.'

I took the tulips from Benjamin with my thanks and, while I was fetching a vase, Dad said, 'Tessa, honey, this is Benjamin Rosenfeld Zarco – he's the man we saw holding the sign on the march, the one about Holocaust survivors.'

'I know,' I said. 'I recognised him.'

'Wow, what a memory you've got!' To our guest, my father said, 'I should tell you that my daughter is an extraterrestrial!'

Benjamin did his best to smile. 'Please just call me Benni. Nobody calls me Benjamin but the mailman.'

While I filled a vase with water, Radley started barking, which set off Mr Cupcake one floor above ours. Dad rushed to his bedroom, opened the door and shouted in Ladino, '*Kaya la boka*!' – shut up – and though Radley obeyed him, Mr Cupcake didn't. His shrill barking always drove Dad into a homicidal fury, so he phoned up to his owner, Daniela, but she didn't answer. On returning to the kitchen, he shook his fists up toward the ceiling and said, 'One day, I'm going to strangle that little monster!' In a calmer voice, he said to Benni, 'My friends call me Morrie.'

Benni handed him the Cagney's Sporting Goods bag. Inside was a bottle of ouzo.

'Oooh, I wish my Grandma Vita were here – she lived on ouzo!

Thank you, Benni. We'll have some after dinner.' Dad handed the bottle to me. 'Do me a favour, Tessa – show our guest around the apartment. And offer him something to drink. And then take Daniela's spare key from under the phone book in the hallway and go upstairs and poison Mr Cupcake with one of my chocolate bars.' He turned to our guest. 'I've got some single-malt whiskey. And a bottle of pretty good red wine.'

Dad shooed us off with the wild hand motions he uses when he's cooking.

Benni sat in the old armchair I suggested for him, with his hands between his legs. I opened Dad's liquor cabinet. 'What'll it be?' I asked, and he replied, 'I'll have what you have,' so I told him that in the summer I generally had a gin and tonic, and he said, 'That's perfect.'

I excused myself to get glasses, ice and tonic water from the kitchen. *Where did you meet him?* I mouthed at Dad, who was frying his fritters.

He took out his pipe just long enough to whisper irritably, 'Can't you see I'm cooking?'

Benni had taken off his suit coat by the time I returned. He sipped his drink with both hands, afraid to spill it – like a schoolboy who'd been punished too many times. I sat on Dad's old velvet sofa. When he glanced down, I saw that the skin of his eyelids was slightly darker than the rest of his face, so that his eyes looked bruised.

By then, Mr Cupcake had given up barking, so I didn't have to go upstairs to yell at him.

After I sat down on the sofa, I told Benjamin he could smoke if he wanted. While he lit his cigarette, I noticed how strong his hands were, which reminded me of his profession.

'So what kind of clothing do you like best to make?' I asked.

Benni thought that over. 'Vests,' he said.

'Why vests?'

'There's a lot of hidden detail that goes into a vest. It looks simple, but it's like . . . it's like making something really complex . . . like stitching together a mystery.'

The Tailor Who Stitched Mysteries, I thought, as if it were the title of an opera.

'Where did you learn to sew?' I asked, and he replied, 'I was an apprentice in a town near Łódź – that's in Poland,' so I said, 'I know where it is. Are you from that area of the country?' and he said, 'No, I'm not.'

I waited to hear where he was born and raised, but he turned to the side and took a long, pensive drag on his cigarette.

'*Nu*, yuhr not going to tell us vare yuhr from?' I asked with a Yiddish accent, hoping to make him laugh.

He smiled, but just to be friendly. 'I'm from Warsaw,' he said, and I told him, 'I'm sorry I was so rude to you the first time we met,' and he said, 'You weren't rude,' but he shook his head too definitively for me to believe.

'No, I was,' I said.

Benni took a slow sip of his drink, and then another. I pulled a few threads out of the green silk pillows – they always had loose threads because of Radley's sharp nails. As the silence closed in around us, I decided that our conversation might proceed more smoothly if I were tipsy, so I downed my drink quickly and poured myself another.

He asked if he could look through my father's bookshelves, and while he was glancing across titles, I chose an album by Patsy Cline to put on the record player. After the first clippity-cloppity verse of 'Walkin' After Midnight', Benni turned and asked me in a concerned voice if my father really wanted to poison the dog who lived in the flat above ours.

I laughed. 'No, he loves Mr Cupcake! Whenever Daniela has to go away – that's his owner – Dad takes care of him. They're friends. It's just my father's sense of humour.'

Benni considered that while nodding, then asked who was singing. I ended Patsy Cline's short biography with her plane crash.

'Gosh, it's awful that she died so young,' he said, and I noticed then that he'd grown pale.

To change the mood, I suggested taking him on a tour of the apartment. On reaching my room, Benni noticed my flute on my pillow. 'Your dad said you're a great musician. Would you play something?'

I noticed then that Benni's hands were shaking. A moment later, he hid them behind his back. His nervousness moved me. 'You want to hear something?' I asked.

'Yes, please. I love the flute. It always makes me think of Shakespeare in Yiddish.'

'Why's that?'

'My cousin Shelly was Puck in a production of *A Midsummer Night's Dream* when I was little, and my parents were so proud of him! There must have been a lot of flute music in it, because that's mostly what I remember.'

His childhood sounded like it had been filled with theatre and opera, which turned out to be wrong, but it intrigued me at the time. I closed the door to muffle the record playing in the living room and considered wowing him with Bach, but I thought a bit of swing might help us relax, so I played the first few phrases of 'Puttin' on the Ritz'.

'That was great!' he said. 'Irving Berlin, right?'

'Absolutely. Do you like him?' I asked, and he said, 'Sure, who doesn't! I met him once, you know,' and I asked him when.

'He came into my shop about ten years ago. He bought one of my ties – red-and-brown paisley. No one was making paisley ties at the time, but I'd made a few just for the hell of it.'

'Good for you!' I exclaimed; an immigrant tailor who liked Irving Berlin and who made things just for the hell of it seemed like someone who could fit in well with my dad's group of oddballs.

From Benni's concentrated look, I expected him to tell me something meaningful about ties or tailoring in general, but he looked out the window.

I picked up my drink and stared at his profile, and after a while, he looked over at me curiously, and our thoughts seemed to come together in the air between us, and mine were, *What I need to tell you is that I thought you were very brave to hold up your sign, and I wanted to talk to you the moment I saw you on the television news*, and his were, *I was just doing what I had to do – it wasn't anything special*.

Benni smiled as though to reassure me. We seemed like two little kids standing at the edge of a great ocean, afraid to enter the water. I noticed a slight tremor in his hands again.

'Do you play an instrument?' I asked, and he replied, 'No, but my grandmother does,' so I asked, 'Was she the woman I saw you with at the march?' and he said, 'Yes,' and I said, 'What instrument does she play?' and he said, 'The piano. In fact, she used to teach piano. In Poland. And for a few years after I brought her here.'

'When did you bring her here?'

'In 1956, after I started earning decent money.'

Benni looked around the room, then stepped to the wall opposite my bed to study a watercolour of red roses sitting in a transparent vase. I liked the way he leaned forward with his hands joined behind his back. He looked like a conductor reading a score.

'I think the refraction is done really well,' I said.

'Refraction?'

'The sunlight is refracted by the water and makes the stems look ... displaced.'

'Oh, I understand,' he said.

After he studied the watercolour again, he gazed down and smiled – though it seemed more like an admission of despair. It was my first experience of what I'd come to call *the smile*.

'Are you okay?' I asked, and he said, 'A memory, it snuck up on me. But it's no big deal.'

'A memory of flowers?' I asked.

He shook his head. 'Of a person I used to know. When I was small. It means nothing.'

Or maybe it means everything, I thought, since I'd already begun to suspect by then that he tended to conceal what was most important to him.

'A relative?' I asked.

'Yes, I was reminded of ... well, my mother.' I was sure he'd say more, but he decided on a diversionary tactic. 'You know, when I was a boy, I once saw a man and his donkey share an apple. The man took a bite, then the donkey. And so on. Until the apple was finished.'

'They must have been close,' I said, hoping he'd laugh, but I only confused him and he asked who I meant.

'The man and the donkey,' I said.

He nodded. 'Yes, that's not so different from what I thought. But you may find this strange ... I considered that the donkey might have once been a person. The man's father or grandfather. They seemed to understand each other very well.'

'That sounds reasonable enough to me,' I said.

'Does it?' he asked, and I had the feeling that he was testing me.

By then, the gin had started to make me lightheaded, so I sat on my bed and put my pillow over my lap, which seemed like the right move, because it permitted me to think I was still a little girl and didn't have any responsibility for the way this conversation meandered.

'Lots of stranger things have happened than a man turning into a donkey,' I told him, and he asked, 'Like what?' and I replied, 'Like . . . like every Passover, Moses parts the Red Sea.' I stepped my fingers through the air. 'And you and I, we follow right behind him as if it's the most reasonable thing in the world.'

'That's true enough,' he said, and he smiled for real.

He looked extraordinarily handsome to me at that instant, and while studying his face, I felt Belle placing her hands in mine and telling me that I had to listen closely to the peculiar things people told me when I interviewed them – because they were letting me know who they'd dare to be if they could be entirely themselves. And asking me to let them become that person.

'Every conversation is an opportunity to help someone be the person they want to be,' she'd told me.

Benni, it's fine with me if you believe that men and women can change into animals, I told him inside my head, but what I actually said was, 'Thank you for holding up your sign at the rally. It was exactly what needed to be said.'

'I hope so. But you know, a few days later, a Hasidic old man recognised me on Second Avenue. He told me that what I was doing against the war was wrong because we were guests in America, and we had to agree with the president, and since then I've been thinking that maybe . . . maybe he had a point.'

'No, he didn't,' I said, and he replied, 'How can you be so sure?'

so I said, 'First of all, everyone is a guest in America except for the Indians. And second of all—'

'That's just what my friend George says!' Benni cut in excitedly. 'He's a Navajo.'

'Well, George is right. And Benni, it's not gratitude to keep quiet about injustice. Gratitude is something completely different.'

'But the Hasidic man was worried about the Jews. That we could be killed here. I felt guilty that I'd made him feel more . . . vulnerable.'

'So guilty that you'd prefer to be invisible?'

'No, I guess not, but being invisible could be a good thing under certain circumstances.' The ash on his cigarette was curling, and he cupped his hand under it and asked me where he could stub it out, so I fetched him my clam shell. We smiled at each other awkwardly after he took a last, greedy drag, and I realised we still hadn't stepped into the ocean. Shortly after that, something out the window caught his attention and he laughed fondly, and when I looked, I saw three little girls playing jump rope.

In profile, he looked older. And quite distinguished – as if he were an aristocrat. And an irrational possibility gripped me: *Maybe his eyes became bruised while he was in the ghetto. Because he'd seen too much.*

'Can we begin again?' I asked, and he said, 'What do you mean?' and I replied, 'We got off to a bad start. And it was my fault.'

Benni's eyes teared up. What I then did would – in years to come – remind me of my dreams of floating, because I did something that I'd never normally do, and with perfect ease: I stepped up to him and caressed his cheek.

Ever since that evening, I have speculated many times about how I could have done something I'd never normally do, and I always come back to the possibility that he was speaking to me at a deep, nonverbal level with his odd smile and quivering hands – in the place inside us where we live out the great myths of recognition and homecoming and kinship.

Benni took my hand away from his cheek and brought it to his lips and kissed the tips of my fingers, which no one had ever done before, and which seemed like a gesture out of a foreign film, and while I was looking into his bruised-looking eyes and considering what he was thinking, I stumbled into the silence we made together, and I didn't try to end it because it made me feel as if I'd stopped running in a race that had already gone on far too long.

Can a necessity become obvious in a single instant? Because for the first time in my life, I realised I could only live with a man who would permit me to get to know him without words.

Benni's quivering silence . . . I said that phrase to myself as if it were the start of a poem, and it made me think that his love, if he ever gave it to me, would come from a world he kept hidden from everyone else. And yet, the coarseness of his hand around mine soon made me shiver, because it reminded me that he was a man and I was a woman.

He let my hand go and studied the girls jumping rope. I understood that it was his way of not having to talk about what had just taken place between us. When he turned back to me, he said, 'I spent too much time alone when I was a boy.' He spoke as if he'd wanted to confess that to me for some time.

'I'm sorry about that,' I said.

'Don't be. I only mentioned it because touching isn't always easy for me. I'm not very Jewish in that way.'

'Not very Jewish?' I asked, and he said, 'The Jews in New York . . . They're often playful with each other – physically. I lost that back in Poland.'

'Maybe you could get it back,' I suggested, but he said, 'I don't want it back,' and when I asked why, he said, 'When I'm touching someone else, I sometimes think I know what that other person would like to say or do if no one was watching – or if they dared. And it doesn't always seem so nice. It's an illusion, I know that – or a kind of invention. But I don't always like it.'

'Now that we've touched,' I said, 'have you learned what I'd want to say or do if no one was watching?'

'No, I didn't feel anything like that with you,' he replied, 'Maybe I was too . . . surprised that you reached up to my cheek.'

'Well, when you find out, let me know.'

Benni nodded, and he might have spoken as well, but my father shouted, 'Where the hell are you two?'

I opened my door and called out, 'In my room.'

'Well, dinner is ready, so get yourselves back here!'

'Do you and your father always shout?' Benni asked.

I laughed. 'Yeah, I guess we do. It's part of our comedy routine.'

I didn't intend to say more about my dad, but as I gestured for Benni to precede me through the doorway, I said, 'Dad saved me after my mother abandoned us. And my little sister, too – Evie. He spent years taking care of us – cooking, doing the laundry, getting us ready for school . . .'

I didn't know why I confessed that. I guess I wanted Benni to know how good a man my father was. And that I wasn't always mean and insensitive.

Benni took my hand and gripped it hard, and while he was staring at me, his magnificent dark eyes seemed a miracle of honesty, because they told me exactly what he wanted, and he leaned toward me and kissed me, and I found myself kissing him back, and the taste in his mouth of tobacco, tonic water and something peppery I would later identify as uniquely Benni made me feel as if I were easing outside my body and floating above us and looking down at a young woman who had no idea where she was headed but who wanted to get there quickly.

While Dad served us his fritters, he explained to me that he'd visited Fourth Street Guitars two weeks earlier to ask if they knew anyone who repaired accordions – he was considering getting his fixed – and when he returned outside, Benni was standing next to the door, studying a poster for an Andrés Segovia concert that had been taped to the window.

'I invited him for coffee, and we hit it off, and that was that,' Dad said. He raised a finger of warning. 'Benni, please don't let me forget to loan you my Segovia album.'

'It's not necessary,' Benni said.

Dad tilted his head like he does when he's about to say something important and spoke one of his mother's sayings in Ladino: '*Necesario no tiene nada a ver com los djestos de l'amistad.*'

'My family was taken from me before I could learn Ladino well,' Benni said apologetically.

'*Necessary* has nothing to do with acts of friendship,' I translated.

After I'd served the wine, we got onto the subject of the Vietnam War, and Benni told us that for a long time he'd refused to watch the news because he didn't want to believe that America had such a shameful foreign policy, but when he found out how our bombers were dropping napalm on the Vietnamese, he started writing letters to Dow Chemical, the manufacturer of napalm, and to President Johnson, telling them that they were acting immorally.

'Ever get any replies?' I asked.

'No. But I think I should have asked a friend to correct my English in my letters. Everyone who read them probably thought I was a nutcase.'

'No, it's typical,' Dad sneered, and in an eager, conspiratorial voice, he added, 'Benni, you know what, the next time you chain yourself to the induction centre, I'm going with you!'

'That would be really good,' Benni replied gratefully. 'Because I get a little scared before I go. Though once I'm there, I'm okay.'

'Dad, that plan sounds really good, but just one question,' I said. 'Who's going to bail you two out of jail? Because we both know Radley is the world's smartest dachshund, but he isn't going to be able to sign any documents.'

'Teresa, the police won't arrest us,' Benni said in a matter-of-fact voice. 'The cop who put handcuffs on me told me it would be bad publicity – for the mayor and even for President Johnson. And Americans are nuts for favourable publicity.'

Dad nodded his agreement, but I wasn't so sure.

'The only problem I really ever had,' Benni said, 'is that some customers who saw me on the news, or who heard about what I'd done . . . They don't want me making their clothes anymore.'

'You see, Dad,' I said. 'It's not as safe as you think.'

'Listen, baby,' he said, 'how about you stop worrying and pour our guest more wine.'

After I topped up his glass, and Dad's too, I asked Benni, 'What exactly did the police do when they grabbed you at the induction centre?'

He stabbed a piece of fritter with his fork. 'They yelled at me as if I were a kid that they wanted to . . . I forget the word.'

'Bully,' I suggested, and he said, 'No, a bigger word,' so I said, 'Intimidate.'

'Not that either,' he told me, 'but it's almost right. Anyhow, a cop named Bianchi was talking rudely to me, so I said, "Look, Mr Policeman, please don't bother trying to scare me. I survived the Nazis and the Polish anti-Semites, and even when you're being nasty you're not anywhere close to how nasty they were, and you're probably an Italian-American, which is almost like being Jewish – if you don't mind my saying so – and you aren't allowed to threaten me with a bullet in the head or a death camp, or even a German Shepherd, so I'm very sorry but you're wasting your time."'

Benni's Yiddish rhythms and immigrant politeness made Dad laugh so hard that tears rolled down his cheeks. As for me, our guest's run-on sentences seemed a revelation.

When Dad got up to fetch the couscous, Benni looked over at me, and it was obvious again what he wanted, which set my heart drumming, and I laughed to myself because I'd thought at first that he looked like a raccoon and now I found him extraordinarily handsome.

After dessert and coffee, Dad handed Benni his Andrés Segovia album and suggested that I walk our guest home. After he kissed Benni goodbye – on both cheeks, in proper Sephardic fashion – he whispered something to me that touched me because it was his way of saying that I'd grown all the way up: 'You don't have to come home tonight. I won't worry.'

At that moment, I didn't think I'd ever love anyone as much as I loved my father.

Benni stopped as we walked down the staircase so he could wipe his forehead with a pink handkerchief he pulled from his breast pocket. He was dripping with sweat, and he looked really pale, too. 'I need a minute,' he said.

He sat down on the stairs, so I joined him. 'Did you drink too much wine?' I asked.

'No, it happens occasionally,' he said. 'My cousin Shelly says I got cracked in Poland.' He showed me a disheartened look. 'Sometimes I leak.'

'What do you leak?'

'I'm not sure – I guess everything I can't put into words.'

I loosened his tie, and dabbed the sweat from his top lip and chin with his handkerchief, and I held his hand. He asked me about my studies, and I told him about Appalachia, and I sang him a ballad about a race horse that Belle had learned when she was a little girl, which made him close his eyes, and after a while he started breathing more easily.

'I like you singing to me,' he told me after I'd helped him back up. 'It's like being blessed.'

At his apartment, we tiptoed around and whispered because his grandmother, Ewa, was asleep. He turned off his air conditioner on stepping inside his bedroom because he said it always gave him a cold if he left it on at night.

I tried not to make any noise while he was fucking me, and so did he, but the only way we could do it was to kiss while he was thrusting into me, so that's what we did, and after a while, I couldn't get enough air – just like him a little while earlier – and we had to stop.

I began sobbing because I'd spoiled everything, and I was too young to realise that wanting another person so badly could play havoc with your emotions, and his cock was throbbing so hard that it must have been painful, but he scoffed and said, 'It's okay, my *putz* has his needs, and I have mine, and sometimes we agree to disagree,' which made me laugh with relief. After he drank a glass of seltzer and smoked a cigarette, he spooned up behind me and told me he was sorry if he'd hurt me. 'It's just that you make me crazy excited,' he confessed.

I told him that he hadn't hurt me at all, but that I'd never felt as naked as I did with him and it frightened me.

We woke at dawn, and we made love as if we'd been hibernating in frozen earth all winter, and he reached someplace so deep inside me that I sobbed afterward, and I had to keep reassuring him that

I was all right. He held me tight, and he smelled like the Greek yeast cake my dad made for Hanukkah, which seemed a favourable sign, and he became the first man whose kisses after lovemaking didn't seem an attempt to trap me or convince me to do something I wasn't ready to do.

While drinking coffee with him that morning, I felt purged of a burden, though I wasn't sure what it was. In a dream I had a week or so later, however, I imagined Benni floating with me and Belle over a wall separating us from a turbulent sea, and all three of us were laughing, and I awoke feeling as if I were living in an enchanted, shimmering world. Late that morning, I called Belle and told her the dream, and she said that the wall had been around what she called my *ascendant heart*, which always beats to the rhythm of the *great waters*, and that it was a very good sign that Benni was floating with the two of us, and she bet that he had dreamed something like that too, because, she said, 'Important dreams come in pairs to people like you and Benni.'

'What do you mean, like me and Benni?'

'The way you speak of him, child – I think he's the man you've been looking for!'

That evening, when I asked Benni if he remembered having floated with me in any dreams, he shrugged and said he didn't, but that in any case he hardly ever remembered them.

There was a catch in his tone – an apologetic hesitance – that made me doubt his assertion, but I let it go; I was learning not to trespass on territories of his heart that he preferred to keep secret. A couple of mornings later, Benni and I took a shower together after making love, and while I dried off he walked naked and dripping into the kitchen and made us coffee – which for him was an exacting and important ritual – and we sat at his dining table over two steaming New York Mets mugs. He closed those bruised eyes of his after each sip, and when I commented that I never saw anyone seem to take such joy from coffee, he told me that it was essential to his sense of well-being, and smoking, too, and drinking wine and beer, and shaving – and having sex, of course – since he had spent years thinking that he would never become an adult and be able to do the things that only grown-ups could do.

In a whisper, he said, 'You know, Tessa, for twenty years now, I have thought I'll wake up one day and realise I'm still in Warsaw, and I've never stopped being a kid, and I'm still waiting for my parents to come home. And I'll understand that all my adult life has been a dream.'

'Do you think of your parents often?' I asked.

He shook a cigarette from his pack and stuck it in his lips but didn't light it. He took my hand and gave it a squeeze. 'I'm sorry, Tessa, but I don't know what *often* means for dead parents.'

He lit his cigarette with his head at an angle, like he always does, and turned away from me.

'Have I offended you?' I asked, near tears. 'I didn't mean to.'

He shook his head. 'No, not at all. I'm very sorry if I made you think that.'

His voice – overly reassuring – made me wonder if there were places in him that I'd never be permitted to see. Still, it pleased me to be able to fantasise about him as a little boy wishing he was old enough to shave and drink coffee and smoke.

A little later, he said in a conspiratorial whisper, 'I nearly always remember that my parents are dead when something good happens. And I don't like it, because it spoils things. So I get angry at them, and I want them to go away, though I know it's not fair.'

'It seems fair to want to be free of sadness,' I said.

'Is it? I think maybe I owe them my sadness and every other feeling I could ever have.'

He stubbed out his cigarette and finished his coffee. My cup was still nearly full, so I lifted it to his lips for him to sip, and after he did, his hands gripped mine. They were chilled and moist, and when I pointed that out, he said, 'It happens when I start leaking.'

After I kissed him, he added, 'Even now, after making love with you, I'm not sure it really happened. I think that maybe this . . .' He waved his arm to indicate everything around us. 'Maybe all I see and hear is an illusion that has been put in my head to protect me from the truth.'

'And what's the truth?'

'That's just it, I don't know. But I don't think it's good.'

I knew I'd have to return to Berkeley in late August, but picturing my goodbye to Benni made me want to run and hide. Why did I have to fall in love now?

I confessed my distress to him one day while we were strolling through Washington Square Park, but he didn't ask me to stay, as I'd expected. Instead, he reminded me that if I didn't go back to school, I'd lose my place in my graduate programme.

'Don't you think I know that?' I snapped.

During the quarrel I then started with him, I realised I wanted him to tell me he wouldn't allow me to go. I didn't confess that to him, however. Instead, I insisted that he was pushing me away. I realised I was being dishonest, but I wasn't yet ready to admit the depth of my ambivalence and fear.

By then, I'd told Benni about how I'd pictured my mother laughing at me whenever I was most upset, so he said, 'Tessa, let me tell you, I know something about what your friend Belle would call a haunting, and I'm pretty sure that your mother is going to start ridiculing you again if you don't go – and all the time. Because you won't be doing what you need to do. And maybe you'll even begin to hate me. And that would ruin everything between us.'

That night, after making love, I realised that he was right not to ask me to stay with him. I told him that it was a new experience for me to be with a man who respected my independence, and I apologised for provoking an argument with him in the park, and he enfolded me in his arms by way of reply, and his warm, protective strength reassured me that everything would be okay.

When I woke up at just after eight, he'd already left for work, which was a disappointment. But Ewa had made coffee and it smelled heavenly. She was seated on Benni's rumpled, brick-coloured sofa, and seeing her smile at me made me feel as if I were about to join her on a grand adventure. As usual, Ewa had surrounded herself with the big, colourful silk pillows Benni had sewn for her, and she was reading a novel in Polish that she'd taken out from the 42nd Street library. She and I had almost always conversed through Benni in the past, since her English was so hesitant, though sometimes she had remained in her room on my visits and never come out. Benni had assured me that it wasn't because she didn't like me, it was simply that her health wasn't so good – she had back and hip problems and high blood pressure – and she had to pace herself. This morning, however, we sat together, and she ended up telling me about her farmhouse in Poland, and how Benni used to catch salamanders at her pond, and how once he'd even brought one inside and lost it, and it took them half a day to find it because it had hidden below her clunky old iron stove. We conversed together like old friends, and after I re-filled her coffee cup, she took my hand and pressed her lips to my palm, just like her grandson, and the resemblance between the two of them made me cry, and without knowing why, I told her that I was in love with Benni.

'I know,' she said with a smile of complicity. And she whispered with great delight, 'He also love you.' She nodded with certainty. 'I see it.'

After I dressed, she asked me to join her at her upright piano, and she showed me an arrangement of 'Air on the G string' for piano and violin, and when she smiled at me, her sharp brown eyes seemed full of sweet-natured mischief, and she said, 'You play violin part with your flute.' There was so much eager hope in her voice – and she made such an effort to speak English – that I couldn't disappoint her.

Her hands stopped shaking the moment they touched the keyboard, and her playing was so calm and trusting that I suddenly realised what it was like to make music with someone who has nothing left to prove.

That afternoon, I took Ewa out for lunch at Arezzo, and she ate her pizza slices with a knife and fork – very dignified – and it seemed obvious then that Benni's aristocratic table manners – the elegant way he held a cup, for instance – had come through her.

Late that evening, before she went to bed, she summoned me away from Benni and the jazz record we were listening to, and asked me into her room. With nervous gestures, she handed me a piece of bluish note paper on which she'd written, *Please always take good care of my Benni.*

'Of course, I will,' I said, and she held her finger to our lips so it would be our secret, which made me tingle, and I embraced her hard. She kissed me on both my cheeks, which kept me up that night long after Benni was asleep, because I had never known my father's mother and this seemed like a second chance for me.

On the plane out to Berkeley, however, it occurred to me – with dread spreading through me – that Ewa's note might have been meant as a request for me to stay in New York.

I slept only a few hours a night over my first week in California. Often, I'd see my mother and Evie in my dreams, and once, after I awoke, I was sure that they'd been quarrelling in my living room, and that Mom had a concealed knife behind her back and was planning on murdering my sister. What's more, I realised it wasn't the first time I'd had that dream.

I managed to reach Evie late that morning and she assured me that she was fine, but the feeling that she was in dire peril remained with me for days afterward.

It was while I was still under the menacing spell of that dream that I questioned Benni about whether Ewa seemed angry at me for going back to Berkeley.

'Don't be ridiculous,' he said, and he assured me that she thought I was the *cat's whispers*, which he knew was an error but which he regarded as far more poetic and amusing than the original version.

One afternoon, I called him on a whim, but I couldn't reach him at home or at work. An hour later, I tried again and Ewa answered this time, and she managed to explain to me in her broken English that he'd been invited to a friend's house for dinner.

I went out to my little garden, and while sniffing at the pink roses my landlord had planted, I surprised myself by picturing Benni with a beautiful young woman.

Thankfully, Ewa had sensed that I'd been upset and had told Benni. He called me at just after midnight, New York time, and he apologised for not telling me about the dinner. He said that the friend he'd been dining with was a professor of Jewish mythology and mysticism. 'He came into my shop the other day, and he wanted me to make him a suit, and we got to talking ... Anyhow, he invited me over tonight.'

I was so relieved – and ashamed of my fantasies – that it took me a moment to ask him if the food was any good.

'Not so hot,' he replied. 'But it didn't matter.' In an excited voice, he said, 'Hey, Tessa, did you know that the kabbalists wrote about angels and devils?'

'No.'

'The professor, he gave me a book by Gershom Scholem. He writes about all this mystical stuff. You know, some of the kabbalists even believed in a form of reincarnation. So maybe it's not crazy for me to think that I was here before.'

'Is that what you think?'

'Well, there are times . . .' he began hesitantly, 'when I seem to remember things – from long ago, before I was born. Vague images – places I used to live. I see Alexandria a lot. I think I used to live there and work in the big library, though I wasn't anybody important. I used to keep the place tidy.' He laughed heartily. 'I was just a janitor. But being around all those scrolls ... Wow!'

His childlike enthusiasm made me want to embrace him. And yet a moment later, sadness slipped between us, and it prompted me to say something that I'd hoped to keep secret. 'Benni, I'm sorry, but I don't know how longer I can stay away from you and continue my studies.'

'What's wrong?' he asked, and I said, 'Sometimes I get worried about what could happen to the two of us,' and he said, 'I'm sorry I worried you – I'll make sure to call you every evening,' and I said, 'It's not that. It's that I don't know what I'm doing here.'

'You're getting your degree,' he said. 'You're doing what you want.'

'What I want is to come back to New York,' I told him.

'No, it's too big a risk. You have to do what you were meant to do, or else . . . or your soul will get all confused, and you'll grow resentful. And you'll regret it all your life. I know it.'

I confessed then that I'd pictured him with a young woman. He thickened his Yiddish accent and replied, 'Zere vas vonce a squirrel who ate nossing but peanuts, efen ven he vas offered big valnuts and hazelnuts.'

'Is this another one of your cousin Shelly's jokes?' I asked in a sinking tone.

'Kind of. But I'm twisting it around. Anyway, ze squirrel's family thought he vas *meshugge*. And his kids, wow, did zey make fun of him! Once, he efen turned down ze most beautiful *mandelbrot* in ze vorld. A *mandelbrot* more beautiful zan Elizabeth Taylor, and more sexy zan Marilyn Monroe.'

'A sexy *mandelbrot*?'

'Vy not?! You got somezing against cake, Miss Ethnomusicologist? Anyway, ze little squirrel, he just kept eating peanuts. And ven his brothers and sisters asked him vy, he said, "Vy should I give up vot I love for vot I don't?"'

I wanted to laugh, but I also knew his explanation was too glib. 'Look, Benni, how do you know you *von't* start looking for peanuts elsewhere?' I asked. 'You might decide that a piece of *mandelbrot* would taste pretty damn good after a supper alone.'

'Teresa, I'm pretty certain you missed the point of the story,' he said with what he hoped was an amusing groan.

'Maybe. But you're sure to get angry at me sometimes – for being so far away.'

'For better or worse, the Nazis . . . they taught me how to wait. I'm world class at it, in fact. All my customers, they say I could win Olympic gold.'

*

A few weeks later, when I began studying Ticuna with Líria, my daydreams about escaping to the Tropics returned to me, and my fears about Benni finding another woman eased off, especially after he flew out to San Francisco and stayed with me for a week in mid-October. One night while he was sleeping, I traced on his back with my fingertip, *I love you, and everything is going to be okay*.

Two days after he returned to New York, however, he called at eleven in the evening, and he told me that Ewa had collapsed at home a few hours before, after eating the spaghetti-with-eggplant dinner he'd made, and she'd died on the way to the hospital. When he said in a whisper that he wasn't sure he could go on without her, I thought, *I was wrong, nothing ever works out like it should*.

Benni's voice was dull and hopeless, and I realised that Ewa had asked me to take care of him for the day when he would sound like this – for right now. Maybe she'd learned from her doctors – or had some terrible intuition – that she was nearing the end.

I said I'd fly to New York on the first plane the next morning, but he replied, 'No, no, no, keep teaching – there's nothing you can do here,' but I said, 'I want to be with you. I can help you.'

'It's not necessary,' he replied, so I reminded him, '*Necesario no tiene nada a ver com los djestos de l'amistad*.'

Benni cried most of the first night we spent together, and even though the weather was muggy, he couldn't get warm, so I piled blankets on top of him and made him drink cup after cup of hot tea. I called my father early the next morning to help me get aspirin and liquids into him, because he refused to do anything to help himself, and he had scheduled the funeral for early that afternoon.

Benni was so exhausted and lost that Dad had to help him dress. He looked handsome in his slate-grey suit and pale-blue shirt, but I wasn't sure about the crimson tie he chose. 'Ewa always liked bright colours,' he explained, 'though she was afraid to wear them herself.'

Benni added a shot of schnapps to his second cup of coffee that morning, and he drizzled in a bit more when he thought I wasn't looking; he seemed to regard staying sober as a betrayal of all he'd felt for his grandmother – which might have been all right, but it also made him morose and weepy. And he was smoking too much, too. I feared he'd make himself ill.

Out of solidarity with Benni, Dad poured schnapps in his own coffee too, and when I gave him a resentful look, he said, 'Tessa, it seems there are things you don't understand yet about men.'

'I'm not sure I like this men-versus-women way of seeing things,' I replied.

He lifted the bottle of schnapps. 'You're absolutely right. Have a shot.'

I accepted his offer, but the drink only sapped what was left of my flagging energy.

Just before we went out to the limousine that Dad had hired to take us to the cemetery, Ewa's doctor called to tell us what he'd discovered about her sudden death. Benni didn't understand the explanation, however, so I took the phone. 'It appears to have been an aortic aneurism,' the physician – Dr Martins – told me, and when I explained to Benni, he burst into tears and said, 'Then it wasn't the spaghetti with eggplant I made? I'd never have forgiven myself if it was.'

Ewa's funeral was held on Wednesday, October 26th at a Jewish cemetery on Long Island, which seemed odd to me because she'd always worn a tiny silver cross around her neck, and I had assumed that she had converted to Catholicism, probably when she'd understood that the Nazi's were about to occupy Poland.

'No, Ewa wasn't a Catholic or a Jew or anything else,' Benni
told me as we trudged across the cemetery to the grave. It had
showered the evening before and the walkways were muddy. 'She
had no interest in religion. Or even mysticism.' He gave a little
laugh. 'She thought that I was nuts for reading about reincarnation.'

'And the cross?' I asked, and he said, 'It was a gift from her
mother,' so I asked if her mother was Catholic, and he replied,
'Yes. But Ewa only believed in Bach and Handel and Mozart, and
what they could teach us.'

'And what can they teach us?' I asked.

He stopped walking and looked down, examining the mud on
his shoes. At length, he said, 'To be very gentle with one another,
because we break very easily.'

I believed that conclusion said more about Benni and the Nazis
than Bach or Handel or Mozart, of course, but I accepted it as an
important lesson to learn from whatever source we could.

Benni had organised a graveside ceremony, and his cousin Shelly
and his wife, Julie, had flown down from Montreal and driven out
to the cemetery in a rental car.

After the gaunt young rabbi that Shelly had hired had told
us about the selfless love of grandparents, Benni picked up the
shovel the cemetery had provided and sprinkled dirt onto the
grave, but he didn't return to me afterward. Instead, he stood by
himself, letting his shadow fall over the grave, as if that were how
he would try to protect Ewa now. Something about his rigid stance
and closed eyes . . . I grew terrified that her death had ended our
chance for a life together.

Right then and there, while studying Benni's purposeful shadow,
I knew I would marry him – that is, if he'd accept a somewhat crazy
and conflicted young woman as his wife.

After Shelly and Julie had shovelled dirt onto the casket, it was my dad's turn, and he spoke a Sephardic prayer for the peace of Ewa's soul, before finally it was my turn. After I sprinkled dirt on Ewa's casket with my hand – I'd wanted to grip the earth as hard as I could before letting it go – I started to sing. I hadn't planned to – I just did. And what came out of me was a lullaby that my father had taught me.

Durme, durme, querida hijica
durme sin ansia y dolor
cerra tus lindos ojicos
durme, durme con savor.
Cerra tus lindos ojicos
durme, durme con savor

Sleep, sleep beloved daughter
sleep with no worry or pain
close your beautiful eyes
sleep, sleep restfully.
Close your beautiful little eyes
sleep, sleep restfully

I sang softly and slowly, and after the first couple of lines I became a melody floating above the six of us, and there, in the air, indifferent to the renewed drizzle soaking into the hair and clothes of the woman I'd been a minute before, I also became aware that a deep force had chosen me to sing at that moment – and it seemed a kind of volition that came and went without regard to my preferences, one that couldn't be summoned or predicted.

Benni came over to me and kissed me, and we walked arm and arm to the limousine. Along the way, he turned to Shelly and Julie

and said, 'Come back to my apartment until you have to leave for
the airport.'

At the car, my father told us that he would pick up some Turkish
food and a couple bottles of good wine. 'Is that all right, son?' he
asked Benni, and he used Ladino word for son – *fijo* – and when
Benni embraced my father, I realised that he and Dad and I had
become family.

That evening, as soon as Benni and I went to bed, he turned toward
me and said in a confessional voice, 'Please, Tessa, don't be angry
with me if I say something you won't like.'

I closed my book. 'What is it?' I asked.

He gazed down shamefully. 'Ewa wasn't my grandmother – not
by blood, I mean.'

I was too shocked to reply.

'She hid me in her home near the end of the war – she was the
piano teacher,' he continued.

'But then why did you tell me she was your grandmother?' I
asked.

'That's how I thought of her. And that's what I told the
immigration officials. I had to say that or she wouldn't have been
permitted to stay with me in New York.'

Though the irritation I felt seemed unfair, I accused him of not
trusting me enough. I might have explained my feelings further,
but he began moaning and pulling at his air. When I embraced
him, he said, 'Ewa and I, we never told anyone because we were so
afraid that if someone found out, they'd send her back to Poland!'

I stayed in New York for a week, and I never left Benni's side. He
was quiet almost all the time, even after making love, which had
previously been the only occasions when he dared to return to

Poland and tell me of his past. Before I left for Berkeley, I had a presentiment of his death, and I made him promise not to hurt himself. 'No, I wouldn't do anything like that – not now,' he said, as if there were many past times when he had, in fact, considered suicide.

I told him to call me anytime – day or night – and that there was nothing he couldn't discuss with me, and I almost asked if he would marry me, but his diffidence – in particular, the cool watchfulness in his eyes whenever he spotted me looking at him – gave me to believe that he might turn me down, either because it was the wrong time or maybe even to punish himself.

Benni stopped answering the phone at home, so when I wanted to speak to him, I called him at work. He said that he wouldn't talk to anyone except me and Shelly and my father.

On my request, Dad checked up on him a couple of times a week, observing Benni from afar as he worked in his tiny shop on First Avenue.

And then, the unexpected intervened . . .

I missed my period two weeks after returning to Berkeley, in mid-November, and again the next month. After a gynaecologist at the student health clinic confirmed that I was pregnant, I flew back to New York for the weekend. It was only late afternoon when I got home, but Dad opened the door in his pyjamas. He was sweating hard, and his hair was plastered to his forehead. 'You been dancing with Radley?' I asked.

'No, I was playing Gershwin – *Rhapsody in Blue*. But what are you doing here?'

'Don't worry – it's good news,' I told him.

He helped me out of my coat and took my bag. 'So, tell me what's up,' he prompted.

'I'm pregnant.'

He missed the hook while hanging my coat and it dropped to the floor. He squinted at me. 'Pregnant as in . . . a baby?' he questioned as if he were sneaking up on a hoped-for miracle.

'Do you know another meaning?' I asked, laughing.

'*Dio Mio!*' he exclaimed, and his jaw dropped open. 'Thank God I didn't wake up dead after my heart attack!' He looked up to heaven and cried out, '*Un inyéto!*' – a grandchild.

Dad put on a record by Astor Piazzolla, and while he tangoed me around the living room, Radley began chasing around us and Mr Cupcake started barking upstairs, and just like that we were back inside the frenzied New York comedy that had been my childhood.

After Dad had retreated – panting – to his armchair, he asked if Benni knew the good news yet, and when I said he didn't, he replied, 'You know what, Bunny Rabbit, invite him over for dinner and tell him here! Get on the phone – quick! I'll get dressed and pick up some champagne.'

'I'm not sure,' I said. 'I think Benni and I ought to be alone when I tell him.'

'How about this – Rad and I will go to the kitchen when you give him the news. We'll only come out if I hear shouting. Or if Benni faints.'

I was too worried about how Benni would receive my news to understand that Dad was joking. I sat down on the arm of his chair, suddenly in terror. 'You think he's going to be upset?' I asked.

'Of course not!' Radley had climbed up on me by then and started licking my face, so Dad circled him in his arms and pulled him back. 'What a silly Bunny Rabbit you are! Benni is a Holocaust survivor.'

'What's that mean?'

'Listen, the one thing I had to do for my parents and grandparents, and for everyone else who was murdered, was to have kids. I could feel the Jews of Salonika counting on me. It became an obsession. Which wasn't so good. Because it made me rush into things that I should have taken at a much slower tempo. *Andante, andante . . .* ! I found out too late that I was a slow movement in a long and gentle sonata, not a big thundering *presto.*'

'What things should you have taken slower?'

He snorted. 'You really want to hear ancient history right now?' I nodded.

'Well, I had maybe six good months with your mother. After that, I began to see that she wasn't the right person for me, and that I wasn't right for her either.' He looked at me knowingly and patted my hand. 'She was young and didn't know who she was or what she really wanted. And I think that maybe I fooled her into thinking I was someone who was going to give her access to really famous people – which was important to her. I knew some big musicians back then – Herbie Steward, Lester Young, Stan Getz . . . Anyway, I went ahead and proposed to her, because that's what she expected. And I got her pregnant one-two-three because that's what I had to do. We had a good half-year, like I said, and after that the Titanic hit an iceberg!'

'Was that what you meant when you told me once that a few months can last a lifetime?' I asked.

'Yeah. But I should have said that a few months can last *three* lifetimes – you, me and Evie.'

Benni came over that evening for dinner. I made him a really strong gin and tonic, and after he'd taken a sip and complimented me on my new recipe, I took a step back from him and said, 'I've got a surprise for you,' and his expression grew dark and he took his cigarettes from his shirt pocket and said, 'I'm not so good with surprises, they usually end up with someone who dies,' and I said,

'But this one is good,' and he said, 'It is?' and I said, 'Yeah, we're going to have a baby.'

His eyes opened wide and he raised a hand to his cheek. 'You're pregnant?'

'Yeah, I checked with my doctor to be sure. You're not angry, are you?'

'And I'm the father?' he asked, and I snapped, 'Of course, you're the father!' and my father shouted from the kitchen, where he was making dinner, 'Teresa, it's a perfectly reasonable question!' so I yelled back, 'Dad, if you don't keep quiet, you're going to be in big trouble!'

He turned the blender on, but only at low speed; he was still trying to eavesdrop.

Benni closed his eyes and whispered, 'Give me a minute,' and after mouthing what must have been a prayer, he came to me and kneeled down, and he spoke softly in Yiddish into my belly, and then he whispered something else in Ladino that I couldn't catch, and when he stood up, I asked what he'd said, and he told me that he'd first thanked the baby for choosing the two of us.

'And the second thing?' I asked.

He shrugged. 'I thanked you for falling in love with the nervous raccoon who tried to pick you up outside a Turkish restaurant.'

After supper, while Dad was in the kitchen checking on his baked apples, Benni and I agreed to have our wedding right away because I'd have to fly back to Berkeley in two days for my final classes before the Christmas break. But by the time we walked to his apartment, the constriction in my chest made me fear that I was about to have a panic attack, so I asked him if we might put off the wedding for a week or two. 'Benni, I know I'm being difficult, but things are happening so fast. I need to get used to the idea of the baby before I can do anything else.'

'Sure, it's not a problem,' he said, and his smile was genuine.

But when I awakened in the middle of the night, he was seated next to me, his legs crossed, and the light was on, and he was holding a book by Gershom Scholem, and he was weeping.

'What's wrong?' I asked.

'Everything was so good, and now you don't want to marry me.'

I sat up and rubbed his back. 'I *do* want to marry you. I just need a little time.'

'Listen, Tessa, I was wrong, I'm not Olympic gold, because I can't wait,' he said. 'We'll be separated and I'll never find you again, and the baby won't have a father, and everything will go wrong!' He jumped up and threw his book against the wall.

I went to him, but he pushed me away when I tried to hold him.

'Benni, this isn't Poland during the war,' I said. 'Nothing terrible is going to happen.'

'Teresa, where we are on the map doesn't change the laws! Don't you know that?'

'What laws?' I asked, and he replied, 'The laws that govern things,' and I said, 'Benni, what are you talking about?' and he replied, 'I'm talking about how things work down here – and maybe in the Upper Realms, too.'

'Benni, please don't take this the wrong way,' I said gently, 'but I think you're reading too much kabbalah.'

He gazed at me, and I could see he was about to yell at me, so I held up my hands like he does to imitate a cornered bank robber in a Western, which – thankfully – made him reconsider.

'I may read too much kabbalah,' he admitted in a calm and

friendly tone, 'but I still want to get married right away. Do I have to beg?'

'That might help,' I said playfully, and as he kneeled down to do so, I saw my mother gazing at me inside my mind, hoping I'd say no, so after Benni had asked for me to marry him, I squatted down next to him and said yes, and that one simple word seemed the greatest triumph I'd ever had.

The next morning was Saturday, and Benni woke me with lots of popping kisses, dressed in his olive-green suit – my favourite – and his crimson silk tie. He'd combed his hair back with water, which he never did, and it made him look like a Jewish gangster from the 1930s – or a slightly smaller and darker version of his cousin Shelly. He was so excited to be going to the marriage bureau to pick up our licence that he couldn't eat breakfast.

I phoned Evie right away and told her that Benni and I were getting married in a few hours and that she had to meet us at the synagogue, because I wasn't doing this without her. Though I'd woken her up, she shrieked with glee and promised she'd drive carefully.

While I was making myself toast, Benni asked me to close my eyes and put out my hand, and he slipped a ring on my finger.

When I opened them, I saw a deep-red ruby surrounded by tiny diamonds, in a squarish, art-nouveau setting. It made me think of a stylised hibiscus flower, and it looked like something that Isadora Duncan might have worn, which is why I twirled around and unfurled my hands to him.

'I know it's small,' he said, 'but it's an antique – from Budapest, the jeweller told me.' He reached into his shirt pocket and pulled out the art deco-style diamond breastpin – shaped like a crescent moon – that her father had given her for her high-school graduation. 'And it'll go perfectly with your favourite brooch.'

'Oh, it's gorgeous, Benni!' I assured him. 'But I've got no ring for you.' In an embarrassed voice, I added, 'Or any present at all – not even a tie.'

'You'll buy me something on our honeymoon,' he said cheerfully.

'Are we having a honeymoon?'

'Sure, I'll come out to Berkeley for a few days. Maybe we'll drive somewhere up the coast.'

Two hours later, Benni and I had the licence in our hands, and after picking up my dad – who'd just purchased our wedding bands in the Diamond District – we took our taxi to the Rodeph Sholom synagogue on West 83rd Street, and we asked for Rabbi Simon, the painfully skinny young man who'd overseen Ewa's burial. He came to our pew holding a white-satin yarmulke in his hand. 'You always forget to bring one,' he told Benni.

Benni put it on and thanked him, then told him that we wanted him to marry us.

'Now?' he asked, and Benni said, 'As soon as Tessa's little sister gets here. It shouldn't be much longer. Is that a problem?'

'No, it's wonderful news!' He took my hand and Benni's and squeezed them tight, and he asked Dad to join our little chain, and then he turned the four of us in a slow circle. On a second gyration, he sang a high, nasal, Arabic-sounding melody. Benni, Dad and I looked at each other because we had no idea what was happening.

'Just something I picked up while working in Istanbul,' Simon said after we'd stopped turning. 'The dervishes – their whirling – is very moving. Did it seem *meshugge*?'

'Maybe just a *bissel*,' Benni told him with an apologetic shrug.

Evie arrived a half hour later, and I hadn't seen her in a dress in maybe five years, and I was so happy to see her looking gorgeous and confident that we jumped up and down together, giggling, just like we used to when we were schoolkids.

After the wedding ceremony, nervous exhaustion overwhelmed Benni, and he sat down in one of the pews with his head between his legs. Dad kept his hand on his shoulder and called him *fijo* in his whispered encouragements, and I couldn't take my eyes from the two of them because they were so handsome together. If I were a composer, I told myself, I'd write a piano concerto about men who support each other at their most difficult times, because there seemed nothing more moving, and whenever I'd listen to it, it would remind me of what good luck I've had all my life.

Over the next couple of days, Benni seemed to be hopping and skipping through his days, and he laughed at nothing and everything, and while he was cooking, he sang Polish songs that Ewa had taught him, and we held hands nearly all the time when we were together, every one of his smiles genuine. But curiously, he never once mentioned the baby.

Whenever I'd ask how he was feeling about having a child, he would whisper, 'Super-duper!' in the voice of an advertising pitchman, and then change the subject. After a while, I began to suspect that there was a great tangle of emotions below his surface – a knot that he didn't dare undo – so on the evening before I was scheduled to go back to Berkeley, I sat him down and said that he had to tell me if he was having second thoughts about the baby. He took my arm and stood me up, led me into our bedroom and eased the door closed, and drew all the curtains and turned off the lights.

'What's going on?' I asked.

He sat me on the bed and whispered that he didn't want to risk bringing attention to me and what he called *our insignificant gift*, because something terrible might happen to us – 'Something *catastropic*!' he said with a grimace.

I reminded him that catastrophic had an 'h' after the 'p', but said he'd left out the letter on purpose, because words spoken aloud had what he called an *arcane power*, and he didn't want to pronounce it correctly in connection with our 'insignificant gift'. He also made me promise to always refer to what was growing in my belly as 'the little nothing' or something equally innocuous, since that would keep the baby safe.

His pleas left me feeling trapped by all he'd suffered in his childhood. 'Benni, what exactly are you talking about?' I asked.

'Tessa, if we draw attention to what's coming into our life, somebody is sure to take it away!'

Benni and I decided that I'd go on teaching as long as I could and then return to New York so that he and my dad could look after me. He seemed happy with that solution, and we made plans for him to come out to Berkeley a few days later, but as I entered the tunnel to walk toward my plane, I turned to wave, and I expected to see him standing where we'd kissed goodbye, but instead there was a group of people looking down at the ground. I rushed back and found him lying on the floor with his hand over his eyes and a young black woman kneeling next to him. 'Do you have any pain?' she asked him.

'No, I'm okay,' he replied.

'That's my husband,' I told her. 'Benni, are you all right?'

'Teresa?' He took away his hand and looked at me with grateful eyes. With a grunt, he fought to sit up. 'I got dizzy while saying goodbye to you. But why aren't you on the plane?'

His face was puffy-looking and sweaty. I kneeled next to him. To the people gathered around us, I said, 'He's all right now. You can go. Everything's fine.' As they dispersed, the woman who'd come to his aid said, 'I'm a nurse – I'm happy to help.'

'Thank you,' I told her. 'But he'll be okay now.' I was about to say, *He gets faint when he leaks*, but that wouldn't have made any sense to her.

After she left, I felt Benni's forehead, and he was cold. 'You need to drink something hot,' I ordered, and he said, 'I'll get some coffee once you go,' but after I helped him to his feet, I realised I didn't want to leave and said, 'Let's go back home.'

'Tessa, please,' he said, taking my hands, 'if you stop what you need to do every time I get dizzy, you'll never do anything. It's no big deal. I'm used to it.'

'No, I can't leave you,' I said.

'You have to. You've no choice. I won't let a little dizziness hold us back. I can't.'

We argued a little longer, but he was insistent that I go. I helped him dust off his jacket, and he smiled his smile that wasn't really a smile, then shooed me off with whirling hands, so I went.

I worried about him over the next few days nearly all the time, but when I picked him up at San Francisco Airport in my old Ford, he was relaxed and happy. I think that those few days we had together in Berkeley were the true start of our marriage, because everywhere we walked I felt a third, very solid presence between us, and I realised that it was what we were building together. Whenever I was teaching or studying, Benni would go for long walks on the hills above the campus – he'd never lived anywhere but on flatlands – or sit with the *New York Times* and *San Francisco Chronicle* at the Caffè Mediterraneum on Telegraph Avenue and drink espresso coffee and smoke and read the news. I hadn't considered until then how hard he brooded over the world's events – the war in Vietnam, especially. At that time, he started underlining words and expressions he didn't understand and would ask me to explain them to him.

Cajole.
Fingerpicking.
Pellucid.
Flunky.

I stashed one of the *New York Times* Arts sections that Benni had underlined in my closet because it reminded me of the enormous effort he always made to speak English, and how proud he was that he could occasionally fool a cab driver or waitress into thinking that he was, as he called it, *a native-born American.*

Benni in his olive-green suit and his sun-god bolo tie, hunched over the News section of the *Times*, wearing the burgundy-coloured beret I'd found for him at the Macy's in San Francisco . . . He looked like a French intellectual among all the scruffy students, and I was proud of his difference.

Over our honeymoon together, I also discovered that he was a talented mimic, especially when it came to animals. Alone in my apartment, he would imitate perfectly the fixed and defiant stare of the opossums that were always rummaging in the back garden.

I also discovered that he adored making me breakfast and serving me in bed, and one morning, as he was carrying a tray of blueberry pancakes, coffee and orange juice, he tripped over a book about Sufi mysticism that he'd left on the floor and everything went flying. The hot coffee splashed over our sheets and the wall, and one of the cups shattered against my bedside table, and I was sure he'd be upset, but after he showed me an astonished face, he erupted into such gleeful laughter that he had to grope his way along the wall back to me, and he said through his merry tears, 'Who knew that screwing up so completely could be such a relief!' He caught a drop of coffee sliding down the wall on his fingertip, and he licked at it luxuriously, like a cat, and then he took the pot of warm milk from the dining table and twirled around and around and said that he had been reading about the whirling dervishes ever since Rabbi Simon had mentioned them. The milk sprayed around him, creating Jackson Pollock streaks across my bookshelves and floor, and I shouted 'No!' and held my hands over my eyes, but soon the pot was empty, and he stumbled around, enjoying the dizzy circles he was tracing, and then he jumped on me, his mouth warm and peppery, just like it nearly always is. As I pulled him into me, he shut his eyes tight and began to sing softly in Polish, and whatever it was made him cry silently. I held him tightly, and he kissed my ears and nose and eyes, and his sudden peals of childlike laughter made me understand that he had found his missing playfulness in the astonishing way our bodies fit together.

Benni flew back to New York on January 2nd, and it soon became clear that the *little nothing* in my womb had re-energised his personal anti-war campaign. He and Dad began standing out in front of Dow Chemical's Midtown offices every Friday before Sabbath, holding up a sign saying HOLOCAUST SURVIVORS AGAINST THE WAR and shouting, 'No more napalm!' More often than not, passers-by were disapproving; some hateful people even threw whatever garbage they had handy at the two of them, and a brawny construction worker in a yellow hard hat once marched right up to them and threatened to clobber them if they didn't, as he put it, *shut the fuck up*. Dad later told me that Benni asked the man if he was a Holocaust survivor, and the worker sneered at him and replied, 'What the hell does the Holocaust have to do with anything?' and Benni told him in his slow, controlled voice, 'It has to do with everything – even with you, as it happens. Because my parents were murdered by the Nazis, and my aunts and uncles, too, and I was a little boy then, so I couldn't defend them. But if you attack me or my father-in-law, I guarantee you that I will find a way to hurt you very badly, if not today, then one day very soon.'

The construction worker must have thought that the immigrant with the bruised eyes in the powder-blue suit wasn't in his right mind, and after calling him an asshole, he walked away.

Dad and Benni also had an occasional triumph. One clear and bright evening in early February, in fact, they got a crowd of about a hundred people chanting anti-war slogans along with them in front of Dow's offices. About ten days later, on Friday the 17th, Benni conscripted me and my sister into his campaign on one of my quick trips to New York, and the four of us chained ourselves to railing leading up to the front door of the military induction centre. I was four months pregnant at the time, and already shaped like a pear, and Benni had brought along a brown-and-black woollen poncho that he'd just made for me and a thermos of coffee. I thought I might feel trapped when we were locked to the railing, but instead I was eerily calm, perhaps because I sensed I was finally doing something not just for the Vietnamese, but also for Dad's and Benni's parents and other relations.

When the police came, they clipped our chains, and a balding, surly cop led me and Evie away from Benni and Dad. He turned out to be from New Rochelle, which was where our mother had been born, and when we were alone, he confessed that he thought that sending our soldiers to Vietnam was a gigantic mistake.

As for my father and Benni, a handful of policemen dragged them into a van and a mean-spirited old officer shouted at them for what he called *making adolescent mischief at your age!* A little while later, at the station, a squat, no-nonsense lieutenant told them that two 'God-fearing Jews,' as he put it, ought to be ashamed of themselves, especially for bringing a pregnant woman into their silly scheme, and on a freezing morning in February no less.

According to Dad, who later recounted the episode to me and Evie and Daniela – who'd heard us giggling with relief in the hallway of our apartment building and come down to investigate – Benni replied that his wife did whatever she wanted, and what she wanted was to end the war in Vietnam. My father told me later that he'd detected Jew hatred in the man's bullying voice, and especially when he asked them if they were *commies*. Dad was sure they were about to be arrested, but in the end, the lieutenant escorted them out of the station and told them that they ought to go to their temple and repent, because they were sinning against the Lord by opposing the war, since the Vietnamese weren't Christians or even what he called *mule-headed Jews*.

I kept up my teaching duties and my study of the Ticuna language until late March. By then, my belly was huge, and Dickson told me what I already knew – that my plans for Amazonia would have to wait. I'd been preparing myself to give up my graduate work for weeks, but after my goodbye to him, desolation started trailing me everywhere I went. And alongside that desolation roamed a question I knew I'd never voice aloud: Did Mom feel the same sense of despair when she got pregnant with me and had to quit her master's programme in English literature at Columbia?

As soon as I returned to New York, Benni cheered me up by assuring me that he wanted me to return to my studies after the baby was born – if not in Berkeley, then at City College or NYU.

'You really want me to go back to school?' I asked.

He gave me an irritated look. 'Tessa, I'll only answer your question if you tell me why you're so generous with everyone else, but so stingy with yourself?'

'I don't know what you're talking about,' I said.

Benni rolled his eyes. 'You let me work at the shop on Sunday and leave my books and newspapers all over the floor, and you eat the dinners I make even if they're not so hot, and you don't make fun of me for dressing like I'm Jay Gatsby, and you—'

'I love how you dress!' I exclaimed.

'That's what I'm trying to say. None of us can do any wrong in your eyes.'

'Who's us?'

'Your dad and Evie and me. But you . . . It's like you're always not good enough. And waiting for someone to punish you.'

His insight was like a slap across my face. But there was an even greater truth hiding below that stinging insight that only occurred to me in bed that night: *It's as if I think that I deserve to be abandoned if I'm not perfect.*

Did lack of sleep contribute to the heavy sense of hopelessness that soon took possession of me? After a night when I couldn't find any comfortable position in bed, I grew convinced that my first field experiences in Appalachia would be my last – that my child would tether me to home for many years, and I'd never again find the courage to take up my studies.

One morning in mid-April, after looking at my photographs of Belle, I grew desperate to hear her comforting voice. I'd last spoken to her just after my wedding. I told her right away that I was pregnant, of course, and after she said how pleased she was for me, she asked me how I felt about becoming a mother, and I said I was often still surprised – that I'd figured I'd be in my thirties before I'd have a child. She detected something downhearted in my tone and told me she needed to hear the truth from the people she loved, so after some nervous hesitation, I told her how worried and sad it sometimes made me to have to give up graduate school.

'Listen, baby, you've no reason be so upset,' she told me. 'That music in you is going to take you places you ain't even dreamt of yet. I'm sure of it! And wherever you go, you'll bring your child with you. You've got options I never had, Teresa. You just gotta grab hold of 'em!'

Belle's faith in me made me shiver, but not entirely with relief; I sensed that there was still far too much about myself that I didn't understand. And maybe never would. I went on to tell her about how happy Benni was, but when we detoured onto the subject of how his family had been sent to the death camps, she let an unnerving silence fall between us. 'You need to be very careful,' she ended up telling me, and when I asked her why, she said, 'Sooner or later, your baby is gonna need you to protect him from all them ghosts in his family and yours.'

'What do you mean?' I asked.

'Benni's kin and yours – that died in them Nazi camps. They got expectations of you. All ghosts do. So you gotta be very careful and watch for any sign that the baby ain't doin' so well – that he's scared of comin' into the world.'

Belle's warning sounded a bit kooky and melodramatic to me, so I didn't tell Benni about it, but it might have ended up saving my life and the life of my unborn child; during my twenty-eighth week, I came down with chills one afternoon, and my legs gave way when I was washing my face with hot water. After I lay down, I felt a little better, and I decided not to call my doctor or husband, but then I heard her telling me that my baby needed me to protect him, so I phoned Benni at work, and he rushed me to my gynaecologist's office. Dr Marsden discovered that my blood pressure was dangerously high and that I had pre-eclampsia. 'Good thing you came in right away,' he said in a grave tone.

He gave me medications for my condition, but my body rhythms must have already been badly compromised, because I went into labour after only thirty-three weeks, on Saturday, June 3rd.

Then, after my emergency caesarean, my blood pressure crashed.

In one of the dreams I had while drifting in and out of consciousness, Benni led me by the hand up a steep burial mound. After we climbed to the top, we looked out over a city that was on fire, and we started to sing, and it was our voices that put out the flames.

The moment I regained consciousness, I asked Benni about the baby, and he told me we'd had a boy, and that he was in an incubator, and that the doctors were doing all they could for him.

Benni's voice was frail and desolate. I forced myself not to cry. And through some alchemy I didn't understand, my thoughts turned hard and resilient and defiant; I decided that because Benni was a Holocaust survivor, our baby would fight so hard to live that no illness in the world would be able to overcome him.

I was aware that I was counting on wishful thinking, but it seemed my only option at the time. After Benni and I talked about the ward where our baby was, I remembered my dream of saving a city in flames, and I started to teach him the melody I'd learned. I figured that maybe it had been given to me for a reason, and that if he sang it to our son, it would help him remain with us. But after the first few notes, Benni stunned me by joining me an octave below.

When I asked him how he knew it, he showed me an astonished look and said, 'I've done nothing but sing it to you all the time you've been ill!'

Benni told me that when I was close to death, he remembered a melody that Berekiah Zarco had taught to Ewa and started to sing it to me.

'How did Berekiah teach it to Ewa?' I asked.

'He appeared to her in a vision – a long time ago, during the war. I know it seems strange. But anyway, when the doctors told me you might die, my heart seemed to explode, and all I could think of was singing to you – that the melody would reach you wherever you were and keep you from leaving me and the baby. I held your hand and I sang it to you for hours, but then my throat got sore, and I could hardly even whisper, so your father took over.'

I knew at that moment that the possibility that our son might die had deepened Benni's belief in magic. And mine, too.

When I asked him to tell me what our baby looked like, he took my shoulder and confessed to me that the first time he saw him, he was so scrawny that he feared he'd die before I'd had a chance to hold him.

'But he's not dead, is he?' I asked fearfully. 'Oh, God, tell me the truth, Benni!'

From the urgent way my heart was beating, I knew that my entire future depended on his reply.

'No, he's hanging on,' Benni told me. 'He's got soft brown hair just like you and a sweet little mouth and . . . and you know what, he's got the most beautiful hands you ever saw.' He started to weep silently. 'I keep thinking of his lungs,' he continued, 'because the doctor told me they're really fragile and tiny, and I sometimes I think that maybe he can't get enough air to go on living, because he inherited that from me, the not getting enough air, and I know that he cries so hard because he's scared of suffocating. And that's my fault, because that's what I felt so often when I was in hiding and couldn't go outside and thought I was going to die.'

While I kissed and comforted Benni, I realised that I was drawn to people who believed in nearly impossible connections between everything that we see and hear and feel – between our own experiences and even people we've never met. Benni later told me that he'd concluded that such linkages were made by what he called *the Incandescent Threads*, and that he had sensed them since he was little and even seen them twice. They were filaments of cause and effect, he said, and they linked people across centuries and millennia, and their light was caused by the heat that was generated at the time of Creation. There was nothing they couldn't bring together. He was pretty sure, in fact, that he and I had met because one of them was stretched between the two of us, or maybe between one of his ancestors and my father. 'We both went to the Bosphorus that night because of one,' he told me. 'I sensed it linking us securely – otherwise I wouldn't have found the courage to talk to you.'

We called the baby Ethan. The name had come to Benni one morning at work, while he was fixing the seams on a pair of my father's trousers, though he didn't tell anyone, not even me. Characteristically, he'd decided that if he kept it a secret, our child would have a chance at life.

The name sounded perfect to me, especially since no one in my family or his had ever had it – at least, to our knowledge – so it didn't come burdened by our past.

Ethan spent nine days in his incubator before the doctors told us he was out of danger. Holding him in my arms, caressing his dark, downy hair, seemed proof that occasionally, and despite all the odds, our greatest hopes can come true.

Once we got him home, I told Benni what Belle had said about the danger that the ghosts of his ancestors had posed to me and Ethan. I was pretty certain he'd react angrily, but he told me instead she was right, that it had often seemed as if his ancestors wanted too much from him.

Maybe even my life, he didn't admit to me, but I could see that worry in his eyes.

Ethan's pale complexion deepened and his cheeks turned rosy shortly after I started to breastfeed him, and his frenzied fidgeting ceased. Still, Benni and I were up many nights calming his tears. Once, he and I tried singing Ewa's melody to him, but it only made him scream louder.

A surprise ... My closeness to Ethan seemed to sharpen all my senses, so that everyone I saw or spoke to – even just the mailman or a delivery boy – became charged with a delicate and abiding love. It was as if I could sense each person's heroism for simply being able to carry on amid all the torments and disappointments of a normal life. Belle told me that the same change had come over her after giving birth for the first time. 'It's the crown of a great truth,' she told me, 'though it doesn't always make things easy,' and I asked, 'Why's that?' and she said, 'Because you'll never again be able to make believe that other people aren't as real and important as you are.'

Evie was staying with Dad for the summer, so she came over every morning to help me. The two of us would go for long walks with Ethan, and we'd always find our way to Benni's shop in the end, and his face would glow with Ethan in his arms, and even the bruised shadows around his eyes would vanish.

After a few weeks, I started shopping in the Asian markets in Chinatown again, and I'd buy coconut milk, dried mushrooms and all sorts of peculiar ingredients, and I began making exotic curries and noodles for our suppers. Sometimes, too, I'd make a recipe from the cookbook Dad had inherited from his mother. In hindsight, I think I needed a way to express my gratitude toward my husband and father and sister – and to the world itself for permitting my baby to live. Benni in particular grew to love those banquets. They may have even become a form of theatre for him – a reproduction of the chaotic, noisy, big-hearted childhood that he had lost. Sometimes I'd watch the way he'd fold Ethan over his shoulder while he conversed with my father – and while spooning up whatever custardy or gooey dessert I'd made to satisfy his sweet tooth – and I'd know that he was exactly where he'd hoped he'd one day be.

If Shelly and Julie were visiting with their daughters, we'd also play charades and drink a lot of Portuguese red wine, and after they'd gone off to their hotel, Benni and I would head to our bedroom and make love amid the extravagant flower bouquets that they'd always bring us.

Playing my flute to Ethan in the warmed, perfumed air of the kitchen – after I'd made one of my exotic suppers – was my most secret pleasure. He'd clap his hands and giggle, and all of him would become laughter.

Sometimes I was struck by the notion that Ethan made time stand still for me, most usually in the night, when I'd listen to Benni's soft breathing and the merciful quiet that surrounded every voice coming from the street, and I was sure that all the universe wished me well, and for the first time in my life, I think, I was not afraid of death.

At the very least, Benni and I have contributed something beautiful to the world, I would think.

And if the worst happens, he and my father and Evie will make sure that Ethan is loved.

Often now, while making love with Benni, I'd feel a soft humming inside me – a subtle energy that I hadn't been still enough to hear before – and it seemed a product of our union.

For months, I gave everything I was to my husband and son.

I held nothing back. And in so doing, I found myself. It seemed my Golden Age.

It would be misleading to claim that my transition to motherhood went completely smoothly, however. Over Ethan's first weeks of life, I found caring for him terrifying, and I even found myself fantasising on occasion about how freer – and more engaged in the world – I'd have felt if I were in Brazil and studying the music of the Ticuna. He was so tiny and fragile, and I didn't ever seem to know what I was doing. Even though Dad taught me how to carry him and change his diapers, I imagined that there was a set of directions to motherhood that my mom ought to have handed down to me and never did. So I was sure that sooner or later I'd make an error that would put his little life at risk, and it took me four or five months to stop panicking every time he developed a cough or soiled himself with diarrhoea. And it took me even longer to realise the obvious – that Ethan's fussing and whining were his ways of teaching me when to give him my breast or his bottle, and how I could make him more comfortable. In short, I didn't need any manual to motherhood, because my son would tell me what he needed in his own eloquent ways.

And then, on the first Sunday in February, everything came undone …

Benni was at his shop, doing some alterations for an important customer, when the intercom buzzed. 'Who's there?' I asked.

'Is that you, Teresa?' a woman's voice asked brightly, and I answered, 'Yes, who is it?' and the voice said, 'It's your mother. I've come without calling first. I hope that's okay.'

The skin of my face began to tingle. And a small, terrified part of me – way below my surface – whispered, *Don't say a word! She'll go away if you don't speak.*

'Teresa?' my mother said. 'Are you there?'

My finger pressed the button to let her in without my willing it to do so.

I wrung my hands while I waited for her. And I realised how cluttered our bookcases looked – and how tattered our Oriental rug. When I opened the door, Mom smiled. Her eyes were lively and friendly, enhanced by a light dusting of blue eyeshadow. Her hair was brown with blonde highlights. She looked a bit like Jane Fonda.

'Wow, you've grown up!' she said with a pleased smile. She opened her arms.

I didn't move. So she came to me and hugged me. She felt as though she were made of something hard and cold – porcelain, it seemed to me.

While I was gazing at her clear blue eyes, I felt the perilous urge to throw my arms around her and confess how much I'd missed her, and hiding behind that urge was the hope that she'd have an overwhelmingly sensible reason for never calling or writing after she abandoned us: *I was very ill, Teresa, and I didn't want you and Evie to see me after my radiation treatments, and the cancer made me depressed for years, so I . . .*

I crouched deep down in my mind and invited her into the living room and asked if she wanted something to drink.

'Yes, some hot tea would be great,' she said. 'With a little milk.'

I put the kettle on. When I returned to the living room with our teacups, Mom was wriggling out of her winter coat, and the way she did was just like Evie, which made me think, *I'll never not want to know anything as much as I don't want to know that she and my sister are so alike.*

I hung her coat on one of the hooks by the door. 'How did you find me?' I asked.

'Evie found me. She told me you'd had a baby.'

That seemed unlikely, but my scepticism withered into a flat-sounding 'Oh.'

Mom laughed and shrugged – at what, I had no idea – then undid the floral-patterned silk scarf around her neck, but she kept it in her hand, telling me in a confiding voice – as if we were close friends – that she froze in New York now that she was used to Los Angeles.

I returned to the kitchen to prepare our tea while Mom looked around the living room. I kept close track of the creaks she made on the parquet floor as if she might be tempted to steal one of the paintings Benni had bought from his old friend George. Or more to the point, as if she might ease open the door and slip away.

Just after I brought the teapot to the living room, Ethan stirred. He'd been sleeping in his room.

'Is that your son?' Mom asked, and when I said it was, she asked in a cheerful voice, 'Should we go see what's bothering him?'

I brought Ethan out to her. He was wearing a blue woollen beanie that Belle had crocheted for him. I'd folded him in his favourite yellow blanket.

'My God, he's beautiful,' Mom said, and she gazed at me affectionately.

Her eyes were keenly aware and intelligent. I hadn't remembered that. And for the first time in my life, I could see why Dad had fallen for her.

When she reached out for Ethan, I handed him to her as if I'd been hypnotised. She cradled the baby in her arms and smiled. 'Hello, my gorgeous grandson!' she exulted.

I wanted to shout at her that she hadn't earned that role, but when she looked up at me, her eyes were dripping tears. I felt as if this was how my life would end – with my baby stolen from me by my mother. And that there was nothing I could do about it.

'How old is he now?' she asked, and I said, 'Eight-and-a-half months,' and she said, 'He has your mouth and hair,' and as if I were making a move at chess, I replied, 'But Benni's nose and dark eyes.'

I poured us tea. Mom sat with Ethan on our sofa. I dropped down in the black velvet armchair where Benni read the newspaper. I felt years distant from the person I'd been just a few minutes earlier.

Benni's cigarettes were on the low table between us. 'Do you smoke now?' Mom asked, and I said, 'No, Benni does,' and she said proudly, 'I stopped, you know.'

I hadn't remembered she'd smoked. How do you forget something like that?

She asked me about Ethan's sleep habits. I found I was talking too shrilly and at some point stopped in mid-sentence. I studied my mother. She was shorter than I remembered. And her tense and wrinkled hands surprised me. They didn't seem to fit with the rest of her.

'When did Evie tell you I'd had a baby?' I asked.

'A couple of months ago. Franco and I had already made plans to come to New York, so the timing seemed right for me to come see you.'

'You're still with Franco?' I asked.

'Yeah, we got married,' she said, shrugging as if the results had been mixed. She brushed the back of her hand against Ethan's cheek. 'He's such a cutie!' she gushed.

As I studied the careful way she moved a corner of Ethan's blanket over his feet, she stopped being my mother for an instant. She was a lonely woman who'd been tugged in two directions when she was too young to know that whichever path she chose would be the wrong one. I leaned forward in my seat and said, 'I think I understand you better now that I've had a child.'

'Understand me in what way?' she said.

Her tone was curious, friendly, eager – which encouraged me. 'I sometimes wish I'd stayed in graduate school,' I told her. 'So I think I may have some idea now about why you abandoned me and Evie.'

'Did I abandon you?' She pulled her head in like a hen and showed me an arched glare.

'You left without warning. I was seven and Evie was five, and you went away.'

She put Ethan down on the sofa. 'Let me tell you something, Teresa,' she said with a firmness that seemed a warning of worse to come, 'you left me long before I left you!'

That accusation gripped me so hard that I couldn't move. It was as if she'd bewitched me. But then Ethan reached out with his hands, and I found myself standing up and rushing to him. Having him in my arms gave me back my confidence. 'Mom, what are you talking about?' I asked as I sat back down with the baby. 'You know you left us. We all know.'

'Teresa, you couldn't get enough of your father. For me . . . You never felt anything for me. I'd try to hold you and you'd push me away.'

'That can't be true,' I said, and she said, 'Of course, it's true! Ask your father.'

'But why didn't I want to be with you?' I inquired.

'How the hell should I know?' she said scornfully. She showed me a haughty look. 'If you think you can always figure out your kids, you're wrong.'

'So you're blaming your seven-year-old daughter for why you abandoned us? Do you really mean for me to believe that I was responsible for your decisions?'

'Believe whatever you want. It makes absolutely no difference to me. But look,' she said in a conciliatory tone, fighting to smile. 'I didn't come here to argue. That's all in the past.'

'Yes, but is what I believe about you really of absolutely no interest to you?' I questioned.

'Look, Teresa, I can't control what you think. I've learned the hard way to let all of that go.'

'What does *let all of that go* mean?' I asked.

'To move on,' she said as if it were obvious, so I asked, 'Does a mother ever move on from having children?' and she said, 'Kids grow up and you move on. That's the way life works.'

I paused while suppressing a shout of protest. 'Evie and I needed you,' I finally said, and I hated my desperate, pleading manner, but I couldn't stop myself. 'She was only five. She used to cry all the time. Dad had to carry her to his bed or she couldn't sleep. We never even knew where you'd gone.'

'Your father knew where I was well enough,' she said, and I asked, 'Did he?' and she said, 'Sure,' so I replied, 'In any case, you made no attempt to see us.'

She laughed scornfully. 'What would have been the point? I wasn't going to stay, so it would just be worse for you if you thought I would.'

Could that be true? I wondered, and I felt all my energy leaving me – sucked out of me as if by black magic. 'This conversation, Mom . . . I can't talk about these things. It does me no good.'

Mom's face turned patronising, and she started to reply, but the key turned in our front door. Benni came in carrying the *New York Times*. To see his face – his deeply loving eyes – was like being rescued from a shipwreck. The foyer wall prevented him from seeing my mother at first. 'I brought you the paper,' he said. He stepped into the living room. 'Oh, hello!' he said to Mom.

'It's my mother,' I told him.

She stood up. Benni walked to her and shook her hand. 'Lovely to meet you,' he said.

'And it's great to finally meet you.'

Benni turned to me, and I saw the concern in his expression for how dazed and disoriented I must have looked. He came to me and kissed me, then leaned down and tousled Ethan's hair.

'Your son is gorgeous!' Mom told him excitedly.

'Thank you. Now, if I remember correctly, you're living in Phoenix these days. So what brings you all the way to New York?'

Benni knew very well that my mother lived in Los Angeles. I was certain that this was his way of making it clear that she hadn't earned the right to be included in our family.

'No, I live in Santa Monica,' Mom said. 'I write for TV. Have you ever seen *Bonanza*?'

'No, I'm sorry. TV Westerns . . . They seem to be made just for kids.'

The phone rang. 'I'll get it,' Benni said, but it was probably Evie and I was anxious to know why she'd told Mom about my baby. I handed Ethan to Benni. 'I'll get it in the bedroom.'

The call was from Rabbi Simon, who'd gotten into the habit of checking in with me every few weeks.

A couple of minutes later, Ethan erupted into whooping cries. I told Simon I'd have to call him back and rushed to the living room. Benni had turned his back to my mother and was trying to calm our son with whispered endearments and caresses.

'I haven't done anything!' Mom cut in as if she'd been wronged. 'It's this husband of yours – he seems to be imagining things.'

Benni whipped around. His eyes were blazing with rage. 'Mrs Sasportes, I've asked you to leave,' he said with deadly calm. 'And I'd be grateful if you did what I ask.'

'I haven't been Mrs Sasportes in twenty years!' my mother told him in a superior voice.

'Well, whoever you are, you have to go!'

'Benni, what happened?' I asked. I tried to take Ethan from him, but he turned away from me and said in a voice admitting no dissent, 'No, I'll hold Ethan until your mother is gone.'

'Teresa, if I go now, I'll never come back,' Mom told me. 'And I'll never phone or write. And if you try to get in touch with me, I won't answer.' Her eyes – cold and threatening – were those of an old enemy.

'Are you really asking me to choose between you and Benni?' I asked in disbelief.

My mother took her coat from the hook by the door. She never said goodbye and neither did I.

When she eased the door closed, I felt as if my heart had stopped. I imagined the unhappy girl that I'd been, and I heard her shrieking for help. And I knew that there was nothing I could now do to come to her aid.

After Benni managed to calm Ethan down, he wiped the boy's puffy, red, tear-stained cheeks with his handkerchief.

I was still standing by the door. 'What did she do?' I asked.

'She said she wanted some more milk for her tea, so I handed Ethan to her. While I was in the kitchen, she began to whisper, and I went to the doorway, and she told Ethan that she could tell you were a bad mother. She said you'd rejected her and were sure to reject him sooner or later.'

'Those were her exact words? Are you sure?'

'Of course I'm sure. She wanted me to hear them. It was her way of getting revenge on me for saying that she lived in Phoenix. Though more likely, she was already angry when she first came here. I don't know. And I don't care. I ran in and took Ethan from her, and she tried to hold onto him, and he got scared, and I looked into her eyes, and what I saw there was . . . I'm not sure what it was exactly, but it was dangerous – like something in a nightmare – and I told her to leave.'

I embraced Benni and thanked him. My relief was like wading into a warm ocean. And it was mixed with gratitude and a host of other emotions I couldn't have put into words, most likely because lonely seven-year-olds don't have the vocabulary to express all they feel.

Later that day, I called Evie and asked her why she'd told our mother about Ethan, but she didn't know what I was talking about. 'Why in God's name would I try to find Mom?' she demanded in a disgruntled voice, and I said, 'So then how did she find me?' and she replied, 'Well, you're in the phone book as Teresa Sasportes, so anyone with half a brain could find you.'

I went to see Dad after that. He had a bad cold and was in bed with Radley and a big box of Kleenex tissues. Elis Regina was singing 'Corcovado' on the record player.

'Have you spoken to Mom lately, by any chance?' I asked.

'Are you nuts? I'm sick but I ain't delirious!'

I explained about her finding me and what she had let Benni overhear, and how he'd rescued Ethan from her. His face grew tense and upset. 'Your mother is toxic,' he told me. 'She's just lucky I wasn't there when she showed up.'

'But did I really abandon her before she abandoned us?' I asked.

'In a way, but you need to know the reason why.' He patted the bed, so I sat with him. 'Whenever you didn't do what she wanted, she'd say you were selfish and mean-spirited. She used to belittle you, and at some point she started calling you a little wretch all the time, and sometimes, if I wasn't home, she'd whack you on the behind – and really hard.'

'She did? How did you find out?'

Dad took a steadying breath. 'Once, I saw the marks on you when I was bathing you.'

'How old was I?'

'Four or five.' He sneezed, and I handed him a tissue. 'I warned her that if she hit you again, I'd grab you and Evie and leave,' he said. 'And she seemed genuinely remorseful for a while – and kind. But then she started up again on you – calling you names when she didn't like what you were doing. I realised then that we couldn't stay together, though I waited too long to make that decision. I kept telling myself that she could change. One good thing I did do was buy you a flute, because I sensed you needed something to block out that awful, belligerent voice of hers.'

'Why did you decide on a flute?'

My father's eyes twinkled and he reached for his pipe. 'Even a tiny Bunny Rabbit can carry a flute around with her anywhere she wants!' he said, and the joy in his voice made me laugh. 'Frank Wess helped me pick out your first instrument,' he continued. 'And it became your shield.' He wiped his hand back through his hair, troubled again. 'If you want to know the truth,' he said, 'your mother was in competition with you. She sensed that you were more intelligent than her, and more talented, too, and she hated that. You know, baby, when your mother called you an extraterrestrial . . . She meant it as great praise at first. She said it with pride – just like me. But then, when you were maybe six or seven and started getting such glowing evaluations from your teachers, she began to say it resentfully – with a sneer. For her, it stopped being a compliment.'

'And did you find out where she went after she left us?' I asked, and he replied, 'I thought maybe she was with her brother, but I never called him and he never called me,' and I said, 'Mom sounded so believable when she told me I'd abandoned her,' and in an authoritative and angry voice, he said, 'Let me tell you something. Your mother lies with perfect ease and without any sense of guilt, because she's certain she's not lying.'

Shortly after Mom's visit, the finality of her threat against me – of my never being able to see her again – sent me into a panic on two successive days, and from that point on, leaving my home – even just to buy the newspaper – would set my heart battering against my ribcage. An imminent and overwhelming sense of danger gripped me whenever I was on the street, and I was constantly compelled to look over my shoulder for someone who might be stalking me.

Do men and women who were abandoned as kids eventually come to believe that the world wants them dead?

That question recurred to me all the time, because it seemed clear now that I might have been in peril as a little girl – that my mother might have indeed harboured murderous thoughts about me. And about Evie, too, of course. In fact, I came to believe that my dreams of Mom concealing a blade behind her back and readying to attack my sister were – metaphorically, at least – accurate.

I forced myself to go food shopping every morning and take Ethan for long, serpentine walks in the afternoon, and I'd feign serenity if Benni or my father came with us, but in truth every step was a struggle against my instinct to run back home.

Worse, as the days passed, my fears didn't diminish.

I never told Benni about them, or confessed my shame and confusion either, but he sensed that I was lost in deep water, and in danger of drowning, and he would hold hands with me nearly all the time, and kiss me for no reason, and clown around for me and Ethan. Occasionally, he'd ask if I wanted to talk about what I was feeling, but I couldn't think of what to say other than what was already obvious. At night, after our son was asleep, he'd read excerpts to me from his kabbalah books, and once – probably hoping to show me a pathway out of my predicament – he told me how the Jewish mystics would repeat prayers to themselves as quickly as they could to escape their usual ways of thinking. 'They were trying to give themselves brand new eyes to see themselves and the whole universe,' he told me.

Benni also taught me a Hebrew prayer that his great-grandmother had given him, and he made me promise that I'd say it to myself when I sensed myself in danger, and I did, but it didn't ever ease my racing heartbeat.

On weekends, he'd plead with me to take a ride with them on the Staten Island Ferry, or hop in a cab with them and go to the Cloisters, and I wanted to say yes, but I didn't. Once, after I'd declined to join him and Ethan on another one of their adventures, he brought my hands to his lips and – with unfallen tears in his eyes – asked if I was dissatisfied with him. 'Do you regret marrying me?' he questioned in a trembling voice.

'No, of course, not,' I rushed to reply, and I embraced him hard, and my reply seemed true at the time, yet I realised long after midnight that night, unable to sleep, that I had begun to find his encouragement – and even his affection – intrusive. And why? Because they drew attention to my limitations and difficulties, and I only wanted to be left alone.

Occasionally, I'd put an interview with Belle on my tape player and close my eyes and imagine that I was sitting with her on her creaky porch. The exquisite pain that would spread through me when I heard her telling me about the ocean she'd always wanted to see – and never had – made me certain of what I needed to do, but I knew I could never admit to Benni or my father that I wanted to return to my university studies so soon after Ethan's birth.

I was so ashamed that motherhood wasn't enough for me that it would make me shudder.

And then a powerful insight came to me while I was listening to Belle telling me about the poverty and hunger she'd experienced as a girl: what I feared most was turning into my mom – that I would one day abandon Ethan and Benni.

Was I going mad? If so, then I grew to learn that madness is only a short distance from the place where each of us usually lives.

Other than my tapes of the singers I'd recorded in Appalachia, my only other solace became reading. I remember lying on the sofa with *The Brothers Karamazov* one afternoon in mid-March of 1968 and hoping the story would go on forever. But then Ethan started to cry, and so I threw the book at the wall, hitting a Japanese rice-paper lamp that Benni had bought in Montreal. The lamp crashed to the floor, and I didn't bother picking it up. When Benni came home, he said 'What happened, Tessa?' and I said in a mean-spirited voice, 'The lamp must have tripped on one of the books you left on the floor,' which gave him a frightened little laugh, so I laughed too. But afterward, when we looked in each other's eyes, we both knew that he was scared of the person I'd become. And that I was as well.

A week or so later, Benni came home from his shop in the afternoon and held out an envelope to me. 'Open it,' he said.

Inside it were plane tickets to Lisbon for me and him and Ethan. We were scheduled to leave in a week. 'What's this?' I asked, and he replied, 'We're going to Portugal,' and when I asked what was in Portugal, he said, 'My ancestors lived there – and yours. I figured it was time we went there. I've been studying Portuguese, too.' He snapped his fingers as if to summon a waiter. In his proudest Portuguese accent, he said, '*Quero um café, por favor. E um—*'

'But Ethan can't come,' I cut in. 'He's too small.'

Benni grinned mischievously. 'I called Dr Allen, and he cleared Ethan for lift-off. He can go anywhere we want to go. The kid is as strong as an ox – just like your father!'

'Dad isn't as strong as an ox,' I said, and he replied, 'Well, he raised you and Evie alone – that's pretty damn strong,' and because he was right, I showed him a resentful look and said, 'I can't just go to Europe like it was nothing,' and his dark eyes grew menacing and he said, 'Teresa, we have to go!'

'But why . . . why do we have to go?' I stuttered.

'Isn't that obvious?'

He gave me a hard look and pinched a cigarette from his pack. Then, without warning, he made a desperate, choking sound, and he thrust his hand over his eyes, and I was certain he was about to burst into tears, but he turned away from me instead and walked to our bedroom and eased the door closed behind him. My heart told me to go to him and confess the truth, but I stayed where I was and started thinking of all the ways I could sabotage our trip.

While I was lying in the dark that night, I realised I wanted Benni to be as unhappy as I was. I'd even been hoping he'd lose interest in making love with me.

It's amazing that a person can live for weeks without being aware of the downward trajectory of all her thoughts – and the devastating effect she has been having on the people who love her. In the end, I agreed to go to Lisbon because I didn't want to become a vengeful and deceitful woman – in other words, my mother – but I resented Benni for forcing me to go.

My father came with us to the airport. We spoke Ladino together in the taxi, and he started to cry when he said goodbye to me, which scared me.

'Dad, is there some problem with your health you're not telling me about?' I asked.

'No, I just want you to be back the way you were – when you were happy.'

I wanted to tell him, *That Teresa is gone for good and I'm all that's left*, which shocked me, but it also seemed perfectly accurate.

On our first morning in Lisbon, it was pouring with rain. Benni suggested that we spend the day inside, and he was keen on seeing the Museum of Ancient Art, so the taxi dropped us there. Just after we got our tickets, Benni told me that a friend of a friend was waiting for us in the auditorium, and it seemed bizarre that he hadn't told me earlier, but I decided not to quarrel. A young woman with long curly hair was seated at a desk in front of the auditorium doors, with name tags spread in front of her. Benni went to her and said in English, 'Hi, I'd like the tag for my wife, Teresa Sasportes.' The woman found it quickly, and she handed him a cloth bag, as well, and he came back to me. Inside the bag – which was stamped *Colóquio de Estudos Sefarditas – Março 1968* in black letters – I discovered brochures about Sephardic music and culture.

Benni took Ethan from me very gently, without waking him, and after he'd secured his yellow blanket around him, he said, 'Your place is inside the auditorium.'

'What are you talking about?' I asked.

'Apparently, the old songs are still sung in places like Morocco and Turkey. And people study them. Isn't that amazing?'

'I don't understand,' I told him, and he replied, 'Teresa, you need to do what you were meant to do,' and I asked, 'Which means?' and he said, 'There's a vibration inside you, a kind of singing, even when you're silent, even when you don't know it's there.'

His words seemed to be spoken to the deepest and most hidden part of me, but they also made me uncomfortable, as if he had learned too much about me. 'Just how long have you known about this conference?' I demanded.

'Your dad found out a while back through his Sephardic contacts.'

'And you two decided I should be here?'

'I guess that one thing just led to another.' He made an imploring gesture with his hands. 'Tessa, Morrie told me that he's known what you needed to do since you were seven years old.'

'So you both think that I wasn't meant to be a mother?' I asked, and inside that one simple question was every wrong idea I'd ever had about them or myself.

'No, you're a great mom! Our little nothing adores you. This is something else.'

'I don't understand.'

'Tessa, when we first had dinner together, you told me to tell you when I knew what it is you really wanted.' His bruised eyes grew deadly serious. 'So I'm telling you now. You need to study music – Sephardic music. That's why you took your classes in Portuguese. And why you started fantasising about Brazil. And if you don't mind my saying so—'

'I fantasised about the *Indians* in Brazil,' I cut in.

'Yeah, you got that a bit wrong,' he said with a merry laugh. 'Maybe the truth needed to come disguised – like angels. Did you know that angels put on clothing so that their light . . . so it doesn't blind us?'

'Benni, I'm sorry,' I said with a big theatrical sigh, 'but this is insane.'

'You've told me about the hollow inside you when you picture all the cousins you'd have in Greece if Hitler didn't come along. So, what kind of music did they sing?' he asked defiantly.

I didn't give him any reply because I sensed that he was steering me in the right direction, and I didn't want to go there. My fears apparently had their own perverse gravity.

'Exactly, Ladino songs,' he announced. 'But you know what, we can't go back into the past – at least not little people like you and me. So the way I see it, you've only got one option, and that option is waiting for you inside the auditorium.'

I held out my hands for Ethan, because I was going to return to the hotel with him, but Benni gripped my wrist. 'Months ago, your father and I went to see one of the organisers of this conference, a big-shot professor in New York. He's really nice. His name is William Armer. I got in touch with him again just before we left. He's expecting you.' In a gentler tone, releasing me, he said, 'Today is the first day of the conference. You haven't missed anything.'

'Benni, I know you mean well,' I said, smiling falsely, 'but I can't just start over. I can't just barge in on a meeting of specialists. They'll think I'm an idiot.'

'You're not starting over! You were raised on Sephardic music. And Armer says he needs someone who speaks Ladino and Portuguese, and who has a great ear. He's expecting you.'

The terror in me was like a crow flapping around in my chest. *Where does all this fear of revealing the truth come from?* I wondered, and I only noticed I'd started crying when I tasted the salt on my lips. 'Benni, what have you done to me?' I said with a moan, though as soon as that cry of distress came out of my mouth, I realised – cringing – that I sounded like a line my mom might have written for *Bonanza*.

'You seem to have forgotten that I'm on your side,' he said. 'And so is Ethan. And by the way, you can stop trying to conceal what you're feeling from me. I'm not a dummy. I know how to detect a fake smile far better than you do!' In a whisper, he added, 'And I know you listen to your tapes of Belle when I'm not there.'

'And . . . and you're not mad at me?' I asked in disbelief, and he said, 'Why would I be mad?' and I said, 'Because it means that I miss my fieldwork.'

'Look, Tessa, it's time you told Zencefil the Witch to go strangle herself, don't you think?'

'Zencefil?'

'Your mom.'

'My mom?'

'Yeah. After the day she visited us and said such insulting things about you to Eti, I put two and two together. I mean, I saw what a menacing woman she was. And that she wanted to punish you. I realised that that damn doll your dad put in his puppet show must have seemed like her to you when you were a little girl. So it's time you cut her strings and told her that she can't insult you any longer. And that you never liked marionettes in the first place!'

I shivered. And my feet felt rooted to the stone floor, because I knew he was right about Mom's mesmerising power over me – over even my dreams.

'I'm scared,' I confessed. And it seemed the most honest thing I'd said in a long, long time.

'So be scared!' Benni said without sympathy. 'When you're perfectly safe, being scared isn't such a terrible thing. For Christ's sake, I'm scared every day.'

'You are?'

'Sure! When I think of my childhood, I sometimes want to run and hide. You think you're the only one who looks over her shoulder on the street? And I have to get a little tipsy before I can chain myself to the induction centre. And half the time, I live on pancakes and toast because I don't think I can keep down anything else. So be scared! And then do what you were meant to do!'

I then told him what I never thought I would: 'Benni, I'm most scared of abandoning you and Ethan – like my mom. At night sometimes, it makes me want to shed my skin.'

'No, you'd never abandon us,' he said confidently.

'But maybe I'm not so different from my mother. Maybe she wanted things that she was afraid to tell my dad. So she left.'

'Sorry, I don't buy it! And anyhow, what your mother wanted back then ... it has nothing to do with you. *You* need to live out your dreams. Everything will be okay if you do that.' He flapped his hand at me. 'Besides, you're nothing like your mother. You're like Morrie.'

'Is that true?'

'Are you kidding me? You and your dad are like peas in a pod!'

Benni kneeled and set Ethan down gently on a chair at the side of the room, and after he returned to me, he kissed me on the lips, and he didn't permit me to back away, and I kissed him back, and I re-discovered the wonderful, intimate taste of tobacco and coffee and pepper in his mouth. And I realised that he was right when he said that he could win an Olympic gold medal at waiting, because he had shown me only devotion and kindness over the last two months, and I said to myself, *It's true that he attracts all that's unlikely to him, because here we are in Lisbon, and I'm about to do what I didn't think I'd ever do.*

He went back to Ethan and picked him up. The boy stirred but didn't awaken. 'There's a Hieronymus Bosch triptych of Saint Anthony in the museum,' Benni told me as I joined him. 'And my mom once showed me a photograph of it when I was kid back in Poland. So I'm really excited that Eti and I are going to finally get to see it. We'll catch up with you at the hotel in the evening. If there's a dinner for the participants tonight, go. Don't worry about us. The little nothing and I will be fine. I know how to prepare his bottle.' Ethan chose that moment to yawn and stretch his arms and legs, and Benni combed his soft dark hair into bangs. 'Right, Eti?' he said to the boy, and Ethan reached out his hand for his father's nose, which he liked to squeeze, because Benni would make a honking sound.

This time, however, Benni licked Ethan's palm like Radley and barked, which made the baby open his big black eyes – his father's eyes – and shake with laughter.

'See you later,' Benni told me, waving to me with Ethan's hand, and after a few moments, he and our son – a bit confused, just like his mom – walked down the hallway and turned right into one of the exhibition rooms, and just like that, they were gone.

What came into my mind then was one of Belle's songs, 'Lost at the Fair', and how she had told me that there comes a point in nearly everyone's life when they had to pay attention to the voice inside their own heart – a voice they'd denied for a long time. They had to obey what it told them to do or they would never find their way back to themselves. So I eased the door to the auditorium open and slipped inside.

About thirty people were in the audience, and a plump, round-faced young woman at a podium – wearing a long white peasant skirt and a loose, amber-coloured sweater – was talking in English about her fieldwork in Morocco, and showing slides of grizzled old men and women, many of them smiling with concealed amusement, a few of them caught with their mouths open and arms apart, as if they were belting out their greatest hits. She said that they were some of the very kind people from whom she had collected songs, and when I realised that a few of them might have had ancestors in Salonika, way too many emotions started rising into my chest, and too quickly, so I took a seat at the back where no one would see me give way to them.

Near the end of her talk, the speaker explained that the

melodies of the Sephardic Jews have always adapted to the scales and harmonies of the countries in which they've made their homes.

'But the lyrics rarely change,' she added. 'No matter where the Sephardim go, they take their words with them.'

That conclusion seemed like it had been searching for me for years. Indeed, it was as if I'd been waiting to hear that one affirmation all my life, and it was obvious at that moment that I'd inherited the ancient and holy words of the Portuguese and Spanish Jews, even if I hadn't been aware of it. They'd helped to make me the person I was, in fact, because the first songs I'd ever learned were the Ladino lullabies that my grandmother and grandfather had sung to my dad.

Everything seemed to make sense that day. Over our entire stay in Portugal, in fact, I felt as if I'd happened on a world where only positive things could happen to me and Benni and Ethan. I was aware, of course, that that was an illusion, but I was also beginning to understand – in the slow, surreptitious way that insights come to young and nervous mothers – that human beings invented the world they wished to live in, and the most sensible among them populated it with only the people they wanted with them.

While breastfeeding Ethan on our lumpy hotel bed, I observed Benni sitting on the balcony, doing his best to decipher the news of the Vietnam War in the Portuguese newspapers, and maybe I had acquired those new eyes the kabbalists wanted, because he had never been so benevolent and handsome and genuine to me, and when I looked down at our hungry baby, I sensed that my mother no longer had any power over me – that her abandonment of me and Evie would no longer be able to stop me from doing what I most wanted to do. Something had changed since we'd come to Lisbon. Maybe because I was certain now that I was journeying every day farther and farther from the lonely and wounded little girl I'd been, alongside a man who held my hand nearly all the time and a small, tender and needy little creature whom he and I had created, and I said to myself, *Everything is okay now, because everything that's happened to me – even the loneliness and guilt, even my moments of madness – has led me to this place.*

GEORGE FINDS
HIS APOLOGY
(1945-1947)

After my discharge from the army, I returned to Toronto, but my mother's worried eyes pursued me even through the locked door of my bedroom, so I made plans to move to Montreal. 'I'll only be able to start over where no one knows me,' I told her and my dad.

I meant what I said, and I was pretty sure that they believed me, but in truth I didn't know what starting over might mean.

'So you think you'll go back to university in Montreal?' Mom asked.

'Sure, once I'm settled,' I told her in a reassuring voice. But I couldn't imagine I'd ever sit in a classroom again.

Since I was a kid, I'd been certain that I'd move to my father's hometown when the time came to leave Toronto; the dry heat and towering red cliffs around Moab, Utah, always made me feel as if I'd arrived in paradise. So I surprised myself by choosing Montreal. In part, I was afraid of leaving Canada again so soon after coming home from Europe, but I also secretly believed that I hadn't done enough to earn all the warm light and colour of the desert.

My first lodgings in Montreal during that summer of 1945 were at the Pension Honfleur, a gritty flophouse on the rue Drolet where I shared a bathroom with a colossal Ukrainian boxer named Fedir Petriv. Fedir dyed his hair with shoe polish, flossed his gold-capped teeth at breakfast and smelled in the day like talcum powder and in the evening like bourbon. After a week of timing my comings and goings to avoid what he called his *kitten taps* on my chin, I was able to rent a one-bedroom apartment above the Patisserie Les Anges two blocks down the street. I chose a French-speaking area of the city because I didn't want to understand casual conversations, had no desire to make any friends and didn't want to risk bumping into anyone from home – or worse, from the army.

The neighbourhood streets were potholed and dirty, and a lot of the shops were woefully neglected, but it was an area of Montreal that seemed perfectly frank about life's difficulties, which was a relief. Homeless old men – *clochards* – in moth-eaten sweaters and fraying trench coats seemed always to be drinking beer or wine by the post office on the rue Saint-Hubert, and the oldest of them – a white-haired, bushy-eyebrowed leprechaun with a map of red veins on his cheeks – welcomed me to his territory by giving me the wilted pink carnation from his lapel when I handed him my spare change. I particularly admired the local kids and how they flew by on rusted bikes and roller skates, shrieking and giggling, communing with the god of danger that they had every right to worship at their age. On Saturday nights, I'd occasionally see a fist fight outside one of the scruffy, down-on-their-luck bars or hear some foul-mouthed commotion involving a sequined hooker, and it was then that our streets seemed the perfect locale for a blood-drenched film about Montreal mobsters and lowlifes. But in the daytime, with crowds flocking to the fruit-and-vegetable stalls in the Jean-Talon Market and clustering around bargain bins on the rue Saint-Hubert, I could more easily imagine a rags-to-riches Hollywood musical starring Bing Crosby and Judy Garland.

I was fairly certain that everyone who took notice of me pegged me as a lonely drifter or a mild-mannered nutcase, which was just how I wanted it. The only drawback to my new neighbourhood was the stench that often soured the air and made my nostrils itch; as the *clochards* explained to me, the nearby quarries had all been turned into garbage dumps in recent years.

My bedroom had only one small window facing north, so that it had the tranquil and isolated feeling of a cloister. In compensation for the darkness, the rent was next to nothing and the landlady – Madame Fourier – agreed to have the cracked white enamel in the bathroom sink fixed right away. I bought a scarred wooden desk and wicker chairs at a nearby pawn shop, and I found a serviceable mattress and clean blankets at the big, bleach-scented Salvation Army store on Sherbrooke Street. At a Chinese shop just a block away, red and green rice-paper lanterns were hanging in the window, and I was certain I'd seen them before, but I couldn't place where. Had Mom lit our porch with them when I was little? I hung them from the cracked ceiling in my bedroom, and gazing at the gentle, unambitious mixture of light they spread across my bed made me certain I had my own home for the first time.

My dad came to visit me a few weeks after my move and said my flat looked and smelled like an opium den, but he meant it with good humour. Over the spaghetti lunch he made us the next afternoon, he asked me to join him in the moonflower ceremony at sundown. His father – a Navajo healer – had taught it to him.

We drank Dad's bitter elixir out of a mason jar while sitting on the front steps of my apartment house. The billowy clouds coming in from the west started revolving around me a half hour later, and my tongue seemed to turn into a rubbery little lizard. Dad helped me up to my flat and handed me a glass of water, then began smoking his pipe like a demon and chanting in Navajo. Sometime after he asked me to take a few puffs, time slowed down, and the walls added their resonant, cello-like voices to his, and their low, purposeful, dirge-like singing continued even when he grew silent.

Dad had spoken to me in Navajo as a boy, so I knew that he and the walls and even now the ceiling were asking the spirits of the moonflower to descend from out of their canyons in the sky along the cord we'd extended to them with our hearts. Their supplicating voices exhorted the spirits to be gracious and merciful to us, as well.

I soon began to see fluttering lights everywhere I looked – emerald green and yellow – and when the hundreds of points of radiance grew tails and snouts and horns, I broke out into a cold sweat. Dad gripped my hand tight and assured me that they were sentinels from the world of our ancestors sent to watch over us, and that they didn't sting or bite. A number of them soon crowded around a piece of bread on the cutting board I kept by the sink, though it seemed more curiosity than hunger that drew them there.

When I went to the window for air, I saw a great stone arch in the distance, and the sky was the blue of fantasy summers, and I discovered that I was outside, in the Utah desert, and the sun was like burning metal against my face. A little while later, a cool rush of air shook me, and wings beat up by my ears, and I was flying over the main street in Moab. In the window of a shop was an ancient silver-and-turquoise necklace of stylised squash blossoms, but when I glided into the store I discovered I was in my room in Montreal. My father waved to me, and I turned back from a bird into a man, and I saw that I was back at my window.

'You all right?' asked Dad, and he patted my back.

'I was flying,' I told him.

'Yeah, I could see that in your eyes.'

A short time later, while I was washing my face at the sink, everything in my vision went white, even when I closed my eyes. I'd have never believed it possible.

I thought I might be blinded, but Dad said that the whiteness was the gate to another world. 'Walk forward in your mind,' he told me, gripping my shoulders, and when I did, the stark brilliance deepened to a black so complete that it seemed endless and eternal.

I knew that Kokopelli was hiding somewhere in that darkness

because I could hear him playing his reed flute. And I knew, too – though I didn't know how – that I had entered the world that awaits us after death.

My body had grown chilled and heavy, so my father helped me into bed. After Kokopelli's melody faded to silence, I sensed someone beside me, staring. When I turned, I expected to see my father, but a little boy with great black eyes gazed back at me. Had I already fallen asleep?

'Who are you?' I asked.

He shook his head as if he dared not say and stood up, and he walked forward. As I watched him, I saw that my apartment was just outside the wire fence of Bergen-Belsen. I wondered why I hadn't realised that earlier, and I understood now that the camp would forever accompany me. The boy – who looked to be seven or eight years old – summoned me forward through the gate with a wave, but I shook my head and said I wouldn't enter there ever again. Without speaking, he told me that he would go on alone – I could hear his thoughts – and as he walked among the starving prisoners, it seemed that the muddy ground and the wooden cabins and the barbed wire and everything in the camp was made of the same element. And that element was betrayal.

'I hadn't known,' I called to him. And what I meant was, *I hadn't known that it was possible for men and women to betray nature itself.*

I awakened after sunrise. My father was standing at my stove, stirring scrambled eggs. He was bare-chested, and he'd tied his long dark hair into a ponytail. 'Welcome back, son,' he said with the quick and eager smile that I've always associated with him. He'd made us strong coffee and handed me a cup. We ate while seated together on my bed. While I was wolfing down my eggs, he asked if I recalled what I'd told him the night before.

'No, I don't remember saying much of anything.'

He said that I'd described a bit what I'd seen in the death camp and told me that he understood me better now and that he would help me. He made me promise to call him once a week even if I didn't want to. He explained that the spirit of his father and other Navajo shamans would enter his voice and find a way to heal me.

'Over the phone?' I asked sceptically.

'If I can hear you, they can,' he replied with a good-natured laugh. 'And they will know what to do. Don't forget, they've had to deal with a great deal of cruelty.'

He didn't need to add that the American government had murdered tens of thousands of our ancestors – millions if we included the other tribes – and forced them onto reservations.

Dad took me out for pizza that afternoon and then we walked to his car, so he could get back home that night. Once he was settled in the driver seat, he said he understood that I needed time on my own, without being watched. He reached into his coat pocket and handed me a bolo tie of a Navajo *kachina* to protect me.

'It's from your mom,' he said.

The *kachina* had turquoise eyes and a headdress of red coral. 'She sees even in the moonflower darkness,' he said, 'and I expect she'll send you a warning if you're about to take a misstep.'

He pinched my cheek and told me I could use a shave, and his eyes moistened, and I knew it was because I was a man now and there was less that he could do for me than he'd hoped. 'When you're feeling down, tell yourself that you and I and your mother are one. You understand?'

After he left, I sat by my window, and my father's great love for me made me want to weep, but I didn't permit myself to do so. Before I could give way to tears, I needed to apologise to all the living and the dead that I had seen – especially all those tormented and starved prisoners that had been tossed into the burial pits I'd helped to dig.

Mom and Dad and I are one. When I was particularly depressed – unable even to get out of bed – I told that to myself, though it didn't seem to do me much good.

The slightest rumble of a truck or birdcall would tug me out of sleep, and I ended up with insomnia, so I was often lying in the dark, or reading a cheap paperback, and sometimes I'd listen to street conversations in French. *Il est vraiment sympa ... C'est une très belle maison ...* Words clung to my thoughts as if to summon me out into the world, but I wanted only to stay home.

Sometimes I'd picture myself finding refuge at a farmhouse at the edge of the sea, and after a while I realised that across all that cold grey water was my previous life.

My high-school French teacher was named Zotique Groleau, but behind his back we called him Monsieur Exotique Go Slow, because he was from Paris and had straggly grey hair that he often wore under the burgundy-coloured beret of French paratroopers. Also, he had a bum right leg and walked with a limp, especially during the winter. I was very curious about his long, pensive pauses, which made me think he was recalling his youth, but I'd never found the courage to talk to him about anything but conjugations and tenses. Now that I heard French all the time, I often wondered if he was still teaching. And if he forgave me for being such a poor student. It seemed sometimes as if I had learned nothing in high school or my one year of university that might have prepared me for what I saw in Europe. But very probably there's no preparation for mass murder.

One particularly warm dawn, I went for a walk down the rue de Bellechasse in only my pyjama bottoms and carpet-slippers. An old woman peeling an orange asked me in French and then in English if I was lost, though I think what she really meant was, *Do you want me to call a doctor?*

She was built like a bulldog and had two blue clothespins attached to the collar of her apron.

'*Non, merci,*' I replied, though I wanted to say, *I think I've just got to keep walking.*

A few blocks further on, I found a red vinyl armchair amid a pile of junk on the sidewalk, waiting for the garbage pick-up. A calico cat with fearful eyes was sitting on its arm; it hissed at me as if I had murder on my mind and dashed away. A half-filled box of pastels was under its seat cushion, and written on the cover in blue was the name Guy Mercier.

I wondered right away what the name of the boy I'd seen during my moonflower vision might have been – the young man with the big black eyes and hair cut in bangs.

I pictured Guy as fair and tiny, and he wore big tortoiseshell glasses. I saw him lying on his bed beside his lazy old Persian cat, drawing them both. But I could tell just by thinking of his name that Guy had not lived to adulthood. Then, when I picked the box up, it seemed scented with my dad's particular brand of pipe tobacco, which seemed impossible. I grew dizzy and troubled, and I sat down on the sidewalk to keep from falling.

After a while, I remembered that my father had told me that the moonflower spirits might come to me again on occasion and give me their insights. So I closed my eyes and welcomed them, and the dizziness soon subsided, but I never figured out what they wanted to tell me, unless it was simply that I ought to take the pastels home with me.

All the way home, I daydreamed of little blonde Guy in his hospital room, and I saw the ashen, downturned faces of his parents, and I knew they were thinking of all that their son would never become. Most of all, he'd wanted to be a pilot. And because I could see the dark hollows around his eyes so clearly, and hear him asking his grandmother for chocolate, and understand everything he said in French, I suspected that I was losing my mind.

I began drawing colourful landscapes on the walls of my apartment. A tree was a single green-and-blue curve, the horizon a long yellow line. I was trying to see if I could evoke and even shape my feelings about the world with just the slightest of gestures.

After covering one entire wall with my landscapes, I realised I had adopted a coded language of colour.

Red = fear
Sky blue = peace
Purple = wisdom
Olive green = relief
Yellow = longing
Burgundy = mystery

A little later, I began to draw only anger. That was a surprise; I hadn't known I was hiding any.

My anger was brown and black. Shadings of midnight blue turned it to rage; dark green turned it to sputtering, mindless, self-loathing fury.

I was reading a book about ancient Pompeii and Herculaneum at the time, and I drew Mount Vesuvius behind my bed as a brown-headed cyclops with a wrinkled blue eye. He was spewing burning rain over the townspeople.

The molten rain was orange and red. The people of Herculaneum folded themselves around their sons and daughters to shield them, but their air became so hot that it scalded their lungs. *Sometimes, there is simply no escape.* That was the moral I took from what I drew.

When I told my father about the deaths I'd depicted, he told me to walk east, toward the sun, every morning, and west in the evening. He said that my drawings of the victims of Vesuvius were telling me that hunkering down and curling over my hopes was the wrong strategy. He taught me prayers to the sun god and told me to chant them in my spirit voice when I was walking. As for Mom, she had realised that trying to cheer me up on the phone wasn't going to work, so she channelled her love into packages of food, mostly dried mushrooms and tomatoes that she had learned to make herself. She also started sending me her favourite novels.

Over my first months in Montreal, I often tried to get the shopgirls that worked on the rue Saint-Hubert into bed, but my courage would vanish while I was chatting with them. The first of the girls to agree to venture home with me worked at a sad little women's clothing shop named La Femme Moderne and had grown up in Trois-Rivières. She was slender and slow-talking, and she wore bright red lipstick, and she sniffled a lot because of her allergies. In profile, she looked like Olive Oyl from the *Popeye* comic strip. After we made love, she touched the cyclops I'd painted behind my bed with her hesitant fingertips. I understood then that I'd created him as a warning to all those who entered my flat.

'He's not so bad – it's me you've got to worry about,' I told her, but she thought I was joking and started to giggle.

Cerberus ... I drew him on the inside of my door as an additional warning. His thrashing canine head dripped rabid saliva. When I'd finished the high curve of his whip-like tail, I thought, *Did the Greeks get you all wrong? Were you only trying to protect the dead from further harm and humiliation?*

I walked toward the sun every morning, as Dad had recommended, but thunderclouds packed my head, and I could feel the flaming rain falling inside me nearly all the time. I was sure that it had been coming down ever since I first caught sight of Belsen and that it would never cease.

Everything I drew with my pastels – even the burnt-out wooden synagogue I'd seen near Kraków – seemed a reflection of something inside me, a mirror image of all that was broken or ruined in my mind, and that would never to be repaired.

Outside and inside share the same horizon, and that horizon is me, I wrote above Cerberus, and I wondered why I hadn't understood that earlier.

The second of the girls I managed to get into my bed told me she thought I was handsome and funny, but I told her I wasn't ready to date anyone on a steady basis.

'You don't like me?' she asked sadly.

'No, it's not you. It's me. We like to believe that we can recover from anything, but we can't.'

'Recover from what?' she asked.

'I wish I could explain, but I can't,' I told her.

A secret . . . After we made love, the desire to end my life washed over me. I imagined myself slitting my wrists and blood-painting more victims of Vesuvius on the walls of my bedroom until I lost consciousness. That was the real reason I didn't want her coming back.

A few days later, I sought help in my drawings for the first time; I sketched a little blue finch perched on the roof of the domed synagogue in Bialystok. I figured I was waiting for the old rabbi to come out and spot me above him and teach me the prayer of apology I needed so badly. Once I had spoken it in the language of birds, I would ask him to take me in his hands and toss me high in the air and send me back across the ocean to my childhood.

But I knew that he couldn't come out to me; the Nazis had locked him and two thousand other Jews from the city in the building and set it ablaze.

I began to add myself to some of my previous landscapes. I

drew myself as a crimson-coloured fish swimming in a sluggish river bordered by mangroves and a bobcat leaning over the rim of a sunlit canyon. I was always alone. I was always waiting.

Sooner or later, someone holy will find me, I thought – *the Paiute prophet Wovoka, or maybe Saint Francis, or . . .*

Or even Marian Anderson.

Was Marian Anderson a strange choice as my saviour? Probably, but she was the first person to teach me that the human voice can soar into places of the heart where nothing else can go.

Mom was a sixth-grade teacher at the Allenby Public School in Toronto, and she started me and her students on poetry with the Old Testament and Marian Anderson's 'Ave Maria'. And then she played us Negro spirituals like 'Go Down Moses' and 'Nobody Knows the Trouble I've Seen'.

I painted Marian on my bedroom door, with her arms raised over her head, summoning the new Creation that I needed so badly.

When I told my dad about her in our weekly phone call, he said, 'Yes, son, you should join your voice to hers like you and I used to do.'

To give me that advice, my father used the speech rhythm of the shamans, which was slow and precise. He often spoke in Navajo, because he couldn't find the English translations for what he wished to say.

'Do you have enough money to buy a record player?' he asked.

'Yes,' I said, but I lied. I was running low. Soon, I'd have to find work.

Three days later, a short, middle-aged man with stiff grey hair and a hooked nose knocked on my door. He said his name was Darryl and that he and my father had worked together at the Toronto Brick Company before I was born. He was carrying a big box. In it was a record player. I invited him inside but he said he was double-parked and couldn't stay.

'How did my father know I was lying?' I asked.

'I don't know, maybe you haven't yet learned how to lie convincingly,' he said, and with an affecting, high-pitched laugh, he added, 'A couple more years in Montreal, and it'll come more naturally.'

I called up my father to thank him, but he wasn't home. My mom got me talking about the vegetarian cookbook she was organising to raise money for her synagogue. It was her way of reminding me to eat well, and I assured her that I was making soups with her dried vegetables. In all that she didn't dare tell me, I sensed the length and breadth of her hopes for me, and I tried not to be oppressed by them, but I failed.

After I finished my book on Herculaneum, I started an anthology of short stories by Willa Cather that I'd found in a charity shop just around the corner from my flat. I was reading it by the light of my mom's menorah – her parting gift to me – and drifting off toward sleep when I came to the following paragraph in 'Flavia and Her Artists':

'Laughing, Flavia started the ponies, and the colossal woman, standing in the middle of the dusty road, took off her wide hat and waved them a farewell which, in scope of gesture, recalled the salute of a plumed cavalier.'

I don't remember standing up, but I do remember the feeling of something warm brushing against my thoughts. A man's hand?

I picked up a pastel from my desk and slashed two orange lines and then a third. They seemed to form a long feather, and I imagined it floating down into my hands. So I filled in its contours with tight strokes of white and black pastel, then smudged them together. I turned the orange to russet by rubbing in a little brown.

Russet and grey – it seemed a mix of fear, anger and melancholy.

The next day, I sketched a line under the feather, and a little while later, I turned the line into the outlines of a fedora. I surprised myself then by drawing a woman's gaunt profile under the hat. In the story I told myself about her in bed that night, she'd put it on to cover her hair, which had begun falling out. I imagined that she was dying, and she wished to tell me her last wishes, but she didn't believe that I would understand her Yiddish.

I didn't think much about the woman I'd drawn until about fifteen months later, in the late winter of 1947. By then, scores of scruffy Italian immigrants had settled in my neighbourhood. The men who hadn't yet found jobs stood around on street corners, their cheeks and chins unshaven, smoking and murmuring and scoffing. I was working as a waiter at the Fiore d'Italia, a home-style restaurant owned by a Sicilian family just a few blocks from my apartment.

I'd moved on from creating frescoes on my walls to paintings on canvas, and though I'd decided to make street scenes in Montreal my overarching project, some vestige of Bergen-Belsen would suddenly appear – leaving poisoned clots of paint – in even the most tranquil of cityscapes.

Some days, I woke up oppressed by the knowledge that I was doing very little with my life that anyone would consider useful. On such mornings, I sensed that I was drifting toward a future of failure and frustration. I still spoke to my father every weekend, and it was reassuring to hear his voice, but my relationship with my mother had degenerated. In the awkward silences that punctuated our conversation, I sensed her desperation for me to come home, but that was the one thing I couldn't do.

After my evening shift at the restaurant, I generally headed straight back to my flat, but one particular Friday night in early March, I walked past it, drawn by the full moon. Its glow was so soft and near that it seemed to be the kind-hearted and benevolent moon god that my grandfather had told me about when I was little.

I turned left on the rue Dante because I heard singing coming from just down the street, and it sounded like gospel music. Crusted snow and sheets of ice covered the sidewalk and streets – it was a frigid night. My steps were brittle but sure.

After I passed the first houses, the voices faded. Were the moonflower spirits playing tricks on me? That's what I assumed, since the only song that I could hear now – faintly, from a top-floor apartment – sounded like a big-hearted French crooner wooing his sweetheart.

I'd never been on the rue Dante before, and at the corner of the boulevard Saint-Laurent, I discovered a billiard parlour with a pink-and-green neon sign reading BAR BILLARD LE TROUBADOUR. It was still open, and I wouldn't have normally gone in, since I didn't play pool, but I figured that a mulled wine or grog would be just the thing to warm me up.

The bar was smoky and smelled faintly of marijuana, which I was able to identify because I had gone to a jazz club downtown on a few occasions. The bulky metal ceiling lamps made the green felt of the pool tables look electrified. Two scruffy-looking young men were playing at the table farthest from me, and an old man wearing a fuzzy cap was seated on one of the stools at the back, snoozing. At the bar was a boisterous, slump-backed group of middle-aged drinking buddies, and at the far end, around its curve, sat two young women, both in tight skirts and dark stockings, and wearing way too much make-up.

The place had the lonesome, forgotten feel of an Edward

Hopper painting. I shuffled up to the bar and used my pidgin French to order a grog.

I sat on one of the stools near the snoozing old man until a young guy whom I hadn't noticed before – had he been in the bathroom when I'd entered? – sauntered up and asked me something in French that I didn't catch. He looked vaguely familiar, but I couldn't place him.

'I don't speak French,' I told him with an apologetic nod.

'I ask if you want to play billiards with me,' he said with a thick accent. His *if* was *eef* and *billiards* sounded like *beeyar.* He smiled in an inviting way, but I hesitated. 'Come on,' he said, 'I promise you I will not take your money!' He introduced himself as Shelly, and I told him my name.

'It is nice to meet you, George,' he said.

The French way he pronounced my name – that soft initial G – pleased me, perhaps because it convinced me that I was having an adventure outside my usual territory. Very soon, I discovered that he could speak English only in the present and future tenses. 'The past is beyond my comprehension,' he told me, laughing freely.

When he took off his jacket to reveal his T-shirt, I saw that he was lean and strong. His dark eyes had the longest lashes I'd ever seen, and his short, curly hair shimmered under the lights over the pool tables. As he racked the billiard balls, he asked me if I was studying at McGill, and I told him that I was a waiter at Il Fiore d'Italia on the rue Saint-Hubert.

'*Merde*!' he exclaimed. 'When you come in, I am sure you are from McGill!' he said with an irritated twist to his lips.

'Maybe I'll go back to school one day, but not just yet,' I told him.

In reply to his other questions, I said that I was from Toronto and had moved to Montreal a year and a half earlier, after my stint in the army.

Shelly told me he was a gardener at the Montreal Botanical Garden. He said he loved his job because he was able to work outside most of the day, and because the young women who came to admire the flowers were in such a relaxed mood that they didn't mind him flirting with them. After we started playing billiards, he jerked his hand back and forth along his cue stick and said that two weeks earlier he'd fucked a girl from Calgary in the palm greenhouse. 'Jane,' he said. 'That is her name. She is a princess in the rodeo.'

He told me that the scent of moist, fertile life of the palm greenhouse made it the best place in the world for sex.

'You ever fuck in a greenhouse?' he asked me as he lined up a shot.

'No,' I said.

He sent the cue ball shooting across the table. 'I am shit tonight!' he snarled when it failed to send the ball he'd been aiming at into the side pocket.

As I scanned the table to see which ball I ought to try for, he put a stick of gum in his mouth and said, 'When I'm with a girl who wants a second guy, I invite you. *Tu vas adorer*!'

There seemed to be something bigger than life about Shelly, and unflappable, too – as if he would perform his heart out even if only one person were watching. I was especially impressed by how he could talk with a cigarette dangling from his lips and wield his cue behind his back to make trick shots. In the film I imagined about Montreal mobsters, he quickly took on one of the starring roles – the up-and-coming young hustler who planned to sneak off to Hollywood with his girl as soon as he'd siphoned off enough money from his bosses to buy a big house on the beach.

After he'd beaten me at billiards, I confessed that I was a bit drunk and needed to get to bed, since I was working the next afternoon and evening, and he told me he'd walk me home – 'To make sure you not get lost,' he said.

As we started off, he asked where I lived, and when I told him my address, he stopped in his tracks and told me in a shocked voice that he lived just around the corner. In fact, we had to pass his apartment house to get to mine.

When we reached his place, he said, 'This is my home. Top floor.'

'So your place is the one with the bright blue curtains?' I asked, pointing at the flat I meant. It was too dark to see the colour of the curtains, but I'd noticed them before.

'Sure,' he said. 'You like them?'

'Yeah.'

'I make them myself!' he said, beaming.

'You sew?' I asked – astonished.

'*Bien sûr.* Saves money. And I'm good at it.'

A billiard champ and hothouse gigolo who sewed his own curtains . . . That made me laugh pretty hard.

'What's so funny?' he asked.

'You! You defy expectations,' I told him.

'At least I'm good for something,' he said with a mischievous smile.

I told him I could make it home from there, but he wanted to see my place. Inside my flat, he turned in an astonished circle around the living room. 'So all these crazy drawings . . . you make them?' he asked.

'Yeah.'

'What is their meaning?'

'I haven't got a clue.'

'You must have *une idée,*' he insisted.

'They're places I've seen,' I added. 'Landscapes inside me.'

I figured that if I couldn't sound confident, like him, at least I could seem mysterious. He nodded pensively, as if he knew exactly what I meant. When he noticed my mother's menorah standing on my desk, he picked it up. 'You a Jew?' he asked.

'I'm half-Jewish. My mother's Jewish and my father is Navajo.'

'Navajo?' he asked.

'An Indian tribe.'

'*Ah, oui*! That's fantastic!'

'Is it?'

'*Absolument*! Wow!'

'But there are hardly any of us left,' I pointed out.

'Yeah, I know – it's a crime what they do to you.'

'And what's your heritage?' I asked.

'Me, I'm Jewish – a hundred and fifty percent.'

'Why the extra fifty?'

'For the ones the Nazis kill,' he said, and his eyes – catching mine – were deadly serious.

He put down the menorah and took both my hands, and he swung them between us – like a child's game – and to my surprise, he leaned in to kiss me. I pushed him away, but he grabbed my shoulders and said, '*Ecoute, mon ami, je sais ce que tu veux.*'

It was true that I'd been semi-hard most of the evening and that I found him very attractive, but the idea of actually acting on my hidden desires had always terrified me, so I frowned and replied, 'How the hell do you know what I want?'

He pointed to his eyes, then mine. 'I see your thoughts.'

'And what do they look like?'

'They're skinny. And scared. They prefer to be *cachées*. But you do not need to hide them. I like you a lot. And I'm very good at fucking.'

'But I'm not interested in . . .'

'Please, George, you not waste more time. You must learn to do what you want. I will help.' I discovered his mouth tasted of tobacco, whiskey and the cinnamon gum he'd been chewing.

When he gripped my cock in his rough hand and gave it a squeeze, my heart began to race. 'You like that, don't you?' he whispered up at my ear, then gave it a lick.

I nodded, but he didn't grin as if I were a conquest, as I might have expected. He caressed my cheek and said, 'George, everything is okay. I just want to make you happy.' He showed me a generous smile. '*Tu es très beaux, tu sais?*'

'I've never been with a man before,' I whispered.

'Then you come to the right place,' he said with a proud grin, and he dropped to his knees and took me in his mouth, which seemed the most exciting thing that had ever happened to me.

'This seems wrong,' I told him.

'*Au contraire, ta queue est parfaite!*' he said. He licked the tip of my cock. 'She tastes like ice cream!' He raised a finger of teaching. 'You need to listen to your cock and not your head.'

A few minutes later, when he entered me, it burned.

'I will not move,' he said. 'The pain will go away. *Tu vas voir.*'

'Maybe I don't want it to go away,' I told him. 'Maybe I want you to hurt me.'

'And maybe you're a little *meshugge*,' he said, which made both of us laugh, and that seemed a good sign.

Lying on my belly with Shelly inside me, I gave up on trying to control who I was and where I was headed, and I was able to relax for the first time since I'd entered Bergen-Belsen. But the hollow after he'd come inside me and pulled out was devastating, and I began to sob.

Shelly kissed my hands and said he was sorry if he'd hurt me, and I wanted to say he hadn't, but the tears were dripping from my eyes, and I thought, *So this is what it means to start over*.

That night I went to sleep in the arms of a man for the first time. The bristle of his chest hair against my back seemed unlikely and wondrous – and the answer to questions I'd never dared ask. Even his snoring seemed beautiful.

We both called in sick the next morning, and we made love on and off all day, and all my previous sexual experiences seemed delicate and pale in comparison. That evening, we went to a movie – *The Best Years of Our Lives* – and we held hands in the dark and both started weeping at the same tender moments. Looking back across my life, I decided that I'd never had a true friend before.

We made love once more that night, and I woke up just after dawn to discover Shelly was studying the hollow-cheeked woman in the fedora that I'd drawn shortly after I moved in. He was naked, and I saw that if I were to sketch him, I'd start with the sleek, powerful curve of his back and his amazing eyelashes, and he would be scarlet, amber and burgundy, the colours of fear, longing and mystery.

'You like my work?' I asked.

When he turned, his face was pale. 'I think I know her,' he said in a menacing whisper.

'What do you mean?' I asked, sitting up.

'She has a hat . . . it's the same. *Et tu as dessiné son profil.*'

'My French should be better by now, but it isn't.'

'You make her profile,' he said.

'Whose?'

'*Tia* Graça. She is married to my uncle – my father's brother. *Tia* . . . it means "aunt" in Ladino.'

After Shelly explained to me about the origins of Ladino, I said, 'Well, in any case, it's just a drawing I made. It's not anyone special.'

'Nothing is *just* a drawing,' he said as if nothing could have been more obvious. He found his cigarettes on my desk and lit one.

'Where does your aunt live?' I asked.

'Dead. They all are. I go to Poland just after the war. My parents, my aunts and uncles . . . I find no one.' He drew in urgently on his cigarette, clearly wishing he could have told me a different story.

'But what were they doing in Poland? I don't understand.'

'My family is from Poland. I grow up in Warsaw.'

'So you're not from Quebec?'

'No, of course, not.'

'Then how do you speak French so fluently?'

'My mother is born in France. I escape the Warsaw ghetto and go to *Algérie*. I work there while the war . . . while she is going, then come to Canada. My accent isn't Quebecois. You cannot hear the difference?' he asked disbelievingly.

'No, I'm sorry – I guess my ear isn't very good.'

He sat on the edge of my mattress. He put his hand on my leg and squeezed it. His fingers were icy. 'Please, you must tell me about this woman you draw,' he said pleadingly.

I explained about sketching the feather and the hat and finally the hollow-cheeked woman. I said that I had the feeling that she was wearing a hat because her hair was falling out. And that she needed to tell me her last wishes.

'Last wishes?' he asked.

'What she needs to tell me – or have me do for her – before dying.'

'So what are they?' he asked.

'I don't know. She didn't say. Maybe she knew I wouldn't understand her Yiddish.'

He looked back at her for a time. 'Typhoid fever,' he said definitively.

'What about it?'

'It makes the hair . . . the hair fall. I read about it. The people in the camps have diseases.'

'Look, Shelly, I don't know if she was ill. I don't know anything about who she was.' I shrugged. 'I make up things about the people and things I draw. They're just stories.'

He looked at me as if my reply were wholly insufficient. And maybe a bit stupid, too.

'When I'm working, images just come to me,' I insisted. 'I don't know why.'

'Are you telling the truth?' he asked.

'Of course, I am.' But I wasn't – not entirely; I was aware that I'd drawn her because I'd seen so many dying prisoners at Bergen-Belsen.

He stood up and walked to the window. In profile, he looked as if he were readying himself for a battle. When he turned, he said, 'I live so close. We can see my apartment. And you draw *Tia* Graça. That means something.'

'What's it mean?'

'I don't know. I need to think about it.'

I was tempted to tell Shelly that I'd been present for the liberation of a Nazi camp, but I didn't want to venture anywhere near that hell ever again, so I took him out for coffee at the Fiore d'Italia, where we wouldn't be able to discuss serious matters.

That night, after we'd made love, I was lying on my back, drifting off. He was caressing my chest and telling me in a resentful mixture of French and English that his father had kicked him out of the house when he was sixteen, for sleeping with a girl and her older brother who lived in the flat above theirs.

'Both of them at the same time?' I asked.

'*Oui, bien sûr. Porquoi pas?*'

'I don't know. It seems . . . risky.'

'It is not risky,' he scoffed. 'Brother and sister both like me. So why choose?'

My laugh came tinged with envy. 'I guess that's logical,' I said.

'*Tia* Graça, she saves me,' he told me.

Shelly explained that his aunt had permitted him to stay with her and her husband for as long as he wanted. He'd ended up living with them for two years. 'They become my second parents,' he said. 'And Benni, he is just six years old. He becomes my little brother. I read stories to him. And we talk of all the voyages we take. So many hours we have together of *voyages-rêves.*'

'Where did you want to go?'

'I want to go south . . . to the sun. To Italy, Spain, Greece . . . Portugal. Our ancestors are from Portugal. I tell Benni, "I take you there one day. We live on the beach, we eat lots of fish." But the boy is crazy for Egypt. He wants to see the pyramids and the Nile and all those statues of gods – you know, with the heads of birds.' Shelly flapped his arms. 'The kid wants to fly!'

So maybe the sluggish river I've drawn in my living room is the Nile, I thought with a sense of arrival, but then a moment later it seemed a silly notion.

When I looked at Shelly, his eyes were troubled. 'George, if Benni is dead too . . .' He wiped a hand back through his hair. 'I not go on.'

I sat up and took his shoulder. 'Listen, let's talk of other things. And let's have some sherry as a treat. My dad gave me a bottle and it'll calm you down.'

'No,' he said, shaking his head. 'I don't want to be calm! I want to find Benni and my sister and everyone else.' He switched on the reading light on my night table.

He wouldn't look at me, so I apologised for trying to divert his attention. 'What's your sister's name?' I asked.

'Esther.'

'And how old would she be now?'

'Nineteen.' He gazed down, puzzling something out. At length, he said, 'You know, George, if anyone survive, it would be Benni.'

'Why?'

'He's alive in my dreams.'

'And that means he made it?'

'If he is not alive, I think I dream he is dead.'

What he said reminded me of a quote from Willa Cather that I'd written down in my journal. I got the book out from the bottom drawer of my night table. '*It does not matter much whom we live with in this world*,' I read, '*but it matters a great deal whom we dream of.*'

'*Absolument*,' he said with a knowing nod, but he stood up and stubbed out his cigarette as if he were angry with himself. Almost right away, he tapped out another one from his pack. 'Sometimes I wake in the night,' he said, 'and I'm sure I'm in Warsaw. I start to go to his room, but then I remember I'm in Canada. And I feel...' Shelly searched for the right words while swirling his foot over the floor. 'I feel that the night, it is falling on me.' He patted his chest. 'I cannot breathe.'

'Where is Benni in your dreams?' I asked.

Shelly lit his cigarette and funnelled the smoke up toward the ceiling. 'I don't know. I think in Poland – maybe Warsaw.'

His lips had begun to tremble, so I fetched him a glass of the sherry I'd offered him earlier. As I handed it to him, I said, 'When you went back to Warsaw, did you leave your address with the people you knew – and who knew Benni?'

He pinched a bit of tobacco from his tongue. 'No, I do not have an address yet. I am trying to make it to Canada. I speak to only two men from the old days – Nowak and Wieczorek. Before the war, Nowak owns a shop that sells fabric. But there is not much decent fabric, so he sells fruit.'

'And Wieczorek?'

'He's a baker. He looks like hell, but he is alive. I buy him beer to celebrate.'

'Could they tell you anything about Benni or his family?'

'No, nothing.'

Shelly sat back against the windowsill and took a sip of his sherry, then stuck out his tongue and made a sound of disgust. '*Trop doux*!' he told me.

'I've got rum. Would you like that better?'

'Yes, please,' he said like a hopeful schoolboy, which made me laugh.

How easy it was to imagine Shelly as a ten-year-old terror charming everyone in sight!

I took my rum from the bottom drawer of my dresser. After I filled a shot glass for him, he sniffed it and smiled. 'Ah, *oui*!' he enthused. He knocked it back in one gulp like a gunslinger, then asked for more. He downed it in the same fashion and held out his glass once again.

'You sure?' I asked.

'George, I survive the Nazis, so I think I survive your rum,' he said, rolling his eyes. This time, however, he took tiny, grateful sips. I sat down again on my bed.

'I tell Nowak and Wieczorek to tell my parents or Benni or anyone who comes home that I am alive,' he said. 'I say that they find me through the French Embassy in Montreal.'

'And they agreed to do that?' I asked.

'Yes, but . . . they are frightened. Nobody talks openly because the Red Army is all over the place. But they seem like they will help if they can.'

'When exactly did you speak to them?'

'Right after the war ends – in the middle of June, 1945. Then I visit a distant cousin in Łódź. His dad is Polish, his mom is half-Jewish. But she is dead. His family is . . . *très dans le coup*. Religious Catholics.'

'What's *dans le coup* mean?'

'When you know all the right people. And my cousin, Tymon, he is still living in a *très chic* apartment on Piotrkowska Street – which means that he probably joins the Communist Party and works with the Soviets. But I don't ask – I cannot risk irritating him. Anyway, he does not want to receive me because I am a Jew. But I push the door open. He promises to write to me at the embassy in Montreal if my parents or Benni or Esther . . . if they find him. But he wants a lot of money, so I give it to him.'

'What an asshole!'

Shelly shrugged. 'To have Esther or Benni back, I give him anything he wants.'

Shelly sat down next to me. He put his half-full shot glass on my night table and pulled his knees up by his chest as if he were chilled. 'I come to Montreal in early July, and I go to the French Consulate. I write my address. And I give them a list of my family members. I ask them to send the list to the embassy in Poland when it opens. You see, it is closed when I am in Warsaw – no ambassador, nobody. Then I take a bus to New York. I go to the American Joint Distribution Committee. I give a man there my address in Montreal, and my phone – and another list of my family relations. He tells me he has a friend who will go to Poland in a month. But when I speak to him after that month, he says his friend finds no one on my list.'

'It sounds like you did everything you could,' I said.

'Maybe. But I have this strange *certitude* that Benni is alive.'

'What do you mean?'

'George, this is a bit peculiar.'

'Peculiar in what way?'

'Benni, when he is little, I sometimes hear him in my head. Or maybe I just *think* I hear him. I don't know. I don't care. He hears me too. It is like a game. We are like twins. You know, twins who know where each of them is. So now, every night before I go to sleep, I say, "Listen, Benni, I wait for you at the Portuguese synagogue on Stanley Street. I stay all Saturday afternoon." And I tell him, "If you can't come on Saturday, Rabbi Jonathan, he knows me. He will bring you to me. Or, if you prefer, you go to the Botanical Garden. Everybody there knows me. And if you have trouble, go to the main train station and ask where is Stanley Street."'

'When you're talking to Benni, what language do you speak?' I asked.

'Yiddish. He doesn't speak French. Sometimes I add a few words of Ladino, too.'

Shelly handed me his shot glass. 'Finish it,' he said.

My drinking out of the same glass made him smile at me warmly. It seemed a seal over our friendship – and his way of rewarding me for not raising doubts about him and Benni hearing each other's thoughts.

'Sometimes I speak to Benni at night for many hours,' he added. 'Because maybe he is alone, still hiding somewhere. Maybe he has no one to talk to. I know it is silly, George, but I think my words, they travel at night much better . . . more rapidly.' He laughed as if he were close to tears. 'It's like I'm a radio station and he's a receiver.'

'Shelly,' I said, 'if Benni thinks you're dead, he might not be listening for your voice. He might not try to find you.'

'Yes, it's true. But I don't know what else to do.'

He stood up again and gazed out my window as if searching for another strategy. I surprised myself by thinking, *Meeting Shelly and helping him find Benni is why I turned down the rue Dante*. And then a few seconds later, an even stranger thought made me jump to my feet and step to Shelly: *It's why I came to Montreal*.

He gripped my hand and smiled at me as if his only other choice were to start sobbing, and I think it was at that moment that all my resistance to him dropped away, like old clothes that were too tight on me and that I'd never wanted in the first place.

'When I was in the army, they sent me to Europe,' I said, though my voice seemed to be coming from far away. 'I ended up at Bergen-Belsen. I was there for the liberation of the camp.'

His eyes caught mine and held them for a long time, and I saw hope in them, which worried me. 'I know what you're thinking,' I told him, 'but I don't remember seeing Benni or your aunt. Maybe I did, but I wouldn't have known who they were. I didn't know who anyone was. The inmates were starving. And their faces . . . They weren't like normal faces. It was like they'd been hollowed out. You could see the outlines of everyone's skull. I don't think I'd have recognised my own mother if she'd been in the camp.'

He took my hand and placed it flat against his chest, so that his racing heartbeat was in my palm. 'You feel that, George?' he asked in a challenging voice.

'Of course,' I said.

'If anyone is alive, I must find them like my heart keeps beating. I have no choice.'

'I understand. I didn't tell you right away about Belsen,

because . . . it was a nightmare, and it's always with me, and it pulls me very far down . . . I'm sorry.'

'*Oui, je comprends*. But what I need to tell you is that I promise you that my aunt has a hat just like the one you draw.'

I took my hand back because I didn't want to give him false hopes. 'Shelly, no one held on to any hats in the camp. The prisoners were in rags. Or naked. You don't understand.'

'Then explain to me.'

As I spoke of Belsen, the stench of death entered me. When I grew sick, Shelly sat with me on the floor of my bathroom and rubbed my back as I leaned over the toilet.

'What a fucking mess I am,' I said when I was done.

'You'll be okay,' he told me.

'No, I won't,' I replied. 'I'm not who I used to be, and I'll never be that person again. And to tell you the truth, I don't want to be.' I spoke angrily, but in truth it seemed like a triumph to be able to say aloud that Bergen-Belsen had changed me forever – and that I wouldn't want it to be any other way. After all, who would want to remain the same after digging burial pits for a thousand goat-ribbed Jews and Gypsies who'd been abandoned by the world?

When I awakened in the night, I went to pee and a chilling memory made me moan aloud. I sat with Shelly a long time – overwhelmed by my need for him – before nudging him awake.

'What is it?' he asked.

'An English officer took a velvet hat from the commandant's wife. It had a black veil in front.'

He sat up. 'And a feather?'

'No.'

'But listen, the officer, he handed the hat to a young woman . . . an inmate. She'd asked for it. Shelly, she was . . . Imagine a skeleton in pyjamas. With eyes ... experienced, sensitive eyes, like an old woman in a Rembrandt painting. But her shoulders were like coat hangers. And her arms were so horribly slender, like ... like bamboo.'

Shelly winced. In a fearful voice, he asked, 'What does she do with the hat?'

'She spit on it and threw it down. But the force that took ... She started coughing up blood. And it seemed like she was going to collapse, so I steadied her, and our eyes, they met, which turned me to stone. Because I saw that she knew she was dying. Do you understand? Liberation had come too late for her. We were too slow! It was our fault. I wanted to tell her how sorry I was. I wanted to apologise on behalf of everyone in the whole world – on behalf of the sun and moon and stars. It seemed what I had to do – it was the role fate had given me. But my voice was deep down in my throat, and enclosed in something thick – maybe my fear of her. She spit up blood again, so I ran off for a doctor, but by the time I got back, she was lying on her back, and her eyes were closed. A friend of hers – a tiny old man with a blanket over his shoulders, bald, with dull grey eyes – was sitting over her, rocking back and forth. I checked her pulse, but she was gone.'

Shelly gripped my shoulder. 'I'm sorry.'

'I'd forgotten her, but I can see now that she's the woman that I tried to sketch. Though I didn't do a very good job.'

'No, you do good. Your painting is important.'

'Maybe, but what I mean to say ... She's not your aunt, she's the woman who made me want to apologise to everyone.'

'Unless that woman *is* my aunt.'

'Shelly, I'm sorry, but that's pretty much impossible. What are the chances of my meeting her in Germany, then becoming friends with you in Montreal?'

'George, it is the death camps that are impossible! Who can

believe so many millions are murdered? But to see my aunt and then meet me . . . *Je suis desolé, ce n'est pas du tout impossible.* Things like that, they happen all the time.'

'My dad would say you think like a Navajo,' I said with a quick and tender smile.

'That sounds pretty wonderful!' he replied in a pleased voice.

It was the first time anyone I knew had taken Dad's compliment as it was intended. But I didn't tell him that because my last moments with the woman who might have been his aunt were throbbing urgently inside my head.

'What's wrong?' questioned Shelly, and he took my hand.

When I didn't reply, he kissed it twice and placed it over his heart again, and now it seemed the most intimate gesture anyone had ever shown me.

This man is the most open and generous person I've ever met, I thought.

'When I told the woman that I'd get a doctor to examine her,' I said, 'she held me back for a second, and she looked at me as if she wanted to speak, but she never said a word. Though now . . . I think I know what she wanted to tell me – what her last wish was. It seems obvious.'

'What is it?'

'She wanted to say, "Don't forget me."'

Shelly shook his head and whispered bitterly. '*Mon Dieu*, this is all too much.'

'The thing is,' I added. 'I'm sure she didn't mean it as a curse – as something that would condemn me. But I think that's what it has become.'

The next day, my father called just before I left for work. I joked playfully with him for the first time in months, and, in an excited voice, he said, 'Something's changed in you – you sound as if you've been flying over Moab again.'

His affectionate and relieved laugh made me want to throw my arms around him. 'I've made a friend named Shelly,' I announced.

'What's she like?' he asked.

I wanted to correct the pronoun he'd used – I could feel the word *he* sitting under my tongue, but I said instead, 'She works at the Botanical Garden.'

'I bet she's pretty, too.'

'Yeah, very.'

I felt a downward movement inside me as I spoke – as though my disappointment in myself were a kind of fatal gravity – but how could I tell my father or anyone else what starting over had come to mean?

Shelly and I slept together several times a week over the rest of that winter and into the start of spring. He preferred my apartment to his and kept a week's worth of clothing in my dresser so that he could stay with me whenever he wanted. He also brought over three extra pillows, since he needed to build a nest around himself in bed in order to fall asleep.

On occasion, we made love in his palm greenhouse, after closing time, and the humid scent of growth around us was as intoxicating as he said it would be. Amid the tree ferns and orchids, we must have looked like characters in *A Midsummer Night's Dream*, his favourite Shakespeare play.

I started accompanying Shelly to the Portuguese synagogue every Saturday afternoon. We'd bring along paperback novels and sit in one of the pews at the back in case Benni had somehow heard Shelly's instructions for him and found his way to Montreal.

Sometimes we'd converse with Rabbi Jonathan in his cluttered office before leaving. He was a stocky, balding, simian-looking man, with hairy ears and a boyish laugh, and he had a deep knowledge of Jewish lore. He was seventy-two years old and originally from Bristol, England, but he could trace his family back to the south of Spain in the fifteenth century. Once, when I asked him for a prayer for forgiveness, he said in a stunned aristocratic voice, 'My dear boy, at your age, what do you need to be forgiven for so badly?'

'I didn't do all I could to help a good friend,' I said, and though that was a lie, it also seemed a deeper form of truth.

'Then you must ask forgiveness from that friend,' he said.

'I do, but it doesn't seem enough.'

'Tell me what you want to say and I'll write it out in Hebrew.'

We settled on the following words: *I regret all that I did not do, and all I did not say, and all that no one did or said, and I ask for your forgiveness.*

Every Friday evening at the descent of the Sabbath, I'd recite that prayer while lighting my candles. Shelly would often join me, and our voices sounded so right together, and powerful, too – as if our simple words were sustaining the earth itself – that I would think, *This prayer is also why I entered the billiard parlour.* And yet I knew that it still wasn't enough to earn me forgiveness. And that nothing ever would be.

Shelly had warned me on a number of occasions that it would be impossible for him to stay faithful to me or anyone else, but I didn't believe him until he got a few days off in early April and drove down to New York City with a big-breasted Quebecoise bookkeeper named Florence that he'd recently met. He called me from a gas station near the American border to tell me he'd be away for a few days. In the background, I could hear Florence telling him she was hungry.

Over the five days that Shelly was gone, I circled like a vulture around my humiliation. Nights were the worst; the bright blue sheets we'd bought together seemed as if they were made of wrapping paper, and I'd wake from panicked dreams of having failed a school exam with a throbbing head and a sour-tasting tongue, as if I were coming down with the flu. While waiting tables, I'd picture how I'd shout at Shelly the next time I saw him – and give him an ultimatum. But when he called me up on the afternoon of his return, he apologised for hurting me and invited me to join him in the palm greenhouse. I didn't know what to do or say, so I simply got the bus to the Botanical Garden, and we made love just after closing time.

From that day on, I knew that our relationship would probably end in tears, at least for me, but I proved a hope-making creature; I came to believe that he would choose me – and me alone – in the end.

In early June, Shelly and I went camping in Mont-Tremblant Provincial Park. We picked a meadow carpeted with yellow and purple crocuses, by a jade-coloured lake where we could fish. We cooked up our trout in his heavy iron skillet every evening. Temperatures dipped below freezing at night, but we'd brought along sleeping bags he'd borrowed from a friend and cuddled together in our tent. At night, the loons called out as if asking the sky spirits to tell them their secrets, and the great expanse of stars – endless and silent – often questioned me about what I wished to accomplish in my life. I surprised myself by thinking that I'd apply to McGill for entry in the fall. I'd study art, and I'd paint all I'd seen in Europe. It would be my way of honouring all the dead and dying who never got to tell anyone their last wishes.

Gazing up at the Milky Way, trying to fathom the distance between there and here, I knew that it would be my life project.

On our last night in the park, I fell asleep shortly after supper, while sitting by our campfire, and the moonflower whiteness opened over me. When I walked forward this time, I came to the gate of Bergen-Belsen that was always just outside my apartment in Montreal. I sensed a concerned gaze behind me, and I expected to see Shelly, but when I turned, a boy with thick black hair and huge dark eyes waved to me. He was cloaked by shadows. And he was in danger.

A yellow star was sewn near the collar of his oversized coat. I knew right away he was Benni.

Far beyond him, a freight train was moving silently through a German forest, and its steam billowed upward, seemingly anxious to hide the sky. I was aware that Jews were locked on the train, and that they were headed toward death. The only question was: would Benni be forced to get aboard at its next stop?

He walked to me and took from his coat pocket my mother's *kachina* and put it around my neck. '*Elle m'a conduit ici*,' he told me in French, and then in English: 'She led me here.'

A great swell of gratitude to my mother rose inside me, and I realised I'd been unfair to her. I knew, as well, that Benni would be safe – Mom's *kachina* would save him from having to board the train.

The full moon was now shimmering just behind Benni, so I could see him clearly. He was a few years older than when I'd last seen him in my mind; bristles covered his chin and top lip. His jacket was the brown woollen one that Shelly wore on winter evenings.

I pointed out the moon to him because its radiance was tinged blue, and I told him it was the colour of watchfulness. 'Shelly and I will keep waiting for you at the synagogue every Saturday,' I promised.

'*Quelle synagogue?*' he asked.

'*À* Montreal.'

'*Mon Dieu, c'est très loin!*'

When I heard stirring behind me, I turned, and my father held out his pipe to me, and I took a few puffs. Dad smiled at me as if to reassure me that Benni would be all right. I wanted to tell him that Mom's *kachina* had led the boy to me, but I woke with Shelly shaking my shoulder. He held a lantern in his other hand, and its glaring light seemed to be the same as the moonflower's.

The light that overwhelms me is inside me, I thought.

Shelly was staring down at me, worried. 'You talk in your sleep,' he said.

'Where am I?' I asked.

'By the lake. With me.'

'What did I say?' I asked.

'I'm not sure. I hear only one thing clearly – "*À* Montreal."'

If Shelly hadn't heard me talking in my sleep, I might have forgotten my dream forever, but I remembered all of it in a single instant. The moon I'd seen seemed to deserve my thanks because it had enabled me to see Benni clearly.

My legs were aching, so I asked Shelly to help me up. Once I was standing, I reached for the *kachina* around my neck and gave her a squeeze. Her turquoise crown pressed into my palm, and the prick of its points seemed to wake me further – and to alert me to the possibility that Benni knew where I was and had heard me speaking to him.

Benni can see my dreams, I thought. *He knows who I am. He sees that I'm with Shelly.*

'George, tell me what you're thinking,' Shelly said insistently.

'I told Benni that we'll always wait for him at the synagogue,' I replied.

'You speak to Benni?'

'I think he's been inside me for months. Maybe since I met you. Waiting for me. I think he hides in the moonflower brightness.'

'In what?'

'Moonflower . . . It grows in the desert. The Navajo make the leaves into a mild hallucinogen.'

Shelly put down the lantern. 'Tell me about Benni,' he said.

'He's inside me,' I said, and I told Shelly exactly what he'd told me.

He made his hands into fists and said determinedly, '*Oui*, I understand now.'

'Understand what?'

'You are my chance to find Benni! You find Le Troubadour because you must help me.'

Shelly's purposeful eyes told me that he had reached the same conclusion as I had about why I'd moved to Montreal, which meant that we were either exhibiting the same symptoms of madness or were both right. 'Shelly, why me?' I asked. 'Why has Benni picked me?'

'I don't know,' he replied, and then he flinched. 'You know, maybe it's not Benni who . . . provokes you to dream of him,' he said in a conspiratorial voice. 'Maybe another person looks for you and counts on you. Someone who loves me and Benni. Someone who is dead.'

'Who?'

'*Tia* Graça.'

In the morning, Shelly and I headed back to Montreal in his old Chevy. He chain-smoked and drove too fast. I kept my window open and listened to a jazz station on the radio.

We got gas at a Sinclair station in Sainte-Adèle. A red-headed attendant with a tattoo of a bare-breasted, dark-haired lollapalooza on his forearm filled up the tank.

'Canada is an odd country,' Shelly told me as he looked from the attendant up to the big green brontosaurus on the station's sign.

'Odder than Poland?' I asked.

'Maybe, but it's also safer, which is all that counts.'

When we got back in the car, he turned to me and laughed bitterly. 'If the Nazis succeed, we are extinct – like the dinosaurs.' He shook his head dejectedly. 'You know, George, I make a big mistake. I should take Esther and Benni with me when I escape from Warsaw.'

I questioned him about whether he really thought he could have made it to Algiers while watching over two kids, but he started up the car and didn't reply. About forty-five minutes later, we reached the outskirts of the city, and he asked, 'Are you sure that Benni tells you that Montreal is *très loin*?'

'Yes.'

When we stopped at an intersection, I guessed from his stern, inward-facing profile that he was picturing his cousin fighting for his life. Fifteen minutes later, he pulled up in front of my apartment.

'I need you in Poland with me,' he said definitively.

'What do you mean?'

'A week ago, a friend tells me that Holocaust survivors are free to leave Poland. I check, and it is true – Jews have no need of a passport. The Kremlin lets them go. So I'm going back to look for Esther and Benni. And my other family members too. If any of them are still alive, I bring them to Montreal.'

'I don't understand – what does the Kremlin have to do with the Jews still living in Poland?'

He showed me a scandalised expression. 'George, don't you read about what's happening in Europe?'

'Not if I can help it.'

'The Soviets run Poland. It's an *Etat fantoche*.'

'What's an *Etat fantoche*?'

'A government that is a marionette.' Shelly made a dangling motion with his hand. 'Stalin and his friends have the strings.'

'I'm sorry, Shelly, but I'm not returning to Europe – not ever. I promised myself that.'

He put his hand on my leg and squeezed. 'You must come with me. I will not find a way to locate Benni – not alone.'

'Shelly, I don't speak any Polish or Yiddish. I'll be of no use to you.'

'George, you won't be in danger. We be together. And we won't visit any of the camps.'

'No, I can't do it. The only things for me there are too many dead people – and even worse, all those collaborators who wanted to turn you and me into dinosaurs.'

I started a sketch of Benni that night, before my internal image of him could fade. It took me three days to get it right. When I handed it to Shelly, I said, 'Show this to people who might have seen your cousin.'

He studied my drawing. 'Is his face truly so slender?' he asked.

'He's growing up,' I said. 'He's becoming a man – at least he is inside me.'

'He'd be sixteen now – almost seventeen. *C'est incroyable*! And Esther, she will be twenty-one in November.'

We huddled together under my bedsheets as if we were children planning a perilous adventure, and he told me how he'd take a boat from America to England and then continue on to Poland.

He said he'd already spoken to a number of Jewish friends about trying to locate their relatives in Poland and written out a list of their names and addresses. These friends would be pooling their money together to pay for his trip. He'd get a bus down to

New York and board the Queen Mary there. He had a ticket for its departure on August 7th.

'I don't know when I return,' he told me.

That hit me hard. But the depth of my despair was nothing compared to his; after making love that night, he surrounded himself with his pillows and turned on his belly and began to sob.

'Are you angry at me?' I asked.

'*Oui*, but mostly I'm mad at myself,' he replied without looking at me.

I reminded him that he'd have probably been caught by the Germans if he'd had his sister and cousin with him when he fled Warsaw.

He turned to me long enough to say, 'So I should stay with them. I go with them to the death camps. They must be so scared. I could help them.'

I took away one of his pillows and lay down beside him. I put my hand atop his head and told him what a wonderful and generous heart he had. He shook his head and said that wasn't true, but he didn't push me away. His eyes were red and tender.

'If you had stayed,' I said gently, 'you wouldn't be with me now. I'm glad you didn't die. And whatever you find in Poland, I want you to come back to me. I will wait for you for as long as it takes.'

He nodded and took my hand and kissed it. Then he closed his eyes. I turned off the lights and spooned up behind him, and in a little while he was asleep, which seemed a great blessing.

Three weeks before his departure for New York, Shelly quit work at the Botanical Garden, and a few days after that he stopped coming over to see me or inviting me to his place. I phoned him several times a day but never got an answer. I figured he was punishing me for refusing to accompany him to Poland. I was desperate to explain myself to him again and ask his forgiveness, so I went round to his flat both before and after work, and I shouted through his door that I was certain he was home, but he wouldn't let me in.

Ten days before his scheduled departure, his downstairs neighbour, a forty-something woman with close-cut, hennaed hair stopped me as I was leaving the building and told me with a scowl that the *le sale Juif* – the dirty Jew – who'd lived upstairs had moved out a few days earlier and that she didn't want me making any more noise in her building.

I could think of no reply equal to my contempt for her, so I simply left.

The thought that I'd never see Shelly again sent me into a frenzy, especially because I'd heard of Jews who'd returned home and been murdered by the Poles who'd taken possession of their homes. Mom had also told me about a recent pogrom in a small city between Warsaw and Kraków named Kielce. In July of 1946, forty-two Holocaust survivors who'd returned to their apartments and houses there were beaten and shot by soldiers, police officers and townspeople.

I rushed around to the restaurants where Shelly and I ate supper on my evenings off and left messages for him. And every night after work, I went to Le Troubadour. I waited hours for him each time, but he never showed up.

Eight days before he was scheduled to leave for New York, I stayed up until early morning, sketching him feverishly all over the walls of my bedroom. In my final drawing – was it the one I'd needed to make all along? – I portrayed him as an inmate at Bergen-Belsen. His chest was sunken and his powerful hands hung down on bamboo-slender arms. He held a book in his hands – *Germinal*, by his beloved Émile Zola.

It made me sick to see Shelly so debilitated, so I covered him over with white paint.

The next night, at just past three in the morning, something heavy crashed in the hallway outside my flat.

'*Oui!*' Shelly groaned through the door. '*C'est moi.*'

When I opened it, he fell into my arms. His eyes were bloodshot and he hadn't shaved. His breath was a fetid mix of rum and cigarettes.

He told me in a slurred and raspy voice – mostly in French – that he was terrified of returning to Poland.

'Because of the Poles who might hurt you?' I asked.

'No, I don't give a damn about the Poles!' he shouted.

'Then what is it?'

'It's all that will not be in Warsaw.' He wiped spittle from his mouth, then swirled his hand in the air like a magician. 'All the things I loved are *disparus* – gone!' He hung his head. '*Mon Dieu*, I detest my life. Do you understand, George – it's just so very stupid!'

Until then, I'd thought of Shelly as utterly unstoppable – the hero of the gangster film I had in my head. Looking at his desolate face, however, my heart seemed to tumble in my chest.

'Only you can find Benni!' he told me, pawing at me.

'That's not true,' I said.

'George, I won't go without you!' He slipped out of his old brown coat – the one Benni had been wearing in my dream – and threw it to the floor.

Terror gripped me. I shivered and went all rigid, needing to defend myself against emotions too dark to allow back into my mind. 'Shelly, we've discussed all this,' I declared. 'It's impossible. I'm sorry. If there were any other—'

'*Tia* Graça needs you!' he cut in. 'That's what she tells you, remember? "Don't forget me!"' He jabbed his finger into my chest with drunken fury. 'She means now! *Tu ne comprends pas?*' Glowering, he said, 'George, if you don't find Benni, it means that you forget her! Worse than that, you ... Oh, what's the fucking word?'

'I don't know,' I said, and I shook my head to indicate that I didn't want to go on with this conversation.

'You fail at everything!' he shouted. Sensing he'd wounded me badly, he continued his onslaught. 'Yes, you fail her and you fail me! *Et encore pire*, you fail yourself!'

The slow poison of his condemnation made me gaze away. When I could assemble a few coherent thoughts, I went to my stove and started to boil water.

'What are you doing?' he asked. When I didn't answer, he stepped up beside me and pushed me so hard that I had to reach out to the wall to keep from falling. 'I hate you!' he shouted.

His face looked possessed. I thought he might curse me or spit at me. I sensed that what I did with my life from now on depended on the next words we addressed to each other. But I didn't want to say anything that might give him hope, because I couldn't go back to Europe.

In the glare from my ceiling lanterns, I noticed how badly he was sweating. And that he'd been crying. I stepped up to him and felt his moist forehead. He was burning up.

'You need to get into bed,' I said. 'I'll make you some hot tea.'

'George, the last thing I want is tea!'

'Shelly, I can't go. In any case, it's too late for me to get a place on the Queen Mary.'

He shook his head with drunken abandon. 'No, it's not – I book a room for two. In case you decide to come.'

'But that must cost a fortune.'

'I paid for it with my own savings. And it's only money. It means nothing.'

'And what about a visa? Canadians must need one to get into Poland.'

'I bribe a man at the Polish Consulate for mine. He'll take money for yours too.' His expression turned resentful, 'Besides, I already tell you, the Polish government wants the Jews to leave. Don't you understand? They want you and me to find Benni and bring him here!' He caressed my cheek. 'George, *je te jure*. I will protect you. Nothing bad will happen!'

I got out a bag of my father's Navajo herbs. 'Shelly, you've got a fever. You've got to rest.'

He closed his eyes and bowed his head – a sign of resignation and defeat – which made me shiver. I went to him and started to lead him to my bed, but with an angry grunt, he struggled free, catching me a blow on my bottom lip, which started to bleed.

'Oh, *merde!*' He reached for my shoulder, but I slapped it away.

Coherent thoughts failed to form for a time. I felt as if I were standing in a no man's land between Canada and Europe, which made me tremble. I went to the bathroom to calm down and wash my lip. At length, Shelly shuffled to the doorway. His expression was regretful and his arms hung loosely by his side, as in the last sketch I'd done of him. I noticed again how powerful his hands were. *He'll squeeze the life out of anyone who tries to hurt him back in Poland*, I thought, and it seemed a very good thing. Except that I couldn't be absolutely sure that he wouldn't lash out at me again, which is why I said coldly, 'No more violence. I won't take that from you or anyone else.'

Tears slid down his cheeks and he said in a hoarse whisper, 'I never do that again. I promise. I'm so sorry.' He took a deep breath and confessed with a moan that he couldn't stop picturing Benni and Esther dying of starvation in a Nazi death camp, which was when I felt a latch of forgiveness opening inside me. He raised his hands into a position of prayer and asked meekly, 'Can I hold you?' His eyes were desolate.

When I nodded, he put his arms around me and kissed me. I kissed him back and then rested my head against his chest. *We've dispelled the barriers between us*, I thought with a deep sense of relief.

When we separated, I saw that his lips were smeared with blood, which seemed a sign from far beyond this time and place – from out of the ancient Navajo stories that my dad had told me as a child, in fact. My bottom lip was swelling up by then, so I continued to wash it at my sink. Shelly watched me with apprehensive eyes. When I returned to him, he apologised for a second time for hurting me. 'Please don't be mad at me,' he pleaded.

'I'm not. I'm just upset – with you, with me, with everything.'

'I feel not so good,' he said.

'Because you've given yourself a fever.'

He'd become completely pliable by then, like a little boy who'd been forced to stay up way past his bedtime, so I sat him down and took off his trousers and socks.

'George, you are my best friend,' he said as if it were a sudden revelation.

I walked him into my bedroom, got him under the covers and made his nest of pillows around his chest. He said he needed to stay awake and talk to me, but I told him he had to go to sleep. 'I'm in charge tonight,' I said.

'Do you want to fuck me?' he asked. 'You can, you know – anytime you want.'

'Christ, Shelly, do you always think about sex?'

'No, of course, not!' he said in an irate voice.

I was glad now to have argued so violently with him – it seemed a test we'd passed. 'I want you to drink some Navajo tea,' I told him. 'And then you need to go to sleep.'

'Whatever you say, *cheri*.'

After he'd had his tea, he whispered, 'If I go alone, I die.'

I was seated on the bed, with my hand in his. 'You're not going to die,' I said. 'You're going to come back to me in Montreal.'

He gazed past me with resigned eyes, as if he were looking at his destiny.

'You'll be fine,' I told him. I moved the blanket up to his chin. 'Now close your eyes.' He did as I asked. I combed his sweaty hair off his forehead with my hand and chanted a Navajo prayer, and after just a few minutes, he was sound asleep. I switched off the lights and took off my clothes and eased in beside him.

My need to protect the troubled man I loved became an ache in my gut, deep and resolute. And I felt that pain altering everything I'd intended to do with my life.

I woke at just after dawn, feeling as though the immense blue sky over Moab were waiting for me to open my curtains. *If I return to Europe, will that same munificent firmament be there, too?* I wondered.

After I'd made us coffee, and while I was frying us some French toast, Shelly stirred and stretched his arms over his head. 'George?' he asked.

'What?'

'Do I come here last night?'

'You stumbled up the stairs and crashed into my door.'

He grimaced. '*Je ne me rappelle pas*. No memory.'

'You were pretty sauced.'

He gazed beyond me at whatever he remembered about the

night before, but didn't find anything he considered important enough to tell me. '*Merde*, my head, she is painful!' he said.

'I'm not surprised she is painful,' I told him. 'You ought to treat her better!'

He laughed, his eyes gleaming with affection. I put the back of my hand to his forehead, which was cool. 'Your fever is gone,' I said.

I went to my first-aid box and took out my bottle of camphor and drizzled it on a tea towel. 'My God, what is that?' Shelly said, and he pinched his nose closed.

'It's my mother's cure. Tie it around your head.'

'Does it work?'

'Shush!'

He knotted the towel around his head and breathed in deeply. 'What a smell!' he said, and with a provocative grin, he added, 'So your mother, she gets drunk a lot?'

'No, but my grandfather liked his schnapps.' I went back to the stove. 'I'll have the coffee ready in a couple of minutes. That'll help too.' A little later, at my signal, he kicked his legs over the side of the bed, and I handed him his steaming mug. He watched me finishing up the French toast without speaking, but he smiled at me gratefully, and I realised that something had changed between us overnight; something honest and permanent that had started to grow between us. I thought, *I'll tell Mom and Dad about him now, and however they react will be all right, because I've found my way forward.*

As he took himself a cup of coffee, Shelly told me in a tentative voice – as if tiptoeing into murky waters – about his great-grandmother Rosa, and how she was able to see people's souls.

'See them how?' I asked.

'Through their eyes. Pretty strange, no?'

'I've heard stranger.'

'Like what?'

'Like that Coyote is very strong in me. My dad tells me that all the time.'

'I don't understand.'

'For the Navajo, the god that plays tricks on everybody is a coyote.'

'Okay, so maybe the Navajo are a little odd too,' he said in a serious voice, though a moment later, he laughed in a big, theatrical burst.

I asked him what souls looked like.

'Rosa says they look like living flames,' he replied.

Shelly said that the soul-flame could flare up and set off sparks at times of great emotion, and it could also die down at moments of hopelessness. He said that each individual soul was aligned to the north, south, east or west, depending on its particular nature. In rare instances, it could also face up or down. From the increasing depth in his voice, I could tell that he was building toward a revelation, and I thought he'd reached it when he said, 'But Benni's soul is even more *insolite*.'

'What's *insolite*?'

'*Mon Dieu*, your French is without hope,' he said, grunting. 'It means peculiar . . . unusual.'

I slid the toast from my skillet onto two big plates. 'Why is his unusual?' I asked.

'His soul changes direction. For example, when he is with me, it faces east – like mine. At least, this is what Rosa tells me.'

'And what does that mean – a soul facing east?' I asked.

'East belongs to the sunrise. So we are optimists. We keep going no matter what happens.'

'And you keep fucking, too,' I suggested.

'*Oui, c'est important, quand même*,' he told me with the smile of a little boy who is greatly loved.

'And for people whose soul faces west?'

'They absorb light from the setting sun. They are habitually melancholic and pessimistic.'

I sat next to Shelly on my bed and started eating. While gazing around my room – at the jumble of clothing on my armchair, the tower of paperbacks on my desk, my red and green lanterns – I thought, *That something wonderful can take place in this little nowhereland means that I can have the life I want.*

How is it that one thought can make us aware that we can do what we never believed possible? For I knew at that moment that I would accompany Shelly to Poland.

'Benni, he is one in a million,' Shelly told me as if he were still astonished by the notion.

'Because his soul faces different directions?' I asked.

'It even looks up and down,' he said, taking a big bite of his French toast.

'Looks?'

'The soul sees things, it observes – even when we sleep.' He pointed to my eyes with the tines of his fork. 'The soul, she watches.'

'Which means exactly what in Benni's case?'

'He can see things – strange things.' Shelly leaned close to me and whispered, 'Rosa tells me that Benni can see a little bit of God's hidden life.'

'Does God have a hidden life?' I asked.

Shelly snorted. 'George, where is your head? Everything that lives has a hidden life!'

'But you told me once you don't believe in God.'

'That's true. But I believe in Rosa!'

'So what does Rosa think that God does in his hidden life?' I asked.

'I have no idea,' he said with a shrug.

Something in the constrained way he faced down and resumed eating gave me to believe that he was feigning ignorance. It was the first time that I considered that there was a deep level of mystical understanding in Shelly – an inheritance from Rosa, perhaps – that he would never reveal to anyone. 'Which way does my soul face?' I asked.

'I have no idea.'

'You've never seen it?'

'No, of course not.'

Shelly devoured his breakfast with such urgent purposefulness that I was reminded that he'd lived through Nazi occupation. 'You've never told me how you escaped the ghetto,' I said.

'Through a tunnel,' he replied, and he stood up to fetch the coffee pot and refill our cups.

'And after that?'

'I go to Algiers.'

'How did you get there?'

'I walk.'

'The whole way?' I asked.

'No, sometimes I take a train. I have French papers. My mom gets them for me.'

'Nobody bothered you?'

'Not so much.'

His matter-of-fact tone made that seem a lie. On a hunch, I asked, 'Did you ever have to kill anyone?'

He started. 'Why you ask me that?'

'I don't know. It just came to me that maybe you had to.'

He looked at me with cold eyes. 'I kill a Frenchman once.'

'Who was it?'

He sipped his coffee pensively. I had the feeling he was considering whether to tell me the truth or not. 'How do you say in English a man who fixes shoes?' he finally asked.

'A cobbler.'

'A cobbler who tries to stop me from . . . from continuing my way.'

'Did you know his name?'

'No.'

'How did you kill him?'

'George, *écoute*, *ça suffit*! I do not wish to speak of this.'

'I'm just glad you survived,' I said. 'Which means I'm glad that you killed him. Though that sounds terrible.'

'No, it doesn't sound terrible. I'm glad I kill him too – at least, most of the time.'

While he licked the cinnamon sugar off his plate, I asked, 'Did you go hungry a lot?'

'George, everyone goes hungry,' he replied impatiently. 'One has little to eat in a war.'

'Want another piece of French toast?' I questioned.

'Yes, please.' He handed me his polished plate.

'Will you ever tell me about the bad things that happened to you?' I asked. When he looked at me with a surprised face, I tried to speak to that hidden part of him that he might never show me or anyone else. 'You can trust me – I won't tell anyone. And I won't judge you either.'

'Maybe some other time,' he replied. 'Now I need to talk about other things.' While I was pouring oil in my skillet, he said, 'When I first see you at Le Troubadour, a comprehension comes to me that is odd.'

'It was *insolite*?' I asked, pleased with myself.

'*Voila*!' he exclaimed with that sweet-natured grin of his that might have made him a leading man in Hollywood if he'd been born in America.

'So what did you understand?' I asked.

'That you are hurt. I say to myself, "*Quelque chose horrible a blessé ce garçon.*" Something horrible hurts this young man.'

I scoffed. 'It's normal to see all sorts of things in people's faces – to read into them what we want to see. Or have to see.'

He shook his fist. 'Not with such a . . . *force fatale*.'

'What did you think had happened to me?'

'I think you lose your family – like me.'

'But no one murdered my mother's parents. They came to Canada long before the war. And my father's parents survived all the bad things that happened to the Navajo.'

'Yes, but you do have a horrible experience – in Germany. And then something else happens that is strange – *quand tu m'a pris.* That first time.'

'What happened?'

'Do you remember that I ask you to stop moving?'

'Yes, you said that you hadn't been fucked in months.'

'Exactly. But I lie. You don't hurt me. I get scared. Because I can feel the death inside you. I can feel my parents, and lots of other people from Warsaw. And I sense that the Nazi camp is just outside your front door, where the other apartments should be. And I can feel all those dead people coming from you into me – one by one. I become very cold. And my erection, she disappears. And that never happens.'

'Never?' I asked, and he shook his head.

When I apologised for scaring him, he said, 'No, I am glad. I want my relations in me. I want to see what you see. That's what I wish to tell you for many weeks. That you give them back to me. I want to thank you for that. I feel them in me now, all the time.'

'Why did you wait to tell me?'

'It isn't easy to say you have dead people inside you. But I know now that you are conscious of them too.'

I waited till his French toast was almost done before speaking again. 'The problem is,' I said, 'I don't think I'll ever get all those dead people out of me.'

'Do you want to make them to leave?'

I thought about that. 'No, if I'm being honest, I want them to stay with me forever,' I said.

I sat with him as he ate. At length, he rested his hand on my knee and said, 'I look in books, you know – at the public library. I discover important things. The Jews who are not killed in the *soulèvement* of the ghetto in Warsaw, they—'

'*Soulèvement*?'

'When the Jews fight the Nazis.'

'The Ghetto Uprising.'

'Yes. The survivors are transferred to Bergen-Belsen. That is how my aunt goes there. If the woman you see is her, I mean.'

Shelly and I spoke no more of his family that morning. After he finished eating, he took off his camphor-soaked tea towel and lit a cigarette. He smoked with an easy serenity, and I could see that the past had released him. Later, on our walk through our neighbourhood, he told me about how much he missed the flowers and bushes at the Botanical Garden. 'I need the palms most of all – they are so soft and loving,' he told me.

'And which way does the soul of a palm tree face?' I asked, which made him pause in his step and laugh in a burst, but then say in a serious tone, 'You know, I do not know – Rosa never tells me.'

At the end of our walk, while we were admiring an old apartment house that had been painted pink and yellow, Shelly said that he had to run some errands and would see me that evening. I took his shoulder and told him then that I'd decided to accompany him to Poland.

He didn't cry; he kissed my hands as if he were enacting an ancient Hebrew ritual, then embraced me.

The next morning, I called my father at work while Shelly was taking a shower and told him I'd be returning to Europe soon.

After a shocked uptake of breath, he said, 'Why in God's name are you going back?'

'To see all the places I missed – Paris, most of all,' I lied. 'Shelly is coming with me.'

'You two won't go back to Germany, will you?'

'No, of course, not.'

'That's okay, then,' he said in a relieved voice. 'Listen, son, do you have enough money to stay in decent hotels? I don't want you staying in places that aren't clean.'

'Shelly's got savings,' I said.

'And you promise to be careful? Some places might still have people that don't like Jews.'

I assured him I would be. And then I paused, because this would be my last chance to tell him the truth about Shelly before our trip to Europe. 'Listen, Dad,' I began, 'I've something to tell you.' But I couldn't go on; my heart was racing, and the words wouldn't form in my mouth.

'What is it, George?' he asked. 'Is everything okay?'

'It's about Shelly,' I said. 'The thing is, his real name is Hershel, though he never uses it.'

'I don't understand,' my father replied. I could hear in his tone that he'd already taken a step back from me in his mind.

'Shelly is a young man,' I said. 'And he's really wonderful.' I spoke as confidently as I could – in a voice that my dad would have to respect – yet I heard it as if I were standing behind a thick glass wall. My legs had begun to shake, so I sat down.

'A man?' my father asked.

'Yes.'

Silence.

'Dad?' I asked. 'Are you angry at me?' I tried to keep my voice from quivering but failed.

He didn't reply. I thought I could hear him breathing hesitantly, but that might have been in my mind. Not knowing what else to do, I made a little jest. 'Mom won't have to worry about me marrying a goy,' I said, 'Shelly is Jewish.'

The continuing silence made my attempt at humour seem like a kind of slow death. 'He was born in Poland,' I went on. 'He's really nice and intelligent.'

'Shelly is a man?' my dad asked again.

'Yes. He's a few years older than me. Listen, I'm sorry I lied to you before. But you'd like him. And he's helped me ... start over.'

No reply.

I started counting. I was thinking that by ten Dad would tell me that my falling in love with a man made no difference to him.

Five, six, seven ... Just after eight, I heard a click and the line went dead.

It occurred to me that my father had hung up as discreetly as possible, as if he didn't want me to know he had left me, and I knew instantly how I would begin telling Shelly what had happened: *It was as if he wanted to try to slip away from me without being noticed and make believe that our conversation had never happened.*

While holding the receiver in my hand, listening to the dial tone, I continued counting, but slower than before: nine, ten, eleven ... I pictured my future self, looking back at this moment, and remembering that it was precisely at the count of twelve that I'd learned that I was separate from everything in the world, but most especially from my father.

By twenty-one, I was pretty certain that I was no longer in danger of collapsing into tears, but I couldn't yet hang up the receiver, since there would be no going back after that; I'd never again be able to think of my father the same way.

Thoughts scattered through my head. I took a cigarette from the pack that Shelly always left on my night table. Was I searching for a way out of myself by imitating him? A little while later, he finished his shower. When he came to me, I didn't mention my phone conversation with my dad. He asked why I looked so pale, and I said that it was because I'd smoked one of his cigarettes.

'You need more practice,' he chuckled happily, and I did my best to laugh too.

A little later, I dressed for work; it was my last day at the Fiore d'Italia.

After closing time that night, I grabbed a beer and locked myself in the staff bathroom. A postcard of Saint Cristina of Bolsena being attacked by fanged snakes had been taped to the wall behind the sink. I wondered how she managed such a contented, beatific expression, then studied myself in the mirror until my face no longer seemed the one I knew. *You are not the man you're supposed to be*, I thought, and my self-loathing seemed violent and unforgiving.

I might have stayed in the bathroom until morning, but Adalberto, the owner, knocked and told me in his Sicilian-accented English that he was dying to pee.

Lying in bed that night next to Shelly, I tried to convince myself that it was wrong for me to feel so protected with his arms around me, but I was unable to do it. And whenever I pictured us in the palm greenhouse, I grew certain that nature itself – every leaf, flower and spore – understood my love for him. In fact, it seemed as if every test of courage and strength that I'd ever given myself had prepared me for these last few days.

My mother called the next morning. We were leaving for New York in four days. 'I need to talk to you,' she said in a hectoring voice.

'Look Mom, if it's to tell me you're upset and disappointed with me,' I said impatiently, 'I already know it. You don't need to say a thing. You can just hang up – like Dad.'

Mom started crying. That hadn't been my intent, but I wasn't sorry, which is how I understand that I intended to avenge myself on my father by being cruel to her.

'I understand how shocked you must be,' I told her.

'You don't seem to understand anything about me,' she replied sadly. And then, flaring with rage, she added, 'I don't care two cents that Shelly is a man!'

I didn't believe her. 'Mom, I honestly don't know what I can do or say. I didn't plan to be this way. But I'm also not ashamed. In fact, I'm—'

'George, I won't let you turn me into an ogre!' she interrupted in an outraged tone. After a moment, she said more calmly, 'It's my fault, I suppose, that you don't know who I am. How did that happen? My goodness, everything used to be so easy between us.'

'Mom, the boy I was is gone.'

She sighed. 'I know. And I know now that I wanted to hold on to him. That was a mistake. I chased you away. I'm sorry. I didn't mean to, but I did.'

I realised I'd been waiting for her to admit that for months. What was astonishing was that all my anger at her vanished the moment she apologised. 'I'm sorry too,' I said.

'It's good for me to know you've grown up – and that you've met a man you like. I want to meet him. I want to be with you both.'

'I guess . . . I guess that when we get back from Europe, we'll come to Toronto,' I said. 'We'll stay in a rooming house if Dad doesn't permit me to come home.'

'George, it's not his decision. This is your house too. And mine. You'll both stay here.'

'But what if—'

'George, listen,' she cut in. 'I have a bus ticket to Montreal. I'm coming tomorrow afternoon. I couldn't live with myself if I let you go back to Europe without seeing you.'

'What about Dad?' I asked.

'I'm coming alone. It'll . . . it'll take him a while to get used to this.'

'I'm not sure he ever will.'

'I know your father, George. Give him a few weeks. He's a good man.'

'Mom, he hung up on me!'

'George, you startled him. Once he gets his bearings, he'll be thrilled you've fallen in love. At the moment, he's battling with some old spirits in that ancestral desert of his, up on top of some mesa somewhere, but I'm quite certain that he'll find the way forward. He always does.'

'But this is different.'

'No, actually, it's not. He's proved how good a man he is many times before . . . how genuine and kind. And he'll prove it again. You'll just have to trust me on this.'

Mom called me from the Montreal bus station at five-thirty the next day to say she'd arrived and would hop in a taxi. Sitting with Shelly at my tiny dining table, pretending to study the Polish visa in my passport that we'd managed to get that morning, I pictured a family disaster heading straight for us; Mom would find Shelly glib and superficial, and he'd find my mother a pretentious snob.

Shelly sensed my tension, of course. 'George, just keep breathing,' he told me, grinning like he does when he thinks he's being charming and devilish.

My mother arrived a half hour later. She'd tied her long brown hair into a tight knot at the back of her head, which made her face seem older and starker than I'd remembered it. She wore a man's corduroy trousers and a loose-fitting charcoal-grey sweater that she must have knitted recently, because I didn't remember it. We kissed, and she said I looked healthy and happy.

When she hugged Shelly, she placed her head against his chest for a moment and closed her eyes, and I was certain she was giving him thanks in her own way for helping me start over.

Her turquoise earrings – in the shape of bellflowers – dangled over her cheek.

Mom has a long Roman nose, deep-brown eyes and an olive complexion, and when I was a kid, I loved to see her wear turquoise jewellery, because the perfect blue of those stones made her look elegant and lovely – and, to my adoring young mind, like one of the wise mothers in the Navajo myths my father told me.

Shelly made a nervous face at me while she was embracing him, but I didn't go to him because I was terrified that he'd kiss me on the lips the moment my mother drew back from him. I couldn't seem to figure out what to do with my hands, so I joined them behind my back. Mom and Shelly seemed like characters from two different plays that had accidentally met on this little stage that I'd built for myself.

After Mom leaned back from Shelly, she lifted up her hand and cupped his chin. She studied his face as though she were a sculptress.

'Good or bad?' asked Shelly.

'Good,' Mom said with a nod. 'In fact, *Monsieur*, you have the most beautiful eyes I've ever seen! *Les plus beaux que j'ai jamais vu!*' she added, which surprised me because I'd never heard her speak French before.

'*Merci, Madame,*' Shelly replied, smiling in his Hollywood way.

'*S'il vous plaît, je ne suis pas Madame, je suis* Irene,' Mom said.

'*Comme vous voulez*, Irene,' said Shelly with a gentlemanly tilt to his head.

Mom turned to me. 'Yes, I can speak French, George. I studied it for seven years back before you were born.' She clapped her hands together and grinned with joy. 'Now, I want to get a look at you together.'

'What . . . what you mean?' I stammered.

'I'm sorry, baby, but you're standing there like a . . . cold radiator, and we've got to end this impasse here and now or I'm not going to be able to enjoy the rest of our evening together.'

'What impasse?' I asked.

Mom rolled her eyes. 'George, *mon amour*, I nursed you through every childhood disease you can name, so don't you think I can tell when you're feeling uncomfortable?'

'Well, what would you like me to do?'

'My goodness, do you really think that you two are the first men I've known who've slept together? You remember my old friend Frederick?'

'Of course, I remember him.' Frederick taught history at a high school in Vancouver.

'He and I shared the same boyfriend for nearly a year – before I met your dad.'

'I didn't know you had any boyfriends before Dad.'

Mom laughed in a gleeful burst and turned to Shelly. In a

scandalised voice, she said, 'Do children always think their parents come to life only at the moment of their birth?'

'Very probably,' he said, and from eagerness in his eyes, I could tell that he had just discovered that he and Mom were both born performers – and might have a long future of drama and comedy ahead of them.

'*Monsieur*, I think you'll have to make the first move,' she told him. 'My son seems convinced I'm someone I'm not.'

Shelly came to me and took my head in his hands, and he leaned in and he kissed me, and he kept his lips on mine until I kissed him back.

'Wonderful!' Mom exulted. 'You make a very handsome couple. *Très beaux*! And now I'm going to take you boys out for a nice dinner.'

Mom took my hand outside the door and gave it a squeeze, and as we smiled at each other, I thought, *Until this very moment, I didn't understand what ought to have been obvious – that for Mom, love and loyalty are inseparable.*

I'd made a reservation for my mother at one of the fancy hotels downtown, but she had two glasses of retsina at the Greek restaurant we chose for dinner and got a little groggy, so we ended up getting her a room just down the street at the Pension Honfleur. In the morning, she came over for breakfast and told us – giggling girlishly – that Fedir the Ukrainian boxer was still living there and remembered me fondly. 'I think maybe he has a crush on you,' she said with obvious delight, which both stunned and pleased me.

Mom cooked us oatmeal while Shelly wove her shoulder-length, greying hair into French braids, explaining that he used to do this favour for his sister Esther all the time. 'Braiding a woman's hair . . . it always makes me feel useful.'

'My God, the beautiful way you speak English . . .' Mom told him. 'I could happily listen to you read the phone book!'

After our lazy breakfast together, the three of us took a taxi to the bus station. Mom's bus to Toronto left at noon.

'Take good care of each other,' she told us as she took our hands for one last squeeze. Just before boarding, she reached into her old plaid suitcase and gave us the presents that she'd nearly forgotten – a big bag of dried mushrooms and her first edition of *The Grapes of Wrath*.

After I hugged and kissed her goodbye, she caressed my cheek and said, 'At your difficult moments, remember that what you feel for Shelly is as old as the stones of the Utah desert. And George, nothing you do could ever shame me.' She turned for Shelly, then reconsidered and reached back for me. 'Oh, and one other thing, sweetheart – I think you will find that nearly everything people say about the way life works is lies, so just do what you have to do.'

Shelly embraced Mom tenderly and whispered in French to her. Later, he told me that he'd promised her to look after me. After they'd kissed cheeks, he put his arm over my shoulder – to show her that I would be safe with him – and we waved goodbye.

We left for New York two days later and stayed in a cheap rooming house just off Houston Street. The next morning, at 11 a.m., we boarded the Queen Mary.

After Shelly and I had put our bags in our cramped stateroom, we rushed back up onto deck – taking the stairs two at a time – feeling as though we were explorers aboard a floating island bound for exotic territories. It wasn't true, of course, but we must have needed to tell ourselves a happy-go-lucky adventure story to keep us calm.

A little later, we pulled out of our berth and slipped into New

York Harbor. Barges and tugs and even a few sailing ships were sliding over the dark water, which seemed to hoist us aloft. While most everyone else waved and called out to the Statue of Liberty, I tried and failed to come to terms with the deep sway and glide taking place under my feet.

A certain lightheaded sense of strangeness – of doing the impossible – overcame me as the towering skyline of Manhattan shrank down to the horizon. But when it vanished entirely, disquiet snuck up behind me. Shelly sensed my mood and led me down to our room, and he assured me that I'd feel fine once we had a nap, since we'd slept very little the night before. He was right; I woke up more determined and relaxed. Over coffee at the ship's cafe, he asked me how my parents had met, and I told him about my mom's father's camera shop in Toronto, and how Dad would go there every day to sneak a look at her.

After Shelly retired to our room to read Émile Zola, I returned to the main deck and gazed out to sea, due east, toward the ruined continent awaiting us. After a while, my father appeared in my mind. I saw him seated by a campfire in the desert, chanting to the spirits of the earth and sky – asking them for the wisdom to understand what he hadn't ever previously considered.

We encountered rough seas over most of the journey and took close to eight days to cross the Atlantic. Shelly was seasick and miserable almost all the time, and my main activity became cheering him up. We played rummy and casino on our bed for hours, and I let him win because I'd learned by then that losing at any game put him in a foul mood, and I read to him from *The Grapes of Wrath*. Had Mom chosen that novel for us because it was about the quiet heroism of the kind of people who rarely appeared in history books?

Shelly asked me every morning if I'd learned anything more

about Benni – from a dream, or burst of insight – and though I never did, I could feel the boy waiting inside me at the gate to Bergen-Belsen. I executed several small portraits of him in my sketchbook but could never seem to get his eyes just right. Shelly kept saying, '*Plus grands encore*,' but whenever I made his eyes bigger, he would shake his head and say with frustration, 'No, they still aren't Benni's eyes,' though he could never tell me what exactly I was doing wrong.

When we disembarked at Portsmouth, Shelly kneeled down ceremoniously and kissed the cobblestones of the quay. At a nearby pub, he was able to eat solid food for the first time since leaving New York. Two days later, he was fully recovered, and we boarded a ferry in Folkestone that took us to Boulogne-sur-Mer, and from there we made our way to Warsaw by train.

At the border crossing between Germany and Poland, our train was stopped and our passports were taken from us by two Red Army soldiers, who promptly marched out of our compartment and vanished. Shelly and I were seated in a foul-smelling compartment with cigarette butts on the floor and greasy streaks on the window. When the train started up again an hour and a half later, our documents still hadn't been returned to us, and a terrifying surge and descent of blood ripped through me. I jumped up, and for a time I couldn't seem to get enough air.

'George, what's wrong?' Shelly asked.

'What's wrong?' I cried out in a suffocating voice. 'They've got our passports! What if we don't get them back?'

'They just want to frighten us,' he answered. 'Our papers are in order. Just sit back down.'

He sounded calm, but I could tell by the rigid set of his jaw that he was steeling himself for a major battle, which set my heart thumping. I wanted to go looking for the soldiers, but he told me I'd only end up arrested. He opened *La Bête Humaine*, crossed his legs and started to read, which created in me a poisonous fury that I knew was unjust, but that I was powerless to fight. I shut my eyes and tried to imagine that I was hiking in the wilds of Mont-Tremblant Provincial Park, but instead I saw the fresco of the rabid Cerberus that I'd painted on my wall.

Two hours later, after we were already deep into Polish territory, the younger of the two soldiers who'd taken our passports returned. When I stood up, he handed them to me with a small bow. While I confirmed they were ours, he addressed Shelly, and his voice soon became secretive and unsure. It sounded as though he might be speaking Russian, but my friend later told me that it was heavily accented Polish – that the young man was probably a Pole who'd grown up in the Soviet Union. The only words I understood were *Montreal* and *Toronto*. Shelly's replies clearly captivated him, however, and he reacted with pleased, grateful nods. At one point, he even permitted himself a glowing smile.

Shortly before leaving us, the solider checked the corridor to make sure we weren't being observed and took out a pen and a tiny piece of paper – no bigger than his thumb. He handed them to Shelly, who quickly jotted down a few words.

'*Dziękuję*,' the solider said as he took back the paper. As he folded it in four, his tongue poked out boyishly between his lips. Was he all of eighteen years old? After the paper was the size of a small postage stamp, he tucked it into his shirt pocket.

When he shook Shelly's hand, hope lit his eyes, and it touched me to see how two strangers might share a meaningful exchange under these difficult circumstances.

Once he was gone, I asked Shelly what the conversation was about.

'He wants to know if we have professional ice hockey teams in Canada. He says he plays really well. He wants to go there, though he doesn't openly say that. He is too afraid to say what he thinks.'

'What did you write down?'

'He asks for my address.'

'You gave it to him? But what if he shows up expecting to become a hockey star?'

'Don't worry. I want to help, but I don't dare. I invent an address. Poor kid – he is desperate to leave this place. And brave, too – he tells me that talking to me could get him arrested.'

We arrived at the ruins of what had been Warsaw's main station on the afternoon of Monday, August 25th, 1947. Policemen – many of them no older than the soldier who'd returned our passports – patrolled the platforms. Their rigid, impassive faces and their tommy guns, slung over their shoulders, spread shivers through me.

Outside, the rotting stench in the streets compelled me to cover my nose and breathe through my mouth. Although about three years had passed since the Nazi destruction of the city following the Warsaw Uprising – when the Polish Home Army had tried to take back the city from the Germans – sewage still seemed to seep out from somewhere beneath the ground.

To get to Shelly's childhood home on Ciasna Street, he led me through what had been the Jewish ghetto, but he had trouble getting his bearings because Russian troops – fearing outbreaks of typhus and other diseases – had bulldozed every last remaining structure to the ground. The gouged and muddy streets reminded me of the mining towns in Wyoming I'd visited with my parents as a boy, except that these streets were bordered by hillocks of broken concrete, brick and shredded metal. Spindly, yellow-blossoming weeds and stunning blue cornflowers grew wherever they had a chance to express their desperate wish for sunlight. Curiously, nearly all the men and women we passed seemed to be on urgent errands, rushing by with their heads down and shoulders clenched. I suggested to Shelly that they'd learned during the German occupation that keeping to themselves would be key to survival, but he made no reply. In fact, his lips had become a slit of forced silence since we'd arrived in Warsaw. I tried to take his arm at one point, after we passed a high mound of rubble on Dzielna Street that he believed to have been the Eldorado Theatre – where he'd played Puck in *A Midsummer Night's Dream* – but he gasped as if I'd burned him. 'I'm sorry, George, I can't be touched right now,' he said, and when our eyes met, I realised that violent and tragic emotions were assaulting him.

At one point, he got out his list of the relations of his Jewish friends and made a big blue X with his pen by the names of those who had made their homes in the area that became the ghetto.

Occasionally, Shelly would point toward a terrain of broken concrete and tell me that this was where the apartment house of a family member or old friend had been – or might have been, since it was nearly impossible for him to get his bearings in the sea of rubble around us.

We each carried a small duffel bag. Now and again, Shelly would put his down and gaze around in a slow circle. His face expressed deep confusion and disorientation.

After about a half hour of trudging through that desolate landscape, he kneeled down by a rusty girder. He picked up a piece of brick and tossed it across the street. 'I'm pretty sure Uncle Henni and Aunt Elisabete have their home over there, with their son, Abe,' he told me. He pointed up. 'Second floor, left. They keep begonias in their window boxes. And they have a fat dog with crooked teeth – Knodl. It means matza ball. They also have a parrot named Glukl – good luck. They do not place her in a cage. She has her own bedroom. She is very old. And she can speak three languages.'

I laughed, but Shelly stared at me as if I'd insulted him. I wished I could find the right words to bring him back to me, if only for a few minutes.

'Abe was the chess player?' I asked.

Shelly lit a cigarette. 'He would have been Polish champion,' he said in a monumental exhale of smoke.

'Maybe we can find him.'

He raised his hands as if he needed to make a momentous pronouncement about his cousin – a declaration about injustice perhaps – but a moment later he simply let his hands drop and shook his head as if it were useless to try.

A hundred paces down the street we came to a giant crater where girders had been twisted into tormented shapes. It seemed like a sculpture meant to symbolise how quickly an entire culture can be reduced to nothing. I followed him down to the crater's centre. We squatted together by a pile of broken glass. 'We come here at Rosh Hashanah and Yom Kippur,' he said.

'Was it a cemetery?' I asked.

'No, the Great Synagogue.' He spread his arms. 'Beautiful building. You can't imagine.'

The remains of the ghetto wall were nearby. Past them was a neighbourhood where some of the buildings had suffered only minor damage. Many shops had opened again.

Shelly bought two apples and bottles of beer for us from an old man with the narrow and wary eyes of a hawk. From the wooden sign above his head – bearing the name Nowak – I realised that he might have been the former fabric seller who'd promised to get word to Shelly about any members of his family who returned. At the back of the shop, Shelly started a conversation with him, and the old man showed him a nearly toothless smile. They talked for twenty minutes or so.

Shelly returned to me with the apples and handed me one.

'Is that the Nowak you spoke to a couple of years ago?' I asked.

'Yeah, he says my parents not come back. Not Benni or Esther either. He says some Jews return, but they leave again.'

'Where'd they go?'

'He is not sure. He says the government takes them to the Czech border, and from there they maybe go to Germany – to the part controlled by the Americans.'

'What about that other man you spoke to, the baker? Maybe we could find him.'

'No, Nowak says that Wieczorek vanish about a year ago. Maybe the Soviets take him. Or maybe he moves somewhere.'

'And Nowak knew your family well before the war? I mean, he'd recognise them.'

Shelly nodded. 'My mother and aunt shop here all the time – when Nowak sells fabric.'

He bit into his apple, so I started on mine; I wanted to remind him that we were on this journey together.

'My mom has a dress that is scarlet,' he said. 'I forget until now. Nowak, he reminds me.'

'What was it like?'

'It has a high collar. And she wears an onyx brooch on it. Scarlet and black – they are my mom's favourite colours.'

'She must have been beautiful,' I said.

Shelly shook his head emphatically. 'No, not beautiful. She is athletic and slender. Though she is an amazing dancer. She studies ballet when she is a girl, and later, when—'

He choked suddenly, and he reached up to his throat as if he couldn't breathe. Before I could get to him, he staggered back and tumbled over. He scraped his right hand badly, and it started to bleed. After he cursed himself, I helped him sit up and undid his scarf. He took a few desperate breaths. In his eyes, I could see that his fortifications against his homeland had crumbled.

He won't survive many days of this, I thought, and I accepted at that moment that it would be up to me to force him to return to Canada no matter what we found – or didn't find.

After I put a bandage on his hand, we started off again. Soon, I noticed a staircase in an apartment house climbing up into the sky – leading only to empty space – and it seemed a metaphor for something absurd and deeply flawed in Poland and the rest of Europe that would never now be fixed. And it occurred to me, as well – with the quiet, steadfast certainty of a revelation – that there was no need for an artist to invent symbols, since the world offered them to us ready-made.

Shelly spoke to an aged grandmother wearing a dirty smock who sold newspapers from a stall made of wooden planks, then every other shop clerk and salesgirl on the block. His first question, he told me, was always the same: *Have you seen or heard of any Jews who are still living in Warsaw?*

While he questioned everyone he could find, I searched a bombed-out building for anything that might be of interest. He returned to me shaking his head. 'Nobody knows of any Jews who come back and stay,' he said, adding with an irritated grunt, 'Though most people close their doors to me.'

'Why?'

'They're afraid of the secret police.'

'They think you're from the secret police?'

'Some do. Though others ask about my French accent and must

think I'm a spy. Anyway, they're obviously scared that if they talk to me, they'll be interrogated. And maybe tortured.'

Hoping to improve his morose mood a tiny bit, I held out a tortoiseshell comb I'd found, but he told me to get rid of it because it might carry lice eggs. Down the block, two young women wearing long elegant coats and lacy stockings were having an animated conversation at a bus stop. Shelly spoke to them, but they looked at him as if he were a bad smell.

'A problem?' I asked when he returned to me.

'They just refuse to talk to me – they tell me to get lost.'

'They're dressed much nicer than a lot of women I've seen.'

'Yeah, they must have good jobs. Or rich parents. Either way, they've managed to get in good with the authorities.'

'Why do you say that?'

'The Communists decide where you work now. And how much of your earnings you get to keep.'

When he told me that, I realised what ought to have been obvious to me – that signs and ciphers were concealed beneath the surface of all I would see in Warsaw. As I turned in a circle to remember that lesson, a hunched little man in ragged clothing, carrying a big brown bottle in a filthy hand, limped past me, and I smiled encouragingly, but he glared at me as if I'd insulted him.

Did he assume I was a Jew who'd returned to reclaim my home? Was he a down-on-his-luck Nazi collaborator who'd partied in elegant bars and brothels throughout the war?

At length, we passed a thuggish-looking young man with long, oily hair, wearing a dusty grey suit that was way too small for him, so that his pink wrists and hands stuck out comically. He was carving off big pieces of a dark sausage and popping them in his mouth. He chewed from side to side, rather like a sheep. His eyes – when they met mine – expressed amused curiosity. A little while later,

I realised that he was following us, so I stepped up to Shelly and whispered, 'The guy behind us has a knife.'

'Don't worry. He's okay.'

'How do you know that?'

'He lets us see him. It's the men we can't see who might make trouble.'

'So we're being followed?' I whispered.

'You do not notice?'

'No.'

'A man in a grey suit watches us since the station – probably from the UB.'

'What's the UB?'

'The Polish secret police.'

'And where is he now?'

'Behind us, but don't look! Just forget about him. We have more important things to think about.'

We turned right at the second street corner, and a minute or so later, Shelly stopped in front of a six-storey building with one side missing and no roof. By then, the thuggish-looking sausage-eater was gone. Shelly pointed up. 'My parents, Esther and I live on the third floor,' he said.

I patted his shoulder. 'Let's go look,' I said. 'I want to see where you were a kid. And if Benni or Esther left you a note, it'll be there.'

'George, I'm not sure I'm ready to go up.'

'I'll stay with you.'

'Give me a minute to smoke,' he said.

When Shelly was nearly done with his cigarette, a little scrappy-looking man wearing a red-and-white armband and a rifle slung over his shoulder came clomping and sliding down a high mound of rubble toward us. His eyes were wild, and his thick brown hair was a mess. I feared he'd demand a look at our papers, but instead he tossed off a sneering remark to Shelly and raced past us. A minute later, he disappeared around a street corner, and I asked Shelly what he'd said.

'Something like, "What are you looking at, asshole?"' he replied.

'Who was he?'

'I have no idea. And I don't want to know.'

Our eyes met, and his seemed to search me for my consent to something I didn't understand, but which might have had to do with my suspending judgment of him and his homeland.

Our knocks at the door to Shelly's old home summoned a woman in her thirties to the door, which she opened just a sliver. Her lips were cracked and her eyes were narrowed by fear. Her red headscarf, tied too tightly, made her face look pinched and judgmental.

If I'd spoken Polish, I would have assured her right away that we were neither the police nor French or Canadian spies. Shelly held up his hands and must have said that very thing, since I heard the words *policja* and *kanadyjski* clearly. But she must have decided he was lying. She tried to press the door closed, but Shelly thrust out his hand and blocked it, then pushed it in.

The woman stood back from us. She wore men's slacks and an old white sweater – moth-eaten and stained green at the collar. She was holding a long carving gouge with a wooden handle. We were in a small foyer. The doorway at the back was open, and I smelled turpentine and something else – a fragrant oil of some kind. Remnants of wallpaper – a fleur-de-lis pattern in gold and red – clung here and there to the walls. Black mould grew on the ceiling.

Shelly held his hands up and addressed the woman cautiously. She spoke to him in a jagged, aggressive voice – giving him a warning, I imagined. He answered her, then shrugged as though to excuse himself, and she told him something that made him frown and shake his head, then speak in a frustrated tone. A barefoot boy in a blue pyjama top but no bottoms appeared in the doorway, holding a piece of white paper. He looked to be about five years old. Shelly spoke to him gently and smiled. The boy – blonde, with reddened eyes – looked from him to me to his mother. Had she kept him home from school because he was ill? He spoke to her – asking who we were, most likely – but she yelled at him and waved him off. His mouth dropped open, and when she shouted again, he ran away.

Shelly spoke again to the woman, but in a friendly and entreating tone this time, undoubtedly trying to reassure her that we had come in peace. But she shouted resentfully at him and pointed her gouge at his face. I may then have gasped or given away my fear in some other way, because Shelly turned to me and said, 'Don't be frightened.' He flashed a smile at me, as well – later I realised it was to put the woman at ease – then lunged for her and grabbed her threatening arm. With brutal quickness, he seized her throat in his other hand and slammed her back against the wall so violently that she gasped and burst into tears. Her gouge dropped to the ground. She struggled against his grip, but he was too strong.

'Shelly!' I yelled. 'Don't hurt her!'

He leaned toward the woman and spoke to her in a dark, poisonous whisper. When he released her, she started to cry silently. He snatched up her gouge, then handed it to me. 'I'm going to look around,' he told me. 'You can stay here or join me. But do not trust this woman. And do not give her back her tool!'

I nodded, and I wanted to ask him what she'd told him, but he rushed into the apartment. The woman spat blood on the ground between us. She took off her headscarf and ran a tense hand back through her thick blonde hair. When she looked at me, her face was compressed by rage.

'This was my friend's apartment,' I told her.

Glaring, she pointed at me and uttered something that seemed a curse.

She turned and stepped through the door at the back into the apartment. I took a couple of steadying breaths and followed her, gripping the gouge in case she came at me. I found her standing by a far window covered by grimy brown curtains. When she made a smoking motion with her hand, I told her I had no cigarettes. As she frowned at me, Shelly called out angrily, 'George, for God's sake, stop talking to her!'

I found him in a room centred by a small bed covered with a fraying yellow blanket. Miniature wooden automobiles and planes were scattered around the floor, and a number of carved animals – I spotted a giraffe and a zebra – were jumbled in a wicker basket standing next to a chamber pot. A pink elephant with big yellow ears stood on the night table, and a paper solar system hung from the ceiling. The sun was about the size of a soccer ball. Saturn's rings had been coloured with crayon or pastel and fastened to the planet with tape.

Had she threatened Shelly to protect her son? But why would she believe that we'd hurt him?

Shelly was standing by a bookshelf, looking at titles. His back was to me. When he turned, I saw that tears were caught in his lashes.

'Shelly, what's wrong?' I asked.

'Dad's books,' he replied in a hoarse whisper.

I went to him. 'That's wonderful,' I said. 'We'll take them with us.'

After he nodded, he turned around to continue reading the titles. At length, I asked, 'So why did the woman who lives here now get so angry with us?'

'She says the Soviets arrest her husband – that they take away thousands of veterans. He was in the *Armia Krajowa*.'

'What's that?'

'The Polish Home Army. She does not see him in a year. She believes he is dead.'

'I don't understand. If he fought in the army to free the country from the Nazis, the Soviets should give him a medal!'

'George, you think like a Canadian,' he said critically.

'Which means what?'

'Any loyal Soviet citizen knows that a Polish army officer is trouble – he might try to fight for the freedom of his country.'

'All right, but what in God's name has all this got to do with us?'

'Her priest . . . he tell her that the Jews control Stalin – that the Holocaust survivors . . . that we go to Russia and tell Stalin to arrest her husband and kill all the army veterans.'

'And she believed him?'

'*Oui, pourquoi pas?*' Shelly replied with the resigned shrug. 'Besides, it's more complicated than you think.'

'Why is it more complicated?'

'There's a Jew named Jakub Berman who runs the Polish secret police,' he replied. 'He is a wretched man – *une abomination*. And a good friend of Comrade Stalin.'

Shelly grabbed a thick volume and examined the cover, which had the title in black Hebrew characters on an olive-green cover. When he opened it, a photograph fluttered out and landed by his right foot. He picked it up and studied it closely. Now and again, he licked his lips. I had a feeling that time had come to a halt inside him.

When I asked to see the picture, he handed it to me, then flipped through the book, though I grew convinced he was studying me.

In the photograph, a man in a high-collared shirt and a woman in a ruffled dress were standing behind a boy who looked to be about seven years old. The man – tall, stiff, elegant, in his sixties, perhaps – has his left hand on the boy's shoulder, to remind him – it seemed to me – not to move while the photographer made ready to take the shot. The woman's eyes were gazing inside. At sad memories? I sensed she was holding back tears, but the boy's expression radiated amusement. His thick dark eyelashes made him look as if he were a character in the *Arabian Nights*. He had a short fringe of dark hair and was wearing a striped, exotic-looking coat – a hand-me-down from a well-travelled relative, perhaps. His right arm was a blur because he had started to bring his hand up to his mouth, presumably to conceal his giggles.

'You're the boy?' I asked.

Shelly nodded. 'I'm with my grandparents.'

'What was so funny?'

'My great-grandmother, Rosa, is next to the photographer. You can't see her. She is pulling faces. She is old, but she is still a clown.'

'How old was she then?'

'At least eighty.'

'Your grandmother looks upset.'

He took the photo back and studied her. 'Maybe she is angry with Grandfather. He always has money problems.' When he turned the picture over, he discovered several lines of highly slanted lettering in what looked to me like Hebrew script. He reached up to his brow with his free hand and moaned. Then he laughed in a burst and turned toward the door. At length, however, his face clouded over and he showed me a confused look.

'What did you see?' I asked.

'*J'ai pensé que Rosa . . .*'

Without warning, his eyes rolled back in his head and he

crumpled. I lunged for him too late. His head hit against the wooden floor with a thud – the sound of billiard balls clacking together, I'd later think. His left arm was pinned behind his back at a painful angle, so I freed it and hauled him up onto the bed. His head wasn't bleeding, but his breathing seemed dangerously shallow and his hands were frozen. I rushed into the sitting room. The woman was filing a roundel of wood with a rasp. I realised – astonished by how slow my mind seemed to be working – that she must have carved the toy animals for her son.

I made a drinking motion. She brushed a lock of hair from her face and walked into a side room. An aluminium pail brimming with water stood on the floor of the kitchen. Laundry hung down from a cord tied across the room. She handed me a white porcelain bowl and a tarnished ladle.

After rushing back to Shelly, I dripped water onto my hand and dabbed his brow. I called his name.

The little boy appeared again, this time wearing his pyjama bottoms. I didn't want to scare him, so I didn't look at his face. I patted Shelly's cheeks and called his name again, and he awakened.

'Welcome back,' I said. 'You'll be okay now.'

'What happens?'

'You fainted.'

'No, that's impossible.'

'Why?'

'I do not faint.'

'You do in Poland,' I said, trying – and failing – to summon a smile from him.

'There is a photograph?' he asked.

'Yeah, and as you looked at it, you seemed to hear someone come to the doorway.'

His eyes closed. 'Rosa,' he said glumly. 'I hear her calling me.

She always calls me *Teivele* – Little Devil. I am sure she is there. But when I look, I see nothing.'

I found the photograph by one of the legs of the bed. I handed it to Shelly and asked what was written on the back.

'It's from my mother,' he replied. 'She warns me to leave Warsaw because it will never be safe for us. She writes, *Make a good life. Do not worry about me or your father or your sister*.'

'So she knew you'd make it back!'

'No, but it is her hope.'

'And she knew that a few of her books would—' I almost said *survive*, but I looked for another word.

'You can say it,' he said.

'Say what?'

'Survive. Rosa says books are the human form of angels – the form we can see and touch. She says that is the secret reason why the Nazis burn them.'

'I get the feeling that Rosa was the poet in your family.'

'More mystic than poet,' he corrected.

'There may be more photographs in the other books.'

'Yes. I should take the books last time I am here. That is a mistake. But I am not . . .' He shook his head and closed his eyes. He was too weak to explain.

'You were busy trying to find Esther and Benni and your parents,' I said reassuringly.

He looked past me because the little boy had found the courage to take a few steps toward us. Shelly summoned him over with a friendly wave. He came to us with very erect posture and his hands joined behind his back – an elfin dancer.

'He's beautiful,' I whispered to Shelly.

'*Oui, touts les enfants sont beaux*,' he replied, which seemed the reply of an older brother who had braided his sister's hair throughout her childhood. He showed the boy the photo and spoke about it in a secretive and tantalising voice. And then he asked his name.

'Bohdan,' the boy replied.

Shelly pointed to himself and said his name, then gestured toward me. '*Georg*,' he said with a Polish pronunciation.

Bohdan asked Shelly a question – if he was the boy in the photograph, I later learned.

'*Tak*,' Shelly said with a good-natured shrug.

It was delight that I saw in my friend's eyes while Bohdan studied the old photograph. And my heart filled with respect for him, for he plainly held no grudge against a Polish child for what had happened to his family.

Shelly asked me for the water and took a couple of sips. He swung his legs over the side of the bed, but he was too dizzy to stand. I asked him for the Polish word for book and returned to the mother. She looked up from her carving with irritated eyes, but when I told her what I wanted, she led me into a bedroom with a Cubist print of a guitar tacked to the wall.

'Braque?' I asked.

'Juan Gris,' she said. She seemed to want to smile at this small triumph over me, but with a put-upon gesture, she pointed me to her dresser. On it were six books, two of them leatherbound, and with gold stamping on their spines.

I gestured toward them, then toward her. 'Yours?' I asked.

She shook her head, so I carried them back to Shelly. After he spoke to the little boy, the child moved his collection of toy animals to the floor and handed me his now-empty wicker basket.

Shelly was able to stand by then, and together we put our books inside. The ones that didn't fit we squeezed into our duffel bags. He took out ten American dollars from his wallet, kneeled down and handed the note to the boy. The child couldn't possibly have understood its value, but Shelly said something that made him jump up and down. His eyes shone with silvery glee.

After Shelly had had a chance to look around the rest of the apartment, the woman saw us to the door. She said nothing. Shelly made no attempt to shake her hand or speak to her.

On the way down the stairs, he read my mind and said, 'When I explain why we come, she tells me there are too many Jews before the war.' He stopped on the first-floor landing and eyed me menacingly. 'She said, "I am only sorry that Nazis did not kill you and your brother."'

Shelly told me that he next wanted to go to the apartment that had belonged to his Aunt Graça and Uncle Adam – Benni's parents. After we'd gone a little ways, he took my arm and said in a sing-song voice, 'Once upon a time, my father and mother have a large library. Mom has French novels and all of Shakespeare in an edition with gold lettering – so beautiful! Dad has books in Yiddish and Polish and German.' He grinned mischievously. 'And also a few in Russian.'

'He could read Russian?'

Shelly jiggled his hand. 'Not so good, but he must have Chekov in the original editions.'

'Your parents may have sold them to raise money.'

'Maybe, but I doubt it. They love their books.' He patted my shoulder and smiled, 'You know, George, finding that photograph . . . Wow, that is some big surprise!'

'You've got *glukl* on your side,' I told him.

He laughed, and his long-lashed eyes regarded me affectionately. It seemed as if the great tragic winds inside him had vanished. Maybe he had just realised that we were together on this journey.

Or perhaps grabbing an anti-Semite by the throat was what he'd needed to do for a very long time.

We were both tired and thirsty by then, and Benni's neighbourhood was still more than a mile away, so we went to a dingy bar to get coffee and a snack. Once we were seated, Shelly put his arm over my shoulder and let his head fall against me, and his breathing against my skin seemed a higher form of trust – so far beyond words that I said nothing. I believed that he was thinking that, as well, but when he raised his head, he said, 'Are we alive, George?'

'Yes,' I said.

'Are you certain?'

'Pretty certain.'

'Good, because I'm no longer sure.'

A half hour later, we discovered that his aunt and uncle's building had not fared as well as Shelly's; the side where they'd had their home was gone.

'Two rooms are still there when I am last here,' Shelly told me, and the forlorn, teary-eyed, constricted way he gazed around gave me to believe that his throat was being slowly slit by his return to Warsaw.

He and I hunted like rescue dogs for family belongings in the rubble beneath the missing apartment but only turned up a pair of tattered socks and shards of porcelain – off-white with a bright red rim.

'*Tia* Graça's china,' Shelly said, and he slipped a small piece into his coat pocket.

Over the next hour, I sat with our bags and books while Shelly asked at all the shops on the block if anyone had seen any of his relatives. His irritated headshakes and compulsive smoking made any questions I might have wanted to ask him about his success unnecessary.

When he finally returned to me, his shoulders were slumped, and his eyes were bloodshot and weary. I said he needed to lie down. 'No more searching today,' I told him.

'Sorry, I must go on,' he replied.

'No, it's out of the question – you're making yourself ill.'

I won our short quarrel, and we moved on to the hotel that had been assigned to us by the Polish Consulate in Montreal. It was called the Hotel Fabryka, and it was on the far side of the bridge that crossed the Vistula River to the Praga district of the city, which seemed to have fared better under Nazi occupation than the rest of Warsaw. Given its name – *fabryka* meant factory – we expected it to be a converted industrial plant, but it turned out to be a shabby, three-storey rooming house with wilted red and yellow geraniums in the window boxes. On the bottom floor was a cheap restaurant frequented mostly by prostitutes and reeking of DDT, which struck us – in our exhausted state – as fantastically comical. For supper, we each ate three bowls of borscht with a loaf of bread. The soup was salty and greasy, but it was all there was and it was hot.

A pale, middle-aged man with a beaky face and short, bristly hair, wearing too large a grey suit, studied us throughout supper. Shelly whispered to me that he was the guy who'd been following us since our arrival in Warsaw.

That night, we sat together on Shelly's bed – we had two small cots – and shook out the books we'd rescued, and seven more photos fluttered out, six with virtually the same message on the back in his mother's handwriting and one in his father's tiny script that said, *By now, I suspect that you are the man I myself once wished to be. Was I envious of your freedom? Can you forgive me for being harsh with you? I hope so. Whatever you do, do not stay in Poland. Go somewhere civilized, with true human*

beings – if there is such a place. Make love with anyone you like.
And accept an embrace from your silly old father, who feels only
affection for you.

Shelly is tiny and naked in the photo. His father – laughing joyfully – holds his baby son high over his head. Shelly's arms are spread before him as if he is about to fly.

After translating the message for me, Shelly said he needed some air and went down to the street. I could see him out our window, his head down, walking in circles, chasing too many memories. Only after he was safely back in our room – a half hour later – did I return to bed.

I awakened long after midnight, and Shelly was standing at the window – his cigarette glowing. I imagined him searching the sky for guidance or solace, but when I asked him what he was looking for, he said, 'Ghosts.'

'Did you spot any?' I asked.

'No.'

'That's a relief.'

'No, you're wrong. I wish to see my father or mother.'

I stood up and went to him. 'What would you tell them if you could talk to them?' I asked.

'I *do* talk to them,' he said. 'All the time. And I tell them I am well.'

I took his hand. 'Did you tell them about me?'

'Of course. It's not possible to keep secrets from ghosts.'

'What do they tell you about us?'

'Until now, my father says he is ashamed of me. But now, after what I read . . .' Shelly's voice broke, and he finished his sentence only after placing his hand flat against my chest and pressing. 'Papa thanks you for coming to Warsaw. And I thank you too.'

I kissed him for his thoughtful words and kindness, and

through him, I also kissed his father for giving the world such an
extraordinarily beautiful son.

The next morning, we walked to the Saska Kępa district of the
city to visit the French Embassy, but the youthful secretary there
was unable to find any dispatches from the consulate in Montreal
mentioning Shelly's search for Benni and Esther. Shelly was crushed,
and he raged at her for the incompetence and ill will of the French.
Terror-stricken tears appeared in her eyes, and she explained in
stops and starts – hugging her hands around her chest – that any
communiques sent by the consulate in Montreal were probably lost
in the confusion of post-war Poland. 'Or blocked by the Soviets
– they censor all our dispatches,' she told him.

      While I was trying to calm Shelly down, the Cultural Attaché
came out from his office to demand that Shelly stop berating the
secretary. He was a harsh-looking man with the brutish, thrust-
out chin and balding head of an expressionist caricature. And I
saw in his cool, predatory eyes – evidencing secret amusement, it
seemed to me – that any apology Shelly tried to make would fail
to breach his contempt for us, so I took my drawings of Benni
out of my envelope. 'I'm sorry that my friend and I have caused
you trouble,' I said in English, 'but all we really need to know is if
either of you has seen this young man.'

      Shelly translated my request, since the Cultural Attaché told us
in French that he spoke no English. He and the secretary studied
my portraits but said that they didn't recognise Benni.

      Back on the street, Shelly apologised for creating a scene. He
also speculated that no one at the embassy would have wanted to
admit that they'd seen Benni because then they'd have also had to
confess that they'd failed to register his name and address.

      Over that afternoon and the next three days, he questioned

twenty-four residents of Benni's old neighbourhood and eleven shop owners in the hopes that one of them could tell him something about his cousin or Esther or any other members of his family. At more than a hundred and fifty other apartments, the inhabitants refused to speak to him.

I know exactly how many people Shelly interviewed because I kept our log.

Seven of the people he questioned admitted that they remembered Benni, and two recalled Esther. But no one had seen them or any members of his family since the end of the war. A diabetic and nearly blind old woman who was confined to bed did claim, however, that she'd heard that Benni had survived. Unfortunately, she did not remember who'd told her that. In the end, she admitted that maybe it was just a wish, because she had always thought he was a *lovely child*, as she put it.

'Speaking to her is a disappointment, but it also does me good,' Shelly confessed to me as we walked back to our hotel, and when I asked him why, he replied, 'She helps me discover again how beautiful is the Polish language.' He opened his arms wide. 'And it is so very big – almost too . . . grand for me!'

'What do you mean?'

He tilted his head as if listening for the answer to come to him from out of his past, then said, 'Polish is a mansion with hundreds of rooms, and in each room is something crazy and wonderful – jewels and flowers and sculptures of the Virgin and ancient manuscripts . . .' He shut his eyes tight. 'And if you go down into the basement, very far down, you find old friends you forget about, and they embrace you, and just for a little while everything is as it should have been.'

Over the next two days, we visited all the addresses where relatives of Shelly's Montreal friends had lived. More than half of the flats had been destroyed; Poles had moved in to the rest. Those few who agreed to speak to Shelly told him that the families who'd been living there had never returned. Some of them might have been lying, of course, but we had no way of forcing them to tell us the truth. A telling detail: although Jews had certainly owned many of the flats in the ghetto in which they'd lived, the Poles always referred to them as *the previous occupants* or simply *the Jews who lived here* and never as the *apartment owners*.

The next day was Monday, and in the morning we went to the offices of the American Joint Distribution Committee on Chocimska Street, and the director, William Bein, was having a busy day, so he entrusted us to an energetic and quick-smiling assistant named Dan Margolis. I handed him our complete list of Shelly's family, and the second list of the relatives of his friends in Montreal. Dan was a retired lawyer from Chicago who looked a bit like Buster Keaton. In his no-nonsense, rapid-fire English – chewing gum the whole time – he promised Shelly that he'd start going through the committee's files that very evening and continue the next day. He patted our backs with grandfatherly optimism and took us for a beer at a nearby restaurant where, he said jokingly, they had grown used to serving him and other American spies.

Dan explained to us that the rifle-bearing man who'd raced past us on our first afternoon in Warsaw – who'd told Shelly that he was an asshole – was from the ORMO, the local equivalent of the Nazi Brownshirts. 'Complete lunatics,' he said. 'You were lucky he didn't take an interest in you.'

His folksy charm and stories of a childhood spent swimming in Lake Michigan soon took our minds thousands of miles from Poland, and we were grateful. But when we returned the next afternoon, he said that he'd been through all his files and hadn't been able to find anyone.

'It's incredible that they are all gone,' Shelly told him.

'No, it's pretty much average,' Dan told us. 'More than three million Polish Jews were murdered. If you want, I can tell you what transport to Treblinka some of the people on your lists were on. Do you want those details?'

Shelly said he couldn't cope with any more bad news, so I spent the next two hours with Dan, jotting down names and dates.

Shelly had waited for me at the pub where we'd had a beer with Dan and was sloshed when I joined him. We trudged back across the city without speaking.

'We are living in *Gehenna* for more than a week,' Shelly told me when we spotted our hotel from down the street. 'And we have nothing.' He showed me an angry look. '*Rien, rien, rien!*' he growled.

'One or two of them must have survived,' I told him.

'If they are alive, they are in America or Palestine,' he said. 'We never find them.'

That evening – September 1st – was clouded over and the stench of sewage along the river became unbearable. I discovered that it is possible to think of an entire city – and all its people – as cursed.

After supper, Shelly told me he wanted to return to the Jewish ghetto.

'But there's nothing there!' I protested.

'I need to walk through the streets and think,' he said.

'Think about what?'

'About anything that appears in my mind,' he said defiantly.

He believes Benni's and Esther's ghosts may show themselves to him there, I thought, so I accompanied him. But the broken-down wall around the ghetto seemed a menacing barrier. When I told

Shelly that I preferred not to go any further, he glared at me as if I'd become his enemy. 'So go – I don't need you!' he said roughly.

I might have gone with him anyway, but he turned and lumbered away. I stood motionless for a time – regretting I'd admitted my reticence – then started back for the hotel. I thought that Shelly might call out to me, contrite, but he didn't.

There are places I'll never be able to accompany him, I told myself, and yet I realised – surprised by my calm – that I had never expected our life together to be easy.

Perhaps ten minutes later, I detoured around a group of raucous Soviet soldiers onto a side street, and I kept walking in what I thought was the right direction, but I soon realised I was hopelessly lost. I asked for directions at a bar where a band was playing an off-key tango, but no one knew enough English or French to help me. I ended up ordering a beer, but the singer – a slender young man in a torn army jacket – screeched on the high notes, and a number of tough-looking men stared at me as if they might want to beat me up, so I took a few quick sips and returned outside.

'The Vistula?' I said to a giggly young couple that passed me nearly right away, and they pointed behind them. Ten minutes later, I reached the river. Just ahead, a dingy red sofa was sitting in a weedy embankment. I imagined it as having fallen there from out of the sky just for me. A few minutes after I dropped down on its lumpy cushions, I realised that the string of lights up ahead was the bridge to Praga, so I headed there.

I was passing below a street lamp when the world seemed to spiral away from me and tumble over. I was on the ground and fighting for breath, and cold, insistent hands were going through my coat pockets. I tried to push my assailant off me, but he was too strong. After he ran away, I felt for my bill-fold of American dollars, but it was gone. Luckily, I still had my wallet.

Had my robber followed me from the bar? It seemed likely, but Shelly would later suggest that the UB man who'd been shadowing us might have decided I was an easy mark.

I could taste blood on my lips and was worried that I was cut badly. Lights were on in the windows of a ground-floor apartment about a hundred paces ahead, so I decided to ask for help. I knocked at the door. A tiny woman with a sheepskin over her shoulders answered. I only realised then that it was a chilly evening. She looked at me resentfully. 'Sorry,' I said, and I told her I'd been robbed and was lost.

'What country you?' she asked.

'Canada.'

She took a quick look left then right – presumably to see if we were being watched – then motioned me inside. After she led me through her foyer, I discovered floor-to-ceiling bookshelves in her sitting room. *And the stranger discovered that the road ahead was paved with books*, I thought, and I decided that this room would be at the centre of a painting I'd do back home about my robbery and rescue.

'George,' I said, pointing to myself.

'Magda,' she said with a timid smile. Her teeth were tiny and brown. She had a round, moon-like face.

'Am I bleeding?' I asked.

'Bleeding?' she asked.

'Blood,' I said. '*Sangue . . . blut.*' I made a scratching motion against my cheek. 'Do I have any cuts?'

'Ah, yes,' she said. She pointed to my ear. 'And here,' she said, touching my brow.

She poured vodka on a towel and cleaned my wounds. '*Przepraszam,*' she said gently whenever I winced. After I thanked her, she told me in a mixture of broken English and hand signals that she'd escort me back to my hotel. But I was to let her walk ahead of me and not try to approach her. She pointed to her eyes. 'Police,' she said.

'*Rozumiem,*' I said, trying out the word for *I understand* that Shelly had taught me.

Magda laughed good-naturedly at my attempt to speak Polish. It seemed as if under other circumstances – back in Montreal or Toronto – we could have been friends.

She left the apartment house first. I followed her at a distance of about fifty paces, and I never looked directly at her. After a minute or so, we came to a building with a flag I didn't recognise in the ground-floor window, but which I would later identify as belonging to Yugoslavia. The flag had blue, white and red horizontal stripes and a gold-bordered red star at its centre. Beside it was a tourist poster of Dubrovnik, a tight jumble of handsome stone houses beside a beach of golden sand. *If only Shelly and I were in southern Europe instead of Poland*, I thought.

Suspecting that this might be a consulate or trade office, I peered through a crack in the curtains, but the darkness inside defeated my curiosity.

As I started off again, I felt Benni inside me for the first time in days. His eyes were closed, and he was hoping that I would understand the reason that he appeared to me now. And after a few minutes of searching – and some gazing back over my shoulder at the poster of the idyllic beach beside Dubrovnik – I did.

When Magda stopped by the entrance to my hotel, she turned to make sure that I understood that we had reached our destination. I nodded toward her, and I was hoping she'd go inside so that I could thank her and give her some dollars, but she hurried away with hunched shoulders and disappeared around a corner.

I ran up the stairs to our room. Shelly answered my knocks

right away, but I waved off his apology. 'It no longer matters,' I said with rising excitement. 'I think I know how to find Benni!'

'How?'

'I remembered where you always wanted to take him!'

Portugal had closed its embassy in Warsaw during the war and had only recently opened a consular office, which turned out to be in a dusty second-floor apartment on the melancholy, weed-infested outskirts of the Saska Kępa district where we'd visited the French Embassy. When we arrived the next morning, the consul was out. A youthful secretary – tiny and quick-moving, like a sparrow – answered our knocks. After ascertaining that Shelly understood Portuguese, she told him she was on the phone and would return to us in a minute. Back at her heavy wooden desk, she resumed her phone conversation.

Her shrill and rapid way of speaking – and the repeated shushing sound of her consonants – made her Portuguese sound like someone scrubbing the floor with a brush. When she was done, she shook our hands eagerly. She had an innocent, eager face. Shelly spoke to her in Ladino.

Later, he told me that he'd informed her that we were from Canada and that his ancestors were from Portugal. She replied with her name – Mónica Lopes – and asked how she could help.

While Shelly explained the reason for our visit, the small Portuguese flag on Mónica's desk caught my attention, probably because it was red and green, the same colours as my Chinese lanterns at home – which seemed a positive omen. The flag extended out of an amethyst-coloured vase, and next to the vase spread a half-unfolded Japanese fan. Beside the fan was an old leather book, and on top of the book was a white carnation.

Is everything we do determined by a world inside us that we know almost nothing about? I wondered, because I sensed that I'd known for many years that I would stand here one day, and that I would cast my hopeful gaze over that green-and-red flag, the Japanese fan, the old book and the white flower, and I would be gripped by what I was now feeling – that these were the simple and beautiful comforts of a civilization that the Nazis wanted to destroy and nearly did.

When Shelly told Mónica Benni's full name, she gasped and brought her hand over her heart.

'*Sim, lembro-me dele – um rapaz encantador!*' she exclaimed brightly. '*Chegou cá logo a seguir a abertura do Consulado. Penso que tenho a sua morada. Dê-me só um segundo.*'

She dashed into a room at the back, and I asked Shelly what was happening. He clasped his head between his hands. 'Dear God,' he whispered, 'what if she cannot find his address?'

'But she knows him?'

'She said she remembers him – that he is a charming young man. She said he came here right after the consulate opened.'

Hope made me lightheaded. I remained very still and silent, and I found myself repeating a Navajo chant to try to remain calm. Mónica darted back into the room waving a piece of paper and laughing with relief, and she handed it to Shelly. *Benjamin Rosenfeld Zarco* was typed at the top. Underneath his name was an address and the name Ewa Armbruster, as well as a date – Friday, May 9th, 1947.

Mónica explained that Benni had come to the consulate on that afternoon in May, accompanied by an elderly Polish woman named Ewa Armbruster, who told Mónica that she was a piano teacher. She also made it clear to Mónica that she was to give that address to anyone asking after Benni.

Shelly jotted that information down in my log. I also wrote it on my hand, just to be safe.

He gripped my arm after I handed Mónica back her pen. And then he did something very unexpected – impossible, even – he kissed me on the lips.

I think that Mónica may have gasped. But when I looked at her, her eyes were affectionate. Maybe she thought that Shelly and I were brothers. Or buddies from the Canadian army. More likely, she understood perfectly well and didn't care; there have always been – everywhere – people who understand.

Just before we left, Mónica fetched us a small bag of Polish ginger cakes to give to Benni, and she sent us on our way with a warning that Shelly translated for me. 'Be careful,' she told us. 'Nobody is safe in Poland.'

We tried to book seats on a train that morning at one of the ticket windows, but the woman there told us we'd have to wait. A policeman soon approached us and hustled us into the office of a railroad official who was anxious to know why we wished to go to Łódź. He and Shelly had an animated conversation in Polish that seemed friendly enough at first, but I could tell from my friend's artificial smiles and nods that careful tactical manoeuvres were taking place on both sides. Our heavyset host had fleshy jowls and droopy eyes. He sat at a big wooden desk eating sticky-looking candy that Shelly told me later were called *krowki*. He smiled frequently and nodded in an avuncular way, but something he said soon started Shelly blinking away tears. After my friend made what sounded like a final, desperate appeal, our host shook his head and reached casually for a cigarette. As he lit it, Shelly pulled a small wooden case out of his coat pocket and put it on the desk. When he lifted the lid, I saw a ruby ring with a thick gold band.

Shelly left the gift on the desk. The official glanced at it quickly, then leaned forward and closed the lid. He addressed Shelly in what sounded like a scolding tone for several minutes, smoking greedily. When he lifted the receiver of his phone to make a call, fear constricted my heart.

A mind retreating from a terrifying situation must share something with the world of our dreams, because the man's voice now seemed familiar – a menacing part of my childhood, in fact.

After he ended his call, he stood up, so we did, too, and he walked us to the door in a chivalrous manner, smiling benevolently, speaking to Shelly in a way that led me to believe he was offering advice. A pale and pimply young railroad official met us in the hallway. As he led us off, I asked Shelly what was happening.

'I'm not sure,' he replied. 'We have to wait.'

A few minutes later, the official escorted us into a small, dingy room with a wooden desk at its centre, and a photograph of the Polish president, Bolesław Bierut, on the wall. Bierut had a moustache and slicked-back hair, and I joked that he looked like a Quebecois car mechanic, but Shelly wouldn't reply.

'You think we're in trouble?' I asked him.

'It's possible,' he said. 'But I told him you had nothing to do with the bribe. All my idea.'

A half hour later, a prim little woman in a police uniform shuffled in and handed us our tickets. Shelly studied them with glassy eyes, then held them over his head and whispered a vow: '*Benni, je viens te chercher.*' – Benni, I'm coming for you.

'I buy the ring at a pawn shop on Clark Street,' Shelly told me while we waited for our train. 'I know the owner – Jewish guy from Lithuania. He gives me a great deal when I tell him I go to Poland to find Benni and Esther.'

We spent the afternoon in a cramped train compartment, grinding and lurching through the verdant farmlands and soot-covered, sewage-scented, miserably poor towns of post-war Poland. Shelly smoked in the corridor and snuck nervous looks at me while pretending to read his Zola. As we neared Łódź, a middle-aged policeman with deep creases in his forehead and cheeks, and a mud-brown, cancerous-looking patch of skin on his nose checked everyone's tickets and identity papers. Across from us sat a kind-faced elderly woman carrying a small bag of eggs and two men with the coarse, handsome, powerful hands of farmers.

Shelly spoke to the policeman while he studied our documents, but he seemed uninterested.

The other three passengers turned away from him, but my eyes met the old woman's for a moment, and she smiled affectionately at me, so I smiled back and made a little wave, and I thought, *There it is – humanity. Surviving even in this awful place.*

The policeman handed Shelly our documents back without raising any problem. When I asked him how he'd convinced the man to leave us alone, he shrugged and said, 'I have no idea. I don't understand how most people here think anymore. I am beginning to believe I have come home to a foreign country.'

We arrived in Łódź at close to six o'clock and dashed to the taxi stand. Ewa's village was about twenty kilometres away, and the second person we stopped there – a young man carrying a sack of coal – was able to tell us where we could find an elderly piano teacher named Ewa Armbruster. He told us that the boy we were looking for was probably her grandson and that his name was Krystian.

The house was less than a mile away. We discovered that it had blue curtains in the windows, and atop the roof was a homemade-looking weathervane of Thoth, the ibis-headed Egyptian god.

Shelly asked the taxi man to drop us at the entrance to the dusty lane bordered by apple trees that led to the front door.

We knew we'd reached our destination not only because of Thoth, but also because we could hear a sprightly melody – Bach or Scarlatti, I guessed – coming from a piano inside the house. We picked up our bags and started down the lane.

The front door creaked open after we'd gone only twenty paces. A young man stepped outside. He had undoubtedly heard the taxi drop us. His hair was cut short. It looked like a black skullcap. He was holding a small white towel in his hand.

Shelly eased his bag down and didn't take his eyes from the boy. 'Benni,' he whispered.

The boy stepped forward and stopped. And then he came running. Shelly opened his arms wide.

Tears were already sliding down my friend's cheeks, but he was smiling.

The moment Benni and Shelly met in an embrace, I knew that – no matter what else happened in my life – I had done one good thing. And each of their kisses told me – free of the constraint of words – there would be many times over the next years that my witnessing this reunion would save me from despair and melancholy. And maybe even find me the courage to keep journeying ahead.

The door creaked again, and a woman in a floral dress stepped outside. She thrust her hands over her mouth.

While Benni and Shelly danced and shouted in Yiddish, I sat on the ground and addressed all the dead and dying I'd seen in Bergen-Belsen. *I witnessed how the world betrayed you*, I told them. *And I'm sorry I could do nothing to save you.*

Did they forgive me?

A minute or so later, Benni and Shelly came to me and lifted me up from where I was weeping, and I realised that I would never know. And yet I laughed when they hugged me, and my relief and joy seemed to contain everything I might one day become, because I knew I'd never again have to be the man I'd been before reaching this blessed moment. In fact, he was already gone.

THE
BLEEDING
MIRROR
(2010-2018)

This Is My Father

After his stroke in January of 2017, my father would occasionally sing to himself in Polish, very softly, with his eyes closed, as if he were tiptoeing across the fallen leaves of a long-distant autumn. At first, he told me that the songs were taught to him by Ewa Armbruster, the elderly piano teacher who'd hidden him in her home near the end of the Second World War. But once, when he was lying in bed and nearly asleep, just a week before his death, he said he'd learned them from his grandmother. Whatever the truth, he'd forgotten about them for many years. In fact, he was astonished that he could still sing in Polish.

Had his stroke opened a door to memories he'd once considered menacing?

One chilly afternoon in mid-April, I brought him a cup of fresh decaf coffee as a treat, and I found him standing by his window, watching the birds at our feeder, humming one of the old tunes. He took my hand and rubbed my palm against the grey stubble on his cheek and told me that he was so grateful for having recovered from his stroke, and the spring crocuses in the yard, and the good coffee, and for Ewa and all the songs he'd ever heard, that there was no room in him for anything but that gratitude. As he fought to smile, his big black eyes filled with tears, and I felt an upward rush inside me. *Yes*, I thought triumphantly, *this is my father free of everything that has ever held him down or sealed his lips or set him trembling.*

At that moment, I imagined that the two of us had entered in a holy space – an *eruv*. And yet I also thought – with a burst of panic – *I'll need this feeling of being united with him to sustain me when he's gone, but will I be able to find it?*

The Incandescent Threads

'Dad, are you afraid to die?' I asked him not so long ago – about three months before he passed away. It was a question that had been hiding inside my chest for more than seven years – since his cousin Shelly's death in the fall of 2010. The eager sun peeking through the pink-blossoming branches of my cherry tree seemed to give me permission to finally speak it aloud.

He was standing on our picnic bench, spilling birdseed into the glass feeder, which we'd hung from a thick nylon cord between our apple trees and coated with olive oil, so that the squirrels couldn't get to it and steal all the nourishment meant for his beloved blue jays and cardinals. I was gripping his slender, pale, bony ankles to make sure he didn't lose his footing. He was having a good day – no discomfort in his back at all.

'Nah, I've died many times before,' he replied matter-of-factly. As I helped him down onto the lawn, he added, 'But let me tell you, I've had times when there was a lot of pain, and that didn't make it such a piece of cake. When I worked at the Library of Alexandria, I'm pretty sure I died of some sort of infection in my gut. God only knows what I ate – probably some badly cooked meat. The Egyptians weren't all that hygienic. Hygienic – is that the right word?'

'It's perfect.'

'Saying goodbye to my family and all those beautiful scrolls . . .' He shook his head at the difficult parting. 'I think that that's why I always have to have a book with me in bed or I get really nervous.' He jiggled the box of seed to produce a percussive rustle and did a wiggly little dance. 'This time, crossing over to the Other Side won't be so hard. After all, you and your family are safe, and I'm too old to keep fighting Mr Trump and all the other leaders who do such awful things.' He shrugged. 'You know, Eti, I tried pretty hard to do right by all the good people the Nazis murdered, but I see now that it wasn't nearly enough.'

'Well, at least, you helped stop the war in Vietnam. That was really important.'

'I did what I could. Anyway, it's time for you and your kids to take over. Your mom and Shelly are waiting for me, and Julie and Morrie and Uncle George, which pretty much makes me the last of the Mohicans.'

Could my father talk calmly about death because he really did believe in reincarnation? Or was it because the Nazis had forced him to face his mortality very early on? When I asked him, he patted my hand and said, 'Both, I think.'

'What about Shelly – was he scared to die? I never asked him.'

'No, he'd made peace with the Angel of Death back in Poland – when he was sure he was a goner.'

'When was he sure he was a goner?'

'A Nazi caught him in the forest – where he was sleeping for the night. He didn't tell you?'

'No. What happened?'

'Shelly played deaf and dumb. He made gagging noises and kept pointing to his ears and shaking his head.' Dad imitated Shelly imitating a deaf man pleading for his life. It looked ludicrous but probably Shelly had been far more convincing; my dad was never as good an actor as his cousin.

'So the Nazi believed that Shelly was deaf and let him go?' I asked.

'No. The bastard shot off his gun by Shelly's ear. And Shelly jumped. The Nazi laughed, because he'd proved that Shelly was lying. But that wasn't so clever. It gave Shelly time enough to pounce on him. He was strong as hell back then. The Nazi got off another shot, but it missed. Shelly punched him so hard that he broke his jaw – he heard the crack – and got the gun and shot him in the head.'

'So he killed two people?'

'Two people? What do you mean?'

'Uncle George once told me that Shelly had killed a French cobbler,' I said.

Dad puffed out his lips and shook his head. 'George would know. But Shelly never told me.'

'So maybe he killed even more than two men,' I said.

'I wouldn't be surprised. No anti-Semites were going to stop Shelly – at least not without one hell of a fight!' Dad motioned me to come closer and kissed my cheek. 'I love it when you haven't shaved for a few days,' he said.

'Why?'

'It means you've become a man.' He took a big steadying breath. 'What a relief it is to know that you'll never die in childhood.' He tapped his fist against my chin to lighten the mood. 'But who the hell knew you'd grow up so damn fast?'

'Dad, what about Mom? Do you think you'll see her again?'

'I'm hoping that she and I will be reborn together,' he replied. 'Or is it she and *me*? My English today is abominable.'

'*I*, I suppose, but it makes no difference.'

'Anyway, when you find your other half, you keep on travelling with them through different reincarnations. At least, that's what some kabbalists say.' He showed me a mischievous grin. 'Hey, you know what was a great day?' he asked.

'No.'

'When we stood out front of Trump Tower with that sign saying HOLOCAUST SURVIVORS AGAINST IGNORANT RACIST BULLIES.'

'Yeah, I had a good time – at least until you got into that argument.'

'Argument? Bah! That was nothing. I've had people spit on me. Some idiot kid in an Abercrombie & Flinch T-shirt screaming at me – that's nothing!'

'Abercrombie & Fitch,' I corrected.

'Whatever,' Dad said dismissively. He trickled a bit of birdseed onto his hand and licked it up. 'I like to try everything at least once,' he said by way of an explanation.

When he handed me the box, I tasted a pinch of the mixture, but it was bitter and I spit it out.

'I guess I'm the only birdbrain in the family!' he observed, giggling merrily, and the fondness for me in his eyes made it clear that he wanted me to laugh too, but a knot of panic had formed in my chest. He stroked my shoulders with both hands and told me that everything was going to be okay.

'It's not!' I said testily. 'So don't say it is.'

'Better I go one day soon than seventy-five years ago in Auschwitz.'

'Are those my only two choices?' I questioned.

He giggled again. 'Yeah, kiddo, given where and when I was born, and that I'm one hell of a nutty Jew, they are.'

Kiddo was what Shelly had always called me. Dad had only adopted the word after his cousin's death. By then, Shelly's wife Julie had already been gone for three years.

I left Dad alone to shoo away the squirrels from the birdfeeder and work on my latest painting. In it, me, Shelly, Dad and Uncle George were weeding a small garden filled with pink-and-white cosmos and golden coreopsis. Behind us was the Alexandria Lighthouse. And Chloris, the Greek goddess of flowers, was supervising our work with a demanding eye. Since George was one of the figures, I'd decided to put the garden inside a death camp. But I was having trouble making the barbed wire seem sufficiently evil.

That night, sometime after I'd added a guard tower to the top of the lighthouse, I discovered my father's light on long after his usual bedtime, so I knocked on his door. He was reading a book on the meaning of the Sabbath in Judaism that I'd purchased for him. 'Too exciting to stop!' he told me.

On his tape player was a recording of my mother interviewing an old man from Izmir about the Sephardic lullabies he'd sung to his children. Dad always liked to hear my mother's voice before going to sleep. Sometimes he'd change tapes throughout the night so she'd always be talking or singing while he slept. I noticed that he'd placed his favourite black-and-white photograph on his bedside table, beside his clock. In it, Mom is bringing him a big cup of just-brewed coffee. Dad is smiling at her with surprised delight and Mom is looking at him with charmed affection. I'm the toothless baby on his lap, giggling merrily, reaching out with his hand toward the photographer, who happens to be Shelly. When my father asked me to have this picture framed a few years back, he said, 'Occasionally, Eti, while we're travelling down our road, we stumble upon a perfect moment. Thanks to Shelly and his old Polaroid, I can revisit this one anytime I like.'

Now, I gestured toward the picture and said, 'I love seeing you smile so genuinely.'

He nodded his agreement and said, 'And this time we didn't even have to do a second take!'

After we'd had a little laugh, I asked him if he'd forgotten his pills, since they were still clustered together in front of his clock, and he said that the yellow and orange tulips coming up in the garden – which he and my wife, Angie, had planted – had convinced him to stop taking all his medications except for an aspirin in the morning to keep his blood circulating. I argued against changing his routine, of course, but he looked at me hard and said, 'I can't let you or anyone else decide how I go. It's too important. And I really don't want to talk about it.'

I frowned because I didn't want to admit he was right, and sat next to him, sulking.

'Hey, I've got something important to tell you,' he said in the tone he always used to cheer me up. 'Just after your mom and I bought our house, back in 1969, I hid a metal box in the basement. You'll find it inside a cardboard box stuffed with two old bedsheets. The cardboard box says *Waldbaum's* on the outside.'

'What's in the metal box?'

'A vellum manuscript. You'll need to get it translated.'

'What language is it in?'

'Ladino mostly, with a little Hebrew sprinkled here and there. Get Isaac Silva to do the translation. He's a professor emeritus of Jewish mysticism in Berkeley. I've spoken to him on the phone and he likes me. Don't let his fancy British accent intimidate you – it's just for show. He says he bought it while he was studying in Oxford.'

'Bought the accent?'

'Yeah, he's from some coal-mining town, and his family was as poor as church mice. He told me his accent was holding him back, so he bought a new one. His number is in my address book.' Dad held up his finger. 'A few years ago, I started using Mom's system, so look under *Isaac* not *Rosa*. Got it?'

'Got it. Where's the manuscript from?' I asked.

'Constantinople. It was written by Berekiah Zarco. My mom

translated it for me into Yiddish when she gave it to me, because my Ladino wasn't so hot. But I didn't keep her translation. I left the ghetto kind of fast. I only took the jewellery that my grandmother Luna, Rosa's daughter, had instructed me to keep.'

'What jewellery – you never said anything about that?'

'I had an old topaz ring with me, but I used that to pay a bribe for a Polish smuggler to get me safely to Piotr's apartment. And a pair of sapphire earrings. I managed to hold on to those. You'll figure out who gave them to me – and why – when you read the scroll. Everything else I might have inherited had to be sold to pay for food and clothing. And for sawdust for those crummy stoves we had. Bah! Anyway, just before I crawled out of the ghetto, I tied the scroll around my belly so it couldn't get lost. Rosa had told me and my mom that it was a powerful talisman. It got a little creased and sweaty.' He grimaced. 'It picked up my lice, too. But those little monsters died a long time ago, *Got tsu danken*. A word of advice, Eti – don't ever get lice!'

'I'll do my best.'

'And tell George and Pi and Violet too, because lice are no good.'

'I'll be sure to tell the kids. So what's the manuscript say?'

'It's got to do with those strings of mine.'

Dad had developed a theory that everything that's ever happened was joined together by fine filaments of cause and effect that we can't normally see. He called them *the Incandescent Threads*, because he said they gave off a warm light, at least to those with mystical vision enough to see them.

Once, when I had the flu and he was trying to make me forget how bad I felt, he told me in a conspiratorial whisper that he'd seen them twice. The first time was when Shelly and Uncle George found him after the end of the Second World War. 'Two faint threads of light stretched from George and Shelly to me, and they were glowing red, and I tried to touch them, but that only made them vanish,' he said.

The second time he saw an Incandescent Thread was while walking through the Alfama district of Lisbon with my mother on their first trip to Portugal. He was exhausted from the plane flight and the uphill climb past the cathedral. He'd closed his eyes to rest, and when he opened them, a filament of curving, highly charged vermilion light made his eyes tear. It had issued from the base of a crumbling old wall.

Dad grew convinced that the seemingly unimportant spot must have had something to do with his ancestors. Maybe it was even where Berekiah Zarco had lived.

Now, I asked, 'Why didn't you tell me about the Waldbaum's box before?'

'Because I don't like the idea of you carrying the extra weight of what happened to me. My past . . . We both know that it's too much at times. So only read the manuscript later, when I'm with Mom. Hey, remember when we went out to Utah and first met George's parents?' he said to change the subject.

'Of course,' I said.

'Weren't they wonderful people? George's grandfather was a powerful shaman, you know.'

'Yeah, he and his dad told me about animal spirits when they took me hiking in Canyonlands National Park.'

My father smiled at me, and I could tell he wanted to say something important, but he also didn't want me asking too many questions.

'Go ahead,' I told him. 'I won't make you go back into the past.'

'Good. Listen, Eti, Shelly's things are there too.'

'Where? In Moab?'

'No, in the metal box – in the basement. The stuff he left for me is in one of the pink boxes they'd give us at the Seven Dwarfs Bakery for a chocolate *mandelbrot*.'

'I was wondering where you'd put his things.'

'Diane knows not to let anyone go near them without my permission.'

Diane was Shelly's youngest daughter. She'd been living in Dad's house for the last eight years. She worked in Manhattan as a travel agent and also served as a guide on tours through Spain and Portugal three times a year.

'I know you think I'm crazy for all this secrecy,' Dad said.

'Nah, I just think you're you.'

'Good.' He gazed off beyond me. 'To tell you the truth, kiddo, I don't even know what crazy means anymore. So many words seemed to have shed their meaning of late. Even when I'm jabbering away to myself in Yiddish, I stop sometimes and think, *That word used to be big and round and important, and now it's just . . . just a microscopic little nothing, and I haven't any idea what the hell it's supposed to mean*.'

I Found Them Spooned Together in Bed

Shelly lived with us for the last three years of his life. At first, he didn't want to leave Montreal and the memories residing in every corner of his house, but Aunt Julie had died and his daughters couldn't take him in since they both travelled so frequently. Uncle George offered him the guestroom in his house in Moab, but Shelly thought that Utah was too far away from his daughters and Dad. Our only other choice would have been a nursing home.

My father suggested we move another twin bed into his room, so that's what we did. But Dad's tapes of Mom singing kept Shelly up at night, so we moved him into the den. I gave him his own portable computer with a big flat-screen monitor and taught him how to watch NHL games and old movies, my son helped him find some pretty good porn sites, and he had his own door to the garden and a small refrigerator, so after a few months of moping around dejectedly and a couple of nasty quarrels with me and my father, he settled into a happy routine.

Dad would go to Shelly's room every night before bed and they would split a shot glass full of Danziger Goldwasser, which I wasn't supposed to know about, but I found the bottle under his bed when I was straightening up his room one day. Sometimes the two cousins would fall asleep in their chairs. Once, about six months before Shelly's death, Dad must have grown too tired to climb upstairs to his room and I found them spooned together in bed, with my father's arm over Shelly's chest.

I got my sketchbook and drew them quickly, but I haven't yet framed it. I'm not yet ready to see all I've lost so clearly. Maybe I never will be.

To Create Something Beautiful

What Shelly loved most was sitting with Benni in the backyard, on one of the quilts that Belle sent my mom, his eyes shaded by his Boston Red Sox baseball cap, sipping coffee drizzled with rum and reading classic French novels or gossiping in Yiddish. Before his bad hip limited his mobility, he also joined Dad as one of Angie's assistant gardeners.

It always used to make me laugh to see Benni and Shelly covered head to toe with dirt and carrying trowels in their hands and asking Angie what she wanted them to do next.

Angie in her blue sweatpants and yellow sun hat, leading the two old men around the garden and pointing with her gloved hand to the overgrown bedding around our apple trees or the circle of tulips they'd planted the previous autumn ... 'Time to get serious about weeding,' she'd tell them as if they'd been shirking their duties.

They adored being ordered around by Angie – you could see it in their eyes. And working in the garden meant they could still help to create something beautiful.

During his final years, Shelly had a problematic liver, and he often suffered with bronchitis, as well – undoubtedly from seventy years of smoking two packs a day. Whenever we had to put him in the hospital, he also developed what his physicians called hospital psychosis and would become pretty loony. Often, he'd whisper to me and Dad that the doctors weren't really doctors and nurses weren't nurses.

'So who are they?' I asked the first time it happened.

'Spies.'

'For which country?'

'I'm not sure. Maybe Russia. In any case, they aren't who they say they are, so be careful.'

Once, when he was in the Intensive Care Unit, Shelly told me of a representative of the Polish secret police named Wieczorek who'd visited him that morning and pretended to be worried about his health. 'The schmuck even brought me a prune *hamantaschen* and thought he'd trick me into eating it in front of him!' Shelly told me. When I asked what he meant, he motioned me close to him and whispered cagily, 'It smelled of rat poison, so I told him I'd save it for later and then tossed it in the garbage.' Dad later told me that there really was a Mr Wieczorek, but that he wasn't – as far as anyone knew – in the secret police. In fact, he'd been the owner of their favourite neighbourhood bakery. After the end of the Second World War, in May of 1945, Ewa had left her name and address with him, and he'd promised to give that information to any relations of Benni's who returned to Warsaw. But a few weeks later, when Shelly arrived in the city and spoke to Wieczorek, the baker didn't tell them that Dad was living with Ewa. 'We never found out why he held back that information,' my father told me. 'He was probably terrified that Shelly and George were spying for the Americans and being watched by the Polish secret police. Though Ewa . . . She thought there was a different explanation. She said that Wieczorek told her he disliked Jews. So maybe he even hated us so much that he didn't want us to find each other.'

On another occasion when Shelly was delirious – or when I presumed he was – he told me of a mirror that bled whenever a Jew was murdered, anywhere in the world, and that he had smuggled it out of the ghetto. I didn't believe him, of course, though I would later find out that he was telling me the absolute truth – at least as he understood it.

The Affection in My Father's Eyes

Uncle George visited Shelly, Dad and me for the last time in early April of 2010. He and Uncle Martin had adopted three kids, and his eldest granddaughter – Irene – escorted him on the flight to Boston from Salt Lake City.

George waved both hands at me the moment he spotted me in the terminal. His arms were pale and frail-looking, and his long grey hair – his 'coyote's tail,' as Dad called it – was gone. *A man stretched too thin by accumulated troubles* . . . That's how I began to think of him, because he'd had a cancerous tumour removed from his gut half a year before, and subsequent to the operation he'd been in bed with pneumonia for two months.

As Irene led him forward, I felt as if I were standing outside in a rainstorm, chilled and alone, watching a disaster slowly come to pass. But on the way to the parking lot, George gave me a hearty pat on the back and told me to cheer up. 'I look like hell, but I'm okay,' he said. I didn't entirely believe him, but I also didn't want to intrude on his privacy.

George was wearing a bolo tie of Kokopelli – the trickster god who's always playing his flute – and after I put the bags in the trunk of my car, I told him it was beautiful.

He took it from around his neck. 'Yes, it's very fine work,' he said, and he handed it to me.

The curved, high-shouldered figure was made of silver inlaid with brown-veined turquoise, and the flute was mother-of-pearl. On the back was etched the initials HB.

'Henry Bizaadii – my uncle,' George explained. 'Dad's younger brother.'

'Wow – I didn't know you had a silversmith in the family!'

I started to hand it back, but George shook his head. 'Listen, Eti, I want you to have it,' he said solemnly.

'No, I can't accept it. It must mean a lot to you – it was made by your uncle.'

'Which is why it would please me so much to see you wearing it.'

I continued arguing, but he told me I'd dishonour him if I refused his gift. After he'd helped me put Kokopelli around my neck, he placed his hand against my chest – an intimate gesture he and I had both learned from Shelly – and said in Yiddish, '*Trog es gezunterheyt*, Eti.' Wear it in good health.

His gift touched me greatly, but on the way home I grew morose, because I remembered how Mom had given away her collection of scarves to Aunt Evie and Angie after she'd learned that her cancer had spread. George spotted me sneaking worried looks at him and said, 'Hey, Eti, let's have a good time together and not worry about things we can't control. Okay?'

I limited myself to nodding at him because my voice was lodged in my chest.

Dad and Shelly were waiting for us on the front stoop of my house. As I walked around the car to help George out of the passenger seat, Shelly got to his feet. His walk had become a fragile balancing act of late, but he tossed away his cane and rushed to us. He threw his trembling arms around his old friend and started kissing him as if he were his long-lost brother. Dad hung back, waiting his turn, so my uncle reached out while he was trapped in Shelly's boa-constrictor hug and grabbed his hand and pressed his lips to his palm, and the affection in my father's eyes was wet and shining.

After the three old buddies had hugged and laughed and cried – and after Shelly had a chance to kid George about his haircut – Dad grew dizzy from all the emotion, so I sat him on the stoop again and instructed him to put his head between his legs, and after a while he could breathe without difficulty.

Irene had just turned nineteen, but she had a strikingly adult profile and reserved manner. Her eyes were deep with silent awareness – like dark ponds – and her face was framed by long ringlets of chestnut hair that reminded me of the nymphs and goddesses in Botticelli paintings.

Her expression turned panicky, however, while my dad was panting. 'It's okay, he'll be fine,' I told her. 'It's always like an Italian opera around here when your grandfather arrives.' She still looked doubtful, so I told her to go around to our backyard to see our flower beds, and that I'd come get her and show her where she'd be sleeping in a little while.

Irene spent that night on a futon in the living room, then got picked up by two friends from college in the morning. They were spending their Easter vacation in the mountains of Vermont.

Around the dinner table on our first evening together, Shelly and George told Irene the story of their trip to Poland to rescue my father, who interjected zany asides about his life with Ewa. He got his biggest laugh when he told us that he used to drive Ewa bonkers by hiding slices of cake around the house and forgetting where they were until they started stinking of mould.

Talking about their mission of rescue seemed Shelly's and George's way of putting the world in order – of arranging the story of their lives together the only way that could make any sense. But they didn't speak of the moment that they stepped out of their taxi and spotted Dad coming out of Ewa's house. Years before, George had told me that it was a moment that could only be approached in silence.

All that he now said to his granddaughter was, 'And then our searching ended, and everything else that would happen began.'

After dessert, Angie and I led George to the cot I'd put in Shelly's room, and he thanked us for dinner. He and I hugged, and for just a second I seemed to scent the desert on him – the baking earth and sagebrush most of all, but also the endless, gravelly roads. That night, the eternal light of the Utah desert watched over the first of my many dreams.

Over our next five days together, I had little time with George alone, but on the sixth day, he took me aside after breakfast and told me he wanted to see my latest work. Uncle Martin had flown in by then – he'd been visiting his sister in Miami – so after breakfast, the three of us drove to my studio in Eagle Hill. I was nervous because the way George had always depicted Bergen-Belsen as just outside his front door or down the street had influenced me deeply and prompted me to put clues about my dad's experiences during World War Two in my cityscapes of Boston. Of late, however, I'd become fascinated by the Greek myths – in particular, by the way they reminded us that there is a limit to how much of our destiny we can control. I'd started setting my favourite of those ancient tales in the intimate, chaotic and congested New York City of my childhood.

George's knees were acting up, so he could only get around my studio with great effort. He didn't speak as he hobbled over the paint-splattered floor, gazing at Persephone transformed into a flowering cherry tree in Washington Square Park and Helen of Troy abducted by Paris while waiting for a train in the 14th Street subway station, so Martin and I talked about a cottage that he was designing for a friend.

While observing George, I realised that my figures seemed too staged – as if they were trapped in a play I'd cast them in – and my shame became a prickly sensation at the back of my neck.

How is it that all our confidence can vanish in an instant?

'Ah!' my uncle exclaimed a little while later.

He'd picked up a small canvas that I'd turned to face the wall, since I considered it a failure.

In it, a naked man – bearded, powerful, with alluring, kohl-ringed eyes – is running with a sprightly little boy across a beach toward a dark-skinned, laughing woman standing on the shore. Behind them is an ochre-coloured cliff, and peering over the rim, crouching menacingly, is a giant wolf with red eyes and a bristling collar of silver fur. Around the angry creature are his masters – the soldiers of an ancient army. The boy is panting from exhaustion, and he has my father's anxious black eyes. The dark-skinned woman, oblivious to the drama taking place behind her, has tossed a ball high into the cloudy sky and is preparing to catch it with cupped hands. To her side, at the water's edge, is a slender boat with billowing sails. Across the windswept waters, a cavern of warm, ecstatic light is opening above a crescent-shaped cove.

I intended the fiery light to serve as a sign – from the world itself – that the man must seek safety in the distant cove, but I hadn't yet found the right combination of form and colour to convey that message. A great deal else seemed wrong with the painting, as well, but especially the wolf, who was too obvious a threat.

'I recognise your father,' George said, 'but who are the others?'

I told him that young man was Odysseus, though I'd been considering giving him Shelly's face just before I stopped working on it.

'And the woman?'

'Nausicaa – daughter of King Alcinous and Queen Arete. I don't know if you remember, but she makes it possible for Odysseus to return home to Ithaca and goes on to marry his son.'

He touched his fingertip to my dad's face. 'The sense of doom is upsetting,' he said. 'I think it could become a very strong work.'

His praise seemed to lift me out of a cramped, dimly lit corner of my mind. 'Yeah, I like it too,' I said. 'In fact, I was obsessed with it for a while. But so much about it seems wrong. Anyway, I've given up on it for the time being.'

'Listen, Eti, would you do an old Navajo Jew a favour?' he asked, and when I agreed, he said, 'Go back to it and finish it any way you like. And don't quit, even if it takes years. All right?'

Leading Dad to Safety

Over the next few weeks, I worked on and off on the small painting, but without success until I added circular brushstrokes in silky pink and violet around the cove to give it the feel of a radiant *eruv*. And then, a breakthrough . . . I painted the wolf rearing up onto the prow of the sailboat, his back and stiff, upraised tail lit by the cavern of light in the threatening sky, staring at my father with keen, curious eyes. This positioning meant that he – the wolf – was in two places at once on the canvas: crouching atop the cliff at the left and on the boat at the right. Only a creature possessed of great magic could accomplish that, which made me eager to learn more about him.

While lying in bed that night, however, I realised that he wasn't a wolf; he was Odysseus's dog, Argus! He had tracked his master to the island of Scheria in order to protect him. And then – in a burst of insight – I understood why I'd painted him in two places at once.

To carry out my plan, I traced a black line down the centre of the canvas the next morning, and it was then that the real painting – the one that had needed me to give it form since the very beginning – came into being.

I created two vertical panels. In the left one, Odysseus carries my father on his shoulders and is racing together with Argus away from an enemy army toward the straining, anxious arms of Nausicaa. On the right, at a slightly later time, Dad, Odysseus, Nausicaa and Argus are all safely aboard the sailboat, making their way across the windswept bay to the light-blessed cove, to which I added sudden strokes of blue impasto to give it the feel of a protected refuge. The dog stands now with his front paws on the railing of the bow, and his wary gaze seems magical, since he is focused on the army gathering on the left-hand panel – in the past.

Nausicaa is now depicted as a lithe, cheerful woman with shimmering, boyishly cut silver hair – my mother just before the return of her cancer – but I'd decided not to identify Odysseus with Shelly or anyone else.

This was my first attempt to depict two different moments in time on the same canvas, and the juxtaposed panels drew my eye back and forth, which gave the composition more movement than any of my previous work. I was certain that I had happened on a way forward – and was so excited, in fact, that I couldn't sketch or paint anything else for several days.

I called the painting *Odysseus and Argus Leading Dad to Safety*. I began to think of it as an illustration in a storybook I might create of my father as a character in the classical myths.

I finished it six weeks after George's visit, wrapped it up and shipped it off to him in Moab. In my note, I told him that I couldn't imagine anyone else owning it.

He called me the day he received it to thank me. 'I love your mom and dad in the ancient world!' he said joyfully. 'And the time change is perfect. And those amazing colours . . . It's great, Eti. In fact, there isn't anything about the painting that doesn't seem just right to me.'

'Did you know it was going to come out so good?' I asked.

He laughed merrily. 'No, my grandfather was the shaman in the family! But you know what? When an artist tells you he's been obsessed with a work, it usually means there's something in it that he needs to go back to.'

Just before we ended the phone call, he said. 'One last thing – when did you decide to put yourself in the painting?'

'Me? I don't understand.'

'Well, you seem to be playing Odysseus,' he replied.

I felt as if something dangerous were stalking the phone line between us. 'I don't know what you mean,' I said.

'Listen, Eti, it's only natural that you'd want to help your dad get to safety. All of us who've known you since you were little . . . We've always sensed how responsible you felt for him. But I never saw you illustrate your caring so clearly – your willingness to even go back in time and help him. It's extremely moving.'

I knew he was right about my feelings, but what he'd found in my painting seemed a projection of his own affection for me. 'Uncle George, I don't know what to say,' I told him. 'I don't think I'm Odysseus in the painting. I don't look anything like him.'

'No, not now, Eti,' he replied. 'But you looked just like him when you were twenty years old!'

Kokopelli's Mischief

What George told me left me stunned. And convinced that I might chance upon some surprising discoveries if I kept painting myself and Dad together.

Unfortunately, George never learned how he'd once again influenced my work; he died a little more than two months later, when I'd only just began my series of paintings depicting my father and me in Greek, Norse and Navajo myths. Uncle Martin called to give us the news. He said that the cancer had spread to George's stomach just before he'd visited us. 'Last night, he told me that it was time to end the pain, so I gave him an overdose of morphine. We'd stored up extra doses of it from our doctor in case we ever needed it.'

Martin's choking voice took away all my thoughts. At length, I said, 'That must have been the worst thing ever.'

'I won't lie – it was,' he told me. 'And you know what, Eti, saying goodbye . . . It was impossible for me. I tried to speak the words, but they wouldn't come out. I held George in my arms, and he fell asleep, and then all of me seemed to go blank, but at some point, I realised I was shaking all over, and I fled outside. I needed to be alone, to escape myself and him – to get away from what we made together. I also think I wanted to test what being alone felt like.' He gave a sad little laugh. 'I didn't like it at all. And it seemed all wrong – as if the world had made an error.'

Had George known he was nearing the end? When I asked Martin, he said, 'Sure, but he didn't want to tell you and your dad and Shelly. He wanted Kokopelli's mischief and laughter to reign over the visit, not Death.'

Maybe I've Lived Too Long

Shelly descended inside himself after I gave him the news. For several weeks, he hardly spoke, even to my dad, and there were many days when he wouldn't even leave his room. I'd hear him pacing at all hours of the night. Whenever I came to him, it seemed that something wild with regret wouldn't let him have a moment's peace. Was it because he hadn't been as kind and faithful a lover to George as he might have been? When I dared to ask him that, he pounced on me. 'No, of course not! George and I worked all that out years ago.'

'Then what is it?' I asked.

In a misery-filled voice, he replied that he ought to have died before George and Julie. 'I think maybe I've lived too long, Eti,' he told me with his head in his hands.

Such a Beautiful Man

Two months or so after George's death, Shelly's daughters Monique and Diane finally convinced him to come outside and work with them in our garden. It was the late summer of 2010, and all the dahlias and freesias had just come up, and there was a lot of weeding to do. Once he started getting his big old hands into the soil, his interest in the world returned, and he started reading the newspaper again and taking Dad, Angie and me out to dinner at his favourite Mexican restaurant, and gabbing on the phone with his daughters nearly every day. After a while, he seemed to be his usual unstoppable self.

And yet there were times when he'd grow quiet in the middle of a conversation and his eyes would gain a faraway look, and he'd let his head fall, and I'd know he was thinking that there was no point in continuing.

Shelly had become forgetful over the previous few years, but about three months after George's death, he started to exhibit more serious difficulties. Once, he started berating Dad in the post office for writing the wrong return address – my address – on a package that he was sending Diane for her birthday; he'd become convinced that he was still living in Montreal. On another occasion, when Angie dropped him at Schoenhof's Foreign Books so he could look for French novels, she returned to him after doing a couple of errands and discovered that he hadn't any money left to pay for the book he'd found; apparently, he'd handed over more than a hundred dollars to a young man who'd asked him for spare change.

Soon after that, Shelly grew plagued by the idea that something monstrous would happen to my father and that he wouldn't be able to protect him. Dad did what he could to reassure him, but by then Shelly was way over his head in a sea of worries. Doctors suggested increasing his dosage of tranquilisers, and that helped a little, but it also made him drowsy a lot of the time.

Several days after his daughters came for a weekend visit, on the morning of November 18th, 2010, I went to his room to bring him his coffee, and I discovered that he'd stopped breathing. When I kissed him, his lips were cold. He was ninety years old – almost ninety-one.

Dad had convinced him to help him plant more than a hundred tulip bulbs in our front yard over the previous few days. They would come up in a few months, and their flowers would be pink and scarlet and purple, because those were colours Shelly picked out at the nursery, and that's what started me weeping more than anything else.

'He was such a beautiful man,' was all my father said when I gave him the news, and he didn't cry, but I read in his blinking eyes and lopsided smile that all his defensive walls were crumbling.

He collapsed a moment later. I caught him just before he crashed onto the floor, but he twisted his ankle badly.

I laid him onto the sofa in the living room. He was groggy and confused. I took his hands and told him he'd be all right. We didn't discuss Shelly's death. I tried to, but Dad closed his eyes and shook his head and whispered. 'I can't go anywhere near that.'

Shelly had indicated in his will that he wished to be cremated. Monique drove down from Montreal to Boston to make the arrangements. Then she, Angie and I drove his ashes up to Canada for the burial.

I didn't want Dad to come with us – his blood pressure was erratic and his ankle was badly swollen – but he wasn't about to let Shelly go back to Montreal without him. 'Anyway, if I drop dead in the cemetery, there'll be less work for everyone,' he said. 'You can just stick me in the ground like a dahlia bulb, with my roots facing down and stem facing up. Got it?'

'Sure.'

'But you have to put me right next to Shelly and Julie so that we can keep each other warm. The winters in Canada are too fucking cold!'

'I thought you wanted to be put next to Mom.'

'Well, that would be my first choice, but it really doesn't matter. You can even send me out to be with George in Moab. I have it on good authority that geography doesn't mean so much when you're dead.'

'Whose authority?'

'My own. I'm old enough now to have figured some things out.'

I rented a wheelchair because Dad wasn't able to put any pressure on his ankle.

After the ceremony, Monique hosted a gathering in her apartment, and it was moving to see how loved Shelly was by the nephews and nieces he had on Julie's side of the family. Diane picked up deli food from Schwartz's, but Dad couldn't eat anything, not even the barley-and-mushroom soup that Angie and Uncle Martin insisted that he try. He asked me instead to make him pancakes with banana or whatever fruit Monique had in her fridge. 'It's the only thing I can keep down when my stomach is like this,' he told us.

'Only pancakes?' I asked.

'Yeah. It's been like this for seventy years.'

When I showed him a questioning look, he nodded solemnly, which made me wonder if his gut had ever really recovered from the starvation he'd suffered in the ghetto. And I couldn't imagine anything more generous and noble than how he'd always used clowning to cover up his fragility.

After Angie and I made my father pancakes with strawberries, Monique's son, Daniel, who was fourteen years old at the time, read a eulogy that he, his mother and Diane had written. Dad looked down and hid his head in his hands the whole time. Uncle Martin stood next to him and kept his hand on my father's shoulder.

'Daniel spoke beautifully, don't you think?' I asked Dad as I wheeled him into the bathroom to wash his face.

'Yeah, I guess so, but it wasn't what he said that touched me.'

'No?'

'That little *pisher* . . . He turns on like a lightbulb in front of other people,' Dad said excitedly. 'And me, I was worried it would vanish. Just goes to show you!'

'That what would vanish? I don't get it.'

'Shelly's personality, kiddo. Danny has it. He loves performing. Which means it skipped a generation. Like your son, George. He has all my athletic skills. Not like you.'

'Your athletic skills?' I asked, since I wasn't aware that he'd ever had any.

'It's a joke, Eti,' Dad said, snorting. 'Now bend down.'

'What for?'

'Just do what I say for once!'

When I bent down, he adjusted my bolo tie of Kokopelli. 'Much better,' he said. 'Now help me wash my face. It looks like a garden snail has been crawling over my cheeks.'

After Dad was all tidied up, Monique and Diane called us into the kitchen and handed him a bakery box tied with string that Shelly had left for him.

He'd written *Benni* on the front in Yiddish.

'Dad left whatever is in it for you nine years ago,' Monique said. 'Just after the doctors found a tubercular scar in his lungs and we all got so worried it was cancer. He said to only give it to you after he was gone. But he sent us a letter to put in it just a few weeks ago.'

Dad sniffed at the box and made a face. 'A nine-year-old *mandelbrot* is going to be pretty toxic. You think your father wants maybe to poison me?'

Monique and Diane didn't realise Dad was kidding until he told them they'd have to eat it first, and that we'd wait a couple of hours to see they survived before having a piece.

I cut the string. Inside the box was a red velvet pouch in the shape of a heart that looked like something Shelly must have pilfered from a high-priced bordello. Inside it were Julie's gold bracelet and Shelly's wedding band, and a pair of diamond earrings. There was also a big white envelope containing five thousand Canadian dollars and a smaller one with a note written in Shelly's jagged, Yiddish scrawl. Dad translated it for us:

Hi, Benni. If you're reading this, it means I'm on my way to heaven. I really hope either Julie meets me right away or that angels know what to do with an erect cock and fine young ass (yes, I'm planning to get younger and a whole lot harder as I make my way into the Upper Realms). Otherwise, what the hell am I going to do every day? In any case, that's not your concern. And George will be there to show me the ropes, so everything should be okay. You know what? I stashed this stuff away for you to give to your grandkids. I've already given my daughters enough for them and my grandson. You remember Berekiah's Rule, don't you? Mesirat nefesh *and all that stuff about sacrifice . . . Anyway, you know I was never very good at writing, so I send a big kiss for Eti and lots more for his children. (Hi, Kiddo!) And I send you everything I ever was, because everything was what I wanted to give you and what you deserved. We had a good life, didn't we? I mean, after that big unfair mess at the beginning. Gosh, what a great day it was when George and I found you! Or did you find us? I've never been sure which way your crazy Incandescent Threads were pointing that day. And then Julie walked into my shop and fell in love with me and put up with me all those years when I couldn't keep my mischief-maker in my trousers. Whoever figured you and I would live together at the end? That was the cherry on top of the cake. Thank you for that and everything else. You know, despite all the* tsuris, *I got all I could ever have wanted. I see that now. What good fortune I had! See you soon! Love, Shelly.*

Do You Have Lots of People's Voices Inside You?

After Shelly's death, I used to check on Dad a couple of times a night to make sure that he was sleeping, and sometimes, if he was awake, I'd go in and we'd sit together without talking, holding hands. If he was upset, I'd challenge him to a scrabble game and let him use the dictionary for help.

Once, after I tucked Dad back in and went back downstairs to the kitchen, I felt as if Shelly were with me, so I whispered to him, 'I miss you a lot.'

This was a little more than two years ago, in late February of 2016, and I knew I was mostly pretending that Shelly was with me. And yet a few weeks later, I was lying on the sofa, taking a nap, and I heard rustling sounds in the kitchen. I thought that a field mouse had snuck inside again, since we'd had problems with them of late. But as I sat up, I felt an unseen presence standing by the window, watching the snow, which was falling so slowly and endlessly that it seemed like a metaphor for all that remains just beyond our reach. And then I saw Shelly's reflection in the window, and he was young again, with his dark good looks and seductive eyes, and he grinned at me and said, 'Your father is eating bran flakes from the box.'

'Is that you, Shelly?' I asked.

'Who else could it be? You know, Eti, your father eats cereal with his hands all the time of late, but only when you're not looking. I think he's becoming a kid again.'

When Shelly grinned, his scent of rum and cigarettes wafted over to me. I jumped up, and that's when I opened my eyes and realised I was still lying on the couch and that I'd been dreaming.

I went to the window and opened the curtains and confirmed that it wasn't snowing.

When I went to the kitchen, I found Dad sitting at the table in his pyjamas, with a glass of orange juice and a box of bran flakes, and he was eating them out of his hand.

Of course, I had probably figured out what my father was doing while listening to the rustling sounds. Yet I also couldn't shake the feeling that Shelly had returned for a moment, in a world where the snow fell with feathery slowness and ghosts could be reflected in windows.

'You caught me!' Dad said, and he held up his hands like a captured bank robber in a Western. 'Don't shoot!' he pleaded in a quaking voice.

'The last thing I want to do is play sheriff,' I said. 'So you can put your hands down, Dad.'

'I'm not Dad, I'm Billie the Kid.'

'Yeah, sometimes I'm pretty sure that you think you're only about twelve years old.'

'Eleven, more likely.'

He didn't need to add that he was that age when his parents disappeared. He held up the box. 'Want some?'

'Sure.'

I sat down and he poured some into my cupped hands. I sipped juice from his glass, and we talked for a time about my latest paintings, and his eyes held mine with so much affection that I decided to sketch him.

'But I look like hell!' he said.

'It's just the bad lighting.'

He giggled. 'If only it were just that,' he said.

I started drawing his eyes, as I always do. If I can get them right, the rest of his face enters the tip of my pencil without much difficulty. Everyone who has ever met my father knows that he begins and ends with his dark eyes.

Like moonless nights, Mom used to say, and she was right.

'You know, it was Shelly who told me that you like to eat cereal from the box,' I said.

He banged his fist on the table, pretending rage. 'Gone for five years and still ruining my fun! You can't tell that man anything. If he were here, I'd give him a piece of my mind!'

'Maybe you can,' I said. 'He told me just a little while ago, while I was napping.'

'I don't get it.'

'I was waking up out of a dream and he told me what the rustling noise was.'

'He spoke to you?'

'Yeah – and very clearly.'

Dad patted my hand. 'That's good,' he said gratefully.

'Why is it good?'

'For one thing, he speaks to me all the time, so it's only fair that he speaks to you too!'

I put down my sketch. 'Have you seen his ghost?'

'Listen, Eti, when people die . . . If we're lucky, the best things about them stay inside us. We take over some parts of who they were. It's how we go on.'

'But what about his ghost? Have you seen him?'

'No, but occasionally I hear him. And once, a few years ago, during the winter, I sensed him climbing into bed with me to warm me up. He was pretty drunk – I could smell the rum on him. We talked for a long time, though I don't think it was really him. I think I was still half asleep. I guess my mind was inventing things for him to say.'

'Do you have lots of people's voices inside you?' I asked.

He flapped his hand at me as if he were disgusted. 'Too many! Your grandparents, old friends . . . Even parrots.' He smiled excitedly. 'Hey, did I ever tell you my cousin Abe had a parrot?'

'Yeah, Glukl.'

'But did I ever tell you how smart she was?'

'No, I don't think so.'

'She could crack open almonds. And speak Yiddish and Ladino. She didn't live in a cage either – she flew around the whole apartment. Abe was going to teach her to play chess, but the

Nazis . . . They didn't think that was such a good idea.' Dad imitated Glukl's croaking voice: '*Fardrey zich dem kup und tu vos du vilst.*'

'What's that mean?'

Playing up his Yiddish accent, Dad replied, 'Don't bother me, do vatever you vant.'

'What colour was she?'

'Green – a beautiful emerald green. But I think her claws were yellow. Is that right?' He shrugged. 'Yeah, I've got Glukl in me, and that sweet old hound that Belle loved so much. And there was a white cat with turquoise eyes that belonged to one of our neighbours back in Warsaw, and she made so much noise, you could've *plotzed* from the racket. You know what, Eti, it's a fucking three-ring circus inside my head sometimes!'

In the End, We Won

Our worst crisis over the course of Dad's last months happened when my son discovered that his grandfather had stopped taking his medications – a diuretic and statin, as well as a multivitamin. George was nineteen years old at the time and studying archaeology at the University of Massachusetts. It was late March of 2017, and my father had recovered almost completely from his minor stroke. His only noticeable after-effect was a slight trembling in his right hand.

I should have been able to predict my son's reaction, since he was very close to my father, but an opaque layer of wishful thinking must have covered over the crystal ball in my head.

A shared love of reading and history had first brought my father and George together. Dad had started giving his grandson picture books on Egyptology even before he started kindergarten, and George would cut out the sceptres and necklaces with scissors, and he'd sleep with them under his pillow, which made us joke that he was going to become the first Jewish pharaoh.

Then, when the boy was nine years old, my father bought him an encyclopaedia-sized primer by E. A. Wallis Budge on the ancient Egyptian language that changed both their lives. Whenever my father would come for a visit, they would study together at the kitchen table, drawing the hieroglyphs and memorising both their phonetic value and their meaning.

They began with Cleopatra's name in hieroglyphs:

Dad never got past the first three lessons in Budge's course, but George forged ahead with that unquenchable, optimistic energy of his, and by the time he was thirteen, he could decipher brief hieroglyphic texts in the extensive Egyptology collection he had on his bookshelves.

That same year, Angie and I took my father and our kids to the Metropolitan Museum and my oldest daughter, Pi – fiercely proud of her baby brother – asked him to tell her what was written in a framed scroll depicting Sekhmet, the Egyptian lion-headed goddess, and while I was listening to George's translation, my dad went pale, and though he told me he was fine, he rushed off to the bathroom. After fifteen minutes he still hadn't returned, and I figured that the Szechuan lunch we'd eaten had upset his stomach, but when I found him hunkered down in a bathroom stall, he said that while watching George and Pi discuss a battle that had happened three thousand years ago, he felt so proud of his grandchildren, and so happy that they'd been born, that he realised he'd beaten the Nazis – 'Me and Shelly both!'

He said that his triumph had made him dizzy, but he didn't want to take the spotlight off George, so he'd stumbled off to the bathroom. 'And it's all clean and polished,' he said happily. 'No bad smells. I'd give it an A. What about you, Eti?'

'Yeah, it's nice,' I agreed, 'but you could've said something to me. I'd have come with you.'

He shook his head as if it no longer mattered. 'We won. Do you understand? Eti, we lost so many good people, but in the end, we won!'

I was about to help Dad stand back up, but a fancily dressed guy with a Spanish accent asked us if we were all right, and Dad said yes and told the man that his pinstriped suit looked expertly tailored, and that his white silk tie was a good choice, and my father asked where he'd bought it, and the Spanish guy said in Madrid, at a Corte Ingles department store, and Dad told him that he had an old tie that would looked great with the cream-coloured pinstripe and could he send it to him, and I started laughing to myself because of how my father could engage anyone in a good-natured conversation at any time, no matter where he was.

I took down the man's name, and he said he was staying at the Hotel Carlisle, and the next day, Dad sent him a gorgeous rose-coloured tie that he'd cut and stitched himself more than twenty years before.

Dad's closeness to George came as a surprise to me and Angie because when our son was a baby, my father's clowning only made him cry. You never saw a kid who resented so fiercely any attempt to change his mood through diversion.

The boy hates me, Dad used to tell me with downcast eyes.

It took us both a long time to figure out that George required something of my father that no little kid knew how to put into words but that had something to do with the size and shape and nature of the world he'd been born into. I think now that what George would have told Dad if he could have found the words would have been this: *I want you to be my storyteller, not my clown!*

I suppose that some children know right away that they want a grandparent who can take them to faraway worlds – and into the distant past.

I remember the first time I knew that Dad had won George's heart. My son must have been about five years old. Dad had him on his lap and was telling him about the big lazy ducks who spent hot summer days in the pond behind the house that belonged to Ewa, the piano teacher who'd saved his life.

'You lived in Poland?' George asked, as if it were impossible – even though, by then, I'd already explained about his grandfather's background and showed him Poland on the map.

'Yeah, I grew up in Warsaw. And I never spoke English.' Dad spoke to George in Yiddish to demonstrate. 'That means, *the ducks are overheated and about to faint*. And you know what, baby, if someone had told me that I'd have a grandson named after a beautiful Navajo man from Toronto, and that he'd grow up in Boston, and that his father would be an artist and a professor, and his mother a world-famous anthropologist, I'd have said that they were nuts!'

George's eyes started glowing after Dad spoke to him in Yiddish. Dad later said that maybe my son spotted one of the Incandescent Threads that connected him to the small pond behind Ewa's house or another of the places that had marked the lives of George's ancestors.

At times, however, George's extraordinary determination could morph all too easily into a belligerence that upset and confounded all of us. I remember that once, when he was fourteen years old, he had a French teacher who occasionally ridiculed the accents of his students, and around March he refused to keep going to class. I volunteered to speak to the school principal about his difficulties with the teacher, but he didn't want me to do that. And when Angie and I pleaded with him to return to class and finish out the year, he stopped talking to us until we settled on a compromise, which was that he would switch from French to Spanish.

George remained close to my father throughout high school, and after he started college, he'd come home a couple of weekends a month to play scrabble with my father and take him to lunch at El Faro Taqueria, and amaze him with his stories about going to college in the age of iPods and smartphones.

So, as I say, it shouldn't have come as a surprise to me that George would drive home right away when Dad told him he had gone off his medications, but it did. After a quick hello to me and his mother, he took the stairs two at a time and barged into my father's room and apparently told him he was being selfish, and my father replied that there comes a time when an old man has to be a little selfish, and George said that he wouldn't go back to college unless he started taking his medications again, to which

Dad said that he wasn't about to take orders from a little *pisher*, no matter how smart he was or how much he adored him.

I stayed downstairs, pacing in the kitchen, until George cried out that he hated my father. When I entered Dad's bedroom, tears were rolling down George's cheeks and his long brown hair looked a mess and he was fiddling with the piercing in his ear, which was always a bad sign. My father was seated with his head in his hands, trembling.

'I'm never talking to him again!' George told me.

Stay calm, I told myself, because I knew my son meant it. 'George, come here,' I said. My intent was to ask him very gently to apologise to my father for barging in on him and yelling. *And then we'll all sit together to work this out*, I was planning on saying.

Maybe he sensed what I was going to ask because he crossed his arms over his chest as if he were preparing for a long war and said, 'What do you want me to do, Dad?'

His defiant brown eyes told me I'd get nowhere with him, so I said, 'Listen, why don't you go to your room for now and let me talk to Grandpa alone? Okay?'

'No!' George declared. 'He's going to die, and he doesn't care. He doesn't care what he's doing or how I feel about it or ... anything else. He's selfish – a selfish old man!'

Dad's eyes grew enraged. 'If you knew all I'd sacrificed to be here with you, you'd be ashamed to criticise me like that!' he shouted. 'Did you know I changed your father's diapers for years, and made him dinners, all the time his mother was studying? And I was in my shop six days a week, scrounging out a living, because a lot of customers didn't like it that I was on TV telling people that the war in Vietnam was sickening and wrong! And now ... Now I just want a little peace and quiet.' He took a panting breath. 'All the damn pills aren't going to save my life, George. Don't you know that? I'm eighty-eight years old! When in God's name do I get a little time off for good behaviour?'

My father's face was so inflamed that I feared he was about to have another stroke. I went to him and took his hands. 'Dad,' I said, 'just calm down.'

'*You* calm down!' he snarled, and he tugged his hands away.

'We'll get through everything together,' I said. 'All we need to do is—'

I wasn't sure what I was going to say, but I never got the chance. 'Eti, no one can request certain things from another person,' he cut in. 'It's not fair.' He looked at George and said in a pleading tone, 'You can ask me a lot, but you can't ask me to take medications that make me feel like shit. I want to feel good and strong for whatever time I have left. I want to eat chocolate *mandelbrot* and drink schnapps and make myself pancakes with egg yolks in the batter. And if I want to, I'll even smoke a cigarette! Christ, why do I have to fight my own grandson? Can't you understand how that makes me feel?'

George started crying harder – had he figured out that his grandfather was right? – then rushed out of the room. I told Dad that I'd handle George and to please calm down, but I had no idea what I was going to do. Back in the kitchen, I sat my son down and talked to him about how being old isn't easy, and that my father missed Grandma and Shelly every day, and that because he had been confined during the war it was very important for him to decide his own destiny now, but I could tell from the rigid set of my son's jaw that I wasn't reaching him. Was he simply too young to understand? When he stood up and told me he didn't want to talk any more about it, I realised I'd lost him. 'All I ask is that you sleep at home tonight,' I told him. 'I don't want you driving back to college alone when you're so upset.'

George nodded his agreement, but while Angie and I were talking about what to do, we heard him starting his car, and by the time I got to the front door, he was zooming off down the street, and when I called his cell phone he wouldn't answer.

Dad and George didn't see each other or speak again over the next five weeks. I'm pretty certain I suffered more than both of them, since they at least had their anger to sustain them.

'Maybe they're too alike,' Angie kept telling me.

What she didn't need to add is that I wasn't like either of them – because I was pragmatic and conciliatory by nature. My mother used to say that I'd inherited Grandfather Morrie's thoughtful and sensible, easy-going outlook.

In early May, George came home for a week before driving out to the West Coast with friends. He'd cut his hair short and put a second stud in his right ear. His face had become too slender and austere for my liking – he'd studied nearly non-stop for his exams over the last week – so I was glad he was going on a vacation.

I thought I might have a chance to broker a truce with my father, but he wouldn't come downstairs to have lunch with his grandson. And when I asked George to carry my father's dinner up to his room, he refused. Angie pleaded with him later that night to share a glass of schnapps or Danziger Goldwasser with his grandfather before bed, thinking that treating the young man like an adult might soften his heart, but he refused.

The second morning, when I brought Dad his breakfast, I asked him to lie – to tell George that he'd gone back on all his medications.

'What would your mother say to that?' he demanded.

Had my father read my mind? In fact, I was doing what I believed she'd want me to do.

'She'd say that it was a practical solution,' I replied. 'And that lying in this case wouldn't do anybody any harm.'

'No, she'd say that I had to be honest. That I couldn't hide things from our grandson.'

'I think you're wrong about that.'

'Have you forgotten how frustrated you'd get when I'd keep things from you?' he asked.

'It's like this, Dad . . . I don't want George living out the rest of his life knowing that he failed you right now. He won't be able to make that up to you or me once you're gone. And I can't let that happen. I'm his father and I can't let that happen! Do you understand?'

Dad frowned at me. I went to the window and surveyed the neighbourhood. Imtiaz, our across-the-street neighbour was mowing his lawn. Next door, the Palermo family's overweight Shetland sheepdog was snoozing on the front stoop with all four legs in the air.

'That can't be comfortable,' I said.

'What?'

'Goldie is sleeping with her legs in the air.'

Dad got up and stood next to me. He put his hand on my shoulder. 'I used to sleep like that,' he said. 'It's nice. It's like your legs are weightless.'

'When did you sleep like that?'

'When I was a dog.'

'And when were you a dog?'

'Hard to say – I couldn't tell time or read a calendar.'

I laughed, and Dad did too. I kissed him and he patted my belly.

He sat back down. I could tell from the way he was rubbing his chin that he was trying to decide what to do. I kneeled next to him, and I was going to ask him again to lie, but he started combing my hair with his soft old hand, and I started to cry.

'Only for you, Eti,' he said in a whisper.

'Thank you, Dad.'

'But listen, I don't want to lie to him. I'm finished with lies. So if you get me a glass of water, I'll take my pills.'

'I'm sorry I had to ask this of you.'

'I know. I'm sorry George and I quarrelled. I know that was hard for you.'

I got him water from his sink. He opened his drawer and took out his diuretic and his multivitamin. He downed them both in a single gulp. 'Eti, I won't go back on the statin. It gives me an irregular heartbeat, and I feel like I'm going to drop dead at any time, and I hate it.'

'Okay, I understand.'

'Now send up George.'

'He might not come.'

'Just tell him I've taken two out of my three pills. And that I never stopped my aspirin. Tell him I need to have a serious talk with him about what he can ask of me and what he can't ask. And you can add that I'm going to beat his ass at scrabble!'

When I told my son that Dad had conceded to his wishes, he rushed out to the yard. When he came back in a few minutes later, his eyes were raw and red, and I said what I'd been wanting to tell him for weeks: 'Love that doesn't cross bridges isn't really love.'

'You mean I should have given in?' he asked.

'I mean that you should have met your grandfather halfway. We have to be generous with the people we really care about – always.'

He nodded, but I wasn't sure he believed me. To make myself clearer, I added, 'Love also forgives.'

'Which means?'

'You need to forgive him for not being able to live forever. And he needs to forgive you for loving him so much that you forgot to be kind.'

He nodded solemnly, and when he passed me to go upstairs, he kissed my cheek. I didn't eavesdrop on the conversation he then had with my father, but about an hour later, I knocked and went in, and they were playing scrabble at Dad's card table.

'I'm killing your little nothing!' Dad said in triumph.

'Only because you cheat so badly!' George protested.

'Eti,' Dad said, 'I've always been allowed to use the dictionary, right? It's part of the rules because English has never really fit inside my head. Go ahead, tell him!'

'I'm afraid Grandpa's right,' I told my son, as if testifying before a judge.

While they continued playing, I sat on Dad's bed and started the Willa Cather novel – *One of Ours* – that he was re-reading. After a while, I closed my eyes, however, so that I could feel what a blessing it was to be able to stay in the room with my father and George without having to say anything. It felt right to have them forget I was even there.

Invisibility has always seemed to me a great blessing.

Near the end of the game, my son started looking over at me, and in his eyes was a dark, dangerous territory he was afraid to visit, and I knew that he was asking me for help.

At that moment, I also sensed that his secret had – through some complex adolescent process I didn't understand – become tangled in his grandfather's refusal to take his medications. That was what had made him behave so ruthlessly!

'Go ahead and tell him,' I said while Dad was adding up their scores.

As George looked between me and my father, the boy stuck the tip of tongue between his lips, which meant that he was frightened.

'What wrong, Georgie?' Dad asked.

'He's got something to tell you,' I said.

'What?'

'It's . . . it's kind of really important,' the boy stuttered.

'Is something wrong with you? Is that why you went so crazy on me?' Dad picked up a scrabble piece in his hand and squeezed it in his fist. When George didn't reply, he turned to me. 'Eti, he's not ill, is he? Tell me he's okay!'

'No, George isn't ill.'

Dad got to his feet. 'And Violet and Pi? Is something wrong with them?'

'No, they're okay.'

My father looked at my son for an explanation. The boy gazed down in embarrassment, then looked up at me with pleading eyes.

'George is gay,' I said.

Dad shouted back, 'But what the hell is the important thing he's got to tell me?' He faced George, who was looking down again, and threw the scrabble piece at him, which hit the boy's shoulder. 'You're giving me a heart attack! Now tell me what's so important?'

'I'm in love with a guy I met at college,' George said. 'I'm going with him on vacation.'

'And you're not ill?'

'No, of course, not.'

Dad dropped down next to me on his bed, and when I put my arm over his shoulder, he started sobbing. George stood up, stunned by the depth of his grandfather's reaction. After a little while, my father dried his eyes and opened his arms to my son. 'If you don't come here and hug me,' he said threateningly, 'I'm going to scream so loud that the police will come and arrest you for terrifying a helpless old man!'

After they'd embraced, Dad held my son away and smiled. 'George, honey, I've known you might be gay since you were a kid. It didn't matter then and it doesn't matter now.' He laughed in a burst. 'Your Uncle Shelly slept with half the stevedores in Algiers before he met Aunt Julie. And it was Uncle George who taught him how to love. And I had my experiences with men too – including Shelly.' He tapped George on the head. 'I guess I should have told you that. But I figured it was personal. Anyway, you're old enough to hear all that now, and to understand what I want to tell you, and it goes something like this . . .' Dad closed his eyes for a moment to find the words. 'Your heart and my heart and your dad's heart . . . They follow the same laws as the earth when it goes around the sun, and the same laws that govern the yellow and orange growth of the tulips in our garden, and the same laws that control the way everything in the universe is attracted to everything else – which we usually call gravity. So you know what, I could never be ashamed of you falling in love with a boy, just like I could never be ashamed of the stars in the sky, or the squirrels in our garden, or the blue jays at our feeder.' Dad looked up at me. 'Could you be ashamed of a tulip, Eti?'

'No, of course, not, Dad.'

'George, we have to appreciate the beauty all around us – and be thankful, and grateful, that we share the world with flowers and stars and squirrels.' Dad combed the hair out of my son's eyes and kissed his brow, then looked up at me. 'Oy, he's too skinny, Eti,' he said, playing up his Yiddish accent. He patted my son's belly and asked, 'Vood it kill you to eat a little more?'

George leaned forward and kissed my father on the lips.

Dad covered his eyes with his hand and started crying again. I hugged him until he pointed to his throat, which meant he was too dry to talk, so I got him a glass of orange juice from downstairs. After he'd taken a couple of sips, he said to my son, 'Now tell me about this boy you've met.' He held up a threatening hand. 'But if you ever scare me half to death again over nothing, boy are you going to get a smack!'

The Perfect Moment

Dad died six weeks after making peace with George. Toward the end, he had crippling back pain that confined him to bed, but he absolutely refused to go to the hospital. George flew home from San Francisco to be with him and the rest of the family.

My father's physician told me that the back pains might indicate lung cancer, which terrified me. But my father took the news with a shrug. 'If that's the costume the Angel of Death wants to wear, that's okay by me.' He motioned me closer and whispered, 'What he doesn't know is that I've got prescriptions for all the painkillers I could ever want!'

Only much later did it occur to me that my father might have suspected lung cancer for some time and had hidden the symptoms from me and Angie. Maybe he'd gone off his medications in the hopes of hastening a more comfortable death.

Dad died at home, with a jumble of Gershom Scholem's books on his bed, one of Mom's interviews with Belle playing on his tape player, his bottle of Danziger Goldwasser on his night table, and a game of scrabble with George waiting to be finished on his card table.

The last thing he said was, 'You're going to have to cut my toenails. They're making holes in my socks, kiddo. And despite the rumours to the contrary, I can't bend over that far.'

I'd just come into his room to check what he wanted for lunch, and I told him I'd be right back with my nail clippers. I decided to make him some fresh coffee, too. I sent it up with George while I went to pee.

'Dad, you better come upstairs!' my son called out a few seconds later.

My father's head was turned to the window, as if he'd dozed off while watching the blue jays making a racket in our cherry tree. But his eyes were open and they weren't focused on anything in this world. Face up on his belly was his photograph of the perfect moment in which his smile is so genuine and filled with delight.

After I took the coffee from George and put it down on the night table, I felt for a pulse, but it wasn't there, so I kissed Dad's eyes and closed them, and then I pressed my lips to his and kept them there until I thought I might be able to separate from him without screaming, because I didn't want to make George any more upset than he already was.

When I stood up, I told Dad that I was just going to fetch Angie and that I'd be right back. I spoke aloud because he'd told me that a person's soul sometimes hangs around his body after death, and maybe I didn't really believe that, but I also didn't want to risk him getting scared that I was leaving him.

George was trembling. His shoulders were hunched and his hands were frozen. I took them in mine and said, 'Grandpa's soul might still be with us, so talk to him while I fetch your mom.'

When I returned to the room with Angie, we discovered that George had moved a chair right up to his grandfather's bed and was lying with his head on his chest. He'd pulled my dad's arms around him, as well, and he was telling him about the hummingbirds he'd seen in San Francisco.

When George looked at me with lost eyes, I felt as if I were choking. And yet it was a comfort to know that he wouldn't have to go through his life thinking he'd disappointed his grandfather just before his death. If I never accomplished anything else in my life, at least I'd done that.

A little later, I combed Dad's thinning hair back over his ears and said, 'Go to Mom and Shelly whenever you're ready. I'll be okay, and the kids and Angie are going to be fine too.'

Then I went to the phone and called my daughters. They both lived just outside Boston and had been to see my father the evening before, but they were working today. 'Grandpa simply stopped breathing,' I told each of them. 'He wasn't in any pain.'

I did my best to sound at peace when I spoke to them, but a terrifying silence surrounded me every time I stopped speaking, and I realised I was living now in a world in which I'd never be completely at home. And that I didn't want to be there.

I fought despair as best I could that day and the next, but my father's funeral down in the New York suburbs bested me, and it quickly became the worst day of my life. My heart felt like it was beating somewhere below the muddy ground of the rain-soaked cemetery. I have no idea what I said to anyone that day. My voice was coming from a cheerful impostor I'd invented so I didn't have to speak of having to live the rest of my life without my dad.

Angie protected me. She hooked her arm in mine and walked me everywhere I needed to go. What I had ordered written on Dad's headstone was this:

Benjamin Rosenfeld Zarco, September 24, 1930 – June 19, 2017.
Beloved grandson, son, nephew, father, cousin, grandfather
and husband.
In the end, he won.

Walking back to the car after the ceremony, I remembered Aunt Julie telling me once, 'Everyone thinks I'm a cheerful person, but it's a lie,' and I wished she were still alive so that I could tell her that I understood her now only too well.

Angie and I drove home to Boston right after the funeral, and the moment we arrived, she went outside and did a little pruning and weeding, and I knew from the absent way she wandered past the apple trees and through the flower beds that she was remembering all those busy afternoons with her assistant gardeners – all those wonderful days that would never come again.

I returned to New York two weeks later to collect Berekiah's scroll and the other things that Dad had left for me. My cousin Diane was attentive and comforting while I was staying at our old house. We took out pizza the first night and talked for a couple of hours in the living room, where she'd put up the rock-and-roll posters from the 1960s that she collected. After our conversation about the Doors and Jimi Hendrix and Manfred Mann, I discovered that she had finally forgiven her father for not telling her and her sister about all he'd suffered in Poland when they were kids.

'I've come to accept that he didn't have any other choice,' she said. 'I get it now that he must have thought that he'd ruin our lives if we knew too much. And he couldn't risk doing that.'

While I was eating spaghetti with her on the second evening – my last with her – she asked me if I thought my father was one of the *Lamed Vav Tzadikim*, the thirty-six individuals who sustain the entire universe. 'I have no idea,' I replied. 'But in any case, he told me a couple of times that he thought that if anyone was a *Tzadik*, it was your father.'

She nearly choked on the broccoli she'd been eating. 'Dad?' she asked. 'Uncle Benni can't have been serious!'

'No, he was – absolutely. If your father hadn't found my dad, I wouldn't have been born, and my kids wouldn't be here, and Mom would never have become a professor of music, and we wouldn't have grown up with Uncle George's paintings, and nothing would be as it was. Your dad made a whole universe come into being.'

The Best Deal Any of Us Ever Made

I found the metal box my father had told me about in the basement, just where he said it would be. In addition to Berekiah Zarco's scroll, we discovered a thick, handwritten score entitled *Variations on an Ancient Melody*. The title page indicated it was composed by Ewa Armbruster. Dad had stapled a note to it:

Dear Eti, While Ewa was alive, she didn't want to show her composition to anyone. She said it was just for her and me – our secret. The melody was given to her by Berekiah Zarco in a vision she'd had back in her house in Poland. Did I tell you that? I hope so. Anyway, after she died, I photocopied it and showed it to a few pianists and orchestra directors, but no one wanted to learn it except your mom. She used to play it on occasion when you were little. Do you remember? If you sing the initial melody, I think it will come back to you. Especially because I also sung it to you when you were a baby and couldn't sleep. Anyhow, if you have the chance, please show it to some Sephardic musicians. Who knows, maybe one of them will be interested in putting it in a concert!

I also discovered a black velvet pouch. Inside it were the old earrings Dad had mentioned – star sapphires dangling from slender gold squares. There was also the diamond brooch shaped like a crescent moon that Grandpa Morrie had given Mom. An envelope with my name on it contained seven thousand dollars in cash.

Inside the envelope was a note:

It just occurred to me that after you read the scroll, you'll want to know what happened to the mirror. Shelly had to trade it to a peasant when he was hiding out in the forest. He was starving. He got an anorexic chicken that was still covered in lice-ridden feathers, and some withered cabbage. Still, that meal saved his life, so it was the best deal any of us ever made! Eti, maybe the scroll will prove to you that I'm not as nutty as it must have sometimes seemed – that the Incandescent Threads are around us all the time, waiting for us to see them and use them to find our way safely back into the past and forward into the future.

I didn't want you to read what Berekiah has to say while I was alive because I didn't want you making any more sacrifices for me. You made enough, especially since your mom's death, and I'm very grateful to you. You'll understand more of what I mean after you read what he has to say.

Live a wonderful life! And don't ever lose faith in your painting – you're a wonderful and brave artist! I love you to the edge of the world and back. And yes, I know you love me the same way.

Kisses for Angie, Pi, Violet and George. Your Dad

Beneath his signature was a P.S. in a different shade of ink: *Just like Shelly, I wish we still had the mirror, but some things are lost forever and there's nothing any of us can do about it.*

The Need for *Mesirat Nefesh*

The writing on Berekiah Zarco's scroll was in the square Hebrew script typical of Iberia, according to Professor Isaac Silva, to whom I sent a scan of its pages. He was certain it was authentic, as he had seen other texts written by Berekiah. Here is Silva's English translation:

A Fair Warning

No demon who forges the Pharaoh's weapons or who worships his idols or who prepares his meals or who shares in his bed shall have any power over the bearer of this scroll or anyone who has read even a single one of its words. Furthermore, should any man or woman endeavour to impede the journey of the bearer of this scroll, or do him injury, or take away his voice, or torment him, or speak evil of him, or maintain him in captivity, this foul being shall fail at once to find his breath, and his arms and legs shall wither, and he shall vanish from the earth and be forgotten by his children and children's children, and it shall be as if he had never existed, and this ban shall be imposed on him by the angel Raziel, who acts in defense of the most fragile of the sons of Adam and Eve. And know this: I, Berekiah Zarco, shall reinforce this ban with all I am and have ever been, and I hereby decree that the ten plagues of Egypt shall cripple all those who try to burn this manuscript or damage it in any way. In the name of Metatron, who writes the story of Creation, I declare that these admonitions can never be lifted, eased or diminished. 'There is no peace,' says my God, 'for the wicked!'

Berekiah's Rule

A deep despair has gripped me these past few days, and since I have grown to believe that its cause threatens all Jews everywhere, even those under the protection of Sultan Suleiman, blessed be his name, I am determined to write of it.

To begin with, however, I must speak of a small round mirror

– with a slightly concave surface – that I inherited forty-two years ago, upon the death of my Uncle Abraham, my spiritual mentor.

My uncle used to gaze into it every morning, after chanting a protective prayer. In his reverent voice, he would speak his oration seven times, in fact – the number of rungs of Jacob's Ladder we must climb if we are to reach the highest Palace of the Lord, where our supplications are more likely to be heard.

When I was a little boy, I asked him what he was looking for in the mirror.

'Sangue,' he'd whispered, and when I showed him a confused expression, he took down the mirror from the wall, handed it to me and explained that it emitted a tiny trace of blood – 'Invisible to the untrained eye, dearest nephew' – whenever any Jew was murdered, anywhere in the world, which was why he called it the Bleeding Mirror. He also told me that during the pogroms that decimated the Jewish communities of Andalusia, Castile and Catalonia in the year 5151 of our era – 793 for the followers of the Prophet Mohammed – the looking glass had wept so much blood that it began to stain the carpet beneath its hanging place and his ancestors had had to move it outside for nearly a month.

After I'd become a man, my uncle also revealed to me that the mirror had a highly polished inner surface that reflected the Upper Realms and was therefore able to absorb the subtleties of God's hidden life, free of the limitations of geography and time. In short, it could detect the murder of Jews in places thousands of miles distant. In a cautious whisper, he added that he'd been told by his grandfather that it could even detect pogroms that would take place in the future, as well.

Only much later, after I was already an exile in Constantinople, did I grasp the significance of what he'd revealed to me: the Bleeding Mirror had been imbued by the Lord with the dangerous gift of prophecy!

*My uncle told me, too, that he'd twice seen the mirror bleed. The
first time was in his youth, when the Jews of Trento were accused of
murdering a Christian child and using his blood to make matza for
Passover, and eight of them were tortured and burned at the stake. The
second time occurred during the forced conversion of the Portuguese
Jews in 5257 of our era – 1497 for the Christians – when a friend of
my uncle's and five other leaders of the Jewish community were buried
up to their necks in the ground and left to die. As to when and where
it was made, his father had told him that it had been given as a gift
to one of our ancestors – Solomon Zarco – by the renowned Sufi poet
and mystic, Jalal ad-Din Muhammad Rumi, which would date it
to the beginning of our fifth millennium. Rumi lived most of his life
in Konya, so perhaps it was made in that city or somewhere nearby.*

*Ever since moving into my present home, I have hung the mirror
in my prayer room. It is nearly four palms in diameter, with a frame
the width of my thumb, and though its surface is cracked in several
places, its glass has not warped. As a consequence, it still returns an
admirable reflection, although each face or object that appears in
it suffers a mild distortion produced by its concave surface. When I
showed it to the Sultan's chief woodworker a decade ago, he told me
that its frame was made of the wood of the terebinth tree, which we
know from the Torah as the Tree of the Knowledge of Good and Evil.*

*Every dawn, just after my morning meal, I speak Uncle Abraham's
protective prayer seven times and gaze across the mirror's surface – and
examine its frame, as well – but I had yet to glimpse its mysterious
bleeding until just before the start of Sukkot, seven months ago.*

Here is what happened . . .

*My dearest friend Farid and I had just returned from a sojourn
in Salonika to see my newborn granddaughter, Tamar. Although
our sea journey had left me weary of body and spirit, I wished to
remain awake so that I could tell my wife, Leci, about my stay in*

my daughter's home, and I chanted hymns in my garden to renew my flagging energy. Exhaustion soon overwhelmed me, however, and I lay myself down on an old rug in the welcoming shade of my Persian silk tree. Leci sat with me, her hand in mine, which was a solemn comfort. For a time, we conversed about Zuli, our daughter, and her baby.

Shortly after I drew silent and closed my eyes, a southern wind blew over me, warm and dry, as though it had travelled across the deserts of Zion. When I gazed around, my wife had vanished and urgent gusts were tossing the branches of the silk tree back and forth, causing them to make a clashing, apprehensive sound.

Something odd then happened: although the wind abated, the silk tree continued to shiver, as though moved by hidden hands, so that I became convinced that some unseen presence was with me. Only later did I realise that I had already descended into slumber and that the troubling wind had been blowing only through my mind.

I must then have fallen into a deeper visionary state, for an old man with a dark beard and large, dark, brooding eyes called out to me from my rooftop, using my abbreviated name, Beri, as though we knew each other, although he did not look familiar to me.

Even though he was standing on the rooftop, he shouted, 'Come down to me!'

I hoisted myself up onto my garden wall and made my way to the roof. When I reached the old man, he took my hand and nodded toward the sun in the east, and it was at that moment that I saw that we were no longer on my rooftop in Constantinople but standing in the tiny square fronting the Great Synagogue of Little Jerusalem, the main Jewish neighbourhood in Lisbon.

I was a young boy again. And I was home. And now, the old man looked familiar to me, though I was unable to recall what place he had in my life.

Menacing smoke was ribboning over our heads, and the smell of burning flesh soon made my legs tense up with the need to run – and convinced me that a pogrom was taking place in the Rossio, the city's central square.

Farid!

I moaned aloud, because his name entered my mind as driven into me on the point of a spear, and I sensed that he was in grave danger – perhaps even being burned alive.

'*Yes, it's time again for you to fight them,' the old man told me.*

'*How?' I asked. 'I am alone.'*

He opened wings that had previously been hidden, and they were black and shimmering. He spread them over me, and his mouth became a beak, and he took on the form of a heron. His amber-coloured eyes radiated a mysterious light.

'*You must come with me,' he said, and when I asked him where, he replied, 'The smoke is coming from a faraway time and place. But I shall take you there. We must save your shadow.'*

'*Is Farid my shadow?'*

'*No, you've misunderstood me. Jews are being killed in distant places.'*

'*Who are you? Are you an angelic guide?'*

'*I Am Who I Am,' the great heron replied, using one of our names for the Lord.*

He turned to the west and then the east, as though considering which way to fly, then looked straight up. As though under his command, the radiant blue sky dimmed and lowered, and when it became a ceiling, I found myself in the cellar of our family home in the Alfama. My uncle was seated at his desk, with his back to me.

When I turned to see the heron, I discovered that he had vanished.

The mirror! I thought. I must fetch it and examine it for blood. And maybe it will tell me, too, where the Jews are being murdered.

I rushed to my uncle and asked to look at the Bleeding Mirror. He was too absorbed by the illumination he was colouring to answer me in words. Instead, he raised his hand to grant me permission.

I took down the mirror and went to our courtyard so that I could examine its surface in the sunlight. But I found no blood, not even while looking through the magnifying glass that I found in my hand.

When I turned the mirror over, I discovered a small menorah etched on the frame, and above its central candle-flame were the Hebrew words for know thyself: עד תא ךמצע.

I was about to return to the cellar and ask Uncle Abraham how to interpret those words, but I was worried that he would grow angry at me for disturbing him again.

And then I awoke.

I was alone. I got to my feet, intending to go to Uncle Abraham and ask him what I could do to protect Farid and my family and all the Jews of Portugal, but when I saw the slender minarets of the Fatih Mosque arrowing into the sky above my garden wall, I remembered that my uncle had been dead for more than four decades. I was myself more than sixty years old!

How strange it is to have lived most of my life exiled from Portugal! *I thought, and in my mind I saw Lisbon and Istanbul as if I were a bridge between them.*

Farid and his lover, Shamsi, lived just a few houses away, so I rushed to his home and discovered my old friend sitting in his courtyard. He had just finished praying and was drinking from one of the old ceramic bowls we'd brought with us from Portugal, when we were both just youths.

Farid was born deaf, but he detected my footsteps in the delicate vibration of his tile floor and turned to face me. His expression was troubled, and in the gestural language that we'd developed as toddlers, he said, 'I had a disturbing dream.'

The beauty of his hand creating the word dream – a widening spiral – made me think, He and all the other people I have loved are my true homeland.

I sat beside him, and he told me what he'd seen: 'We were boys again, and Christian bailiffs arrested you for practicing Judaism. They were going to burn you alive. When I awakened, I was sure you were in danger, so I rushed to you, but you were sleeping peacefully in your garden.'

'How long ago was that?' I asked.

'About an hour.'

Farid and I had shared dreams and visions on a number of previous occasions – we had long speculated that it was because our souls had been intimately linked across many lifetimes – so I did not greet this news with surprise. Instead, I told him of my vision. When I had finished, he said, 'I think your angelic guide is trying to alert us to an imminent menace.' For the word menace he used a variation of our sign for snare, which was a fist pressed into the belly, then turned to the right. In this case, the leftward gyration of his hand was an indication that he believed our danger to be of supernatural origin.

His words summoned what seemed a revelation. 'The guide called me Beri,' I told him, 'so perhaps he was Uncle Abraham in disguise.'

'Why come in disguise?' Farid asked.

'I cannot say.' When I covered my eyes with my hands to see if I could spot my uncle lingering in my inner darkness, the odours of Portugal in my skin – olive oil and yeast, most of all – made me feel as though he were asking me to journey deeper into myself. Was that why he had told me to climb 'down' to the rooftop?

I called out to Uncle Abraham in my mind, but he didn't appear. After I uncovered my eyes, Farid formed in the air a Sufi prayer meant to guard us both from evil, and when I thanked him, I was stunned to see that my hands had grown wrinkled and crooked. My spirit seemed to be shuttling between old age and youth, Lisbon and Istanbul, dream and waking consciousness.

Indeed, while gazing into my old friend's apprehensive eyes, it seemed as if we had both been young men only a moment before. All I'd done between my departure from Lisbon and now – forty-two years of life – seemed but an illusion.

'Maybe Uncle Abraham is telling me that all the terrible persecutions we have experienced are still happening,' I speculated. 'He is asking me never to forget that the Inquisition in Portugal is still ruining the lives of many wonderful people.'

'And yet we've never ceased in our efforts to rescue them,' Farid said. 'In Salonika, we were able to raise a handsome sum for the refugees from Portugal and Spain.'

'Then I'm lost – I don't know what my uncle intends me to understand.'

Farid quoted one of our favourite counsels: 'Knock upon yourself as upon a door,' then added, 'If the Lord grants you grace, the answer will come out to greet you.'

I knew he was right, but when I left him, I was still deeply troubled by the mystery of our parallel dreams.

Back at home, I went to my prayer room and took down the Bleeding Mirror from the wall. I examined its surface as well as its frame with my magnifying glass – the same one I'd used in my vision – but I could find nothing.

Over the next days, I felt as though I was under siege from forces beyond my understanding – by abandoned children I could not see but who were straining desperately to reach me. Often, after my morning prayers, I grew certain that they were calling to me from a place so hidden – in so dark and secluded and perilous a corner of my being – that I had never dared approach it even when in the deepest trance. Whenever their presence would overwhelm me, I would stand and intone hymns for their safety, hoping they could hear my singing.

My obsession with their welfare was such that I began to run a fever and was confined to bed for several days. Often, I would find myself in tears in the morning, and covered in a cold sweat, as if my dreams had been soaked in guilt and sadness.

I need Your help if I am to see who is calling to me! *I told the Lord in my prayers.*

Leci forbid me from leaving our home, and she nursed me until I'd recovered from my chills and fever. Farid and I then visited each of the many synagogues in Constantinople to learn whether a rabbi or hazzan had heard of any violence against the Jewish communities of Europe or Asia, but none of them was aware of any recent massacres or pogroms. Farid and I also consulted the imams of most important mosques, as well our Sufi friends, but once again there was no news of any destruction of a Jewish community in Moslem lands.

Despite Leci's protests, I began fasting and weeping in order to empty my mind and increase my awareness of the hidden kinship between all matter and spirit, and one morning, deep in tear-induced trance, I sensed my uncle shuffling into the room and sitting down beside me. After a moment, he kissed the top of my head and pressed my hand to the surface of the Bleeding Mirror.

Thank you, *I told him in a whisper.*

I kept my hand where he had placed it. And I felt him caress my cheek. And then he vanished.

I slowly lifted my hand away and discovered that its reflection in the mirror was covered with fresh blood. Such was my shock that my trance was broken, whereupon the blood vanished.

That evening was the start of Sabbath, and I withdrew to my prayer room after supper and chanted the Book of Genesis deep into the night, asking for the light of Creation to help me see what was hidden to me, and near dawn, the warm, dry winds of the Portuguese countryside began to gust against my face, so I pressed my hand to the surface of the mirror again, and this time, a hand pressed back against mine.

I recited the Shema *to restrain my growing excitement.*

The hand was warm and smaller than my own. 'Stay with me and tell me what you need me to do,' I whispered in Portuguese and Hebrew and Turkish. And then, gradually, I withdrew my hand, continuing to exhort whoever had touched me to remain with me.

But when I looked into the mirror, I saw only my worried reflection. The silver surface of the glass and the frame were free of blood. On recalling that the words know thyself *had been etched on the back of the frame in my initial vision, I studied my own face, and I vowed not to turn away, and after many minutes of deep, unswerving concentration, an image flashed through my mind: thousands of ragged men and women were burning in an auto-da-fé, but they were dying alone, tied to their stakes, without witness.*

I gasped, then moaned aloud. And I realised then that burning men and women had called out for my help in a dream that I'd had a few days before. It was the heat of the flames consuming them that had drenched me in sweat.

A frigid shiver shook me deeply. And then I saw her – a tiny, gaunt-faced woman. She was seated behind my reflection in the mirror. She had grey hair, and she wore a patterned garment of a kind I'd never seen before, which gave me to believe that she lived in a distant land. She was seated by a window, facing away from me, gazing at the same auto-da-fé I had seen.

'I am here!' I called to her aloud.

But she could not hear me, whereupon tears of frustration began to flow from my eyes. And it was then that she turned to me and saw me.

She fought to stand and spoke, and although I could not hear her, I read her lips: 'I have been searching for you for so long!'

'As I have been searching for you,' I replied aloud.

She gazed at me from inside the looking glass, as if she were my reflection. 'I am here,' I told her. 'I shall not abandon you.'

As she strained to see me, the skeletal hollows around her eyes made me shudder, for I understood that she was starving.

She raised her hand and opened it, and in her palm were sapphire earrings that I recognised immediately. And I knew then that she was a descendent of mine! What a wise and far-sighted woman she was! She had known that I would remember the earrings as having belonged to my mother. I had gifted them to my daughter, Zuli, on the day of her wedding.

Did she own the Bleeding Mirror at a time in the future, and was she looking into it now? I could think of no other way that our meeting would be possible.

Her keen intelligence infused me with hope. I raised my hands above my head – like Moses lifting the tablets of God's law – and I summoned her to me, and when she smiled joyfully, I knew that she had seen my face.

She addressed me again, and here is what she said: 'Bless you, Berekiah, for coming to me! Once, many years ago, I read a manuscript of yours that belonged to my cousin Isaac Zarco, who lives in the city of Berlin. You wrote that the kings and bishops of Europe would one day try to destroy our people. You pleaded with all of the Jews of Europe to leave for lands ruled by the Moslems. It was to be yet one more Exodus for our people. But many of us did not heed your words. Or could not. And now the day of our destruction has come. Do you understand?

'Yes,' I replied. 'You have sought me out because you believe the Jews of Europe shall not survive this new danger.'

She was about to reply, but two young boys – one of them holding what appeared to be a chessboard – crossed the room to her. They spoke to her for a time, and she seemed to offer them consoling words, because the expressions in their gloom-filled faces lightened. After she kissed them, they dashed away with renewed energy.

She leaned again toward me, and tears were caught in her lashes. 'Abraham and Benjamin,' she said. 'Your descendants. Beautiful boys.'

A moment later, her eyes grew confused and distraught. I presumed that her vision of me had vanished, for she soon pressed her hand to the mirror, hoping to re-establish contact with me. I placed mine against hers and prayed for our union. A few moments later, when she withdrew her hand, her eyes opened wide. We stared at each other, and I felt her need to be rescued as an upward movement in my heart.

'I believe that we may soon be closing the final page of our history,' she said.

'Are you being held captive?'

'Yes, and we cannot escape, for we are surrounded on all sides. We have been confined everywhere across Europe.'

'Is this Pharaoh who has confined you very strong?

'Yes, and we have very few weapons.'

I pondered her problem for some time, then asked, 'Can you bribe your captors in order to at least save your sons and daughters and grandchildren?'

'No, we have been reduced to poverty. My children and I have almost nothing left. Just the earrings I have shown you.'

'What is your name?' I asked.

'Rosa Zarco.'

'And where do you live?'

'In Warsaw. It was a small town in your time, but it is now a great capital.'

'Will no army help you, Rosa?'

'No, it is just as you wrote. We are alone. Those who might save us are still too far away. They shall not reach us in time. Here in Warsaw, we may soon arm ourselves with the few weapons we have and engage *the enemy in battle, but I do not believe we shall be victorious. Even our shadows shall be erased from history.'*

My thoughts scattered off urgently, trying to understand how I might help her. I realised then – with a burst of clarity – that the prayer that my uncle had always spoken before the mirror had been meant for her and all our descendants and their friends – for everyone whose blood might seep one day from the mirror. How could I have failed to understand that?

I recited my uncle's prayer slowly and carefully to her: 'The Lord and I are one, and it is He who turns my soul to light, and it is that light that always guides me to safety. And may the Lord gift each soul under threat with this same holy radiance.'

I asked her to teach those holy words to everyone in her family and all her friends.

And then, as though to rescue both of us from the coming destruction of our people, two words entered my mind. Did my uncle slip into the room for a moment and whisper them to me? I know that I sensed him by my side for a single instant.

The two words constituted the most important lesson I'd learned from him: mesirat nefesh. *The willingness to sacrifice oneself – if need be, to suffer the cruelest torments – in order to save the life of even one other person.*

I spoke those sacred words aloud, knowing now how I could help.

As she repeated the words to herself, her expression grew determined, and I told her, 'You must be willing to sacrifice yourself to save at least one of your children.'

'Yes, that is what I'll do,' she replied. 'I swear it.'

My respect for her courage prompted me to close my eyes for a moment and whisper a prayer for her safety, but when I opened them again, she was gone. Instead, I saw the reflection of my own searching gaze.

I summoned her again, but she would not – or could not – return. The future had withdrawn from me.

That night, I realised what ought to have been obvious: that I had been a fool to look for blood on the surface of the mirror and its frame! A mirror reflects – that is its nature – so it was on my own reflected face that I ought to have searched for its prophecies!

For many days afterward, I searched for what else I could do to help the old woman and everyone she wished to protect in the world to come, and, in the end, I realised that my only way to combat a future enemy was to try to guarantee the Jews more safety in my own time and place – thereby altering the circumstances of the lives of all our descendants.

I went to see the Sultan the next morning and requested payment in gemstones for the prayer book I had recently executed for him. He acceded to my wish and the next morning one of his messengers brought me a resplendent emerald, a small but perfect diamond, a star sapphire and a large, fire-coloured topaz.

I had the stones set in gold and made into rings by a jeweller friend. I sent Zuli in Salonika the star sapphire and emerald rings and handed the topaz and diamond ones to Ari, who lived with his family in a small house on the banks of the Golden Horn. I instructed both my children to keep these valuables in a secret place inside their homes in case they should one day need to bribe their way out of mortal danger.

To Farid, I gave a gold and carnelian signet ring that had been my uncle's, and that I'd always worn on the Sabbath. Though at first he refused the gift – knowing how precious it was to me – I told him that I should not wish to live in a world without him – my soul-mate – and that I would sleep better at night knowing that it might one day buy his freedom.

Leci and I hid the rest of our jewellery in my secret prayer room.

I also wrote to my children about the need for mesirat nefesh. *I asked them, if ever the need arose, to risk a journey to the kingdom of the dead in order to save those who found themselves prisoners of Pharaoh. Lastly, I asked them to pass on this instruction in the ways of self-sacrifice to their children, and to their children's children, and to all our descendants forever after.*

Berekiah's Rule, *they began to call it.*

Who was the bearded, long-haired old man who first appeared to me? I presumed he had been my Uncle Abraham until another dream soon presented me with the truth. In it, I saw my wife, Leci, standing in my courtyard and pleading with the very same elderly gentleman – sitting at the top of a Persian silk tree – to climb down. She called him by my name – Berekiah!

The old man had been me!

Was it possible that my own future self had come to help me find Rosa in the Bleeding Mirror? An even more difficult question: why did Rosa Zarco appear to me when she did and not twenty years previously, or ten years into my future? I have often contemplated that mystery, and I have asked Farid and a number of Sufi sages for their opinions, but none of us has come up with what I consider an adequate reply. Indeed, the ways of time remain a great mystery. All I can think of is that my trip to Salonika – most particularly, holding my newborn granddaughter in my arms – forced me to consider the dangers that she will face in the world to come and helped me to sense the urgent needs of my descendants.

Have I done enough to save the Jews? Shall there still come a time when they shall be burnt by the thousands in Lisbon and Rome and Warsaw and all the other cities of Europe? All I know for sure is that

I shall bequeath all my valuables to future generations and preach Berekiah's Rule in the hopes of saving even just a fraction of them.

I ask you who read this manuscript to make ready to sacrifice yourself so that your children may make their way to safety here in Istanbul or elsewhere beyond the reach of Christian rulers. If you remember only two words of this account I have written, remember these: mesirat nefesh.

Blessed are all of God's self-portraits!

Berekiah Zarco 15 Nissan 5308

Why My Father Survived

I was back in Boston when I received Professor Silva's translation of the scroll my father had left me. It left me disoriented and troubled; although I was desperate to share my father's faith in Berekiah Zarco's extraordinary powers, I found it nearly impossible to believe that he could have seen into the future and communicated with Rosa. Wasn't it more likely that she had made a careful study of his handwriting and style of writing, and that she'd forged the account of the Bleeding Mirror? Very likely she'd decided that this was the best way to pass on the message of *mesirat nefesh*. In that case, she would have written her account from Berekiah's point of view to give her words unassailable authority.

Was it possible that she saw the renowned kabbalist in a vision and he'd asked her to create the document on his behalf?

After a week or so, I began to see that the origin of the document didn't matter. All that counted was saving my family and our future ancestors. So as soon as I could bring my children together, I told them and Angie about Berekiah's Rule, and what it meant for us. And I made them promise to abide by it.

To the collection of jewellery that I'd inherited from my father and Shelly, I added an amethyst ring and gold cufflinks that my grandfather Morrie had given me, and Angie added an art-nouveau brooch – inlaid with tiny diamonds and garnets – that had been her mother's. We stored these valuables in a small wooden box in our basement.

And then ... And then I did my best to return to the life I now had after my father's death.

I painted and gardened every day, and when school started up in late August, I began teaching again. But too often my mind was back at the cemetery in suburban New York with my father and mother. I guess I was trying to figure out where I belonged now that they were gone and my kids were grown up.

Berekiah Zarco's scroll made me wonder nearly all the time why my father had survived the Holocaust. After all, Abe and Esther must have been given valuable jewellery as well. And their parents would have done everything they could have to save them.

I could hear my father telling me, 'I'm not certain, Eti, but I believe I survived because Rosa put *mesirat nefesh* into practice at the critical moment, when I was about to be picked up by the Jewish police.

'And because my mother had been good friends with a courageous young man named Piotr, who brought me to Ewa.

'And because Ewa would not permit me to be captured and murdered.

'And because of a thousand other tiny, nearly imperceptible threads that drew me forward into the future.

'And, of course, because I was extremely lucky.'

I believed that before he died, Dad had made peace with his having been saved by Rosa – that she'd given up her life for his – but I couldn't be sure; he was always so good at hiding his deepest feelings.

In quiet moments, and to myself alone, I started calling myself by my Hebrew name, *Ethan ben Benjamin* – Ethan, son of Benjamin. Because I wanted Dad to be with me in every thought I had of myself.

But every time I stepped into his silent bedroom, the emptiness that met me seemed too wide and deep – as if it had been conjured up by a purposefully cruel god. Even his scent – of cereal and old pyjamas and Danziger Goldwasser – seemed to have vanished.

Beneath his underwear and socks, I found a bar of Ghirardelli dark chocolate, an unopened pack of Marlboro lights, and a stack of old photos of my mother, Shelly, Aunt Julie, Uncle George and me.

In his bedside table, I found his tailor's shears and an old parchment talisman of Jewish angels that I had never seen before. Had he smuggled it out of the Warsaw ghetto inside Berekiah's manuscript?

My father had always attracted strange events and extraordinary people to him. But I wasn't like him. I didn't even believe in God. And the differences between us became an aching disappointment whenever I looked through his books.

No, I wasn't a mystical clown. Or even a performer like Shelly.

I needed to spend many hours alone painting in order to feel safe and completely alive – just like Mom had needed to play her flute. I was very much her son in that way.

What My Paintings Were Trying to Tell Me
Very likely to compensate for the hollow inside me – in the exact size and shape of my dad – my work soon grew more crowded. Everything I knew about him and his past entered my mythological drawings and paintings – Glukl the emerald-coloured parrot, the blue woollen sweater Ewa had knitted for him, his cigarettes and lighter, the military induction centre in New York, Shelly's

demanding erections and Uncle George's bolo ties, Grandpa Morrie's photo of Louis Armstrong, the tulips that he and Shelly had planted, the quilts my mother had received as gifts from Belle, his tape measure and favourite sewing machine, the rug in which Piotr had rolled him when they fled Warsaw . . . And his eyes – the moonless nights through which I would forever be journeying.

Everything jumbled together at crazy angles on my canvases, struggling for space, so that the four edges of my paintings began to seem like walls that wouldn't be able to hold up much longer against so much pressure. I couldn't ever seem to cram enough into each painting – my mind was made of thousands of crucial and scattered memories that I had to record.

In the end my only choice was to make each piece of Dad's life very small.

His three-ring circus became mine, and I needed to paint it. I didn't seem to have any choice. But doing justice to even just Dad's sandals would require two or three days of work with the tiny brushes I began using, and each canvas would take several months to fill up, which gave me that idea that my paintings were stories that I didn't ever want to end.

Was I like my son, George, in that way? Had I needed a storyteller to draw me out in the world and give me a home? And carry me into the past?

But Dad was gone – which meant that maybe I was the storyteller now. In fact, maybe that was just what my paintings were trying to tell me.

On the Day He Kissed Me
A few days after my father's funeral, Angie had warned me not to be surprised if I occasionally mistook someone on the street for him. She told me that after her beloved grandfather Francesco died, she

mistook other men for him on three different occasions. 'It used to upset me a lot,' she said. 'Especially the last time, in Provincetown. I was with a girlfriend, and I saw my grandfather stepping off a boat. He had Grandad's crest of white hair, and he was wearing a flannel shirt I recognised. And boom! I started thinking that he hadn't died – that everyone had lied to me! I thought that he'd needed to drop off the grid for some reason. What was amazing was that my mind invented a story – right away – about how the FBI had hidden him away because he knew some secret information about a spy that he'd known when he'd lived in Naples. So a local FBI agent found him an apartment in Provincetown, and he'd been living there under a false name. In less than a few seconds, I invented a whole crazy story! And then something amazing happened . . . The old man who'd stepped off a boat waved to me, and he started rushing toward me with that herky-jerky walk of my grandfather's. But when he got close, I saw that he wasn't Grandpa Francesco. He walked past me without recognising me, of course, and when I turned around, he was embracing a young man behind me. I burst into tears. And I couldn't stop sobbing. And even when I finally did, it seemed proof that the funeral was just the beginning.'

'The beginning of what?' I asked.

'I'm not sure. Of another phase of life, I suppose. Of having to accept what I didn't want to accept.'

I took Angie's warning seriously, but over the next few months I didn't mistake anyone in Boston or anywhere else for my father.

Instead of being content about that, I was disappointed. And secretly surprised – because my father had drawn so many odd things to him. And because, if he was right, there had to be lots of Incandescent Threads stretched between us.

Angie was right, however, about the funeral being just the

beginning. Whenever I'd visit my parents' old house in New York, I'd sit for hours in the bedroom that I'd had as a kid.

Sometimes, I'd lie back and stare at the cracks in the ceiling and wonder how my parents had come and gone so quickly. One minute, Mom was lying on the sofa in the living room, and her feet were on Dad's lap, and he was rubbing them, and they were listening to Sephardic Jews from Morocco singing creaky old songs about Queen Esther and King David, and I was asking them when dinner would be ready, and the next . . . And the next they were both buried in a cemetery in Plainview, Long Island.

On these trips home, I'd spend a lot of my time visiting my father's old hangouts. Sometimes I'd do my emailing in the Starbucks where he'd get coffee and buy chocolate-chip cookies at the Seven Dwarfs Bakery, and even invent reasons to go to the Chase branch on Willis Avenue where he'd had his accounts. Once, I bought a pack of Marlboro Lights at Waldbaum's, and I lit one up to remember what it was like when we both smoked.

The new manager at Chase was named Raslan. He was a Druze with dark skin and a sweet-natured smile, and I knew that Dad would have adored talking to him about the history of his people.

There were so many things that Dad would have still wanted to do. And now he couldn't do any of them.

Unless he'd already been reincarnated, of course – maybe in Egypt, the country he'd always wanted to visit but never had.

'Believe me, it's for the best that your father's ghost doesn't appear to you,' Angie told me once when I was complaining to her about not seeing him. 'So stop torturing yourself waiting for him.'

Then I told her the truth I'd been holding back – and that kept me up at night: 'But sometimes I can't remember what he looked like when he was young. I only see him like he was toward the end. And I hate it! I really hate it! I want him the way he was, when he was strong and funny and crazy with love for my mom and me, and . . . I want to see him like he was on the day he kissed me after I'd fallen on the ice and cut myself.'

'We have lots of photographs,' she replied. 'I can get them if you want.'

I let the silence accumulate between us because we both knew I was talking about an internal image that had somehow dissipated.

The Most Obvious Place

Another few months passed. I finished only one painting the whole time. In it, I'm standing on an island made out of books, and the sea around us is the colour of blood, and I'm looking out at the horizon, and lots of people are dancing together on the far shore. My mom is there, and Grandpa Morrie, too, and Shelly and Julie and Uncle George and a hundred other men and women and children, and they've tossed the masks they once wore to the ground, because there's no longer any need for them to hide who they are now that they're dead. Everyone is there but my father.

Our journey together was over.

So many times I thought of slashing that painting with Dad's old tailor's shears. Or burning it. But that would have been like hurting myself at my most fragile moment. And punishing myself for being honest.

Then, last night, I got up to look at it at three in the morning. On the way to the living room, where I'd hung the painting, I went to the bathroom to pee. I flipped on the light. And there my father was, staring back at me from the mirror above the sink. 'Dad,' I said, as if it was the most natural thing in the world to greet him.

Then I grew frightened; I remembered that he was dead. Yet there he was: his tender, dark eyes and look of bemused astonishment. And his whiskered cheeks.

He looked strong. And strangely innocent – as if none of the bad things that had ever happened to him had any power over him anymore.

And then I heard his voice. He said, *I'm glad you found me, Eti.*

He said it as though he always knew I would – as if he had never lost confidence in me, since that would be impossible.

And then he said, *Your heart and my heart . . . They follow the same laws as the earth when it goes around the sun, and the same laws that govern the yellow and orange growth of the tulips in our garden.*

Yeah, you're right, I told him, and we stared at each other for a long time, and then I laughed; after all my searching, he'd been hiding in the most obvious place all along.

ACKNOWLEDGEMENTS

I'm extremely grateful to Alexandre Quintanilha, Isabel Silva, Judith Ravenscroft, Anna Jarota and Rabbi Jacob Staub for reading the manuscript of this book and giving me their invaluable comments. I also want to thank everyone at Parthian Books, especially its perceptive and hard-working founder Richard Davies and my extraordinarily gifted editor, Robert Harries. Lastly, I owe a great debt to the many Holocaust survivors who have written and spoken about their experiences, especially those who – like the main characters in my novel – grew up in Poland.

GLOSSARY

All words in Yiddish or Hebrew

Baruch Adonai	Blessed is the Lord.
Bissel	A little amount.
Chuppah	Canopy under which a couple stand during a Jewish wedding ceremony.
Dummkopf	Idiot, dummy.
Dybbuk	A malevolent wandering spirit – often believed to be a disembodied soul – that enters and possesses the body of a living person.
Farshlofn	Sleepy.
Gefilte fish	Fish paste generally made of a mixture of carp, whitefish and pike.
Gehenna	Hell.
Got tsu danken	Thank God.
Goy	Christian person.
Goyim	Christians.
Hamantaschen	Cookie filled with prune, apricot or poppy seeds.
Hazzan	Prayer leader in a synagogue. Cantor.
Ikh hob dikh lib	I love you.
Kaddish	Prayer that mourners recite for the dead.
Katchkele	Little duck.

Lamed Vav Tzadikim	Hebrew for the thirty-six righteous ones. In Jewish tradition, thirty-six anonymous persons sustain the world in every generation through their righteous acts. The origin of this concept is the Babylonian Talmud.
L'chaim	To life (often used as a toast).
Mandelbrot	Cake made with almond flour.
Mekhasheyfe	Sorceress or witch.
Mensch	A person of noble character. Someone who always strives to behave compassionately.
Meshugge	Crazy.
Mesirat nefesh	In Jewish tradition, an act of self-sacrifice that might lead to dire consequences. It also implies an understanding and acceptance of those consequences.
Nu	Exclamation meaning, 'So?' or 'What's up?'
Nudnik	Bothersome person.
Pisher	Inexperienced and often presumptuous young person.
Plotz	Faint or drop dead.
Putz	Penis.
Rikhter	Judge.
Schmaltz	Chicken or goose fat.
Schul	Synagogue service.
Sefirot	According to Jewish mystical tradition (kabbalah), the ten primordial manifestations or qualities of God through which we can perceive an otherwise unknowable creator.

Shema	Jewish prayer that begins, 'Hear, O Israel.'
Shiksa	Christian woman.
Teivele	Little devil.
Tref	Food – such as pork – unfit for consumption for religious reasons.
Tsuris	Troubles, woes or distress.
Yarmulke	Skullcap worn by Jewish men and boys.

PARTHIAN Also by Richard Zimler

HUNTING
MIDNIGHT
SEPHARDIC CYCLE

BOOK 2

978-1-913640-65-1 • £10

Paperback

At the dawn of the nineteenth century,
John Stewart Zarco lives out an inquisitive,
naive childhood in his idyllic Porto
community. But societal prejudices
against his family's Jewish faith shatter
his innocence and even come to threaten
his life.

Following the tragic death of his dearest
friend, it is only his unlikely bond with
Midnight, an African healer and freed
slave, that restores a sense of safety. But this fragile, fleeting peace is destroyed when
Napoleon's armies invade Portugal and John suffers another devastating loss – one rooted
in unspeakable betrayal and authored by those closest to him. The revelation sets John on
course for antebellum America, in what might ultimately prove to be a doomed quest for
hope amid unspeakable cruelty and sin.

Rich in historical detail and mysticism, *Hunting Midnight* is Richard Zimler's mesmerising
tale of deception, guilt, forgiveness and devotion, played out against a backdrop of war,
slavery and religious oppression.

'pacey and accessible . . . Deeply moving.' *The Observer*

'Wonderful . . . a big, bold-hearted love story that will sweep you up and take you,
uncomplaining, on a journey full of heartbreak and light.' Nicholas Shakespeare

'A gripping adventure story' *The Independent*

PARTHIAN Also by Richard Zimler

GUARDIAN OF THE DAWN
SEPHARDIC CYCLE
BOOK 3
978-1-913640-66-8 • £10
Paperback

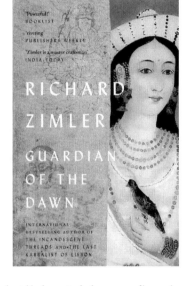

After his Jewish family fled the Catholic Inquisition in Portugal, Tiago Zarco lives a tranquil existence in colonial India, enjoying secret sojourns with his sister into the heady festivities of the local Hindu culture while evading the ruling Portuguese authorities.

But as he comes of age in sixteenth-century Goa, Ti struggles to keep the far-reaching influence of the Inquisition from destroying his family and pulling him apart from the Hindu girl he loves. And when an act of betrayal sees his father imprisoned, he is forced to hunt down the traitor and make an unimaginable choice, triggering a harrowing journey that will show him the depths of human depravity and the poisonous salvation of revenge.

At once passionate, furious and hopeful, *Guardian of the Dawn* is both a saga of horrifying religious persecution and a riveting, tender multicultural love story.

'Zimler is a master craftsman, and this book is Art . . . a riveting murder mystery.' *India Today*

'limpid and encompassing' *The Guardian*

'deeply absorbing' *Kirkus Reviews*

THE SEARCH
FOR SANA
978-1-913640-68-2 • £10
Paperback

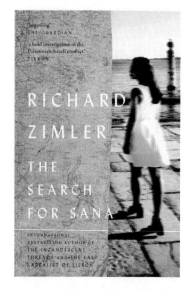

In February 2000, the writer Richard
Zimler met a mysterious dancer at an
Australian literary festival, only to witness
her tragic suicide the next day. This
shocking act was to trigger an investigation
into her past that would alter the course of
his life forever.

His search initially leads him to the
tranquillity and tolerance of 1950s Israel,
where he learns of the powerful sisterhood
forged between two girls – one Palestinian,
one Israeli. But as Zimler is drawn deeper
into their story, he uncovers illusion, deceit
and – most shocking of all – a connection to the most horrifying atrocity of the twenty-first
century.

At once a memoir and a thriller, *The Search for Sana* sees the internationally bestselling
author of the *Sephardic Cycle* create an unflinching exploration of lifelong friendship,
loyalty, cruelty and dispossession.

'A bold investigation of the Palestinian-Israeli conflict . . . [Zimler] writes in
calm, clear prose adorned by the occasional glistening image like a jewel in a
fast-flowing stream.' *Tikkun*

'beguiling' *The Guardian*

PARTHIAN Also by Richard Zimler

THE SEVENTH GATE

SEPHARDIC CYCLE

BOOK 4

978-1-913640-67-5 • £10

Paperback

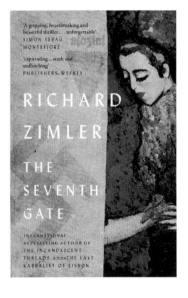

BERLIN, 1932

Intelligent, artistic and precocious, fourteen-year-old Sophie Riedesel dreams of nothing more than becoming an actress and spending time with her beloved Jewish neighbour, Isaac Zarco. But when her father and boyfriend become Nazi collaborators and Hitler's meteoric rise to power gathers momentum, she is forced to lead a double life to protect those closest to her.

Invited by Isaac into the Ring, a secret circle of underground activists working against the government, Sophie soon learns the ways of espionage and subterfuge. But when a series of sterilisations, murders and disappearances threatens to destroy the group, Sophie must fight to expose the traitor in their midst and save all that she loves about Germany – whatever the price.

Thrilling, suspenseful and evocative, *The Seventh Gate* is at once a love story, a tale of fierce heroism and a horrifying study of the Nazis' war against the disabled.

'Zimler's character development is electrifying and his plot rolls along ever faster into the depths of fear . . . unforgettable!' *New York Journal of Books*

'*The Seventh Gate* is not only a superb thriller but an intelligent and moving novel about the heartbreaking human condition.' Alberto Manguel

PARTHIAN   A Carnival of Voices

'For almost thirty years, [Parthian] have been one of the most consistently agile imprints in Wales.' – Mike Parker, *Planet Magazine*

'From the selection of its authors and topics covered through to the editing and production of the books, Parthian exudes quality. It puts out a dazzling, stimulating, thought-provoking selection of books on par with (if not better and more interesting than) the bigger publishing houses.' – Jenny White, journalist

'a vital part of our publishing scene in Wales and great ambassador for the best of Welsh writing.' – Rebecca Gould, Head of Arts at British Council Wales

We have always published first-time fiction and aim to give new writers as much development support as we can. Our recent success includes writers such as Richard Owain Roberts (Not the Booker Prize winner 2020), Alys Conran (Wales Book of the Year winner 2017), Tristan Hughes (Edward Stanford Travel Writing Award – Fiction with a Sense of Place winner 2018), Lloyd Markham (Betty Trask Award winner 2018) and Glen James Brown (Orwell and Portico Prize shortlistee 2019).

We have an ongoing engagement with the literary culture of Wales through our Library of Wales series, which has reached fifty titles of classic writing. The Library of Wales as a publishing project, with support from the Welsh Government and the Books Council of Wales, has been a significant investment in the literary and educational culture of Wales, with over 100,000 copies sold. The series includes books such as *Border Country* by Raymond Williams and Dannie Abse's *Ash on a Young Man's Sleeve*. Recent books include *Dat's Love and Other Stories* by Leonora Brito, *In and Out of the Goldfish Bowl* by Rachel Trezise and *Sugar and Slate* by Charlotte Williams. It has changed the perception of Welsh writing in English, with *Poetry 1900–2000*, a title commissioned by Parthian for the series, being adopted onto the Welsh Joint Education GCSE syllabus, while many of the books are now studied at university level in Wales.

The Modern Wales series, a collaboration with The Rhys Davies Trust, engages with the recent history and culture of Wales. The series includes the publication of major works of biography: *Rocking the Boat: Welsh Women who Championed Equality 1840–1990* by Angela V. John and *Labour Country: Political Radicalism and Social Democracy in South Wales 1831 to 1985* by Daryl Leeworthy.

We aim to produce attractive and readable books in our areas of interest: new writing, the heart of Welsh culture, and fiction of the wider world through the Parthian Carnival.

The Parthian Carnival includes a growing list of fiction and poetry in translation from many European languages. It includes novels and poerty translated from Basque, Latvian, Estonian, Greek, Macedonian, Catalan, Czech, Lithuanian, German, Irish, Welsh, Danish, Spanish, French, Slovakian and Turkish. Most recently, we published a series of books with support from Creative Europe, with a programme of publication over three years and collaboration with the literature councils of many European countries.